A BLACK MATTER FOR THE KING

THE OATH AND THE CROWN, BOOK 2

A BLACK MATTER FOR THE KING

OATH AND CROWN, BOOK 2

BY

MATTHEW WILLIS AND J.A. IRONSIDE

www.penmorepress.com

III

ISBN-13: 978-1-946409-46-1(Paperback)
ISBN-13: 978-1-946409-47-8(e-book)

BISAC Subject Headings:
FIC014000FICTION / Historical
FIC032000FICTION / War & Military
FIC027150FICTION / Romance / Historical / Medieval

Cover Illustration by Christine Horner

Address all correspondence to:
Penmore Press LLC
920 N Javalina Pl
Tucson, AZ 85748

OATH AND CROWN, BOOK 2

"I am afeard there are few die well that die in a battle; for how can they charitably dispose of any thing, when blood is their argument? Now, if these men do not die well, it will be a black matter for the king that led them to it" Henry V, Act IV, Scene 1

DRAMATIS PERSONAE

The Saxons:

Royalty:

Edward the Confessor—King of England 1043–1066

Alfred Ætheling—Edward's elder brother

Æthelred ('the Unready')—Edward's father

Emma of Normandy—Mother of King Edward, aunt of Duke William

Harthacnut—King of England 1040–42

The House of Wessex:

Godwin of Wessex (originally of Sussex)—Jarl of Wessex

Gytha Thorkilsdóttir (JHEE-taa)—A Danish noblewoman, Lady of Wessex, wife of Godwin and mother to nine of Godwin's children

Sweyn Godwinson—(seVEHN) the eldest of the Wessex children, Jarl of Gloucestershire, Herefordshire, Oxfordshire, Berkshire and Somerset

Harold Godwinson (or Harold of Wessex)—Jarl of East Anglia, Hereford and later Wessex

Ealdgyth—(ALD-jheet) Eldest Daughter of Godwin and Gytha, wife of Edward and Queen of England

Tostig—(THOR-stig) third son of Gytha and Godwin, Jarl of Northumbria

Gyrth—(GERTH) fourth son of Godwin and Gytha, made Jarl of East Anglia, Oxfordshire and Cambridgeshire

Gunhild—(GAHNH-hihl) Second daughter of Wessex

Leofwine—(LEOV-wine) sixth child of Godwin and Gytha, Jarl of Kent, Middlesex, Surrey, Hertfordshire and Buckinghamshire

Ælfgifa—(ALF-ghee-faa) Third daughter of Godwin and Gytha

Wulfnoth—last child of Godwin and Gytha

Edith the Fair—(or Edith Swannesha/ 'Swan-neck') wealthy Saxon noblewoman with lands in Cambridgeshire, Suffolk and Essex. First wife of Harold Godwinson

Beddwen—(BETH—wyn) a Welsh woman who acted as nurse to Godwin and Gytha's children and later to Harold and Edith's

Suela—(SOO-ay-laa) a beautiful Ceorl and trusted servant to Queen Ealdgyth

Aofra—(AY- frah) a pretty, ambitious girl, ward of King Edward and married to his trusted Thagn, Bealdric

Camus—(KAM-mus) The royal physician

Alfwine—(ALV-wine) a monk and adviser to Harold in his Jarldom in East Anglia

Caedmon—(KAD-mun) a non-conformist, radical monk belonging to the Celtic Rite Christian Church, resident advisor of Godwin and teacher of Ælfgifa

Nessa—A Pretani born ceorl in Harold's household

Ulfric—one of Harold's vassal thagns

Dubhne—(DOVE-nee) an old blind monk at Westminster Abbey

Berenine—(BEAR-en-een) the now elderly tiring woman to Emma of Normandy

Ulfstaen—(OOLF- stan) a loyal supporter of Harold in Escancaester

The Wealas (Welsh—Cymri)

Gruffydd ap Llewelyn—(GRIFF-ith APP KHLOO-ell-en) King of Gwynedd and Powys 1039–1055, King of Wales (as a united kingdom) 1055–1063

Aldythe of Mercia—(ALE—dith) daughter of Ælfgar, Jarl of Mercia. Married first to Gruffydd ap Llewelyn. Then later she became the second wife of Harold Godwinson

Other Contenders for the English Throne:

Magnus the Good—King of Norway (1035) and Denmark (1042) until 1047

Harald Hardrada—(the hard ruler or the hard counsel) King of Norway 1046–1066

Edgar Ætheling—(ED-gah EETH-ling) also known as Edgar II—last surviving male member of the royal house of Cerdic of Wessex

The French:

Henry I (Capet)—King of France 1027–1060

William I ('The Bastard'/'The Conqueror')—Duke of Normandy

Robert I ('The Magnificent'/ 'The Liberal')—Duke of Normandy 1027–1035

Herleva of Falaise—mother of William I and his half-brothers, Odo, and Robert, Count of Mortaigne

Ralph de Wacey—William's fourth and last guardian

Gallet—a loyal knight of William's

Helisande—daughter of William's master of hounds, later married to Gallet

Bourdas—William's valet and then his squire

Grimoult du Plessis—A Norman nobleman, lord of Plessis

Neel—Viscount of Cotentin, a Norman nobleman

Renulf—A Norman nobleman, the Viscount of Bessin

Hammond ('with the Teeth')—Baron of Cruelly, a Norman nobleman

Guy of Burgundy—a relative of Duke William, the grandson of William's grandfather Duke Richard I

William fitzOsbern—advisor, steward and childhood friend of Duke William, and son to William's former guardian, Osbern

Hubert de Ryes—a knight, loyal to William during the first uprising

Raoul de Ryes—eldest son of Hubert de Ryes, knighted by William

Henry (or Hubert) de Ryes—second son of Hubert de Ryes, also knighted by William

Lanfranc, Bishop of Bec—one of William's closest advisors, educator and negotiator

Raoul de Taisson, a Norman Lord of uncertain loyalties

Roger de Montgomerie—a relative of Duke William and one of his chief counsellors

Mabel de Bellême—wife of Roger de Montgomerie and heiress of lands in Maine

Roger de Beaumont—a distant cousin of Duke William's, and one of his closest supporters, noted for his beard

Robert de Beaumont—eldest son of Roger de Beaumont, he fought alongside William

Jean Bellin, Lord of Blainville—a loyal lord who managed the Duchy while William fought rebellion

Baldwin V, Count of Flanders—Duke William's father-in-law, Count of Flanders 1035–1067

Matilda of Flanders—Married to Duke William c.1053

Berenger—Norman guard at Falaise

Asce—Norman guard at Falaise

Hugh de Grandmesnil—Supporter of William, from a family famous for breeding warhorses

Walter Giffard—A Norman nobleman, later William's standard-bearer

Eustace ('aux Gernons'—'The Mustaches') **of Boulogne** —a relative of Duke William, and Count of Boulogne

Guillaume de Warenne—a youthful Norman nobleman who fought at the Battle of Mortemer

Roger de Tosny ('Old de Tosny')—Head of an important Normandy family, and Duke William's standard bearer

Ralph de Tosny ('Young de Tosny')—William's squire after Bourdas

Herbert, Count of Maine—a nobleman, absentee lord of the neighboring county

Conan II, Duke of Brittany—lord of the neighboring Duchy and rival of William's

Walkelin—Duke William's chaplain

Geoffrey of Anjou ('Martel'—'The Hammer')—Count of Anjou and rival to Duke William

William of Arques—Duke William's uncle, lord of Arques and Talou

Mauger—Archbishop of Rouen and Duke William's uncle, brother of William of Arques

William Talvas (de Bellême)—head of the powerful Bellême family of Maine

Arnulf Talvas (de Bellême)—William's son and successor, lord of Alençon and Domfront

Gui of Ponthieu—Count of Ponthieu, a vassal of Duke William

Saxon place names:

Wintanceastre—Winchester—the seat of Saxon power in the last unbroken kingdom of the Heptarchy, Wessex

Deorham—Dereham, where Harold set his household whilst he was Jarl of East Anglia

Cnobheresburgh—a castrum in the Jarldom of East Anglia where the first Irish monastery was established in 630 AD

Caerdid—Cardiff

Grantaceastr—Cambridge

Gwynedd—one of the Cymry kingdoms in North Wales

Jórvík or Eoferwic—York

Londinium—The Roman capital of Britain, abandoned early in 5th Century

Lundenwic—Anglo-saxon London. The 'city' was established a mile or so from the original site of Londinium in 7th Century and was used as the capital until 11th century.

Westminster—at the time a small settlement on Thorney Island surrounding the early incarnation of Westminster Abbey, where later Westminster Cathedral was built. It is likely Harold Godwinson was crowned here although much of the work was funded by Edward the Confessor during his reign.

Wihtwarasburgh—a fort in or near what became modern day Carisbrooke on the Isle of Wight.

Stamford—one of the Danelaw five burghs, a small walled town in Lincolnshire. Stamford bridge was the site of the battle between Harold Godwinson and Harald Hardrada

Douvres—Dover, part of the Jarldom of Wessex at the time.

Fulford—a small village near York, site of the battle of the same name.

Pefenesea—Pevensey, a village on the coast of East Sussex where William the Conqueror landed his fleet.

Escancaester—Exeter, originally a Roman walled city. It was one of the few Saxon settlements built primarily in stone. After the Battle of Hastings, Gytha Thorkilsdottir fled to Exeter and stirred up rebellion amongst the conquered Saxons.

Hæstingaceaster—Hastings. The town that gave name to the nearby battle of Hastings.

Jarldoms of England:

Northumbria

East Anglia

Wessex

Kent

Mercia

Hereford

Huntingdon

(Norman place names are all rendered much as their modern French equivalents)

CHAPTER 1

The evening was blood red. The falling sun painted the walls of the fort, the shattered gates, the armed men who stood within its ramparts, the prisoners who knelt in the mud.

Victory. A small victory at that, but a victory. Only a tiny fortress, but one step towards suppressing the town across the river. It would be a long siege, but William would make their lives a misery before they submitted.

For a moment all was quiet. A moment later a yell of "bastard!" issued from the crowd and a shape detached itself, hurtling towards William. He had just time to put his hand to his sword, to extend his shield arm. Just had time to take in a bearded fellow in a leather jerkin and leggings, an expression of fury, charging at him.

The impact never came—two of William's guards piled into the man and heaved him to the ground. William let out his breath, a long plume of steam in the cooling air. The attacker was still yelling "bastard!" and "tyrant!" until one of the soldiers picked up his head by the hair and dropped it with a crunch on the ground.

The fury returned in a surge. His own people! Poisoned against him by that traitor Arnulf, making common cause with his enemy, Martel. So the town bordered Maine, but it was held of the Dukes of Normandy by Royal decree. Did that mean nothing to these commoners?

"Let him up," William snapped. "To his knees, mind."

The guards hauled the bearded man up.

"He had this, my Lord." Henri de Ryes offered up a long knife with a broad blade, so curved it was almost a hook, the cutting edge on the inside and so keen it had almost thinned to nothing.

"What is it?"

"A pollarding knife, my Lord."

"Pollarding? What's that?"

"I understand the foresters round here cut the limbs off the trees with knives like this so they grow straight and thin."

Hides for the Tanner! Hides for the Tanner!

Those words now seemed to drift around the inside of the fort, as they had when men had taunted him while hanging hides over the ramparts before the battle. It was silent. All were waiting to see what he would do. No one spoke. And yet the words *Hides for the Tanner!* thundered as if God himself had torn open a cloud and screamed it down from the heavens.

They insulted him. But they didn't just insult *him*. They painted his mother as a grasping whore, his father a slave to his lusts. And William, as the worthless spawn of their filthy union, an upstart runt trying to convince the world he was noble, while they laughed behind their hands at his antics.

"I see." William examined the knife, then looked at the man kneeling before him. If he couldn't punish Arnulf... Or perhaps he could, in a way.

Anyway, it wasn't just Arnulf he wanted to punish. Had this man been among those who had hung hides over the walls?—a common enough thing to protect against blows from siege engines, until they had begun to shout their personal message to him, telling him exactly what they thought of their Duke. He looked from knife to man, to knife.

"Let me see, Master Forester. You hung out hides for the tanner earlier, which was most appropriate to your guest and liege lord. I wonder how I ought to treat wayward foresters in a manner that would be as fitting?"

The man's eyes had widened, and he tried to pull away, but the two men holding him gripped harder. William waited until he was still again. "Pray, tell me more about 'pollarding'."

He looked at the prisoners, and before them, the man who had gone for him. None spoke. All had turned white beneath the crimson glow from the sunset. The would-be assailant's mouth flapped.

"If it's hides for the tanner, it should be pollarding for the forester, should it not?" William scraped his thumb gently across the knife blade, careful to keep the movement perpendicular to that horrid edge. The roughness against his skin betrayed just how keen, but the thickness and curvature gave strength to it. It must slice through green wood beautifully.

William was about to ask him to swear his allegiance to his liege lord or forfeit his life and let the man go when he saw a hardening in the fellow's eyes. The hatred was still there. The contempt. For a second he was everyone who had ever sneered at William's birth, who had failed to accord him the merest shred of the respect he was due. It wasn't just that Arnulf had poisoned their minds. They'd always held him in contempt, and thrown off his Lordship of them at the first opportunity as if it were nothing.

William jutted his chin at the other prisoners. "Take them away. And make sure they know well that any man who calls me bastard shall suffer the same fate. And him…"—William gestured at the forester—"hold him down. Someone find something to put his arm on. I'm going to practice my pollarding."

The man began to thrash and scream, not in anger or hatred this time, but pure terror. William hardly heard. Dimly he was aware of shouts of alarm from the other prisoners as they were herded out of the gate The clamour of *Hides for the Tanner* echoing in his mind was deafening. Someone brought a chopping block, a rough section of tree trunk, and thrust it beneath the forester's arm. The guard struggled to hold him down, finally managing to secure his wrist against the scored surface. His screams had dampened to sobs when William made the first cut. Then the screaming started again.

It was as he had suspected, the knife cut superbly. It sliced through skin, flesh and muscle. Hot blood began to spray over William's hands. The prisoner gave another thrash then fell still, passed out. The tendons proved a tougher challenge, and even with the wonderful sharp edge, it took a good deal of sawing and hacking to get through them. "I suppose there's a knack to getting through anything tougher," he muttered. The knife was down to bone now, and that took his whole weight until, crunching and squelching, the blade worked its way between the edges of the joint. The scraping of metal against bone put his teeth on edge, and then there was more gristle and tendon to slice through, before finally the blood-slicked ruin of a hand plopped into the mud.

"I'll try to get the next one neater," he said brightly. "Put his other arm on the block please." One of the guards vomited.

The second hand took a little less time. William was going to leave it there, but the vitriol sting of fury had not passed, and he decided to do the feet as well. The blade finally broke a little way into the second ankle, so William used his sword, which frankly was much more efficient. He stood, wiped his brow and realised he'd smeared blood all over his face, then began to laugh.

Gallet knelt by the prostrate forester, and snorted. "Bloody flux! He lives!"

William sighed. If he survived the aftermath of his wounding, he'd wish he hadn't. "Bind his wounds. Take him away. And clear those up," he added, pointing to the mangled hands and feet.

"What do you want done with them?" Gallet sneered. "Shall I have them mounted?"

William shrugged. "Stick them in a mangonel and throw them over the walls, why don't you."

"Very well, Lord."

"I didn't mean... oh, do what you will."

William stormed to the spot they'd chosen to set up camp, demanded some water and cleaned the worst of the blood off. He saw the way some of the men looked at him, and he stared back until they blanched, looked away. And as he saw the blood staining the water, soaking into the earth as he tipped it away, saw the reddish tinge in his skin where it had soaked too deep to clean away. He had really done that? Mutilated a man for an insult? Rendered a person a helpless cripple for a look of hatred? Could it be justified? The rage that had taken him over, soaking deep into his bones until he was made of it. Could be be a Duke over all of Normandy when he could not be master of himself? To take a man's hands and feet. All of them! Would there ever be any atonement for that until the last judgement? Probably not.

Good God. What had this Dukedom made of him? But the words of his former guardian about being a good lord, about treating your vassals and serfs well...? How hollow it rang. If you treated people well, they took it as weakness. He would fight until he was the undisputed sovereign of all his territories, but to do it and avoid sin? He silenced the small part of his thoughts that said the man had deserved all he had received and worse.

William called for de Ryes to come to him. "Find the most senior men among the prisoners and bring them to me," William demanded. Now they had some captives, he might as well press them for information. Some among them might know who had betrayed him and passed his plans to his enemies. It was unlikely—probably only Arnulf and a few of those closest to him knew that—but there might be a hint or two that would allow them to narrow it down.

But when two prisoners were brought before him, they were so incoherent as to be useless. Sobbing, grovelling wretches, attempting to prostrate themselves before him. For a while, hardly anything they said made any sense at all. And then one of them collected himself a little. "My Lord, please! Do not take our hands! We are truly sorry for the insult you have suffered. We have been poor servants but we will make amends if only you will let us. We will do you fealty, do service to you all our lives, we swear on the Holy Martyr!" he snivelled.

William frowned. What was this?

De Ryes leant down and whispered in his ear. "Sorry, my Lord. I had to separate the prisoners into small groups as they were a bit of a handful. But they each thought the rest were being taken away to be... ah, pollarded in turn. They're still a bit agitated."

"Hmm. I'll bet they are," he replied. He glanced at the prisoners. How easily they'd submitted when they thought they were going to be treated the same way as the bearded forester with his hate-filled eyes and foul mouth... "Tell me, have the bodies from the fort been disposed of yet?"

"Ours or theirs?"

"Theirs. Either."

"Theirs have been put in a pile to deal with later. Ours are being buried now. Why's that, Lord?"

"I think I may have an idea to ensure Alençon is in our hands by this time tomorrow."

The morning dawned clear, a little chilly, and very, very quiet. The sky, once again lurid through the low-lying mist, dyed the mud outside the gates of Alençon red. William hoped they could see it from the town.

The calmest mornings could be prologue to the most violent days.

William loosened his sword in its scabbard. "Tell them again."

Gallet cleared his throat. "You've had our message. Those are our terms. Open your gates. Hand over Bellême, and any of Martel's people, or every man, woman and child within the walls will suffer the same fate as the... messengers."

The message was not conventional, but it was clear enough.

No one responded. It was as if the town was deserted. And then, with a creak and a scrape, the gates began to shift. William tightened his grip on the hilt of his sword, but this was no last, desperate sally.

"We're bringing you Bellême," a voice drifted out of the mist. "Spare us, Lord!"

"Any man concealing arms or showing ill intent will receive the same treatment as those who defied us yesterday," Gallet shouted back.

"And those who offered insult to the Duke must be given up," William added. Gallet looked sidelong at him. "Or there will more bloodshed."

There was a pause. Then, "Aye, aye, Lord, you shall have them."

"More pollarding, Lord?" Gallet asked. "You have a taste for it now?"

William stared at the knight. Such insolence! And yet wasn't that why he kept Gallet so close? "I haven't decided. I may prune a limb or two. I shan't take all of them."

"The Duke is merciful."

"It's such a lovely morning I'm in a good mood."

Gallet laughed. "And how do you know they'll give you the right men?"

"Does it matter? As long as an example is set?"

Gallet pondered that for a moment. "I suppose not."

"All right, enough of this. We go in."

Henri de Ryes cleared his throat behind them. "They could still ambush us, Lord."

"They wouldn't dare."

They pushed in through the gates. The truth was that William half expected a hail of arrows or a shower of hot oil, but he was committed to showing these people they were beneath his fear, that they had no power to hurt him and he knew it. How different from yesterday...

William called Montgomerie to him. "You have the terms of surrender, Cousin?"

"Yes, Lord. Although I still think–"

"Have Bellême sign them and bring him to me in the town square. Have the whole town assemble."

Montgomerie's shoulders slouched a little. "Yes, Lord."

"Such a touching family reunion," Gallet muttered.

"What a way for Bellême to find out his sister's married my cousin," William replied under his breath.

Soon the surrender arrived in the shaking hands of a scribe with the ink still wet and smudged on the parchment. William took one look at the meaningless scrawl and handed it to someone. He didn't even see who took it. A moment later the man who had signed it appeared before him, propelled by two large Norman infantrymen, Montgomerie trailing behind. Arnulf de Bellême, the Lord of Alençon. A wretch grovelling in the mud.

"Full and unconditional surrender of the town, its fortifications and garrison, Lord," Montgomerie said.

"Good." He drew his sword and stared down at Arnulf quivering before him, chains clinking as he shivered. It was not that cold. Lord of Alençon? William's nose wrinkled. The man wasn't even lord of his own bowels by the smell of him. William hefted the sword and let it swing to his side again. It didn't hurt to keep Arnulf guessing as to its purpose a while longer. He felt the gaze of the mute mass of townsfolk boring into the back of his neck. Many of their former number were less whole than they had been before the butcher Bastard of Normandy had come here. Some by his own hand. Holy Christ, the things he'd done. Such was the price of betrayal. And an insult. And in a day, the tale had grown in the telling. Who knew what savagery would be attributed to him by the time they returned to Falaise?

The truth was that one forester had lost his hands and feet with his own pollarding knife for the sake of an insult. Soon the tale of how all the prisoners had been mutilated to a man and to a limb echoed round the army like the man's screams had echoed round the fort. It was too good a story to deny. And what did it matter if most of the hands and feet they'd catapulted over the walls had come from the already dead? There were enough of those. And plenty to send on to Domfront along with the ever-growing tale. Perhaps his moment of brutality might win two cities.

What was love and respect next to the power of fear?

William let Arnulf kneel in the mud, imagining all the things that William the Butcher might be about to do to him. Arnulf's eyes bulged and his breath came in short, jolting huffs. William looked down at the man and remained silent for as long as he could bear to. He hefted the sword again. "Do you renounce your treachery and promise in all things to be faithful to your liege lord?" he asked, eventually.

"Yes! Yes! Oh, Lord, anything... I... swear... yes. Oh, God, Oh Saints. I swear it! I swear it all. I... renounce... Lord, please... I beg... I beg... faithful... pledge... service." He continued in that vein for some minutes until enough of the words of the oath of homage had been uttered, in close enough to the right order. William tapped him on the shoulders with his sword and sheathed it. He heard Montgomerie sigh behind him. His advisor had been all for executing Arnulf without delay. God's bones, the man was Montgomerie's brother-in-law! He did not want to think on what Mabel, currently making a nuisance of herself back at Falaise, would say to the news that her husband had killed her brother.

No, there had been enough savagery during the brief fighting, and afterwards. That had given Arnulf plenty of reasons to stay loyal, and clapping him in chains had given him more incentive still. In any case, if he was allowed to return to Alençon it would be under the watchful eye of the new Norman garrison, drawn from the soldiers who had defeated him.

"Good," William repeated. "Now, I would ask a boon of my loyal servant."

"My Lord?" Arnulf said, puzzlement briefly in his eyes, before they glazed over with terrified gratitude once more. "Anything!"

"I want names," William hissed. "Someone has betrayed me. You know who they are."

"My Lord?" Arnulf's eyes widened.

"Someone's been feeding you and Geoffrey Martel information. Someone told you we were marching on Domfront. Then that we were coming here." He leaned forward. "Who?"

Even now, Arnulf hesitated. Could it be that for all he feared William, standing before him with a sword and drenched in the blood of his townsfolk, the man feared Geoffrey Martel more? Or was there another reason?

Was his betrayer standing nearby?

"Gallet," William called, "do you still have the pollarding knife that forester attacked me with?"

"I do, Lord," the knight growled. Vicious in battle, he clearly disapproved of other kinds of violence. No matter. Someone smirked behind him. It sounded like Odo.

"Lord, please!" There was pleading in Arnulf's eyes. He seemed to have soiled himself again. "Our scouts reported your army's whereabouts and—"

William silenced him with a look. "Your 'scouts' were seen conversing with... *elements* from my army. It had every appearance of a planned meeting. Do not spin me tales, Bellême, I know I was betrayed, and you know by whom. And if you won't tell me, perhaps your son can. Perhaps he can't, but I won't be sure until I've had a conversation with him."

Something changed at that moment. Arnulf did not move, yet something in his aspect revealed a decision taken. He would throw in his lot with William, for now, and take his chances with Martel's wrath.

This was the moment. William's breath quickened. Would he have to put his cousin Montgomerie to death? Please God, not Gallet!

"Your uncle," Arnulf almost whispered. "The Baron of Arques. He has sworn himself to Martel but agreed not to reveal himself yet."

"I knew it." Gallet issued a stream of language so foul and furious the meaning was only apparent from his tone and the saliva spraying anyone within six *pieds*.

God's balls! William caught Montgomerie's eye. His cousin had the same idea. Arques was back at Domfront and his men outnumbered the rest of William's. They might already have joined with Martel's men in in the town and slaughtered his army! He felt no anger this time, just a slow plummeting sensation. He might already have lost the Duchy.

"Montgomerie?" William gestured to his advisor. "Arrange a garrison. Do it quickly. It may have a third part of all the men, but from the foot. I need all the horse—de Ryes can stay to command, though, I want you by my side." *And in my sight.*

"My Lord," Montgomerie nodded and hurried away.

"Gallet, find Odo, have the rest formed up and ready to march on Domfront at once."

***

William began the march back to Domfront within the hour. Domfront's townspeople should have heard what happened here by now, the disaster that had befallen their

26

neighbors, and if it did not shake their resolve, they would be under no illusions what faced them when the walls eventually failed. A few terrified men had been set free on condition they run to Domfront, and only to Domfront, would see to that. And if they were not persuasive, the severed hands and feet thrown over the walls would bear a starker message.

But on the other hand, maybe all his men were killed or put to flight and he would be met on the road by an army ten times the size of this little band, the combined forces of Martel and his uncle. The world would never remain still. For all that sieges could last years, like the mistral wearing down rock, sometimes things could turn on a moment. A moment of fury. A moment of insult. A moment of betrayal.

When the messengers were first spotted racing along the road from Domfront, William wondered numbly if he was even still Duke of Normandy.

The heralds that met William, Gallet and Odo on the road bore two pieces of news.

"What of the army? Is all well? Has there been any fighting?" William demanded before the man was able to finish his address.

"Fighting? No, Lord." The lieutenant declared, turning slightly ashen. "We carried out your... orders, and Domfront immediately offered terms for its surrender."

Terms? They have seen what will happen if they resist, and they offer terms? For a moment, Arques was forgotten. The impudence! "Are the terms favorable to us?" William asked, teeth gritted.

"Yes, Lord. They wish only that the citizenry go unharmed. They are willing to hand over any remaining Angevin loyalists... in fact, a few were thrown over the walls before they let us in to negotiate..."

"Very well. They will submit to a Norman garrison."

"They will, Lord," said the lieutenant even though it had not been a question.

William let it pass. "Good. See to that, if you please. But what of our forces? The Baron of Arques? All is well?"

The lieutenant turned a shade of green, and William thought he might be about to vomit. Christ's boils, was there another sickness spreading through the army? Or was it even worse?

"Duke William, I am also... I am also commanded..."

"What is it?" Gallet frowned. "Spit it out, man."

"Aye, sirs. The Baron of Arques... during the night... he left his post. As did his vassals. Most of them."

An odd sort of silence descended. William realized he was holding his breath, and noticed that most of the others were too. A moment's relief, then the fury returned. "Left his post? Where is he?"

"Gone, Sire. Lord fitzOsbern sent scouts and messengers to find out where he was going and bring him back. Those who overtook him... Killed, Lord."

"He betrayed us?" Odo squeaked. William realised his brother had not believed it until then. "Our uncle has betrayed us? Blasphemy! I'll have him excommunicated!"

"No doubt marching with all speed back to his castle," Gallet added. "He'd better run, or when we catch up with him he'll wish he'd never been born."

William realized they were all looking at him. Waiting for the storm. Yet within him, he felt a strange almost-calm. It was certainty. Yesterday he'd been wondering whether it might have been Montgomerie, Gallet, Fitz who had been selling him to the highest bidder. Now he knew the betrayal had come from his uncle. It all made sense. Arques had always been the most likely. He had the opportunity to send warnings to Domfront and then Alençon that William's army was on its way. Details of the Duke's plans, manpower and location. He should have had the man watched more closely.

And yet how much could he still trust the others? These men… how much love did they have for him, really? They knew his every secret. Knowledge like that was valuable indeed should they turn their coats.

He loosened his fists and cleared his throat. "There's no need for you to look at me that way."

"Have you orders, Lord?" Montgomerie asked, inclining his head daintily. His silky voice was particularly irksome at that moment. William kept his jaw clamped shut while the urge to tell him to divorce his cursed wife and cut himself off from the whole Bellême clan passed.

"Yes, Cousin," William answered eventually. "Return with the foot to Domfront as quickly as you may. Gallet? Gather the horse to me. We ride for Arques.

"Lord?" Montgomerie was keeping the breezy tone in his voice at some effort. "To face all your uncle's men with threescore horse exhausted from riding… Is there no other way?"

William chose his words. "None that your Lord commands."

"Aye, Lord. It will be done." Montgomerie had turned as white as the lieutenant.

The cavalry maintained a brisk pace through the forest-flanked roads. William could feel the nerves among his captains, Gallet and Odo. It was a fearsome risk they were taking. All Arques needed to do was leave a handful of skirmishers in the woods with bows and his men could be decimated. And yet William was certain Arques would not. That his uncle did not even expect him to pursue. But the apprehension of his captains was like a shadow, and he instinctively drew his horse ahead, picking up the pace.

In that moment he was back in the moment four years ago—or was it five?—at the hunt at Valognes. The day all this had begun. A carefree pursuit of a stag for no better reason than the sport of it, while behind him, his sworn men plotted his destruction. It felt as though it was someone else's life. The sun dappling through the trees, the pounding of his horse's hooves on the hard-packed earth of the road, the beast's breath jetting into the air. What was this constant struggle even for?

Why keep fighting? He could surrender his titles, retreat to a mansion somewhere beyond the reach of his opponents... the men who were fighting so hard to displace him. Let them have it all. Go to a place with a forest for him to hunt in. The life of a country gentleman... would it be so bad?

The heat rose gradually in his chest, neck, face. No. Good God, no, never. He was the Duke! That meant something. It meant something to his father. It meant something to Gallet, who'd risked his neck to spirit him away from assassins. It meant something to his nobles—the loyal ones—to his soldiers, to the people who relied on him for protection.

No! He would fight and fight and fight and defend his Duchy to his final wheezing breath, and if it was not safe, secure and prosperous, then he could meet his ancestors in the knowledge that he had done all he could... ALL he could, to be worthy of what they had built.

The volume of hoofbeats rose to his left, and when he glanced back, Gallet was drawing alongside. William eased the reins a little and sat up. "I know, I know," he said before Gallet could catch his breath. "I'm too exposed and tiring the horses."

"Arques left after Vespers, by all accounts. With all his footsoldiers we'll catch him before noon. No need to knacker ourselves before we get there."

"No, you're right. But stop worrying, will you? It's annoying."

Gallet grunted. "You don't actually aim to give battle do you, Lord? It'd be suicide."

"That it may be, but I don't intend to make it easy for him to get away." Gallet pulled a face at that, but did not respond. "Think about it," William added. "He's fleeing. That means after hearing how we took Alençon he's shitting himself. He could have taken his men, joined up with Martel and torn us to shreds."

"Hm. True. Unless this is a feint and Martel is coming around behind us."

William laughed, a little wildly. "He could be, couldn't he? But I don't think so. He's lost two towns in one day, and what I've seen of the man tells me he's cautious. Too cautious. Arques wasn't expecting us to take Alençon so quickly, which means Martel didn't either."

The horses broke out of the trees into an open stretch of fields. William glanced at the sun. He estimated it was around halfway through terce. Another couple of hours would potentially see them catching Arques' rearguard. All right. He started to run through plans in his mind, depending on how Arques might respond to a party of cavalry appearing in pursuit.

"So why not let Arques bugger off? What harm can he do in his castle? He'll be trapped there like Guy de Brionne. Another siege. What joy."

"My Uncle wasn't acting alone," William said. "He holds his titles and lands on behalf of the Duchy. I could take them away with a word. The fact that he's defying me at all means he has supporters in Normandy, and I don't want them feeling too comfortable."

"Yes, that's true. Every time we uproot one cursed weed, another five seem to spring up."

"It's time to deal with Arques' troublesome brother, I think."

"Archbishop Mauger? Good. I can't stand the weasel. It's probably Mauger that talked Arques into breaking with you. Not to mention sending those assassins."

"I see now that my uncles were only ever waiting for their chance. Martel moving in Maine gave them the opportunity they'd been looking for."

And even that was no coincidence. Mauger had likely negotiated with Martel to protect Arques if he had to raise his hand against his liege lord. Probably Martel. But there were other possibilities... Greater men still who might wish to see him destroyed.

"Anyway. Your plans, Lord?" Gallet broke into William's thoughts.

"Make it look as though we're going to charge the rearguard. Then at the last moment, approach with a small group under flag of truce. A score of men, mounted on coursers. To discuss my uncle's conduct."

"Aye, Lord. And if he takes a more... belligerent approach?"

"That is why I suggested fast horses."

At the next well, they stopped, allowing men and horses to rest and drink, but William did not allow them to stay for long. The men with the fastest and freshest mounts were assembled and detailed to ride with William during the parley, and they armed and set off again.

The sun was not long overhead when an incongrous grey smudge could be seen on the road in the distance. "Pick up the pace," William ordered. The more dust we can kick up, the more men they'll think we have. The cavalry formed fluidly into battle order and they rode down on the waiting army. Though they could not yet see, William imagined the effect their charge would have. If they were lucky—very lucky —the men might take flight before they arrived. But it was not to be. As they approached, he saw the rearguard forming a line, pikes driven into the ground and raised. He swung his spear upward, a signal to his men and revealing the white banner at its head.

At that, the majority of the men reined in their horses, and the small party at the head trotted into earshot of the defensive line. What thoughts were going through their minds now?

"Normandy!" William called, "Normandy!" That would set the cat among the pigeons he hoped, revealing that the Duke himself was pursuing them. "I demand to speak with my vassal, the Baron of Arques! I require that he explain his actions, present himself to me at Falaise and repeat his oath of homage!"

A ripple went through the pack of men lined across the road, and the larger mass behind. Messages being passed, options discussed.

"Do you think he'll comply?" Gallet asked.

"If he has any sense, he will. But I fear things have gone beyond that point." William was sure of that. His uncle had seen what became of traitors. "He may feel the only thing that will protect him now is the stoutness of Arques castle's walls." *And allies who could break a siege?...*

The line ahead parted and three men, one carrying a flag of truce, emerged. William could already tell his uncle was not one of them. Disappointing.

The men approached, and saluted them, a little apprehensively. *They will have heard about Alençon,* William thought.

The envoy in the centre met his gaze, and swallowed. "Lord, I am commanded to inform you that my Lord of Arques does not recognize your right to the Dukedom of Normandy, and will not submit to your request."

"T'was a demand, not a request."

"Yes, Lord. My Lord of Arques requests that according to the laws of nobility, he be left free to return to his castle free of harassment."

Gallet gasped and William laughed.

"You may tell my uncle that if he does not submit, he is no Baron, and that the lands, titles and castles he previously held of me will be forfeit. I will give him one day to reconsider his impertinence. One day, mind. At noon tomorrow, having not received his embassy, he will be held to have committed treachery against his liege lord. He and his men will be harried day and night until they leave Norman lands." He leaned forward slightly. "Any men who remain with my uncle will be held to have sinned equally. Any who renounce their false Lord and present themselves to me will be treated mercifully. Tell my uncle."

"Aye, Lord."

As they withdrew to the main group, Gallet muttered "that was well done. I wasn't sure how you were going to get out of that and save face without attacking."

"Thank you," William chuckled. "I'm glad you approve."

As one difficulty was overcome, another arose. But despite it, William felt a kind of wild jubilation. Perhaps it was the euphoria of battle and chase with too-little sleep, but he did not think so. His enemies, Arques and Mauger at least, were now out in the open, not skulking round, undermining him from nearby, destroying trust in those around him. And he had forced the great Martel onto the defensive.

"So what do we do next?" Gallet asked. "We need more men if we're going to keep this up."

"Yes. But I know how we can attract thousands of men to us."

"Oh yes? How is that?"

"With one woman."

Gallet chuckled. "She must be some beauty to draw all those men to us."

"It's not for them. She's for me."

Gallet doubled over with laughter. "Oh, Lord! You'd sacrifice your freedom for your Duchy?"

William shrugged. He may have lost one lord's armies, but there could be another's marching under Normandy's banner. A much greater lord than Arques, with battle-hardened forces. "Dispatch an emissary to the Count of Flanders sending word that I wish to complete our arrangement."

In the midst of war, it was time for a wedding.

CHAPTER 2

Ælfgifa had not slept well since she had overheard the guard Berenger's account of William's actions at Alençon. It was well enough in the day, when she had the distraction of work and Helisande's company. At night, when she laid down on the hard cot in the bare and tiny chamber that had been allotted to her, Ælfgifa found her imagination running riot. It was all too easy for her mind's eye to see how it would have happened. The miscreants who had insulted William's parentage. The curl of the pollarding knife, gleaming in a sideways silver grin. The screams, the blood, the stench of burned flesh as extremities were removed one by one. Had all the offenders been punished at once? Or had each had to wait his turn, watching with horror the fate that awaited him. Soiling themselves or vomiting. Adding those human stenches to the air already rich and reeking with human blood, boiling oil and seared flesh as the wounds were cauterized... The fate of those who betrayed the Duke. What, she wondered, might be the fate of a spy?

The faint scratch of nails on wood made Ælfgifa start up from her pallet.

"Psst, Lady?"

Ælfgifa drew a deep breath and glared at the door in annoyance, furious at having been caught so unawares in the heart of enemy territory. "What is it, Helisande?"

"Please? Will you just come with me?" There was an ill-disguised chuckle, muffled by the door.

Ælfgifa rolled her eyes, wondering what mischief her friend had planned this time, and let her in. Helisande surprised her, one small hand grasping Ælfgifa's wrist and drawing her silently into the corridor, motioning for Ælfgifa to be quiet and hurry. Helisande led the way to the ladies' quarters, away from the bed chambers.

The door to the solar was locked, just as Ælfgifa had expected. Lady de Bellême made a great show of the keys entrusted to her care, as if keeping the key to the spice cabinet and the much larger key to the solar marked her out as a special functionary in the Duke's household. Ælfgifa privately wondered if the lady fancied herself mistress of Falaise. God knew how she would act when William eventually brought his Duchess home. Still, she had been uncertain about this piece of mischief and was just as glad to turn to her companion and say, "Come, Helisande, it was a noble attempt but... Helisande?"

The girl reached into her girdle and drew out two long thin pieces of metal. One came to a fine point, the other was wider, stronger. "Keep watch," she murmured to Ælfgifa.

"Helisande! What are you doing?" Ælfgifa hissed, casting a hasty glance along the dark and empty corridor. They were alone. All the castle were abed—as they should have been themselves.

"Opening the door, of course. One moment... ah!" Helisande had inserted the broader strip of metal into the lock with a slight wiggle. The fine, pointed length went next. She wriggled this a little too, as if feeling inside the lock with the tip. Ælfgifa heard a faint click as something inside the lock slid home. Forgetting her nerves, she watched in fascination as Helisande applied pressure to the broad strip whilst simultaneously smoothly lifting and turning the thin piece. There was a satisfying snick from inside the locking mechanism and Helisande grinned. "Try it now," she urged.

Warily, Ælfgifa tried the door again. It swung open with a low, sleepy creak. She shook her head at Helisande. "Where did you learn to do that?"

Helisande chuckled and hurried Ælfgifa into the dark solar, shutting the door behind them. "Papa taught me. Noblemen are always losing their keys, he told me, although I think he learned so he could sneak into the castle at night to visit my mother before they were married." She grinned impishly and Ælfgifa found herself reluctantly smiling in return. "It was an easy lock. Only one pick and a tension wrench. I could have opened it with a dagger and a bone hair pin if I'd had to."

"Is Sir Gallet aware that his wife carries the tools of the thief's trade in her girdle?" Ælfgifa asked, raising an eyebrow.

Helisande chuckled again. "If he gets anywhere near my girdle, those are not the contents he is interested in."

"Are you going to tell me why we are here?" Ælfgifa asked with heavy patience.

Helisande looked up at her in surprise. "To play a trick on Lady de Bellême, of course. Why else? I am sick of that fat sow talking about you as if you are a bête. Why do you never speak to her in Frankish as you do to me? She thinks you little more than an imbécile."

"The less I speak to Mabel de Bellême, the less I will have to speak to her. Let her think me an idiot if I might have some peace out of it." Ælfgifa thought she might as well get something out of the arrangement. Pretending not to understand the ladies when they gossiped over their needlework certainly wasn't yielding fresh sources of intelligence. Any gleanings were few and far between.

Helisande glanced up from where she knelt in front of Lady de Bellême's work box. "She had one of the kitchen girls whipped when she found her kissing a drover's son. As if it was any business of hers, the vicious old bitch."

Ælfgifa narrowed her eyes. "What did you have in mind?"

With an expression somewhere between grinning determination and a moue of disgust, Helisande picked up the sack-cloth wrapped bundle she'd brought with her. Gingerly, she peeled back four layers of wrapping before exposing the brown-stained linen package at the centre. Long before she had got that far, Ælfgifa's nose had told her exactly what was in the bundle. *I suppose she is a kennel master's daughter,* she thought.

"Dog shit, Helisande?" she said wearily.

"Yes. And offal from that pig butchered yesterday."

I've stood before a man physically holding his guts in but I swear I've never smelt anything that disgusting. "Wait!" Ælfgifa said, as Helisande reached for Lady de Bellême's embroidery.

Helisande pouted at her. "I thought Saxon women were bold and fearless."

"And I thought you were original," Ælfgifa retorted. "Who do you think will be blamed if Mabel finds her precious needlework smeared with dog excrement?"

"She will think one of her horrible little lapdogs has got into her work box," Helisande said with true kennel master's distain for any dog smaller than a wolf hound.

"Not if you add pig guts," Ælfgifa said in exasperation. "I assume you do not wish to be whipped like that kitchen wench?"

"She would not dare!"

"Perhaps it is better not to find out," Ælfgifa paused, the glimmering of an idea hovering in her mind's eye. She shouldn't do it really. She ought to be superior to circumstance and let Mabel's slights and barbs pass her by. And yet a fine thread of recklessness was uncoiling in her gut. "Helisande, is there parchment and ink here?"

"No," Helisande said in puzzlement. "But there is plenty in the priest's room down the hall."

Ælfgifa smiled wickedly. "Good. Go and fetch me some while I put things in order. And dump the dog shit out of the window while you're at it."

It was a foolish game, Ælfgifa was well aware of that. Later she would wonder whether it was truly Lady de Bellême she wished to strike at, even in so childish a fashion as she was considering. It would occur to her that what she really sought was a release for the tight knot of tension since hearing of the Duke at Alençon. To act instead of this infernal, perpetual waiting. Mabel with her small-mindedness, her narrow intellect and her petty cruelties was an ideal stand-in for both the restlessness of Ælfgifa's captive state and a target possessed of far more brutality. Ælfgifa wished for once to do and not consider every angle in advance—precious little good such previous consideration had done her until now, after all. She stifled her caution and began to compose a missive in her head.

As she folded away the fine lawn, with its half-finished design stitched in brilliant threads, Ælfgifa could admit that if there was one thing that was good about Mabel de Bellême, it was her needlework. Bolstered by her mischievous plan,

Ælfgifa was not too proud to admit that Mabel was easily as skilled as herself.

Helisande returned with parchment and quill. As she explained what she intended to her giggling friend, it occurred to Ælfgifa that she had sacrificed much in the pursuit of intellectual accomplishment. Here, a hostage in a precarious position, charged by her brother to spy for him against a rival, burdened with both the secret of this purpose and with the conflict she felt at the dishonor of her actions, Ælfgifa felt truly young for the first time. Her muted laughter joined with Helisande's.

***

Mabel de Bellême took a great gulp of air and pressed a hand over her heart, staring down into her work box as if it contained a coiled viper. Ælfgifa bent lower over her own needlework and forced down a laugh. Next to her, Helisande shook with repressed giggles. There was no way Ælfgifa could kick her ankle without drawing attention so she prayed that the sight of Lady de Bellême in a state of shock would occupy the other women enough that they wouldn't notice the tears of laughter running down Helisande's red face.

Ælfgifa had told Helisande what the note said as she wrote it. Crying with laughter, Helisande had gulped out suggestions for choice phrases concerning Mabel's ample attributes. Ælfgifa had her doubts about whether Mabel would find some of the ostentatious comparisons flattering. Comparing the lady's broad behind to the flanks of a fine mare had seemed extremely amusing last night, but now it seemed so ridiculous as to be unbelievable. Surely when the shock of having received so personal and intimate a letter from an admirer who could not possibly be her husband

41

wore off, Mabel would fly into a fury and start looking for culprits.

"What is it, my lady? Why do you grow so pale?" little Idette asked, coming over to Mabel and peering into the work box. "Is that a letter, Madame?"

Mabel slammed the lid of the box so sharply that Idette almost lost the tips of her reaching fingers. "It is nothing. Really, child, why are you forever prying into those things which are not your concern? If you paid your needles half so much mind, that altar cloth would be done already!"

Idette was young, willowy and naïve. Mabel had made a pet of her and never spoken to her so sharply before. Her huge blue eyes filled with tears and she swallowed hard.

"Oh, go on with you. Take a turn spinning for a change," Mabel said, giving the girl a little push away from her—and the work box. Helisande was almost doubled over her needlework now. A strange whooping noise escaped her and Ælfgifa set her jaw. When she dared look up again, she noticed that several of the ladies had set about their own work with expressions that ranged from perplexed to mildly annoyed. It was quiet, none of the usual chatter. And Mabel sat in state as usual, embroidery forgotten in her lap as her eyes peered into a distance no one else could see and a wistful, tender smile played around her thin lips.

Helisande leaned closer to Ælfgifa on the pretext of showing her a stitch. "You cannot stop now," she whispered, the words tickling Ælfgifa's ear. "You must see how far this will play."

***

Over the next few weeks, Mabel de Bellême often found 'tokens of love' in her work box. Mostly these were letters carefully penned by Ælfgifa with a few suggestions from Helisande, but sometimes there were small posies of flowers, sweetmeats, a silk ribbon. Mabel guarded the letters jealously, though only one or two of the other ladies could read. Encouraged by Helisande, Ælfgifa wrote appalling stanzas of poetry in Mabel's praise, imitating the travelling bards she had once heard at her father's house, who as a gesture of respect always modelled the beautiful ladies of their songs and tales on her mother, Gytha. On occasion, when Mabel was behaving in a particularly foolish manner and the other women began to whisper that Lady de Bellême had a lover, as unlikely as that seemed, Ælfgifa felt a pinch of conscience. What had started as a fine joke to make a fool of a small-minded and spiteful woman could do real damage. How awful when Mabel found out, as she must, that there *was no* admirer. Then Mabel would speak sharply to one of the others or she would revile Ælfgifa for her face and her barbarism, and Ælfgifa would agree with Helisande that Mabel deserved one more letter. Ælfgifa sighed over her needlework—fine embroidery now that Mabel had seen what she was capable of. She knew that using her wits in such a petty deception was wasteful. It diminished her to stoop to such tricks but she could not bring herself to stop because it so amused Helisande. It soothed the wounded, restlessness within Ælfgifa herself, to be striking out even in so petty and juvenile a way. And so she vacillated between shame and amusement, and made no decision.

On that morning Mabel had not sat wearing her customary moon-eyed cow expression, despite the foolishly sentimental and somewhat explicit letter Helisande had folded into Mabel's embroidery last night. *In fact*, Ælfgifa reflected, *my lady de Bellême has not worn so sour an expression since she was instructed to house and shelter me.*

She soon found out what ailed the woman. Mabel had Idette sit with her as they worked but her voice was pitched deliberately loud enough for everyone in the room to hear.

"He'll be bringing the chit here, no doubt. Or she'll follow with an entourage if she has the effrontery to insist on a full wedding after the merry dance she's led his lordship on," Mabel tutted savagely and shook her head.

"What do you mean, Madame?" Idette said in her soft childish voice. "Do you mean the Duke?"

"Yes, the Duke! Who else should I be speaking of? He's on his way here as we speak and his wedding to the Flanders girl has been settled upon—not that Rome approves," she muttered darkly.

Ælfgifa bent over the fine linen she was working on as if setting a difficult stitch. She had mixed feelings about Duke William's return. The story she'd overheard the guards tell had made her freshly wary and more anxious of her predicament. She still wasn't sure what to make of the affair. *I'll stay out of his way on his return. He will not seek me out, especially if he has nuptials to plan.* She could become next to invisible if she chose. Avoiding his lordship seemed the most prudent course. Perhaps he had a bent toward unpredictability that she'd not sensed? *And no wonder Mabel looks as if she's had to swallow a pickled toad. She is used to being mistress here and Matilda of Flanders will outrank her. If this Matilda has any taste at all, she'll find a use for Mabel far from court.*

"I wonder that his lordship goes ahead with this marriage. Any maiden who spreads her legs so easily can hardly be the mother of future dukes," Mabel went on.

"I don't understand," Idette said.

"Word is Matilda is a spirited girl," old Clothilde creaked from the corner. "Kept his lordship on his toes about whether she would have him or no these five years. Never liked to be told he couldn't have what he wanted. Heard that she worked him up into such a rage with her teasing that he took her then and there. Consummated the marriage in advance as it were. Only wants the priest's words to be official."

"Oh, Clothilde, he didn't! Surely if they... they had congress," Idette's voice dropped to a whisper and she colored fetchingly. "If any of that were true, it must be because they have affection for each other..." She trailed off.

Clothilde laughed. "Don't know if it's true or not, but what I heard was he wanted her spoiled for anyone else. Her father approved the plan. Must have been despairing of getting the girl wed, for I hear she's a clever thing with a sharp tongue."

Ælfgifa felt sick. This was the second brutal rumor she had heard of William and she did not like it. While she acknowledged that such a deplorable act was possible, she did not put much credence in William having done so. This was the gossip of spiteful women, jealous of a new, young woman who would be their mistress. This was the whispering rumor of ignorant fools who must have entertainment and diversion from their mundane lives. Worse, Mabel was deliberately, and not at all subtly, undermining her new duchess before the girl even arrived.

What then? Ælfgifa wondered. *Will she play the friend to a lonely, isolated girl when all the time she set her on a wrong foot? Siphon power and influence away from William's wife that way?* It was too despicable for words.

As for William, he may well allow such a rumor to stand if it kept rivals away, if the only way to ensure obedience was through fear of what he might do next, but she didn't believe him to be brutish or stupid enough to start a marriage at such a disadvantage. For a moment she hated these Franks with their Latin Church masses and their belief that clever, articulate women should be put in their place.

"Either way, I would have thought the Duke could do better. If she's let one man in, there must have been others. Probably many." Mabel's vindictive gaze tightened on Helisande who had gone white, shaking so hard she stabbed a finger with her needle. Crimson drops dotted the fine material. "We must hope the Duke will think the better of it. A man who takes the leavings of others can't be much of a man. Don't you agree, my dear?" Her smile at Helisande was a vicious red slash.

Helisande sat in mute mortification under the cruel attack. Ælfgifa felt a rage so pure that for a moment she saw white.

"And as for your goblin friend from England—" Mabel started again.

"I find I must commit the dire offense of interrupting you, my lady de Bellême," Ælfgifa said calmly, eyes fixed on her needlework. "But I have oft heard you remark, Saxon swine cannot be expected to have manners or breeding, so I imagine the impoliteness will not trouble you too greatly." She spoke flawless Frankish and slowly raised her eyes to meet Mabel's horrified gaze. *Yes, every word, every insult, every snub you have leveled at me, I have heard and understood. Your sadly lacking hospitality has been registered. And I owe you no loyalty of silence.*

"What—" Mabel spluttered.

"I beg your pardon, Lady, but I have not finished. Since you are far more well-bred than I, you will not interrupt me." Ælfgifa set another stitch without bothering to look at what she was doing. "Your words have been most troubling. The future duchess might even find them poisonous? No, forgive my poor Frankish... treasonous. Treasonous is the word I wanted. I am certain it would be the word his lordship, Duke William would use." Another stitch, another pause. The blood drained from Mabel's face until she had all the color of a corpse.

"Since I am here under sufferance and therefore dependent upon his lordship's good countenance, I feel honor-bound to repeat such murmurs to him and let him decide. But there is another, more troubling matter," Ælfgifa said, pausing again to knot her thread and bite it off. "I have heard rumors that you yourself have a lover, Lady. I would not bend an ear to such idle gossip save that you have acted most strangely of late. Is it the butcher, perhaps? Or are the letters merely tokens from a most devoted husband?"

Mabel's mouth opened and closed several times but no words came out.

"That must be it then. I am relieved. Considering the content of the letter I spied in your workbox this morning when I went to borrow thread... one would not wish to share such intimacies with any save one's husband. Of course if it was a lover, I would be moved to appeal to the Duke to be housed elsewhere. I could hardly trust you as a guardian of chaste young maidens, myself included, in such circumstances." Ælfgifa smiled, close-lipped and savage. "Really, my lady, you look quite faint. It's early days yet but you may be with child. Perhaps you ought to have a posset made with honey, and lie down. Some sweetening and time to reflect, and you will be quite well again, I am sure."

She folded her work. "I think I will go down to the still room now. Helisande? Will you help?" They rose, leaving the room and Mabel de Bellême—white as salt and strangely collapsed in on herself—behind them.

As Helisande gave way to her mingled relief and mirth, Ælfgifa felt the tremors of rage leaving her body. More petty acts and those women were tinder waiting for a spark, as like to turn on each other as on a newcomer. There was something greasy about the feeling. She had been contaminated. Ælfgifa was furious with herself now. True, her tedious mornings in the solar had yielded little in the way of intelligence for Harold, but it was the greatest folly to give herself away in that fashion. All that patient waiting now wasted. Mabel would not speak incautiously around her again. Probably none of the ladies would. Her fine plans to give the duke a wide berth were fraying at the edges. They would collapse still further if she burned any more sources like that. And yet she could not be entirely sorry. Mabel had needed a severe shock. It wasn't as if she was more Ælfgifa's enemy now than she was before and the look of fear on Mabel's face had been unbelievably sweet. The encounter sat ill with her, however, and she realized that the rumors about William had disturbed her even so. She renewed her plans to avoid too much friendliness with him if she could not avoid his person, and tried to concentrate on Helisande's chatter, pushing the matter to the back of her mind.

CHAPTER 3

The train could be seen winding its way through the streets below and out into the countryside. Great God, how big a retinue was Baldwin bringing? Seven nights of feasting and then the whole party would decamp to Eu for the wedding itself, and then more feasting. No wonder Fitz was tearing his thinning hair out at the cost of it all.

The finery was ostentatious even from this distance. The sun breaking through the cloud picked out deep reds and blues adorning the horses and their riders.

William sensed, rather than saw, the presence beside him. And something else. A new awkwardness. "Lady Ælfgifa. You've been avoiding me."

"I am sure my Lord has not wanted for company since his return."

Must every conversation start with this jockeying for position? He growled in the back of his throat. "Company is never the problem. What do you make of all this, then?" He swept his arm at the approaching procession.

"The Count of Flanders is very keen to impress, is he not. One might gain the impression that this marriage is as important to him as it is to you." Ælfgifa smiled, a sight William was almost used to now. "Though I am sure his

Grace will make it very clear that he is doing you a great honor by dragging his entire household all this way and spending your money like water."

He laughed. "You're sure you've never met the Count?"

"No, Lord. Not this Count."

"You must have heard much of him, though? There was that business with your brother, Harold. And didn't Edward have an ambassador to his court? Some fellow with hair like straw. Brihtric?"

A moment's silence from Ælfgifa. Just an instant, but it was enough for him to know that she knew more than she had let on. Did she know about the rumors then? Of Matilda and the Saxon? Idle gossip, no doubt, and if anyone knew that idle gossip could be utterly untrue, it was him. But the stories had sown a seed, and what grew from it had taken painful root.

"I never met him," Ælfgifa said, tone even. "My position in the court was not so important."

Excuses? How unlike her. William turned his attention back to the Flemish procession, keen to pull his mind away from the thought of his bride's sometime lovers. What was it to him, anyway? This was a diplomatic business, and God knew, he needed Baldwin's support in the field. There, right at the head of the column, was Baldwin, and beside him, Matilda. When he saw the palfrey she was seated upon—delicately, sideways on an elaborate chair built on the saddle tree and led by a groom—he let out an involuntary snort of amusement.

"Lord?" Ælfgifa turned back to him. This was something she didn't know about.

"Forgive me, Lady. I see my bride comes to me on a white horse."

"It is customary, is it not?"

"Yes." He looked at her. She didn't appear to be testing him. "You haven't heard how my mother came to be my father's concubine then?"

"No, Lord."

Hm. Hadn't everyone heard that story? Evidently the people of Alençon had heard a version of it. "My mother was daughter to my father's steward. Not a tanner, as the base rumors have it—but her father was the son of a furrier, which I suppose is where it comes from. My mother caught Father's eye and he summoned her to share his bed. But she insisted on coming to him through the main gate on a white horse."

Ælfgifa laughed. "Is that so, Lord? I think perhaps I understand a little more now."

"Really? About what?"

She smiled and leant on the parapet, not meeting his eye. "Norman custom."

"Yes, well..." He folded his arms. "You see the grooves cut in the stone down there—on the forecourt below the ramp?"

Ælfgifa stood on tiptoe and leaned farther over, holding her plain headdress against the wind with one hand.

"Careful, Lady, I wouldn't want to have to explain to your family how you came to fall from the rampart."

She gave him a withering look, and seemed to be calculating whether or not to speak. Eventually, she said, "I see them, Lord. The grooves. What are they for?"

"Dyeing leather. The whole court is flooded with dye and the tanners trample it into the leather with their feet. The grooves allow the excess to run away."

"I see. How fascinating."

William forced himself to unclench his teeth slightly. "So you see how easy it is for people to suppose that the Lord of Falaise castle might spy the daughter of a tanner, uncommonly fair, raising her skirts to stamp the leather in the dye, perhaps showing more of her ankles than is becoming?"

"Ah. Yes, Lord."

Was that sympathy in her voice? From one who was said to be born of a demon or nymph?

"The white horse is true, I believe," he said. "Not any of the rest, though. None of it." He snorted. "Where do these prattling small folk think a tanner would come by a fine white palfrey?"

She looked at him, and seemed to be evaluating again. "A Lord's people will have stories about him. He is the most important person in their world, in many respects."

"You don't expect me to be happy about it?"

"No, Lord. But the trick is to make sure the stories are the ones you want them to tell."

"Like Alençon?" Scene of another victory. But not a glorious one like Val es Dunes.

"Perhaps. If that is how you want people to think of you. I can see how it might have... advantages." There was that slight reserve again. Fear? Or disgust. The man who won by mutilating his prisoners. The tale had spread far and wide already. Ælfgifa evidently registered the look on his face, as she quickly went on, "Will your mother attend the wedding, Lord?"

Would she? The Viscountess would, but his mother?

"When did you last see her?" Ælfgifa asked, clearly not content with his silence.

"I'm not sure I remember the last time," William said. "I think it was at a feast at Valognes after a hunt. She was introduced to me as the Viscountess of Conteville, and as such I addressed her." *When was that? Four years ago? Five?* "She was a proud woman. The stories I heard from my father and my guardians when they thought I wasn't listening testify to that. The white horse, and so on. I don't remember the color of the horse she rode to Valognes on that day. I doubt it was white. Oh, I'd seen her once or twice since she married the Viscount. Only on occasions such as this. I knew she was my mother, but the idea didn't seem to mean anything. She was a tall woman with noble bearing. The lady of one of my nobles. Not the granddaughter of a furrier, or anyone's mistress. Never that. The commoner who had caught one Duke and given birth to the next? She was some creation of the stories of small folk. Perhaps she vanished when I was born. Perhaps I have no mother and never did. I know I was only three when she married the Viscount. She is the mother to my brothers, Odo of Bayeux and Robert of Mortaigne, but mother to me?" *Good Lord. Now he was spilling his thoughts and memories like a drunken squire at a feast. Fool!*

Ælfgifa shook her head. "A mother is like a weapon. They can protect the holder, but also cause harm, and few people are schooled in having a mother, they do not train every day to avoid wounds. You do not appear to have suffered materially from the lack, Lord."

William laughed, and after a while had to work to stop himself. "No. No, indeed. Tell me, my Lady, do you believe a wife can cause harm in like manner?"

"Undoubtedly, Lord."

There spoke the voice of experience. *It must be a great advantage when people don't want to look at you,* William thought. *The things you must see when others are trying so hard to ignore your presence.* It was not a problem, or an advantage, that he was familiar with. "You offer little comfort."

"It is my curse, Lord. One of them."

"You know I do not even have permission to marry yet? Some distant familial connection, you see. We are cousins in some remote degree. I have a priest in Rome arguing for it." Surprisingly, Lanfranc had seemed perfectly happy for William to go ahead with the wedding before Rome had agreed. He seemed to regard it as inevitable—something that would be agreed to given only time. Then again, perhaps Lanfranc was less interested in the immutability of God's law than he used to be. Bec was now a very rich and powerful see, more so with every passing year.

"Is that so? What will you do if permission is not forthcoming?"

Worry about it later. "Try again," he said. Lanfranc had not been wrong yet. If this attempt failed, he would think of something else.

Ælfgifa looked thoughtful. "It was not so long ago that your people would not have troubled about what Rome thought of your matches, and simply married in the Danish style. Did you consider such a ceremony?"

"Danish style? I confess, Lady, I had no idea there were different ways to marry."

Ælfgifa looked at him in genuine surprise. "Really, Lord? And not five score years since your people came from the North lands? Are all marriages conducted in the Latin way now?"

"Every marriage I've ever known. Of course, some do not marry... What is this Danish style?"

"It allows a man to set aside his wife should he have reason. Or take another wife. It is the case in some English marriages, even those in great houses. But the Church does not recognize it. My brother, Harold, was married *in Daneco.*"

William smiled broadly *Ha!* The thought of what Baldwin of Flanders would make of such a thing! "I can't see my father-in-law agreeing to that. He wants to make an alliance with a great house, and would not look kindly on a match that could be so easily dissolved. In any case, the Church is... influential. Increasingly so, it seems. I would cause myself even more grief if I tried that."

"Does Rome have so much power?"

A good question. The lady had a habit of cutting to the heart of things. "A deal of it, and they want more. There are churchmen with the power of Counts and Barons. But while I am in the Church's favor I may appoint bishops and benefit from their tithes and rents. I could not be without their income, I think."

There was more to it than that. William had been obliged to offer to establish and endow an abbey to sweeten the Church's attitude. And Lanfranc had suggested Matilda make the same offer. It would with be his wife's private funds, but yet another abbey in his Duchy, with another Abbot, yet more land, and yet more taxes he would have to give up to Rome. While other nobles sought to steal his birthright by force, the Church sought to steal it through sleight of hand. Still, he was fortunate in one thing—his enemies enjoyed the Church's favor no more than he did. Geoffrey had been excommunicated for imprisoning the Bishop of Le Mans, so at least there would be no Holy Crusade to disinherit him.

There was something else. Something he dare not tell the daughter of Wessex. Baldwin had finally consented to the marriage before Rome agreed only on being told that William was Edward's nominated heir. The appeal of his descendants being kings rather than mere Dukes was too hard to resist. Whether he would ever negotiate the serpent-windings of Saxon, Frankish and Norman politics to actually take up the Crown... well who could say?

The vanguard of the Flemish party was a minute or two from the gate. "I should go down and greet my Duchess-to-be," William said. "Will you join me, Lady?"

Ælfgifa curtseyed, and the gesture seemed less of a challenge this time. "If it please your Grace, I shall remain. The Count may not appreciate seeing a relative of his erstwhile adversary."

It was probably for the best. He bowed his head and hurried down to the courtyard.

***

William was not sure how the slight Matilda was able to wear the vast velvet robe, embroidered with gold and pearls, without collapsing. It looked as though it weighed more than a mail hauberk. Clearly she was tougher than she looked. A useful thing to know. He had already seen the keen edge behind that sweet smile. Despite Ælfgifa's words a week ago, he could not stop himself from smiling back. Matilda had a very sweet smile.

At least his own attire wouldn't disgrace him in this company. Fitz had surprised him by presenting him with a mantle set with precious stones and a helmet to match, polished to a high shine and sparkling with jewels. It was bizarre, but the assembled nobles seemed to be responding to the pomp and ceremony. To William, it was ludicrous. Wasteful. False. But the grinning faces throughout the church made him feel, in a strange way, like a Duke for the first time. It wasn't a bad feeling.

The priest intoned in Latin. William wasn't paying close attention—there was too much else going on, and his mind was spinning—but he caught the gist. The church of Our

Lady was huge. Would the one he built to secure permission from the Pope be as big? Could he just build a small one? No, that wouldn't do. He was the Duke. Grand gestures must be his portion. The priest had stopped talking. Was he supposed to say something? Damn. He should have been listening properly. A question, there had been a question. Something about age. Were they both of age? Yes, that was it!

"Yes, Father, we are of age."

"Does the bride have the permission of her father?"

"Yes, Father, she does."

"And you are not related in any way that would impede you, in accordance with God's holy law, from marrying?"

If it wasn't true now, it never would be. "No, Father, we are not."

The priest read out the dowry, which caused William to smile again, then he handed Matilda a bag of gold to distribute to the needy. He kissed the lips that had insulted him so gravely at their first meeting, and placed a gold ring on her right hand.

If they could only get this interminable ceremony and the feasting over with, he might be able to take part in a hunt or two before he had to march again, to deal with his rebellious uncle. Twice he had sent to Arques with a demand to re-affirm his fealty. The first time he had received no answer. The second time, a string of insults. The only consolation was that Arques' brother, the treacherous bishop of Rouen, Mauger, had fled to join him, and William was relieved not to have to look at the bishop's scheming face a moment longer. And imprisoning the bishop might have upset the Church.

But it would mean another siege. More fighting. He would need more men. More weapons. And the Lord God only knew how much more time. There would be fresh attacks on his Duchy, he could be sure of that.

Compared with everything that he knew was to come, the prospect of his wedding night with Matilda was only mildly terrifying. What if she remembered that night at Senlis when he had forced his way into her boudoir? Reminded him of it? He fixed his mind on the boar hunt that he had planned to follow the ceremony.

And then, that evening at the wedding feast, news arrived that Henri had declared his support for William of Arques against the upstart bastard of Normandy. William was at war with his own King and liege lord.

CHAPTER 4

Ælfgifa's decision to avoid William had evaporated on his wedding day. For one thing, she'd needed a way of gauging just how strong an alliance he now had with Flanders. While Matilda had not been impolite or hostile, she had certainly not encouraged intimacies with Ælfgifa either, holding herself cool and aloof from the outcast Saxon princess in her court. The young Duchess was unlikely to be a source of information. Ælfgifa supposed she would have to find a way of building on her curious friendship with William and was pondering over it as she worked in the herb garden. It was very early. Most people were sleeping off the effects of too much ale and wine after the wedding. It wasn't much of a wedding, Ælfgifa thought, yanking a weed up by its roots. She'd been surprised when William had left his bride shortly after the stilted, formal Latin service to partake in a boar hunt. It was impossible to tell if Matilda was offended. Her small features had remained perfectly composed. Privately Ælfgifa thought William might have made more of an effort to welcome his lady. She was, after all, in a new home, a strange place with people she did not yet know and few of her own retainers. Most marriages amongst nobles were political affairs but the Duke might have made it less obvious that his new wife was little more than acreage, alliance and womb.

Ælfgifa straightened up and stifled a gasp as she recognized the figure standing in the rising dew of the herb garden. *What in God's name...?* The Duke wore a bemused expression, his dark hair stuck up at angles all over his head and his right cheek bore four livid parallel bars. *Nail marks.* Ælfgifa wondered if he had spent his wedding night in the stables. She put the small knife she'd been using to cut stalks of tansy into her basket, before dropping a curtsey. "A good morning, Lord, and felicitations on your newly-wed state." Ælfgifa couldn't help her eyes grazing over the scratches on his cheek and remarked wickedly, "I had thought you would still be abed, but perhaps your bride is also an early riser?"

William glowered at her but there was no heat in his glare as he trampled a bed of chamomile and dropped onto a stone bench. "No. Absolutely not, Ælfgifa. Not today."

"My Lord?"

"No games, do you hear me? I've had precious little sleep, my household has turned into a treacherous quagmire where I cannot even get a piece of bread and a mug of ale, and I am in no mood for half answers and riddles!" He groaned and raked his hands back through his hair. "My head is fit for splitting and I drank not one tenth of what Gallet did."

Ælfgifa raised an eyebrow and decided that last comment was not directed at her. "Very well, Lord. My wedding gift to you shall be my silence—for now at least." She turned back to her tasks but thought she heard a muffled 'Thank the Lord God' from the Duke. Wryly amused, she picked up her knife again, kneeling on the folded edge of her gown to reach the tansy. She forgot all about the Duke. Indeed he was so quiet that when she paused almost an hour later, she wondered if he had finally found sleep. She was surprised to find him watching her.

"What is that? That plant you harvest?" William said unexpectedly.

"There are several. Tansy. Motherwort. Penny royal. Raspberry." She eyed him shrewdly and decided he must want a distraction. Well enough. She would oblige since it suited her. "Helisande is with child again. I prefer to be prepared early."

"*Again?* Gallet's seen her less than half a dozen times during these interminable skirmishes. He's only been home this time a few weeks."

Ælfgifa was painfully amused at his reaction. "It would seem that Sir Gallet is most... er potent."

"I suppose the child *is* his?" William grumbled, then stopped as Ælfgifa fixed him with a very frosty look. "Ah well, yes, of course it is..."

"Hmm." Wiping her hands on her apron, Ælfgifa unbent slightly. "I suppose you are not quite yourself at present, Lord. It is to be expected." *Although I cannot recall Harold moping in the herb garden after wedding Edith.*

"Is it always like this, Lady?" William looked at her as if willing her to spill answers to questions he could not bring himself to ask.

"Marriage? How in the world would I know, Lord? Thankfully, I am like never to undertake the sacrament." She let the sting leak out of her tone. "If I might ask a question?"

"You promised me silence, Lady," William growled.

"And your Lordship has had a good hour's worth, a greater gift than I gave any of my siblings upon their nuptials I assure you." Ælfgifa half-smiled. "I was puzzled that you chose to go hunting with your men so soon. Indeed I do not think the wedding vows had finished echoing in the chapel before you were astride your horse."

"What the devil should I have done?" William demanded, annoyed and, Ælfgifa thought, a little defensive. *Here is the heart of it.*

Ælfgifa shrugged. "Just as you please, Lord. But there was a wedding feast and fine wine. I rather wondered that you did not dance with your bride. Then again, I am a Saxon. Perhaps we bring too much merry-making into a matrimonial arrangement. Your lady seems clever and sensible as well as beautiful. No doubt she gave you her blessing and was content to wait for your return."

William traced his scratched cheek and then realized what he was doing and thrust his hand angrily into his lap. "Lady Ælfgifa, for once will you stop speaking like a sphinx and say what you really mean!" He paused and drew a deep breath. "You think my duchess was insulted by my actions?"

"I think her father, the Count, was," Ælfgifa said frankly. "As for my lady Matilda, it would be hard for even me to tell but were I in her place I should have been... less than pleased."

"Confounded women," William ground out. "Will nothing please any of you?"

Ælfgifa laughed at him, hard and dark. "If I must answer on behalf of my sex then pleasing us is no difficult task for the most part. I will say only that if she were a prize brood mare, you might have stabled her without troubling yourself over her feelings. I know not whether there is any affection at all in your alliance, it is no business of mine. But had you writ it large and illuminated it in vermillion and gold leaf, you could not have said more clearly that your new duchess was merely a political matter."

A wave of red suffused William's face and his eyes flashed dangerously. "You suggest I lie, Lady?" he said softly.

Ælfgifa canted her head to one side, regarding him. He was very nearly as tall as her even seated. "Nay, Lord. But allowing the illusion would have been wise. She will have twice the work establishing herself as head of your household if your people think you do not value her person or that her word carries no weight with you."

"I think you were correct before, Lady. It is no business of yours." William said coldly. "How you will go on with your twisted female logic. What gives you the effrontery to do so?"

Ælfgifa smiled and gathered up her basket, drifting to the gate. "Why, I needed no effrontery, Lord. You came down here to ask my opinion and quarrel with me—I imagine I am a safer target for disagreements just now than your wife—and so you have had both. Now I must go, but pass on my congratulations to your lady, please. God give you joy of each other." Still smiling, Ælfgifa left the Duke sitting in the damp garden.

CHAPTER 5

Gallet climbed up off his belly and moved at a crouching run back to where William and Beaumont stood, a little way back from the crest of the ridge.

"What's happening?" William said softly, not sure why he was keeping his voice down except that it seemed the thing to do.

"Our men are falling back. In some disarray, by the looks of things," Gallet answered, brushing twigs and dirt off his hauberk. "The cavalry are a quarter of a league West already, outstripping the infantry."

"They've abandoned the footsoldiers?"

"Yes, Lord."

"And is the enemy in pursuit?"

"I'd say so, but I couldn't tell for certain. My advice would be to consider they are. I'll go back and look, with your permission."

"Yes, go ahead." It looked bad. Very bad. The force besieging Arques was in headlong flight from the advance guard of Henri's army. With no cavalry in support, the infantry would be vulnerable to a rout.

Good. Everything was going to plan.

"Mount up!" Beaumont called, and went to take his place on the right of the line. William nodded to his squire, who helped him into the saddle. The squire was a new fellow, Ralph de Tosny, son of his standard bearer. William had knighted Bourdas after Mouliherne, and his former squire was down there somewhere in the fleeing rabble with Montgomerie. He hoped the lad would be all right.

Gallet returned. "They're following, just coming round the bend. Only cavalry. The vanguard, I'd say."

"In good order?" William asked. "Is Henri with them?"

"Tolerably good. No, I didn't see Henri's standard. You know what that preening dandy is like, he wouldn't get into a cavalry charge if he could help it."

"That's your king you're talking about!" de Tosny laughed.

"Sorry, you know what that Royal preening dandy is like."

William sighed and shook his head. "When I'm King of England I won't tolerate that kind of talk. Go and mount up, you'd better not get left behind."

Gallet turned to head over to the left of the line, muttering. William caught *"...And when I'm the Holy Roman Emperor you'll all kiss my ring,"* before the knight was out of earshot.

When seated on his destrier, William could just see over the top of the rise, but not far enough to make out the road down below. He called for quiet and listened. The sound of galloping horses could be heard distantly, building gradually. He didn't want to go too early, or Henri's men would have time to turn into the attack. On the other hand, too late and they'd just get into a chase, probably sacrificing all the infantry below as well. When it sounded as though the horses below were almost level with them, William yelled "Dex Aie!", spurred his horse and rode over the rise.

The valley was spread out below, and almost directly in front, a thousand pieds or so, Henri's advance guard, pursuing the fleeing footsoldiers who, by now, did not have much of a lead. But Montgomerie had them drilled well. The ambush had been his idea. Almost as one, the seemingly disorganized infantry turned, formed a line and raised pikes.

The onrushing horsemen seemed to falter, and at that moment, someone down there must have seen William's cavalry plunging onto their flank. In an instant, the vanguard went from an organized rank to a mess. William could only hear the thundering of the horses around him, his own heaving breath in his ears, but he could imagine the shouts and crash of colliding horses, men, weapons.

Some of Henri's force seemed to have tried to turn to face William, while others had turned away, fleeing to the right, the only exit remaining open. The result was chaos. As he tightened his grip on his lance, he saw an armored knight thrown from his horse, curving slowly through the air. Another was dislodged by a bucking, riderless horse, and he heard the metallic thunk of horseshoe connecting with helm. William picked a man who was still seated, almost stopped, and trying to free his sword from its scabbard. He looked up in horror to see William bearing down, lance raised, and froze. The spear caught the man full in the chest, and he flew out of his seat just before the two chargers collided. A glancing blow, but William's leg caught on something that wrenched at it. He lost a stirrup, grabbed at the bridle, just hung on. God! The lance was gone. He scrabbled for his sword, and three times his fingers closed around nothing before be managed to pull it from its scabbard. De Tosny was still next to him, swinging and lunging at a man in Capet livery. William spurred his horse, raised his sword, saw something from the corner of his eye. More Capet yellow flashed and he parried a desperate blow from a young knight. Two more easy parries and his assailant seemed to be moving sluggishly. William deflected the slowing blows until the knight raised his sword high above his head, leaving William time and room enough to swing the tip of his own sword at the other's throat. The edge bit and the force carried the man off his horse almost gracefully, his head hinging back to reveal a gaping, surprised second mouth before he thumped into the mud. William had time to hope he hadn't killed a relative of Henri before nudging his horse into a less exposed position.

The fighting had diminished into knots, and the Norman infantry was coming back in support, jabbing spears and swinging axes. William could see that most of Henri's horsemen had fled, and the majority of those who remained were either dead or had been captured. A few minutes more and the rest surrendered. He gathered a few of the fresher of his knights together to ride back in the direction of Arques, harry any fighting men retreating in that direction, and gather news of the main force's whereabouts, while William, Gallet and Beaumont organized the cavalry back into some sort of order, disarmed the prisoners, made plans to send them on to safety from whence they could be ransomed. Half an hour later, the pursuivants returned, reporting that Henri had turned about and was marching away, minus the greater part of his cavalry.

"You've won, Lord. Again!" Beaumont beamed at him. The swift victory must have felt very different from years in the mud outside Brionne.

"Yes. I suppose I have." William wasn't going to let himself get too carried away. All they had done was prevent Henri from relieving Arques today. He might try again tomorrow, though William doubted it. And there was still a siege to conduct. With any luck they'd be spared a repeat of Brionne. Or Alençon, come to that. If Henri did decide better of trying to relieve Arques, the rebel lord might be persuaded very much more easily to come to terms.

A gasp and a scream that degenerated into sobs issued a short distance away, where the surgeons were now at work. "Holy Christ! My eyes! I can't see! Lord have mercy!"

William shuddered.

"You know what they'll say about you, Lord?" Beaumont went on, oblivious, the excitement of the fight clearly still in his veins. "That you've never fought a battle you haven't won!"

"No," snarled Gallet. "And you know why that is?"

"Excellent strategy and talented captains," Beaumont replied, smoothing his beard.

"Well, yes." Gallet paused while he handed his sword to his squire to clean before turning back to Beaumont. "But also that the first battle you lose tends to be the last one you fight."

Beaumont snorted, but his chest was no longer as puffed out as it had been.

William smiled, grimly. For some reason, Ælfgifa jumped into his thoughts. Perhaps because her skills as a herbalist would no doubt be needed when they returned, but possibly for other reasons. "I think I know what they'll say. That Mauger may have a demon at his command, but now I keep one at Falaise too."

With the King now in open warfare against him, William felt he needed all the allies he could gather. Even a demon. And as Ælfgifa had suggested, the right story told about him could help his cause too. Let them believe he had raised a devil. Let them fear.

CHAPTER 6

The changing color of the forest canopy had marked out almost the entire turning of a year. The leaves had been touched with bronze when Ælfgifa had arrived at Falaise. From one of her favorite nooks on the battlements, she had watched them turn red and gold before falling in drifts, leaving the dark, naked branches pleading with the sky, which covered them in frost and snow. The faint, fuzzy pale green of spring had crept along from twig to bough and Ælfgifa had felt a renewal of hope shooting up within her like a seedling. But bud, blossom, leaf had burst into full summer before being touched with pale, tired gold once more and the spark had been quashed.

There had been little word from England. Brother Dubhne's careful, pricked messages on the edges of Ealdgyth's bland missives, had bade her keep courage and be watchful—hardly useful advice, however kindly meant. Sometimes the old monk would add a line or two of news about Harold or her father, more to say that they were well than to communicate any news of moment. Ælfgifa felt the sting of being kept out of their plans whilst acknowledging the sense of doing so. She was rational enough to know that she would have acted the same way. It did not lessen her feelings of trapped frustration.

There had been rumors from other sources. Harold was now in Ireland. Her father was then in France. One report placed them for a time in Norway. If any of those reports were to be believed, Ælfgifa thought that they were trying to raise support; an army large enough to force Edward to welcome them back to England. She could not imagine Edward allowing their return on any other pretext, so hardened was his antipathy to the house of Wessex.

Shivering a little in her cloak against the wind, Ælfgifa admitted that it was autumn once more. Small twigs had broken and fallen onto the stones of the battlements. Absently, Ælfgifa arranged them to form the year she had been sent here, then twisted the twig that formed the character '1' into a '2'. *1052. I never thought to be here so long.* She finally allowed herself to truly entertain the idea that she might be here for many years. That her life from now on may well be shut within stone walls, stealing scraps of information and sending on such tid-bits as she could. It was not enough for her. It would never be enough.

If William's initial behavior toward Matilda had put the Duchess at a disadvantage, she did not remain at one for long. Ælfgifa admired the way in which Matilda took the ladies in hand, allowing far less idle gossip and spite, and encouraging more thought and activity outside the solar. It had amused Ælfgifa greatly to see the squawking Mabel de Bellême put so thoroughly and deftly in her place, although she was less pleased when she learned that Mabel would take a turn in the still room with her every week. Glancing at Matilda, Ælfgifa had seen a knowing glint in the young Duchess' eyes and had realized she was being tested. There was no malice in the way Matilda regarded her and Ælfgifa saw that she was being kept at a distance because the Duchess was wary of her—of her astuteness and cleverness, not just of her being a Saxon and a relative of an erstwhile enemy of her father's. She accepted the situation with good grace. Matilda would warm to her or not. Meanwhile she could not complain of her treatment, which had vastly improved under Matilda's example and censure.

Then too, there was the strange tradition of William coming into the herb garden early in the morning, ostensibly for quiet but he always had a question or comment for Ælfgifa. Since he knew that was where he would find her, Ælfgifa did not think it was chance that brought him. The Duke's visits were infrequent and he was still from home much of the time but Ælfgifa knew he sought a way to ask her advice without seeming to do so. Used as she was to being at the beating political heart of matters and starved for conversation of moment, Ælfgifa was usually happy to play along with his ruse. There was a secret pride in her on the occasions when he seemed to act in accord with her suggestions. Not that she ever gave up needling him. She could no more resist poking at his conceits than she could change her own face, but then that seemed to be the second reason he came. The Duke appeared to enjoy a good argument with Ælfgifa as much as she did with him.

None of which was but a small consolation in her current mood. She tried not to be melancholy. She tried even harder to squash the sick desire for home. Helisande might have teased Ælfgifa out of her ill humors but then Helisande was not herself. It had been a difficult pregnancy, an exhausting labor and nothing to show for it. The small, wrinkled red son had never drawn a breath. Ælfgifa had feared the child had died in the womb and when Helisande's birth pains had come too soon, she'd known there would be no happy outcome. There was no herb or philtre that could start life once it was gone. Helisande grieved and nothing Ælfgifa did could comfort her friend. There was only time and now Ælfgifa looked at the plain and unadorned truth. She had been distracting herself with trivialities whilst awaiting a summons back to England. A summons that was not coming.

"You were not in the garden this morning."

Ælfgifa scrambled to her feet, mortified that she had been so absorbed with dark thoughts that she had not heard the Duke approaching.

"My... Lord..." She fumbled, sketching a hasty, clumsy curtsey.

William peered down at her frowning. "You are pale. You do not sicken for something, do you, Lady?"

"No, I am well enough, Lord," she replied baffled by his unaccustomed concern.

"Good. I have need of your services." He eyed her as if measuring her small stature—smaller still now since she had lost her appetite and grown thinner with it. "The dun mare, I suppose. She should not be too strong for you although she is a little tall. We have no smaller horses at present."

"I... are you sending me somewhere, Lord?" Ælfgifa said, thoroughly wrong-footed.

William flashed a sharp grin, pleased at having confused her for a change, no doubt. "*We* are visiting an abbey, my Lady."

***

Ælfgifa had not been on horseback in a year and even the comparatively short distance to La Trineté left her aching. The mare William had decided she should ride was indeed too big for her, but she was an older horse, used to ladies, and Ælfgifa had no difficulty controlling her. She refused to ask the groom for the mare's name as she might once have done.

It was a small escort that saw her and the Duke to the Abbey. By the time they arrived and their horses were taken, Ælfgifa had guessed the purpose of this sudden demonstration of freedom. William still had no skilled scribe. Whatever he wanted to send now must be extremely delicate. So much so that he wanted someone entirely accountable to him to write it. There were worse ways to be used, Ælfgifa reflected cynically. Besides she might learn something of import. That thought acted as only a transitory stimulus. Her weariness of her double role and hostage state seemed all-encompassing, swallowing even the bright autumn sunlight.

There was a tension about the monks of La Trineté. Ælfgifa thought that it was a reaction to finding a Saxon barbarian—a woman no less!—in their midst, requesting parchment and ink. But as she observed the way they moved around the Duke, she decided it was more to do with William's presence than hers. Again Ælfgifa was struck with strange familiarity. The monks tonsured their heads in the Latin style and lacked the freedoms and friendliness in their manner of the Celtic rite. But their robes and their way of living, even the beautiful calligraphy, were so similar to their brethren in England that Ælfgifa felt a sharp pang of homesickness. She was not left to wallow long.

Leaving his escort outside, William ushered Ælfgifa into a small chamber, half warmed with a low fire. There was a bench and table, trimmed goose quills and fine parchment. *Too fine for a mere message, Ælfgifa thought. This should be a page in an illuminated manuscript.* "What would you have me write, Lord?" It was no hardship to be patient. The longer

William took to dictate this missive, the longer she was outside the walls of Falaise.

"Terms," William replied. "Terms of surrender, in Latin if you can manage it, Lady."

"Certainly," Ælfgifa replied mildly, un-corking a bottle of ink that had already been mixed. She thought she heard a faint shuffling sound from behind an oak screen at one end of the chamber but William fixed her with a gimlet stare, demanding her full attention.

"I am trusting a great deal to your discretion here, Ælfgifa. If details of this missive were to go astray I would be... *displeased.*" William laid the last word down like a heavy burden.

Ælfgifa fought the involuntary urge to laugh. Did he have any idea how preposterous the situation was? He had an entire Abbey full of monks at his disposal, not to mention lawmen and priests in his retinue. In fact, did not his wife also read and write? She forced the humor from her voice. "You may be assured that not a breath of this missive shall ever leave my lips. My word as a daughter of Wessex."

William eyed her dubiously and again Ælfgifa fought the urge to smile. The Duke gave a short nod and proceeded to dictate the terms of surrender he expected William of Arques to acquiesce to. It was easy work and Ælfgifa found herself once more wondering about the Duke's manner. Why her? Of all his retainers, why a Saxon hostage? Did William trust her over his own people? Or did he think her scope for damages too limited to be concerned about? Then again, he had stooped to attempting to intimidate her into silence, something that was hardly necessary. *I suppose,* Ælfgifa thought, dusting fine white sand over the letter to dry it, *that it may merely be the Duke's way. How many times has he ever accomplished what he wished without showing the stick as well as the carrot?*

Another faint sound from behind the screen. Ælfgifa stiffened. "Lord, we are not alone. A spy sits behind yonder screen."

William merely smiled thinly. There was a scrape as of a stool being pushed back against a stone floor and an old monk with a lame leg emerged from behind the screen, leaning heavily on an ash wood staff. "Ah, the ears of the young."

"Brother Herluin would you be so good as to read Lady Ælfgifa's letter?"

A test, to see if I am indeed reporting accurately. "Hold it flat, brother, it is not quite dry yet," Ælfgifa said, trying to hide the pique in her tone. It was hardly anything to become upset over. She had just been pondering over the unlikeliness of William trusting her after all.

Herluin glanced at the letter and then focused on it more intently. "You have a very fine hand, Lady. God has blessed you."

Ælfgifa forced a sickly smile. *Yes, God undertook the long hours of calligraphy and Latin study that I might not have to!* She glanced up to catch the Duke looking at her with a half-disguised smirk and wondered how plain her thoughts had been on her face. A dull flush crept up her neck.

"Lord William, this is a fine, accurate piece of work. I could have done no better." Herluin smiled at Ælfgifa in what was doubtless meant to be a kind way but which she was too grumpy to appreciate. "You would have made a very fine monk, Lady Ælfgifa."

"You are too kind. Truly," Ælfgifa said, biting back further words.

William sealed the letter. "Be so good as to send this, Brother Herluin. And not a word about the letter or the lady."

As they left the chamber, Ælfgifa burned to ask William just who on earth he did consider a loyal follower? To needle at him for the secrecy he had demanded without giving any trust or license in return. Her melancholy was forgotten in irritation. She opened her mouth to speak but the sound of feet pounding in haste made her whirl to look behind her. William had already turned. A novice skidded to halt in front of them, gasping and red-faced. *Not even old enough to grow a beard*, Ælfgifa thought irrelevantly.

"Sorry, Lordship, but they said the Lady Ælfgifa was here? This just come." He held out a tiny scroll of parchment. "Pigeon landed but a moment ago. They said I might catch you, Lady."

"My thanks." Ælfgifa took the scroll and the novice bowed clumsily, cast a frightened look between her face and the Duke, and ran away. "May I, my Lord? I doubt it is of moment but some news of home... perhaps I might send a swift reply if needed?"

"Of course, Lady." William raised an eyebrow. "I, too, would like to hear how your family does."

Ælfgifa broke open the scroll and read it in a single gulp. It was short and to the point. She pretended to take a little longer reading it, worrying at the edges for the pricked message Dubhne had added. She supposed she looked like any woman fretting at sudden news.

"It is from my sister, the Queen." Ælfgifa said at last. "She writes that my father and Harold, my brother, have returned to England. The king has most graciously lifted his decree of exile and they are now once more on their own lands." She looked up into the Duke's face.

"I see," was his sole reply.

No doubt you do, Ælfgifa thought. *No doubt your fine grasp of strategy has already told you that so complete a pardon, from a person with so bitter an acrimony against my family, was only granted at sword point. I wager you know to the man and the bow string just how great a force my father and Harold raised in order to force the king's hand.* "Ealdgyth has re-joined her husband. She ends by saying that this time of reflection has been a benefit to all; our family ties are stronger than ever for the mending of a misunderstanding."

The words clung to the inside of her throat. She should be glad, she knew she should. Instead it felt as if she were falling and every new line in the note was a tree branch that arrested her fall, then broke and sent her plummeting down again. Because Dubhne's message was the one that mattered.

Gifa, the usual channels confirm that your host was offered the crown. Accident or intention matters not. He will not be pleased at your family's return to power. Be on your guard. I will ask the Queen to send for you. The King will see even more value in the hostages remaining guests of Normandy now. Have courage. All may yet be well.

Dubhne.

William was silent on their ride back to Falaise but Ælfgifa's mind was in too much of a whirl to pay attention to the fact. *I will ask the Queen to send for you.* Dubhne thought he would need to ask? Why in fact had she not been sent for already? Why had her father, Ealdgyth, Harold... why had they not sent for her and Wulfnoth already? Harold. It all came back to Harold. He must have some reason for her to continue here or, even with Edward's desire to have at least some hold over the house of Wessex, she doubted not that she would be on a ship home even now. *Damn you, Harold, just what game are you playing now?*

CHAPTER 7

If Ælfgifa had known then just how long she would have to wait for news that would summon her home, she might have despaired. As it was the year turned through another cycle of seasons and she was still the guest of the Duke of Normandy.

Since what she now realized had been a trial of her abilities and discretion, Ælfgifa had often found herself writing documents for the Duke. He once favored her with the answer that good scribes were not easy to come by, certainly not those who produced superior work. She supposed that was true and then supposed more cynically that skilled scribes one did not have to pay for their craft were likely even harder to come by. She kept her word; not a breath was uttered by her of the contents of the documents she created at the Duke's behest. But she sent regular missives to Ealdgyth and Harold via Dubhne, and each message contained a pricked secondary and secret message which frequently did contain gleanings from the Duke's papers. Ælfgifa knew she was obeying the letter of her promise not the spirit and it sat ill with her. A growing resentment threatened at times to choke her, for here she was at Harold's command, playing the friend and confidante to the Duke whilst searching for his weaknesses to pass on to her brother. It was a conflict compounded by the fact that William was kind to her after a fashion, certainly kinder to her than many had been and she could number members of her own close family in that reckoning. It occurred to Ælfgifa, somewhat ironically, that William employing her as a scribe was an attempt to avoid allowing a spy so close to the heart of his household. A scribe would be ideally placed, providing an enemy could find and hire a skilled enough person. It made sense that William would make use of a skilled hostage. Ælfgifa wondered at Harold's foresight. Had he factored her skills and her need to be useful into his schemes? If her brother had recruited the Lady Matilda as his creature, he could have done no better. Shrewd the Duke might be, but he was not as cunning and designing as Harold. Ælfgifa felt almost shamed when she compared the two men in her mind. William most likely did have spies but she doubted he had ever considered sending his sister. Of course that might be less a matter of honor and more to do with William's low opinion of women in general.

Her hands paused over the pestle and mortar, as she stared at a distance only she could see. A sharp rapping at the still room door jolted her back to the present. Her heart hammered at her ribs. There was no need for fright she told herself. No reason to think that there was anything wrong at all. Nothing except the cold claw of foreboding that tightened its grip as a page handed her the small scroll, just then delivered from La Trineté.

***

Grief, if it was grief, was a thick, numbing mist. Invisible. Insidious. Muffling her words and thoughts and deeds. Ælfgifa could not quite recall asking to speak to the Duke. Could not recall how she came to be seated, cradling a goblet

80

of good red wine and herbs from which she did not sip. Thoughts slipped through her mind like foxes disappearing into the thickets at dawn.

"Lady? Are you well enough to speak now?" William was frowning but it seemed more in bafflement than annoyance. Ælfgifa swallowed hard, trying to find her scattered thoughts. With great effort she forced her gaze up to meet the Duke's.

"My father is dead," she said in a low, steady voice. "Jarl Godwin is dead."

"Are you certain?"

"I have no reason to doubt it. The letter was scant in detail but he was... allegedly afflicted with a palsy as he dined with the king. He died later that night without ever speaking." Her lips, tongue, face felt numb.

"Allegedly?" William picked out the most pertinent word. "You suspect that it was not by natural means."

"You are astute as always, Lord. That is my suspicion." She attempted a wry half-smile but from the way William jerked as if he were fighting not to recoil, she could only imagine the expression had appeared ghastly, perhaps ghoulish, on her deformed face.

"Your brother, Harold. He is your father's heir? Is he not already Earl of East Anglia? Wessex as well will be a great holding indeed–" William mused.

"My lord, I beg your pardon for the interruption but I must speak plain while I have wit to do so. I beg a boon of you, Lord. It is not an inconsiderable one, I know." Everything she must do, every action she must take laid itself out in a neat path before her. A path it would be easier to follow with William's assistance.

"Go on," the Duke said in a forbidding tone.

"I ask you to release me. Let me return to England." Ælfgifa watched William's expression shift until it settled into something hard and questioning.

"King Edward has not sent for you."

"No, Lord. I doubt if he recalls exactly who you are housing." *Let him realize what inconsequential fish we are to the house of Wessex and to the throne.*

"I confess I do not fully understand your reasoning, Lady Ælfgifa. You wish to pay respects to your dead father? Are daughters so important in England? Were you so close to your father then? I see you do not weep."

"I have never mastered the art of weeping, Lord," Ælfgifa said in a brittle voice. "But once we were very close." Her throat tightened. *Not my little Blackbird.* "I do wish to pay my respects. More importantly, I wish to thwart further mischief. If I had been there then... but it is useless to suppose. I have suspicions without proof. And that I may only gain in person. Will you let me go, Lord?"

"Ælfgifa, you must consider..." William read her expression and changed tactics. "If I agree to this, then it must be a temporary arrangement. Speaking plainly, Lady, you ask me to give up what may yet prove to be a great advantage without my cousin's approval, though you would have me think that you are of little value." His tone hardened.

"I know what I ask and I do not ask lightly. Choose, my Lord." Ælfgifa paused and then added softly, "Please."

***

Ealdgyth had changed in the two years Ælfgifa had spent in Normandy. She had not noticeably aged. She was in fact as lovely as ever, but it was a frozen beauty now. As if a layer of ice had formed around her, preserving her but leaching away

82

warmth and animation. Ælfgifa, who had only stopped in Wessex long enough to pay respects to Gytha and to visit her father's resting place before heading to her sister at Lundenwic, felt her heart drop in dismay. *Not Ealdgyth too.* Gytha's reception was exactly what she had expected. A chilly kiss of welcome on the cheek that seemed to be dismissing Ælfgifa before a word was spoken. Gytha was furious that Wulfnoth had been left behind and held Ælfgifa entirely responsible. Explanations, pleas, entreaties for Gytha to hear how well her youngest son did, of how he had made companions of the young Norman boys and was happy, all fell on deaf ears. Ælfgifa had not been home half a day before she was completely aware that she was not wanted. That Gytha would have preferred Wulfnoth had returned instead was a distant pain now, the bite gone out of it as spring draws cold from winter. Grimly, Ælfgifa had sworn to herself that she would not stay in Wintancaestre any longer than necessary. Not even to see Harold, who was on his way to pay a visit to their mother.

"Sister," Ealdgyth came forward and took Ælfgifa's hands, kissing her cheek in a manner so coolly like Gytha's that Ælfgifa felt a knot of cold twist in her stomach. "We did not expect you." She regarded Ælfgifa gravely, measuring, deciding. "The King has not given orders for your release, I think?"

A flood of hot fury washed the icy homecoming anxiety away. Ealdgyth had not even tried to have her released! All along the road here, Ælfgifa had been caught in a cloying tangle of relief and love, loyalty and fury over Harold, who had used her and would doubtless have kept her in Normandy, a game piece in reserve. It had never occurred to her that Ealdgyth had not even spared her a thought.

"The Duke was most magnanimous. He allowed me to return to mourn our father." Ælfgifa's tone rivalled her sister's for frost and steel.

"You came far for it." Ealdgyth sounded almost callous and then her tone changed. "Of course, you were always a favorite of his."

Not knowing what to say in reply to this, Ælfgifa fell back on unrefined bluntness. "Sister, may I stay or may I not?"

"I would have expected you to return to Harold's household. Are you not a close pet of our brother also?" Ealdgyth's blue eyes were hard.

"Harold's household is now Wintancaestre. Or will be when he organizes his affairs. I do not expect a great welcome there—our mother was pleased to see me leave once more." Perhaps if she reminded Ealdgyth of how much Gytha loathed her, her sister would unbend. "Truthfully, sister, I would rather not see Harold at present. I am not sure his aims and mine are in alignment."

The coldness left Ealdgyth's face by slow degrees. Ælfgifa had finally said the right thing, albeit unknowingly. She managed to drag a full breath into her tight chest for the first time since she had entered the Queen's solar.

"Is it so? Then stay, Sister, and welcome. I will smooth your presence with the King." She embraced Ælfgifa with slightly more warmth.

"Ealdgyth? I'm... I'm so sorry. About Suela."

The Queen gave Ælfgifa a tranquil look, devoid of emotion. "She did as all good servants must do." Ælfgifa felt the hair on the nape of her neck prickle. "We must all be good servants in the end, Gifa. Come, I will show you to your chamber. There have been changes here at court."

Somehow the use of her pet name did not ease Ælfgifa's disquiet at all.

CHAPTER 8

Edward had not paid any attention at all to the sudden appearance of the queen's sister at board that evening. After several days of this treatment, Ælfgifa shrugged off his lack of interest and turned her attention to more immediate concerns. Ealdgyth had warmed towards her no further since her arrival and Ælfgifa was forced to conclude that her sister's interests were entirely—perhaps desperately—tied up with Edward's. The Queen's ties to the house of Wessex were slender and frail now. A chance movement might cause them to snap.

Ælfgifa refused to examine her feelings on this lukewarm home-coming. It had not been a mere desire to pay her last respects to her father that had prompted her to beg a favor from William. A favor that in the fullness of time might prove to be costly indeed. She watched Camus narrowly as he grabbed handfuls of roast fowl with his filthy fingers. Ealdgyth had already mentioned that Godwin had been attended by the king's personal physician. Ælfgifa had barely repressed a shudder at the news. Ealdgyth had seen Ælfgifa's frown and shaken her head. "Godwin was old. He was ailing. That very night he complained of a headache or some such. Camus made him a posset before dinner."

Ælfgifa had said nothing. A sharp headache may have been an indicator of the palsy to come. Her father would not have known. It may not have made a difference in any case. How many people knew how to prepare hawthorn and foxglove in the right way to stave off such an attack? And it was effective less than half the time even if there was a skilled healer nearby who did know. So it may have simply been God's will. Ælfgifa snorted to herself. More likely her father had a pain and Camus gave him an overdose or the wrong herb... Her thoughts fractured. Godwin had forced his way back into England. Godwin was popular amongst the Saxons who neither liked nor entirely accepted, rule from a Norman-reared king. In fact, was not Godwin the rallying point for anti-Norman rule? Just how had the small folk reacted to Edward's exile of their favorite after he'd championed his own people? Godwin had been in Edward's way. Too dangerous. Too popular. Too wealthy. Edward's grudge against Godwin for his brother's death was almost incidental.

He waited, Ælfgifa thought, slanting a glance towards Edward. *All the time he had a grudge against my father and he waited, like a pike. Quiescent, camouflaged. Until he saw an opportunity and he turned just as swiftly and aggressively.* It fit. The king had wanted Godwin gone even as he wed Ealdgyth and awarded lands to the Jarl's sons. Exile was almost as good as death and Edward must have thought Godwin gone for good. Then Godwin had returned and weakened the king by forcing him to return the lands he'd confiscated. Edward had not been so patient this time. A mere year of waiting. Ælfgifa forced her hands to unclench from the board. She had clutched so hard her nails had been forced back and her fingertips were numb.

It did not make sense, though. If you were stooping to assassination, why wait until your enemy sat down to dine with you? Few people would point a finger at the king but even so the risk was foolish. Unless there was a third party, working by the king's desire but without his knowledge. Edward was unlikely to have arranged an unnatural end for his enemy himself, Ælfgifa reflected bitterly. No, the king's apparent displeasure in the right quarter would have been sufficient. She couldn't be sure. If she had been able to see Godwin's body, she might have recognized some sign, some indication on whether it was a natural death. But her father was long since buried. Even if he were not, too much time had passed to be sure. All she could do was what she had always done; watch, listen, analyze. *Perhaps*, Ælfgifa mused, noticing how the King's ward Aofra's hand brushed Camus' arm in a way that no doubt she thought would not be seen. *Perhaps this time, I will act*, Ælfgifa thought, and she wondered, cynically, just how long Aofra had waited for her bed to cool after Garyn's death, before inviting Camus into it.

***

Spring had been well established for some weeks when Harold came. Almost as if in parody of the habits of the Duke of Normandy, he loomed out of the early morning mist as Ælfgifa attacked the overgrown herb garden behind the kitchen. It was one of those moments when she seemed to be looking down on everything from a great height, standing outside and above herself. On the surface a prosaic scene; a brother and sister, long parted, reunited once more. Staring at each other across the herb beds as if unsure how to greet each other after so long. Yet Ælfgifa had a sense of impending destiny, as if much hinged on this moment and how she moved now might affect the rest of her life and her brother's as well.

Then Harold grinned and he was just her brother again. There was no fate, no moment of decision. What a ridiculous notion! Ælfgifa flung herself across the garden into her brother's arms, both of them gasping out laughter that would have sounded like sobbing if they had been different people.

I am home, Ælfgifa thought. *I really am home.* The knot of insecurity that had wound tighter and tighter under Ealdgyth's cool reception and cooler regard, came undone and she was certain that she had been right in coming back to England, and not merely following her own homesick inclinations.

"Gifa. Gifa," Harold said, raising her head so he could meet her eyes. "I am so glad to see you." His words were balm. Someone wanted her here. "But Gifa, why are you here?"

A faint chill prickled at the base of her spine at Harold's words. "Duke William of Normandy allowed me to return. To pay respects to our father." Harold looked skeptical and she found herself rushing on. "His Grace had been very kind..." Well to her, anyway. "He knew my family would need me..." She trailed off, aware that she skirted perilously close to outright lies now. The Duke would have preferred she stayed both for her quill and her tart advice. Perhaps even out of friendship, though she was hardly sure whether to call it that herself.

Harold held her at arm's length, examining her as if she were a puzzle even to him. She drank in his features greedily. He was still handsome, her brother. He still radiated an almost tangible glow of charisma. There were new lines on his face but it only made him look more definite. A seasoned man—one others would easily follow. Decided in his character. The red-gold of his hair and beard were undiminished in brightness. His eyes were still a clear, piercing blue. His mouth still held a secret curl of smile as if he laughed privately at the world. Yes, Harold looked the picture of what such a powerful man should be. Ælfgifa could not help comparing him to William. Where Harold had been born with the full complement of heaven's gifts—family, connections, intelligence, skill and athleticism—William had had to claw his own abilities out of a seething miasma of discontent and betrayal. The two faces seemed to flicker back and forth in her gaze. William's blunt features. Harold's fair face. A dark, heavy scowl. A sardonic but merry half-smile. The strategic mind, running hot and cold by turns as rage and then indifference fueled it, carved from necessity. The quicksilver intelligence, pleasant manner and playful cunning. She was going to be sick or fall...

Harold caught her and helped her to a bench. "I am all right, brother. I did not stop to break my fast. That is all." Ælfgifa's words were calm but her thoughts ran faster than hares, jinking and dodging as she tried to follow them.

"Why are you here, in any case?" Harold said, a faint frown now marring his high forehead.

"I told you. William let me leave–"

"No, Gifa. Here in Lundenwic. If you are not to use your considerable talents in Normandy, then why not employ them in Wintancaestre?" Harold was smiling but Ælfgifa felt the full meaning of his words and was cut by them.

My brother would rather I was still a hostage. He believes I came here on my own inclination. I am a game piece to him. It was not merely Ealdgyth who would not sue for my release. Harold had me exactly where he wished me to be and is peeved that I have upset his plans.

"Gytha made it abundantly clear I was not welcome in Wessex. I came to my sister," Ælfgifa said stiffly.

"Yes, and the queen has you digging herbs. A worthy use of your time and mind," Harold scoffed.

"Why, brother, I never thought you one of those men who thought so little of a healer's art until they needed a healer's services." Ælfgifa raised an eyebrow. She was rarely ever sarcastic with Harold but a small, hard stone of fury was rattling inside her ribs, becoming louder and louder the more his words shook her.

"Gytha is no longer lady of the house," Harold went on, ignoring his sister's anger. "Edith would welcome you. You have another nephew now too. You should be with your family, Gifa."

My family, Ælfgifa smothered a snort of derision. *My family who exchanged me for their own safe passage, guarantee of their good behavior. My sister who holds me distant. My mother who has ever hated me. Harold who would have preferred me to remain a hostage. And if any of my other brothers are there... Leofwine or Gyrth, I do not know any more. Tostig I do not care to see again, the brute.*

"Ealdgyth is also my family," Ælfgifa forced herself to say.

"Perhaps," Harold said darkly. "But are you certain that her intentions and plans align with yours, little sister?"

No. But no more am I sure that my plans align with yours, dear brother. "I will come eventually, Harold. But not yet. There is something I must yet do here."

Harold eyed her and then nodded. "Well enough. Now I must find the king," his lips quirked in a playful smile. "I would not like to deny the old goat even a moment of private irritation as he confirms me Jarl of Hereford." He winked at Ælfgifa, clearly expecting her to follow.

Ælfgifa stood unmoving, struck by the full import of her brother's words. Jarl of East Anglia. Jarl of Wessex—the greatest of the old kingdoms. Jarl of Hereford. Harold had far more land and support than Edward now. Those who were against Norman influence would be rallying behind Harold as they had behind her father—only many hundreds stronger.

My God, Ælfgifa thought. *Edward must be pissing in his breeches.* And then she realized the full truth; Harold and Ealdgyth were no longer in accord. One day, perhaps soon, she would have to choose between them.

CHAPTER 9

The first thing William thought on taking in the site for the Abbaye aux Dames was that someone had got their pieds mixed up with their toises. But seeing how Matilda beamed to show it to him, he realized it must be correct. The church really was going to be this big.

He remembered Ælfgifa's words that day back in the herb garden, about the importance of appearances in the matter of his marriage to Matilda. Well, let men look at this and say he did not value to his wife, listen to her counsel.

Matilda seemed comfortable on her horse despite the fact that she was now obviously carrying another child in her belly. *Please God, another son.* He had prayed more for a son in the last six months than he had prayed for anything in the rest of his life, and now he had one—young Robert. But a second would be wonderful, and bringing the unborn child to the site of the Abbey he was building to atone for his uncanonical marriage... well, it could not hurt.

"Try to imagine it, my Lord," Matilda said, indicating the lines scored into the cleared earth with a graceful flick of her arm. "Here will be the ladychapel. Here the chancel, there the choir, and the altar shall be at the far end, you see, near where those men are digging?"

William peered at the distant, insect-like creatures doing something with tools. "Heavens above! It will be bigger than Rouen cathedral."

"Yes! It's wonderful, isn't it?"

William fixed the priest, Walkelin, standing a little way off, with a stare. He'd appointed the man as his chaplain—Matilda insisted he needed one—as he seemed trustworthy, and Lanfranc had recommended him. The priest grinned as widely as Matilda had. Well, at least it seemed he was not robbing the Duchess to line his own pockets. All her money was clearly going into this vast church.

"What are they digging? A crypt?" William asked, trying to think of something to say. As he said it, it occurred to him that one day, not too far off, his remains might lie in such a place.

Matilda laughed. "No! They are merely probing the rock beneath to judge the best position for pillars. The foundations must be dug first."

"God will ensure a solid foundation for your church, as for your marriage, my Lady," Walkelin said.

"I have no doubt of it," Matilda replied, favoring William with a small, private smile. "But God would not wish us to be reckless in the building of His house."

"No, my Lady, absolutely! You are wise beyond measure." He laughed, and his chins wobbled. "Her Grace is become quite the expert in architecture, Lord," he added, addressing William.

"So I see," William muttered. Well, at least it was her money that would pay for this extravagance. But still, how many cavalry horses could be bought for all this stone and labor? How many mail hauberks? Swords and lances? How many fine ships to carry an army far and wide?

And yet... William had learned in the last year that the straight approach did not always render the quickest or best results. With the support of the Church turning from grudging to unstinting—something Matilda's generosity and open displays of piety had done much to achieve—his nobles were more inclined to support him. Revenues had actually increased in some places where he had gifted land to the Church and given up their rents, as the church seemed so much better at extracting funds. Although how much of the seemingly new revenue could be put down to the absence of Mauger, it was hard to tell. The connection could not be easily be discounted. It seemed that the bishop had found innumerable ways of drawing wealth to him beneath William's nose, and only now he had been forced to abandon his many offices did the scale of it become apparent.

At least the matter of the marriage seemed all but settled. William had feared that taking the Church's assent as granted would provoke the Pope. Given how much he needed Baldwin's men and money, there had been little choice, but an angry response from Rome could have been disastrous. As it happened, the Church seemed ready to agree. Once William had provided just a few more prebends here, of course, a grant of land there, and a bolt or two of samite for altar cloths as befit the status of the giver...

The Church seemed to have changed its mind about William for another reason as well. As news of his candidacy for the throne of England spread, he received greetings from more than one cardinal, offering their compliments to the Christian Duke of Normandy, trusting that when he ascended to the throne across the sea, he would weed out those heretical bishops appointed without Rome's assent. And no doubt yet more prebends and grants of land. It did not feel very Christian. Was nothing simple?

But, as they moved around the site, seeing more foundations being marked out—good Lord, there was more! A refectory, living quarters, Chapterhouse, even a huge kitchen just for the Abbot—William could not help but be impressed with how his wife had managed the business of the construction. Since the wedding—and, truth be told, the less than straightforward wedding night—William had found himself haunted by Ælfgifa's words when they had first met: *an unhappy wife can be creative. I would advise you to find out exactly what women of sense and reason actually do. I fancy the answer might surprise you...* The words had echoed around his thoughts and he found himself increasingly apprehensive of what a wife of sense and reason —and Heaven only knew, Matilda had those qualities in abundance—might inflict on him. He had seized joyfully on the construction of the two promised Abbeys as something Matilda might take upon herself, when she had started to show an interest in the plans and expressed some frustration that they were not proceeding faster.

Trees had been cleared and the timber would be put to good use, after being seasoned, as scaffolding or taken away for shipbuilding. A trackway to bring stone from the quarries nearby was under construction, and stonemasons and carpenters from all over Normandy and beyond were arriving at the site, more every day. Too many for comfort— the bishop of Rouen had already bent his ear about how he had had to increase the wages of the masons working on the cathedral to stop them being tempted away by the constructions at Caen. Despite having been started in William's grandfather's day, Rouen was still not finished, and never would be at this rate... And while William had offered Fitz's services to help Matilda organize the construction, she had barely called upon him, and then only to find out who she might speak to about this or that. The result... well that would not be apparent for many years, and perhaps not complete in William and Matilda's lifetime, but in any case it was evident that the church here made the great keep at Falaise look like a shepherd's hovel in comparison.

If it kept his wife occupied and out of boredom and mischief, it was a good thing, and it seemed to be generating benefits all over. The management of the ladies at court had certainly improved since Matilda arrived. He had far less trouble from the odious Mabel de Bellême now, anyway. Apart from the odd complaint about the Saxon hostage forced to share their quarters, and even that had now stopped, after he had released Ælfgifa to return to the Saxon court. Unsurprisingly, he had received no communication from Edward asking what his cousin meant by releasing a hostage without leave. He had little communication with Edward at all these days. William supposed his cousin had other things on his mind, for he had some very, very powerful figures in his orbit. Harold of Wessex not least of them.

And in any event, Wulfnoth and Håkon were still safely 'mewed up'. Both boys had turned into fine young men, fairly competent with sword and spear, and their horsemanship was better than he would have expected of any Saxon. He had put them under Fitz's wing for the completion of their education. For some reason, his steward thought it was a good idea for both of them to learn to read, though William did not challenge Fitz's ideas. Time would tell whether it was worth the trouble. Neither of them would ever be the scribe that Ælfgifa had been.

In truth, the Saxon woman had been on his mind more often of late, for other reasons. He had felt her lack almost as soon as she had left for England. Not just in her abilities as a herbalist, healer and scribe—though in all those cases the court suffered noticeably. It was her ability to see the truth and speak it to him without gloss that he missed. Oh, Matilda never dressed up her opinion on anything, and Gallet could be relied upon to speak his mind, but neither of them had Ælfgifa's sagacity or sharpness of perception. He had received a few communications—not-quite-stiffly formal greetings—and he had made it clear that he intended her to return, subject to the wishes of his liege Lord Edward, of course. He wondered what might be going on at the English court. The messages from his spies, infrequent and contradictory though they generally were, revealed that all was not well. Godwin's death appeared to have driven a wedge into the Saxon nobility. It seemed that if you were a great man, you were either for the Crown or you were for Wessex. No-one was fighting about it, but no-one was entirely neutral, either. William wondered where Ælfgifa fitted within that circus.

Here, in the mighty clearing fringed by forest, with the clamor of happy industry and the great works of God rising from the ground, Normandy almost felt peaceful in contrast to what he knew of England. He wondered what Ralph would make of it all? He must go and see his former guardian one of these days. They could hunt in the forests of Wacey. He'd let Ralph break the stag...

The peace was an illusion, of course. The victory outside Arques and his uncle's surrender had won some breathing space, but beyond the forest to the East lay Henri, and to the South lay Martel, both bloodied, humiliated even, but undefeated. This church would help him build the kind of Duchy he knew Normandy needed to be—secure, prosperous and with powerful allies—but he would still rather be out in the field with a lance in his hand, looking his enemies in the eye.

And yet... was it so bad to build something that would last? He could not wait until all threats had been destroyed before looking to his Duchy—he might be waiting until Christ returned.

"My Lord?"

He turned to his wife. "Sorry, I was lost in thought. About... the glory of God."

She smiled knowingly. "As I thought. I apologize for disturbing your prayers. There is one thing. This site where we now stand..." She gestured around the space their horses had been led to. "Does my Lord not think it would make a fine hospital for the blind? Of the many men injured in your service in battle, no small number have lost the use of one eye or both."

William made a noncommittal noise. It was true. An arrow even at extreme range could easily put a man's eye out. At closer range it would just kill him of course. Perhaps not quickly, but surely.

"And the small folk and noble alike may be struck down by sicknesses that rob them of sight. It is surely the Christian thing to do to ease their suffering."

Of the battles he'd fought... skirmishes and brawls though most of them had been... the worst thing after the joyful moment you knew you'd won was the cries of your own men and enemies alike. *My legs, my legs! Surgeon, help me!* And inevitably, somewhere, *I can't see! I can't see!*

"Of course, my Lady," he said. "Spare no expense."

After all, one day, soon, he might need it himself. If there were to be new conquests, there would be battle. And there would be conquests.

CHAPTER 10

For a moment Ælfgifa lay in the dark, eyes open but disoriented. She could not say what had woken her. There was a heavy, muffled thud as if something large had fallen against her chamber door. Knocking. She had been dreaming about someone knocking on a door except perhaps it hadn't been a dream?

"Gifa?" A low groan came from the other side of the door. "Gi... Gifa... please!"

"Harold?" she whispered. Ælfgifa threw a cloak over her shift and drew back the heavy bolt. The door swung inwards and a seated figure that had been leaning on the door fell at her feet. "Harold! What is wrong?"

"I do not... not feel at all w-well, G-Gifa..." Harold's breathing was labored. His face was gray, his lips turning almost blue at the corners. He was drenched in sweat. Ælfgifa's hands flew to support him. He burned to the touch but his limbs shook with fine tremors. Could his heart be failing him? Surely not. He was as fit a man as you could hope for. Not yet five-and-thirty. Her mind jumped, began running faster, and suddenly there were only the facts surrounded in cold, blue, crystalline logic. Harold was well enough earlier. He was well when he dined with the king—

though he ate and drank little. There was no reason to think this was a disease—it had struck too fast. Harold did not suffer from a damaged heart as Wulfnoth did but all the symptoms suggested his heart was struggling. Ælfgifa pressed clammy fingers to the pulse in her brother's neck. Slow, uneven and thready. His heart was weak. That left one other option. As if to prove her suspicions correct, Harold turned in her grip and vomited copiously onto the floor next to her. As he moved, his loose shirt lifted, revealing a tell-tale red rash of pin-prick burns.

Poison.

"Harold? Harold!" He had slid back in her grip and his eyes were opening and closing almost at random. The pupils were so dilated that only the thinnest circlet of blue ringed them. Ælfgifa shook him and lightly slapped his face. "Harold this is important. Where did you go after supper? Who did you see? Did you eat or drink anything?"

"S'lotta questions, sister. Wine... good wine... with... Eeffa? Aohra? Can't remember her name... Pretty thing."

"Aofra. You had dinner with the king and then let his ward entertain you?" Ælfgifa's heart was a cold stone in her chest. "Who else was there? Harold, who?"

Harold squinted against the rushlight Ælfgifa had hastily lit as if it pained him. "No... no-one," he slurred. "Private. Not like I n-need help. Been doing it long enough."

Harold, you festering idiot! She wanted to scream at him. But there was still time to save her brother. Harold was far too big for Ælfgifa to move by herself, so she rolled him onto his side, tilting his head back slightly and pillowing it on a blanket snatched from her bed.

She paused in her headlong flight to the still room. If it was poison, as she felt certain it was, then she must be careful. Only those she felt she could trust must be woken.

The girl she had been training in herbcraft. A boy from the kitchens whose hand she had once sewn up and a friend of his whom he swore could be trusted to be silent. And Ealdgyth. She sent a messenger to tell the queen that she herself was ill and needed her sister. Irregular, but better a rumor of that circulated than the alternative. However unsure she now felt about her sister's loyalties, someone had struck with murderous intent in the queen's household. Surely on this, she and Ealdgyth would see eye to eye.

The two lads were big enough and strong enough to maneuver Harold's long frame onto Ælfgifa's bed. She then set one of them to boiling water and the other to grinding charcoal as finely as possible. Her still room assistant cleared away the vomit and held a basin as Harold purged again and again.

"Lady, mayhap it were something he ate?" she suggested. "My cousin were like this after eating the wrong berries. We gave him salt water."

"Which I might do were he not already purging. Too late for making him sick to do much good. The poison is no longer in his gut. It's found a way into his blood." Ælfgifa paused and wiped her damp fingers on the gown she had hastily thrown on. She was mixing specific quantities of very strong herbs. A wrong measure now would see Harold in his grave.

The charcoal first, Ælfgifa decided. Thereafter followed a half hour or more that Ælfgifa didn't later care to remember. They were all spattered in thick, gray-stained bile by the time Harold could swallow the antidote Ælfgifa had made.

Where is Ealdgyth? Ælfgifa thought, the first edge of desperation crumbling into annoyance. It was not the way of things to summon the queen, especially in the middle of the night, but in this case her sister might have made an exception. *She never used to be cold and disconnected. She has sat up with fever-stricken ceorls in the past.*

Some time before cockcrow, Ælfgifa sent the boys back to their beds with three silver coins apiece. She would have given them a gold coin each if it would not have meant a great deal of questions and possibly a whipping for theft for the young men. The herb girl helped Ælfgifa clean Harold's limp form and tidy the chamber. Then she sank into an exhausted doze upon the stool in the corner. Ælfgifa allowed herself a full breath for the first time since she'd awoken. Harold's color was more natural—pale but without the ghastly gray tinge. His pulse was slow but strong. Unless he reacted to what she'd given him, she thought he would be well enough soon.

"Gifa?" Ealdgyth's voice was small and uncertain from the doorway. "Are you... What in God's name is our brother doing here?

Ælfgifa gave her sister a measuring look then glanced over at the herb girl who had been startled awake. "Thank you. You may go now. Make sure you sleep. There's a pallet in the still room."

As the chamber door closed, Ælfgifa turned to the queen but said nothing.

"I came when I could. My lord... paid a call on me last night. The message was delayed." Ealdgyth was almost as pale as Harold.

Or the King paid you a visit to keep you occupied. Possibly he even told you what the outcome would be. He would not let you come until he thought it was all over. "Did you know, Ealdgyth?"

"Know what?" the queen replied a little too quickly.

"About the poison. Harold does not serve Edward's interests, does he?" Ælfgifa said watching Ealdgyth blanch further. She shook her head. "Forgive me. I speak out of turn. It was a long night."

Ealdgyth either could not or would not answer. She moved to the bed and rested a hand on Harold's brow. "What has happened?"

"Aconite. A rare plant here, so I can only assume it was the yellow variety, Wolfsbane—the one trappers use to tip their arrows with, because it is the only poison which will act fast enough to drop a wolf in its tracks. Had it been the purple flowered variety, not all my skill would have saved our brother."

"How did you save him?" Ealdgyth raised a troubled gaze to Ælfgifa's grim expression.

"Nightshade. And other things. One venom thwarts another and the heart is the victor—in a strong man's case at least." Ælfgifa dropped back onto her stool, hardly caring that she had left the queen without a seat.

"You cannot believe I would be a party to this?" Ealdgyth said fiercely.

"I do not." Ælfgifa looked at her sister unhappily. "But to speak plain, Your Majesty, I wonder how greatly you would grieve if the poison had done its work. Not for your brother— I know you would be most grieved to lose another brother. But to lose the Jarl of Wessex, Hereford and East Anglia?"

For just a moment, Ealdgyth looked stricken. Then the beautiful frozen mask was back in place. "It is as well you were here, Gifa. You might even have saved our father. But you are exhausted. I have never heard you speak nonsense before. Little wonder after last night. Rest, sister. I will find someone to watch Harold."

"With respect, Your Majesty," Ælfgifa said in an iron tone. "This story must go no further than this room."

Ealdgyth gave her a hard look, weighing up the possibilities, then with a short, hard nod of agreement, she left.

"The queen is no kinslayer, Gifa," Harold's voice drifted weakly from the bed.

Ælfgifa turned and met his blue gaze, thankful that his pupils had shrunk back to their original size. "No. But she has a finger on the pulse of all that goes on here. It may be that she heard a far-fetched tale and gave it no credence. Or perhaps it came to her ears too late. But she knows there is a poisoner—likely one in Edward's employ—here in Lundenwic." At Harold's puzzled expression she went on. "She recognized the rash, Harold. I was not here but will lay good silver on Godwin bearing that same rash to his grave. Ealdgyth is no fool. She will have had suspicions. That rash occurs when you poison someone with wolfsbane mixed with rue, and probably other things so it tastes well in wine or food." Harold's eyes were cold blue pits in his white face. Ælfgifa swallowed. "Most often it kills in a few hours by stopping the heart. But sometimes it causes palsy. It's rare. Unless a skilled herbalist knew what she was looking for, it would look not like poison but like a natural death."

"That little bitch!" Harold might have sounded more impressive if he was not so weak.

"She is a cat's paw. Although certainly not an innocent." Ælfgifa looked at Harold with a mixture of love and exasperation. "You almost followed your cockstand into the next life, brother. While you are here, I suggest you keep it in your breeches!"

She got up stiffly while Harold laughed in surprise at her crude speech.

***

Ælfgifa convinced Harold that his best course of action was to appear as if the poison had been administered incorrectly or not had any effect. He could see the sense in this. A whiff of weakness at a critical stage might sink his grand plan, the shape of which Ælfgifa was beginning to appreciate with dawning horror. Her brother chafed at not meting out retribution to Aofra and by extension, Camus, but he could see accusing the king's ward and his personal physician was unlikely to get him very far. It was not so long ago that he had lived in exile after all.

When Harold returned to Wessex, Ælfgifa elected to remain, saying she had a further task to accomplish. With Harold gone, Camus and Aofra lacked any target save herself and she felt sure she could stay one step ahead of them. What to do about them was the problem. It was not that Ælfgifa had qualms about poison being the weapon of cowards and women. Properly applied medicine was an artform and an exact poisoning that was undetectable was something she could not help but grudgingly admire. She was also sure that in the realms of defending herself, she would employ any means necessary. What was knowledge of poisons but one more weapon? But murder...? How to make her conscience quiet on that score? Weeks passed, then months and though she watched and listened, she could not fix on a course of action. Ælfgifa decided one late summer's day, to ride to the Abbey at Westminster. She was not ready to admit that she was seeking Brother Dubhne's advice on the matter but she had not heard from him in some weeks nor seen him since her return.

The abbey looked both strange and familiar, as if she were returning after many decades rather than two years. There were so many faces amongst the monks that she did not recognize. They regarded her with a mixture of frank curiosity and hastily stifled revulsion, turning quickly back to their tasks. More than one brother crossed himself involuntarily. Ælfgifa smiled to herself without mirth and tossed the reins of her bay gelding to one of her escorts, bidding them see to the horses and take their ease for a time.

No one challenged her as she made her way to the scriptorium despite it generally being off-limits to women. There was a wounded, disorganized feel to the abbey. With the fewer brethren and new faces Ælfgifa wondered if there had been a sickness there whilst she was in Normandy. The scriptorium was deserted. No monks practicing calligraphy as an act of worship. No novices tracing their first letters in trays of sand. The hush of the place was a dead thing, not alive with the creation of fine work. It felt haunted and forlorn. Ælfgifa shuddered and turned away. The pigeon cote was next. The young novice Ælfgifa found feeding the birds stammered out an explanation, looking frankly terrified of her. Dubhne was not here. He had grown too frail to climb up to the pigeon loft anymore. He was very ill. "Like to die," the novice said, looking down at his sandals.

Bound again in a sense of impending doom, Ælfgifa found her way to Brother Dubhne's cell. She paused at the door, which was ajar. A deep, rich voice intoned prayers from inside. "Kyrie eleison. Christi eleison..."

Her heart leapt into her throat. Was she too late? Then Brother Dubhne's wry, once resonant voice broke weakly through the chanting. "You must pause now, Brother Cuthbert. The Queen's sister is here to see me."

He knew. He always knew when she was there. Ælfgifa felt a wave of relief. Perhaps he was not as sick as the novice had said. She barely glanced at Brother Cuthbert who made a hasty retreat once he realized who she was. Ælfgifa softly shut the door and turned to the pallet which dominated the tiny room. Along with a stool and a plain oak chest, it made up the entirety of the furnishings. The man on the bed was a creature of parchment and bone. Ælfgifa was glad Dubhne could not see her expression. For once she could not school it into a calm mask. She moved slowly toward the stool and sank onto it. "Brother, I have returned to England."

"No one would mistake you for a spirit, child." Dubhne laughed wheezily. "I doubt you need my instruction anymore but I fear we will not be continuing our lessons. God has decided to call his servant home." Ælfgifa did not know what to say and then Dubhne startled her by chuckling again. "He takes His own sweet time about the business, I must say."

Ælfgifa reached forward impulsively and caught up one skeletal hand as it lay on the blanket. Dubhne squeezed her hand in return but there was more strength in a child's grip.

"Perhaps a draught of–"

"Rest easy, child. Not even your skill will keep me here now God has seen fit to remove me." As if he knew that her throat ached with the blockage building there, where grief for her father was still raw and warm, and summoned more grief for her mentor, he smiled sightlessly at her. It was a corpse grin, missing many more teeth than it had a few short years ago. "You forget how old I am, child. I was starting to despair that our Lord would remember me long enough to send the angel of death for me. Don't grieve."

"I can make no promises," Ælfgifa said with a touch of asperity. "Brother, why did you not send for me?"

"One does not send for the Queen's sister. Not a lowly friar such as myself. And I knew you would come before the end."

"I would have come before this. I do not care for conventionalities!"

"Hush. Tell me, now, what advice is it you seek, Lady Ælfgifa?" Dubhne's sightless eyes turned toward her.

"You know me far too well, Brother." Ælfgifa sighed and told him about the attempt on Harold's life and how she felt that her father had been assassinated. Swallowing hard, she told him about the attempt on her own life before she had left for Normandy.

Dubhne was silent a moment after she finished and she wondered if he drifted on that silent sea between life and death, the twisted net of pain keeping him from floating free entirely. His voice was clear when he replied though. Even a little sharp.

"Do you seek pre-emptive absolution, Lady Ælfgifa? I cannot give it even if I were inclined. You would need a priest and probably a papal agreement. The Latin church with its snares and bureaucracy."

Ælfgifa half-smiled. "I am not asking forgiveness in advance of sin, Brother. I am trying to decide whether to sin at all."

"'Vengeance is mine,' sayeth the Lord," Dubhne said in a mocking tone.

"And justice? Protection? Defense?"

"The Lord is admittedly somewhat hazier on those." Dubhne drew a labored breath, yellowed skin pulling tight over his skull. He was vellum that had been scraped and reworked too many times. He had been written on by too many years and was now too fragile to bear more. The air crackled in his chest as if someone carelessly clutched a sheaf of parchment there. "This physician and his mistress—is she his mistress?"

"I am not certain but I believe so."

"They are dangerous together. Part them and you may have solved the problem. It's the girl, isn't it? She goads others to act for her. No doubt she believes herself very clever while being used in turn. And yet she has attempted murder three times at least." Dubhne sighed.

"I do not know what to do, Brother. She is too dangerous to be left at court. Maybe if she were exiled? Less power and influence..." Ælfgifa trailed off.

"You merely make her the queen of a smaller, less impressive kingdom. She has learned manipulation as a way of life. And the physician... he is against his order. It would be easy to blame all on the girl but he should know better than to be tempted. Where did he come by wolfsbane? The Camus I know of is regarded as a weaseling incompetent."

"There were Jewish merchants passing through Lundenwic. Their physicians and herbalists are superior. I doubt not the root was sold in good faith—it does have medicinal use after all." Ælfgifa frowned slightly. "I confess, Brother, I had hoped for more direct advice than this."

Brother Dubhne choked out a clogged laugh. "How I have missed you, Gifa. I will attempt not to allow dying to divert me from the point any further." His voice was full of mirth. There was more color and animation in his face.

Reluctantly Ælfgifa chuckled. "What would you do?"

"Me? Why nothing. I am a monk. But you, Lady, are an important person and player of political games. You must make the best choice you can and learn to live with it." He paused to cough again and flecks of crimson dotted the blanket. "Choose to act or not, in accordance with what will do the least harm. Do you understand? You must apply that admirable brain to the task and look forward, see the possible outcomes."

"I understand," Ælfgifa said and turned their last talk to other, happier matters.

CHAPTER 11

It was both easier and more difficult than Ælfgifa had imagined. A few weeks after Brother Dubhne's death, a scrawny boy covered in bruises and dirt tripped over a loose stone in the herb garden. Helping him up, Ælfgifa recognized the orphaned twelve-year-old who slept on the floor outside Camus' chamber and acted as a runner for him. Camus had made a great show of taking in the boy and training him as an assistant but Ælfgifa was certain the boy had learned nothing except how to dodge the physician's flying fists. And he had not learned that especially well by the look of him.

"Here," Ælfgifa said, helping the boy to his feet. "Why are you in such haste?"

The boy looked up at her and froze. Internally, Ælfgifa sighed. Doubtless he had heard the tales about the queen's demoness sister. He looked to be a simple lad. Apparently his tongue had glued itself to the roof of his mouth. "Why are you in the herb garden, boy?" Ælfgifa said patiently. "Did Camus send you for something?" Much as she loathed the physician before he poisoned her father and brother, she had had to bite her tongue over Camus taking what he thought he needed from the garden she tended. Not that Camus was much of a herbalist. Twice in the past Ælfgifa had steered him away from a foxglove to a comfrey plant. No doubt that was why Camus had taken to sending one of the servants.

"Chervil, Lady," the boy mumbled. "Master Camus says he must have it for his fowl. The kitchen don't spice them right and he wants greens."

"I do not have chervil. Or carrot for that matter. It has gone to the kitchens." The boy looked so woe-begone that she relented a little. "Boil up the leaves of Great Parsley—that should be close enough to flavor fowl." A little fed up with how the boy's eyes swept over her face and away and then back, Ælfgifa gritted her teeth and gestured over her shoulder. "The tall, woody plant with the long fronded leaves. You will not need much. He won't want to eat the flowers."

She turned back to what she was doing and when she looked up it was to see the boy trotting away, hands full of foliage, casting anxious looks in her direction as if she would turn him into something small and crawling. There was something about the picture that was wrong somehow, but the boy's fear had so irritated her that she couldn't work out what it was. Shrugging she returned to weeding. The wind picked up a gust of scent, bruised and fresh and unmistakably reminiscent of urine. Ælfgifa looked up. The scent was coming from the corner where the more poisonous plants were grown. A dawning suspicion saw her making her way toward the scent. Woody stems. Long fronded leaves. Strong smelling. Not Great Parsley however. The boy had taken the wrong plant.

Ælfgifa rocked on her heels a moment and then having debated that the likelihood of Camus sharing the fowl and greens with anyone was extremely low, calmly and precisely went back to her own work. *In God's hands,* she told herself. *Besides, he should be able to tell the difference between*

Great Parsley and hemlock. But she could not lie to herself. She had not handed poison to Camus herself, but she had chosen to do nothing while he blithely ate it.

Camus was absent from dinner that night. By the following day, Ælfgifa heard that he'd been vomiting and convulsing. "Like a palsy," one ceorl said as she plucked a goose. "Can't breathe, can he? Only we all know that means he's angered the Good Folk. Stroked him they have."

Ælfgifa nodded to herself. It was not entirely inaccurate from a certain point of view. Two days later, Camus was dead. Ælfgifa felt Ealdgyth's eyes on her often after that but the queen never asked her what she knew of the physician's death.

Ælfgifa made no excuses to herself. Perhaps God had indeed decided to intervene, or at least shown a way, but she herself had made the choice not to interfere, so she counted Camus amongst those she had personally sent to God. Aofra was more tolerable after Camus' death. She clearly suspected something—a guilty conscience will all too often make one suspicious—but she did not have the knowledge necessary to begin to unravel what had happened. Ælfgifa wondered if it might be possible to leave Aofra alone.

***

Years began to pass like days. Ælfgifa found plenty to occupy herself aside from tending the herb garden and treating the afflictions of ceorls and serfs. There was a new brother to train in the ways of the dove loft. Pigeons came regularly carrying news and Ælfgifa sifted it for importance as before, teaching the monk she had chosen to read the code. He had none of Dubhne's acerbic wit and she never truly warmed to him, or he to her. Perhaps competence and discretion were the most that could be hoped for but she found herself missing her mentor like a severed limb.

Sometimes Ælfgifa thought of the Duke of Normandy and whether he felt that her carefully worded promise—to come back when she was told to by her king—was in breach. But surely he was much occupied with other matters. He must have heirs by now. It was doubtful that he spared a malformed, caustic Saxon wench much thought. She did feel a pinch of guilt at leaving Wulfnoth, but then he would now be a young man. Hardly in need of her anymore. He had been happy in Normandy.

So Ælfgifa let time slide by like a great eel, smooth and too slippery to catch hold of. She never regained her closeness with Ealdgyth but she found that this didn't matter greatly. A change had occurred somewhere within her. If she had been a fruit tree, the branches that craved affection and friendship had withered and been pruned away. There was duty and learning, and there was knowledge. Ealdgyth sought her advice as before and accepted Ælfgifa's word on any intelligence brought to her. But it was a relationship of necessity with none of its previous warmth and humour. Harold seemed to be much occupied in building alliances with rival Jarls, consolidating his power base. The shape of his great plan shimmered like the skin of a great wyrm in Ælfgifa's mind as she watched him from afar. Sometimes she was moved to admiration for the careful way he executed his ambition. And sometimes she was seized with dread. Both made her delay her departure for Wintanceastre again and again as the seasons circled and circled once more. She did not wish to look forward at all the possible outcomes, nor choose the likeliest path. It was all too apparent that a final test of her loyalties was coming to strike a mortal blow to her peace forever. But she was once again at the heart of matters and in her homeland, free to roam as it suited her. Ælfgifa told herself that was enough for her life.

And then, a few years after Camus' death, Ælfgifa observed Aofra slipping a vial of some liquid in a cup of ale intended for her husband. She did not spare any thought for who Aofra had her eye on now or whether she was merely tired of the middle-aged thagn she had married. Ælfgifa rose quietly from where she had been sitting unobserved, crossed the outer kitchen and walked straight into Aofra. The ale soaked into the fine pink woolen over-gown Aofra wore and she turned a feral expression on Ælfgifa.

"I beg your pardon, Lady Aofra. I did not see you."

"It was an accident, I see that," Aofra said sweetly through gritted teeth. But the look that she turned on Ælfgifa was venomous. *Why are you alive,* it said. *At every turn I find you in my way and I paid good silver for your death.*

Ælfgifa watched as Aofra turned on her heel and stormed from the room.

"You wanta watch that one, m'lady," an elderly cook observed. "Nasty little cat, she is. Full of spite."

Ælfgifa turned to the old woman. "My thanks. I will bear that in mind." She slipped out of the kitchen and into the herb garden. Aofra's husband, Thagn Bealdric, had been ill for some time. Ælfgifa cursed her own blindness. Bealdric was past his fiftieth year but had always been hale. The last few months, where his appearance at board had grown more and more infrequent, Ælfgifa had thought that perhaps he was feeling the pangs of age early. Aofra maintained it was gout, when she deigned to speak of her husband at all. Ælfgifa had heard her say this so often as the ladies gathered in the queen's solar, that she had stopped paying much attention. Too much time spent watching Aofra with others, discovering sordid secrets of a more mundane kind. It had never occurred to her that Aofra would have the wit or the will to slowly poison her husband to death. She had assumed, naively she now realized, that there were lines even Aofra would not cross. Unfortunately Bealdric was one of those who believed that the Queen's cunning woman sister, was a *wiccae* of some kind. That Ælfgifa's touch would bring malady and that her success in curing those who did come to her was proof of her witchcraft. How else could someone so plainly marked by God's displeasure, marked as one of the devil's own, ever heal another? It was a popular opinion in some quarters and Ælfgifa avoided the people who held it. So she had not seen Thagn Bealdric closely enough to determine what ailed him. She wished now that she had found a pretext for seeing him.

Sinking onto a stone bench, Ælfgifa had a sudden longing to be away from here. It left her breathless with its strength, and with surprise, for one of the places that flitted through her mind was Falaise. She did not wish to be a hostage again but... but there had been less game-playing and maneuvering there. Many of the women had hated and feared her, but she had been left to her own inclinations. William had quarreled with her and blithely used her skills as it suited him, but he had spoken to her like an equal, almost as if he didn't realize he was doing so. In short, their conversations had been full of barbs but little in the way of pretension. *I am being foolish, Ælfgifa told herself. William turns on a knife point between unsubtle brute and clever, scheming strategist.* But there was something honest in that as well, was there not? He had taken no pains to hide any facets of himself. Here, in Lundenwic, Edward's court was full of those who spoke fair words and hid knives behind their smiles. It was not the Saxon way. Ælfgifa snorted at the irony. Doubtless William would not be flattered to learn that in some ways he was living as a barbarian better than those he regarded as such in England. It was hard to compare Helisande's honestly offered, simple friendship, with Ealdgyth's calculated and cool affection. Harold's charming, mercurial regard, with the Duke's blunt and unrefined respect, so much more prized for its honesty.

I do not know where I belong anymore. Ælfgifa clenched her small hands in her lap. *I no longer see a right path shining amongst the tangle of wrong ones.* That was the heart of her problem and for the first time she truly did feel cursed; cursed to see both sides of a situation, feel for both parties and be required to act anyway. She could see now, that if she continued in this vein, she would always be killing half of herself over and over again. *Perhaps there is no right and wrong, no good and evil. Perhaps there are only choices. Perhaps God and the Devil tired of watching us many hundreds of years ago. We are alone and can only act and live with our decisions.* Ælfgifa swallowed hard against the terrible, blasphemous thought, then set her jaw with determination. Aofra must be dealt with. It was clear that she would not stop. Curse Camus for putting the idea of poison in her head! *But afterwards,* Ælfgifa decided, *after Aofra is no longer a threat, I will fade into the background. I want no more blood on my hands.*

***

"Do you not see what he has done?" Ealdgyth was almost screeching in Ælfgifa's face. It was so unlike her normally perfectly composed sister that Ælfgifa was lifted out of her torpor into something like interest. There were a few fine silver strands in the ripe gold of Ealdgyth's hair. A few spider-web fine lines at her mouth and the corners of her eyes. When had Ealdgyth started to grow old? It wasn't pronounced yet. Ealdgyth was as active and energetic as ever. It startled Ælfgifa to realize that the queen had passed her fourth decade almost two years ago. Ælfgifa herself was a scant year from her third decade. Instead of feeling a sudden and gripping panic at how much older she had grown—without even realizing it—Ælfgifa found herself horrified to realize that she had let herself languish here for nigh-on ten years. It was a moment of terrible clarity. Ten years since William had released her. Nine years since Dubhne had died. Eight years since Aofra had been sent in disgrace to a convent in Escanceaster, with a little prodding and scheming on Ælfgifa's part. And after that... what? What had she, Ælfgifa, done that made a merit of her existence?

Buried her mind. Suppressed her curiosity and her desire for knowledge, Restricted both her schemes and her advice to the most banal and facile of matters. Faded into the background, limiting herself to embroidery, herbcraft and occasional calligraphy. Offered no brilliant insights on the intelligence she gathered. Made no great attempt to steer the course of events but instead watched them play out in a jaded fashion so long as they did not interfere with the now. She had stopped looking ahead. In short, she had become just what Duke William of Normandy had once expected women to be, confining herself to the narrow catalog of approved skills for a gently reared maiden. *An old maid, now.* The thought was involuntary and tasted bitter. *You have wasted the best part of yourself here.*

"Gifa!" Ealdgyth nearly screamed with frustration. "Do you attend my words at all? Harold has married her!"

"Aldythe of Mercia? The widow of Gruffydd ap Llwelyn?" Ælfgifa confirmed. It felt as if her mind were unfolding and stretching itself like a too-long caged hawk, now freed.

"You were never slow, sister. Why do you play the simpleton now?" Ealdgyth leaned away from her sister, eyes darting to the fine tapestries that adorned the ladychapel. Just one of the religious improvements Ealdgyth had ordered. "Harold led the campaign against the Wealas—even my lord husband approved it. But to marry the widow!"

Ælfgifa felt a stab of annoyance. "There is a precedent for such things, Ealdgyth. Besides, the Wealas king's position must have been precarious. I heard Gruffydd made enemies from Meirionnydd to Gwent. No real surprise that his men turned on him in the end, pinned against the mountains in winter with Harold hemming them in with his fleet–"

"Wealas!" Ealdgyth spat. "They'll slay their own king if it suits them—they sent Gruffydd's head to Harold as a peace offering. Ungodly, low and wretched creatures!"

Ælfgifa was stung by a memory of her childhood nurse, Beddwen, who had been one of the few truly kind people in her life. How quickly Ealdgyth forgot. "Gruffydd ap Llewelyn took Gwynedd by force and slayed the rightful ruler. He was not appointed by a Witenagemot nor by God. The Wealas have a long and proud tradition of killing their kings. Hardly for us to judge, sister. We have enjoyed peace under the King Edward but it is not likely to last!"

Why had she said that? Ealdgyth was the same age as Gytha had been when their mother bore Ælfgifa, but still Edward had no heirs. Ealdgyth was old now for a first child. Ælfgifa saw her sister suppress a flinch and rushed on, hoping to divert the conversation. "Ealdgyth, Gruffydd made himself unpopular by taking and dominating the other Wealas kingdoms—Powys, Ceredigion, many others. He wanted a united Wealas kingdom but the people did not. They cling to the old ways." She shook her head. "Why are you so troubled that Harold married Aldythe? She is not like to leave Gwynnedd. Nor is Harold like to put Edith Swannesha away." Harold had six children by Edith now—as well as a number of bastards who had been taken into his household with their mothers. Edith had been sanguine about the arrangement in her letters. Ælfgifa could not imagine fits of jealousy over what was clearly a political alliance. One of Harold's more sensible decisions, in point of fact.

Ealdgyth's fury returned like the tide. She grasped Ælfgifa by the shoulders and actually shook her, slim white fingers biting into her sister's spare flesh. "Aldythe has children by Gruffydd. She is well liked and respected in Gwynedd. It is probable that until the succession is decided that she will act as queen regent. If she gives Harold children too, then that gives Harold an unprecedented amount of influence in Cymru."

"You do not wish for Harold to play kingmaker." It was a flat statement. Ælfgifa felt a slow, chill rage of her own creeping up her spine.

"It does not serve Our interests," said Ealdgyth, releasing her sister. "It cannot have escaped you how much power Harold has amassed already. Any more... and..."

"You fear the Witenagemot will name Harold as heir to the throne. Now why would you fear that, sister?" Ælfgifa asked in the calm, silky tones of absolute fury. "Why *not* Harold?"

Ealdgyth was silent. Her reply did not need to be voiced aloud.

You have changed, sister. Ælfgifa thought. *You crave power now you have tasted it and will not relinquish it willingly. You do not believe Harold will fall in line with your plans. No more do I. Or is it something sadder than that? Is it that so much of you is tied up in creating*

Edward's legend that you cannot bear for a great man to come after him, a man who could become a greater king who might blot out that memory?

"I have never had the courage to ask you before, Gifa, but as your queen I demand honesty now," Ealdgyth began. "Did you... *remove* Camus? And Aofra—that had your hand upon it. How was it effected?"

Ælfgifa looked at her sister rather scornfully. "Camus was not so learned as he liked to pretend and poisoned himself. No one thought to send for me, the queen's devil-sister." No need to admit that she could have stopped Camus ever ingesting those leaves. "Aofra was pleasuring herself with a younger man than her husband—one of many in a long line, I understand. Her husband's servant sought her one night as I was working in the still room and I pointed him in the direction of the stables. Was I to know that he would find her in the arms of her lover?" Of course she had. She had made certain of it and of the servant's loyalty to his master before arranging matters. "She does penance now in a convent as the king commanded and her husband deemed fit."

Ealdgyth took a breath as if to stop herself from saying something she would regret. "Ælfgifa, if I cannot trust you then I cannot house you. I must have your complete loyalty. It was no ill-deed that took either Camus or Aofra from us but... You must obey *me* if you are to be a member of my household." She moved towards Ælfgifa, smiling through gritted teeth and putting an arm about her as if they were close once again. As if they were friends.

Ælfgifa leaned into the embrace for a moment. *Remember this. Remember what weapons will be used against you should you take up the threads of influence and foresight again.* Then she stepped away, cold, alone but beholden to no one. "I cannot promise what you ask,

Ealdgyth. I belong to the tree, not the bough. But I see your perspective, truly I do. Farewell, Sister. I shall not be at board tonight and I expect to leave before you have risen."

And with that she curtsied to the queen and left.

***

There had been occasional letters over the last few years but Ælfgifa had not seen Edith the Fair since before she was sent to Normandy. She wondered now at the madness—for surely it was a sort of madness—that had led her to shred the ties of her old life and step away from intrigue and strategy. For what other purpose had she been made? Ælfgifa swore to herself that whatever she now did, it would be as she believed right, and hang convention and propriety. She felt a little nervous approaching the great house at Wintancaestre though, and smothered it with a layer of belligerence. They would not turn her away, however grudgingly they took her in.

She left her mare with a stable hand and proceeded toward the long house on foot, feeling ever more timorous the closer she trudged. Ælfgifa expected to slip in unnoticed, or half expected to be met by Gytha at the door, her mother wearing the special expression of displeasure reserved solely for her deformed daughter's presence, and be turned away or sent to a cold, hearthless cell, having been told that she was not required at board. Ælfgifa swallowed against the dryness in her mouth and tried to straighten her shoulders. She was no longer a child. In fact at nine-and-twenty she could no longer claim even to be a young woman. *Mother has no power over me, nor is she mistress here anymore,* she told herself. *Harold has wanted me here long since. I will not be intimidated.*

"Gifa!" The cry rang out from behind her and all Ælfgifa's resolve turned to ash and blew away. For an instant she wanted to flee, but she forced herself to turn as a second "Gifa!" was called after her. Edith was still fair, even mud-streaked and pink-faced from running. She laughed breathlessly and Ælfgifa's fears crumbled as certainly as her belligerence had. She found herself half-laughing, almost sobbing in response as Edith struggled the last few feet toward her, skirts held up in one hand in a vain attempt to keep them out of the mud, black hair trailing out of its braids into impossible elf-locks and tangles behind her. Ælfgifa didn't realize that she had reached out her arms until Edith had folded her in a fierce hug, stooping so that Ælfgifa could rest her head on her shoulder.

"I had all but lost hope of you coming here," Edith said, pulling back to look at her sister-in-law. She examined Ælfgifa minutely but her next words were warming. "Gifa, what have you been doing to yourself? You look worn ragged."

It had been so long, Ælfgifa realized, since anyone had cared how she did, had welcomed her presence without reserve, that she had almost forgotten what it was to be liked and valued. Edith's words were balm on a wound she had not known she carried.

Tucking Ælfgifa's arm through her own and leading her to the great house, Edith said, "I am glad you are finally come, sister. I have missed you."

It was the first time since she had returned from Falaise almost ten years ago, that Ælfgifa had felt she was home.

***

Harold stayed in Gwynedd for several months. It was both odd not to have the Jarl in residence and at the same

122

time, utterly familiar. Ælfgifa still tripped herself up expecting to find her father rounding a corner or examining a stallion in the stables. It continued to feel like Godwin's house, though in truth, it bore little resemblance to Ælfgifa's childhood home. Edith had had the great hall enlarged and several chambers added. The old kitchen was now a store room and a larger, more commodious kitchen had been built. It was clear that Harold did not lack for funds and Edith had made sure his household in Wessex reflected his power and wealth.

Privately Ælfgifa thought that Edward would have an apoplexy if he visited Wintancaestre in the near future and saw how great that power and wealth had grown. Certainly Ealdgyth would be unable to disguise that wounded, peevish look she had so often worn before Ælfgifa left Lundenwic. A look that said life had not used her well and that she thought little of those on whom fortune seemed to smile. It troubled Ælfgifa a little, especially combined with the influence Harold would now command in the kingdoms of Cymru, but she told herself not to be foolish. Ealdgyth may have been correct in her assessment but she had been wrong in her actions. *You made your choice,* Ælfgifa told herself. *Now to live with it.*

On the whole it was easy to forget political machinations for a while. The house teemed with children—both Edith's and several other ladies', married and otherwise. While Edward's household had seemed perpetually gloomy and cold as a crypt with its silence and its increasing focus on prayer and holy relics, Harold and Edith's household was the complete opposite, full of activity and laughter and swearing and children romping with dogs. It put Ælfgifa in mind of the old *Pretani* tales of the courts of the *Good Folk*—the summer and the winter—and once the image occurred, she could not shake the unfavorable comparison.

Ælfgifa found herself the subject of much childish curiosity. To start with, her horde of nephews and nieces, packed out with the throng of servant's children and Harold's illegitimate offspring, regarded her with fear and awe because of her marked face. Then by degrees the bolder ones led the others in approaching her and soon they all called her *Wyrm-Fanthu*—'Dragon-Aunt'—regardless of kinship. To her chagrin and surprise, Ælfgifa found she could rarely go anywhere in her brother's high seat without trailing at least four children of varying ages. Often there were more. Somehow she had become a general favorite. The elder children seemed to like her especially because she spoke to them as equals and because she was very nearly of a height with most of them. Ælfgifa supposed in some way this made her one of them in the children's eyes, or at least that she was their special property. She found she did not mind the constant interruptions despite the fact that now she could only accomplish a bare third of her daily tasks. She clamped down relentlessly on the small, still voice that wanted to ask whether she would have liked children of her own. It was not to be and she would not taint the gift of this grubby crowd's regard with longings she should be long past in any case. The first time Edith came upon Ælfgifa as she tried to gather lavender, aided by a dozen pairs of small, willing and ultimately clumsy hands, she burst out laughing. Ælfgifa watched her sister-in-law with wry amusement. Finally Edith got herself under control, wiping her eyes and restricting her laughter to the occasional hiccough.

"I am glad to be such a jest to you, sister," Ælfgifa said without rancor.

"Oh, Gifa, I know I shouldn't laugh..." A burst of giggles escaped Edith again and she choked on her next words. "But it's like watching a flock of goslings following their mother and you are the most unlikely goose I ever saw! If the thagns and ceorls and Jarls at the next Thing saw you thus..."

Ælfgifa rolled her eyes but couldn't avoid a close-lipped smile of her own as Edith doubled over with laughter again. Finally Edith managed to get her mirth under control and shooed the children out of the garden with promises that *Wyrm-Fanthu* would play with them later.

Ælfgifa put her small knife in the trug at her feet and wiped her hands on her apron. "You have come with news of Harold."

Edith regarded her, traces of a smile still curling the corners of her lips. "How well you read me, Gifa. Yes, my lord and your brother returns from Gwynedd even now."

"I wonder he stayed so long. It has been many months since the wedding..." Ælfgifa bit her lip and glanced at Edith uncertainly. Edith smiled again but this time there was a cynical edge to it.

"Do not trouble yourself to worry for me, Gifa. I am quite tranquil on the matter. Harold and I discussed the possibility before ever he went to war against Gruffyd ap Llewelyn. The marriage was the best move but considering there is so little to cement it, I told Harold that if he did marry the Wealas king's widow he had best not return until he was sure she was with child."

How practically minded, Ælfgifa thought, keeping her expression smooth, for such a level of scheming came as a surprise even to her.

"I'm only surprised it took Harold so long to be sure. Generally he only has to hang his breeches on the end of the bed and whatever poor girl has succumbed to his charms that week will have a belly rising under her chin by the next saint's day."

To her mortification, Ælfgifa felt her face begin to burn at this frank admission and callous disregard of Harold's philandering by his wife. In that moment she was almost a little afraid of Edith. Ælfgifa rarely underestimated people or misread them but here was an ambition that matched Harold's own. Powerful enough that logic and cool reasoning conquered the least hint of wifely ill-feeling.

"Have I shocked you greatly, Gifa?" Edith said with a hooked smile.

"Yes, a little. I am not so foolish as to believe the great love songs composed about you and my brother—it is hardly surprising a skald would choose you as a subject after all. Or Harold for that matter. But I had thought the match hinged on affection as well as advantage." Ælfgifa paused.

Edith's smile broadened into something with fewer briars in it. "The love I bear your brother is greater now than when we wed. But I am not going to keep a man on a leash like a dog. He comes to heel when I call in all that matters. Besides, allowing him to roam without complaint has always meant he is eager to return to my bed."

"So he returns soon?" Ælfgifa said almost desperately. After the episode with Aofra, she really did not wish to hear any more of her brother's bed sports or companions. If Edith was not threatened by this Wealas queen then well and good. The plan was obviously sound.

Edith gave her a knowing look that made the color rise in Ælfgifa's cheeks once more. "No lover has taken your fancy yet, then sister?"

Ælfgifa did not believe there was any malice in Edith's teasing, only genuine curiosity. And really, if she was going to blush like a novice every time Edith made a ribald comment then it was no more than she should expect. On the other hand she was not going to leave this line of questioning open. Ælfgifa made herself give a hard, mocking laugh. "Only point out a man who can keep up with me in wits and I shall be happy to keep up with him in the bed chamber! Alas all men of such caliber seem to have sworn themselves to God. A sore waste, think you not, Sister?"

Edith chuckled. "I always thought a monk's life was a waste and I take your point, Gifa."

Do you? Ælfgifa wondered cynically. *Is it as well that I have wit enough to know that no one would have me but for great intelligence as compensation? Or is it a further cruelty on God's part? Perhaps if I had been born stupid as well as ugly I should have endured less and been happier.* She shook off the leaning toward melancholy. Useless musings. She would no sooner give up her wits and her influence than she would cut off her own hand. Ælfgifa linked arms with Edith and walked back into the house.

CHAPTER 12

The messenger held out the dispatch to William, who took it and, without a glance, handed it to Fitz. It was not that he could barely make sense of it—one word in five, perhaps—but that he did not want to be the one to see the news. If he looked at the scrap of parchment, the words would look a certain way, the ink settle itself onto the surface never to go back. If someone else looked at it, it might be different. His heart was drumming in his chest which felt oddly light, hollow, like a bird's.

Fitz let out a long breath.

"Well, don't stand there sighing like a spurned lover, what does it say?" William barked. While they sat here by the coast, trailing Henri's army round like a shunned puppy and powerless to do anything about it, a second army might already be tearing into the Duchy from the South, advancing on Falaise before they could return. To his wife. His *sons*, who must be protected above all else. Young William, the third boy, he'd barely seen before he'd had to leave. Curse Henri.

And if they did return to Falaise, King Henri and his Northern army would be at their backs. He felt suddenly cold, a sweat springing from his skin in moments. He had to know.

"The King's Southern army under Rainauld has been defeated," said Fitz, sounding as though he did not believe the words he was speaking. "Completely. It's... gone!"

"What? How?" Defeated? It must be a mistake. Only days ago had they heard the news of Rainauld's force near Neufchâtel-en-Bray. A second French army entering Normandy and all William's forces concentrated leagues to the North and West. It was like a nightmare.

"There was a battle, it seems," Fitz said, sounding like one who has awoken from the midst of a dream and was not sure what was real and what was not. "Instead of advancing, the army set up camp near Mortemer and began ravaging the countryside." Fitz read down. "Much burning of houses and crops... Slaughter of small folk... Theft..."

Saints' bones! As if Henri's ravaging of Normandy was not enough. "Who fought them?"

"Ah, let me see. The Count of Eu—the dispatch is in his name—Hugh of Gournay, Walter Giffard... Some others... Guillaume of Warenne. Guillaume? Why, he's only seventeen. Anyway. Eu writes that they raised levies to stop the French preying on the country. Combined their men with those of Roger of Mortemer and fell on the French camp yesterday afternoon. Rainauld could not maintain discipline, and the army disintegrated. Fled. There was a rout. A total rout."

"And Rainauld?"

"Escaped."

"God's bollocks. That would have been a pretty capture to wave in Henri's face."

"Gui of Ponthieu surrendered, though. He's in chains, Giffard's bringing him to Falaise."

"Well. that's something." One by one the treacherous barons were being weeded out.

A breeze rose momentarily, rippling the long grass and wafting cool air with the tang of sea-salt over them. William took a lungful of it, and another. He had been caught out, and badly. So focused on chasing Henri out of Normandy, looking for a chance to deal a serious blow despite a lack of men, he'd missed the second army wheeling round his flank. It should have been a fatal error. He looked around him at the army. Gear and armor was worn and scuffed. On every face was an expression of calm and determination. It was a force that had been tested and honed during the long campaign against Henri and Geoffrey. And it was in the wrong place. He'd got his strategy wrong. Gallet had been right—the first battle you lose is the last one you fight. In this case, he'd nearly lost his first battle without even being there to fight it. And yet somehow a victory had been won for him. He could not puzzle it out. God's will, perhaps?

If it was, the Almighty had suffered Henri to trample round Normandy for months before allowing William his victory. Months! In which the King had not sought to do anything but plunder and destroy. William had sent swift instructions to all towns and castles to bring in stores and bar their gates. To expect sieges and raids. Meanwhile, he had raised his army, yet again, and cautiously taken the field. They had stayed close to the French army as it wrecked villages and small, unfortified towns, burned crops in the fields, and carelessly slaughtered peasants throughout Hiesmois, the Bessin, even as far as the river Seule, and towards Caen. Then turned for Lisieux, then Varaville. The presence of the Norman army had at least stopped Henri from laying siege to any of the larger towns, or from getting well enough established to threaten Falaise, but Henri's force was more than double the size of William's army and he could not risk pitched battle, even if he'd been permitted to. He'd managed to stage the odd nighttime raid here, ambush a foraging party there, but otherwise Henri had been permitted to run riot. It was intolerable. William thought he would never get the smell of it out of his nostrils. Burned fields. Burned wattle-and-daub houses mixed with the burned flesh of their inhabitants. Ripening corpses, blood and shit.

Fitz and Montgomerie had been firm with him—as had Matilda—that he must not face any force containing the King. That would make him a traitor, even with that same King riding roughshod over his Duchy. The King meant to humiliate him, they insisted, but he would leave in time. What would Ralph have made of this? Was this the proper order? He felt fury beginning to build. A tension in his arms, then his chest, then a pressure, building, building... He sent Fitz back to the main body and pondered for a moment.

"Where is the King's army?" he asked.

Gallet called over a scout who had been standing nearby. "No formalities," the knight snapped, "make your report."

"The army was approaching the Dive, at the ford, Lords, when I last saw it." The scout paused. He was a local man, and very familiar with the conditions here it seemed. "The tide is due to turn soon, though. If they intend to cross, they'll have to do it quickly."

"All right. I want a report as to exactly what they are doing now, though. We have scouts in touch with the enemy?"

"Yes, your Lordship."

"Then send someone out to them now. As quickly as possible."

The man touched his forelock and ran away to arrange the report. "What's his name?" William asked.

"Roger of Mesnières. His family has a little land on the Bray not far from here."

"He's a good man. We'll see that he's rewarded if we get out of this alive."

Gallet looked at William. "You're not thinking of attacking them are you?"

Dear Christ, he wanted to. But if he led an army directly against Henri, he would lose the support of the Church, and make enemies of the Holy Roman Emperor and a dozen other rulers. Not to mention his father in law.

"No." *Not unless the right opportunity presents itself.* "But there's no reason we can't advance a little. Just to make sure they cross, after all. Knowing Henri he'll be vacillating and all his counsellers arguing. Let's give him a nudge in the right direction."

Gallet called the vanguard into battle formation and William gave the order to advance. The land round here was flat, low-lying. A hummocking of sand dunes a few score toises on their left was the only elevation. There was no way of seeing farther, assessing what they faced. The victory at Mortemer might count for nothing after all.

"Lord William!" Gallet called, breaking into his reverie. "Our scouts, I think." He pointed ahead of them, and a little to the right. Two men on foot, loping in their direction.

William raised his arm. "Halt!" There was a clank of weapons being readied. They might have to make a stand here if the French were hard on the scouts' heels. The men seemed to spot William's standard, borne by faithful old de Tosny, and shortly were jogging towards them.

"Has the army crossed?" William asked, breathlessly.

De Mesnières nodded. "Yes and no, Lord. That is to say, they began crossing, but the tide is coming back in. A part of the army is still on the near bank. The rearguard and baggage train."

"Hmm. How much of the force is across?"

"More than half, your Lordship."

A plan was forming. The situation had changed. The King did not seek humiliation but domination—the second army under Rainauld proved that. It made hurting Henri militarily imperative. And now it may still be possible for William to maintain his ludicrous responsibilities to his overlord. "Has the King crossed?"

"Yes, Lord. The rearguard looks like it's under the command of Theobald of Aquitaine. Those were his gonfanons we saw."

"Do they know we're here?"

"Hard to say, Lord, but I'd think not. They pulled their scouts in when they started to cross. Now they've just got a picket a little way from the bank."

"Hmm. All right." William turned to Gallet. "We're going to attack."

Gallet raised his slab of a face and chuckled. "At last! Much as I've enjoyed my tour of ruined villages, I was wondering when we'd start killing Frenchmen. Do you want me to call up the main body and the cavalry?"

"No, we go now. The vanguard will have to do."

Gallet leaned towards him they marched. "They may surrender rather than fight, Lord, if there are so few. Shall I give instructions to show mercy?"

William looked his steward and friend in the eye. "You shall not," he said. "No prisoners. Not even noble ones. Kill everyone."

He imagined the look on Fitz's face, thinking of all those ransoms going begging. Well, it was too bad. "And we should go now. If Henri really is withdrawing, I want him to see this before he leaves. The King will learn what happens to those who try to invade my lands. Call the advance."

The men at arms of the vanguard pressed forward. If they were tired, sore from being in the field for so long, they didn't show it. William sensed the excitement running through them. A fight at last, after months of having to stay a league or two distant from the men who were trampling their land, killing and raping. William called Ralph de Tosny over and changed his broadsword for a short stabbing estoc on the move. This was going to be a close-quarters brawl. He hefted his shield on his left arm, flexing the muscles, making sure he could move it freely. "Keep the banners lowered," he said to Roger de Tosny, still his standard bearer after all these years, and father of his squire. "I don't want them to know we're coming until the last moment."

"Aye, Lord William," the standard bearer replied, brightly. Even the elder de Tosny seemed full of vigor today.

Before long, they were approaching the lip above the Dive's bank. It would have been a sensible place to mount a defense, but the scouts confirmed that the French were down near the river's edge, seemingly insensible of the army marching towards them. If it wasn't a ruse, they were making a catastrophic error. "Send the archers out to the flanks, and have them move forward to the bank," William ordered. "Tell them to keep low. Take down as many infantry as they can until we get there, as well as the King's archers. Then concentrate on the archers when the mêlée begins." The instructions filtered out and soon the vanguard's contingent of archers was darting out ahead.

A shout of alarm drifted back on the breeze, then more joined it. The archers had taken up position and in a few moments began to shoot.

"You can raise the banner now," William said to his standard bearer, as he waved his sword over his head. "Dex Aie!" he shouted as he broke into a jog. The vanguard pushed forward and they poured over the bank, down the sandy beach to the river's edge where the King's rearguard was hastily arranging itself into a line. They had only managed to take a couple of steps forward before the Normans crashed into them. There were a few archers down there. Shooting? Didn't look like it. He raised his shield as the two lines clashed, and felt the impact jar through his shoulder. For a moment, everything was sensation—the great shoving at his shield, bellowing men, soft, yielding sand underfoot, sound of blade hitting blade, shield, flesh. The man opposite William was pushing with his shield, planting his feet apart, grasping an axe, trying to free his right arm from the press of men beside and behind to swing it. William jabbed up under the broadest part of his leaf-shaped shield with the short sword, felt it scrape against mail. The soldier locked eyes with him and for a second, William saw fear. *How dare you?* He thought, *by Saint Romanus' bladder, you've been slaughtering innocent unarmed serfs and the first time you get into a fight, you're* scared?! The anger bloomed and roiled around, steam in a boiling pot the moment before it blows the lid off. William screamed and brought the sword back up and stabbed downwards into the knight's neck. No coif. Unprotected. It went in half a pied, as if into butter, before meeting something solid. If the knight uttered a sound, William didn't register it. A spray of hot blood jetted into his face. Filthy Aquitaine scum! He raised his foot, planted it against the knight's shield and shoved it back. The corpse toppled into the French line and William followed it, slashing and jabbing with the sword.

Scum! *Slash*. Wretches! *Swipe*. Murderers! *Thrust*. For a few glorious moments he could go where he pleased, hacking his way through the King's men as though they were a field of wheat. Then a barrier—*thud*. A heavy shield under his sword, something swinging through the sky up to the left and —*Christ, Savior!* William swung his own shield round and ducked just in time to parry an axe stroke that sent a buzz through his arm, then almost wrenched it out of its socket when the axe was pulled out again. Now the short sword seemed a pathetic weapon against the axe. He jabbed the point of his shield into the ground, ducked behind it and tried stabbing up underneath the boss again, but the blow was knocked aside. Another swing of the axe, up to the right this time, and he launched himself away from it, feeling the wind as it passed his face and a bite to his thigh as though a great snake had dug its fangs into him. He heaved a breath in reflexively. The leg had gone burning-hot-freezing-cold, would not take all his weight. The axe was coming back but seemed to jerk in flight, and the blow fell harmlessly beside him with little force behind it. The big Aquitainian man who had wielded it had a stick protruding from his face. Arrow! William lifted his shield out of the ground and pushed at his adversary with all his weight, but the knight did not budge. His eyes turned on William, face twisted with the arrow lodged in it, and he began to raise the axe again. This time he was slow, and William had plenty of time to jab his sword into the man's armpit and push, push, twist...

"Lord! Lord William!" A shout came to him from somewhere ahead, to the left. He realized he had been hearing it for some time, glanced around. Gallet, swinging his broadsword like it was a mace and thrusting with his shield like it was a dirk. William fought his way to the knight and without a word they took up a mutually defensive stance. It seemed like hours they stood there like that, back to back, William stabbing and slashing, Gallet swinging, both covering each other with weapon and shield. The lines had broken down somewhat in the mêlée, but over time the two of them managed to shuffle closer to the biggest mass of Norman men at arms.

"We're winning," Gallet panted, after a while.

"Shut up. Kill more," William huffed, redoubling his efforts. But Gallet was right. There was quite a pile of dead in Aquitaine colors lying in the mud or swilling back and forth in the lapping waves of the Dive. The water was now a muddy brown with scrolls of red looping through it, meaningless writing on filthy parchment. Eventually the King's rearguard had become a cluster in the water's edge beset on all sides by Normans. The cluster became a knot, then a handful of men around Aquitaine's banner. Gallet cut down the standard bearer as he begged for mercy, shouting "I yield! I yield!".

A strange, oppressive quiet settled over the vanguard, broken only by the slopping of ripples in the river around the French corpses. William looked across the river. It was lined by silent figures. Men-at-arms, nobles. They had just watched a massacre of their own men. Good.

William's breath slowly returned to him, and he limped forward to the fallen banner. Holy Saints, but his leg was in agony. He picked up the standard, shook it angrily at the French across the river, yelled "Dex Aie!" one more time and flung the banner as far into the river as he could.

***

The joy of victory, if it existed at all, was short-lived. There were wounded men to pull out of the mud and treat. Dead enemies to bury, too. Much as he would have liked to let the Franks and Aquitainians rot, he would not have them doing so in Normandy, the smell of which would breed a plague in his own lands.

William suffered de Tosny to bind his leg. The pig of a Frank had managed to cut into the calf, and after trying to pull out all the threads of his breeches that had got into the wound, William snapped at the squire to have done with it and bandage the cursed thing. He'd taken wounds before and they'd healed. There was work to do.

The army trudged back towards Falaise, and mercifully there was a horse for him. William couldn't have walked another step. Relief at the two victories, the promise of home and his family, a comfortable bed kept him going as the army pushed onward.

But soon, William began to feel that all was not well. The wound stopped stinging, but began to ache. That was normal, wasn't it? But should it be so hot? His entire calf had begun to burn. It was hard to the touch, like wood, and the slightest contact sent nauseating waves of pain through his leg. It wasn't misty, was it? There was a sort of grayness to everything. The sun was out, though. Strange.

"Lord? Lord?"

William looked up. Fitz was riding beside him, brows knitted. "What?"

"I've been calling to you for a minute," Fitz said. "What's wrong, you didn't answer."

"Nothing."

"You're very pale, Lord." Fitz leant in. "And you're sweating."

"It's hot. Damnably so."

"Lord, it's quite cool for the time of year." Fitz pursed his lips. "Let us stop for a rest."

"Fine. Fine to keep going." Need to get back to Falaise. Fire. There was a fire. And a plague. All the dead at the river. They would come back and rot, poisoning the air. Everyone would choke. The air was on fire. No, not yet. Burn the bodies on a fire, and that would stop the plague. "No, no go back, dig Franks dig Henri burn fire plague stop kill–" He tried again, but the words weren't right. It was important. Everything was gray and he had to stop it. It was crowding in from all around now, like fog but warm. William had a strange sense of falling back into himself before the gray swept over everything and blotted him out.

He staggered out of the gray, back by the banks of the Dive. Where was his horse? Gone. There was the river. Had to find them. All the Franks. Burn them. There were the graves, the body-sized mounds up atop the bank. And another mound, low, circular, where they had thrown all the severed hands, feet, arms, legs, the odd head. They must be reunited with their bodies. They could not be burned separately, or it wouldn't work. He dug, pulling out arms and legs as he found them, but there were always more, and the earth was strangely sticky and kept sliding back.

By God, he was thirsty! He staggered into the waters and plunged his hands in to scoop out a mouthful. Warm. Hot. The river was... Holy Christ, it was blood! William barked in anger and fear and staggered onto the land. Had to finish. Must finish to get out of here. He plunged his hands into the soil again. There was... Something soft, yielding. Saints' bowels, what was that? White, small... William yelped. The arm in his hand must have belonged to a child. Not a youthful squire, a child of only a few years. Who in his army had killed a child? He would punish them. Have their insides ripped out! Where was the grave that this belonged to? He ran up to the row of mounds. There! A mound only a few pieds long. He started scraping at the earth, heaving chunks of soil and wildly throwing them away. A face began to peep out of the red earth. Familiar. Surely... What had young William been doing in the battle?! Oh, Holy Father! Who had brought his son here? Who had killed his youngest son! Who?! He would slaughter them all! William could not tear his eyes away from the smooth skin of his boy peeping out of the earth of his Duchy, and felt a scream building in his chest. It would not come out. He could not make a sound. No breath came. But someone was shouting. Somewhere distant. And then there was a strange rushing in his throat and something he could not see had gripped his shoulders and—

"Lord! William! Lord!"

Fitz! "Why are you shaking me?" William rasped. He threw the covers of the bed back and tried to sit up, but the effort sent everything spinning and he had to rest his head again.

"Lord! You're awake!" Fitz started laughing, and then it could have been weeping.

"Of course I'm awake, you were shaking me." William rubbed his face. Heaven's dunghills, he had a beard! What in the devil had happened? What was...? He thought back... last thing he remembered... Battle, and... something about digging? The vague image of a pale face in red receded and he could not hang onto it.

"Where?"

"Falaise, Lord. We brought you here after... you passed out on the way back from Varaville. Almost fell from your horse. Would have done if..."

"How long?"

"Three weeks."

"Good God!" He had missed three weeks? What might have happened in that time? "Where is Henri? Did he retreat? Anjou? What of the King's brother?"

"Do not worry, Lord." Fitz smiled ruefully and made calming gestures with his hands as if patting a ghostly dog. "Henri is at Senlis. He disbanded his army a fortnight ago. And there was nothing left of Rainauld's army to disband. Martel has made no moves to raise a new army—he's still in Angers. All is safe, Lord."

Relief washed over him. William made another effort to sit up, and succeeded this time. "So you've kept things in good order?"

Fitz laughed, shook his head ruefully. "I'm not sure I would have without Lady Matilda. She's had the grands eating out of her hand and kept them away charmingly whenever they demanded to see you. Things are going quite well. I don't think I've seen the household running so well. Which is astonishing considering how much time she spent seeing to your care."

William huffed, which left him out of breath. "It was my leg, was it? That Aquitainian brute with the axe?"

"Yes, Lord. Corruption took the wound and a great black fever came upon you."

"But..." he tried gingerly moving the leg, then touched the calf. He could feel stitches, but nothing else to suggest anything was wrong with it. "It's all right?"

Fitz smiled. "Yes. The corruption is gone. The healers treated you with herbs and the like from the garden that the Saxon hostage used to keep, according to instructions she left for treating wounds. It seemed to work well, and your delirium passed. Though we began to worry when you did not wake."

Thanks to God and thrice thanks to Ælfgifa.

The door opened. It was Matilda. "Lord! You are awake!"

"Yes, Lady." Just to see her made him smile. "It appears I have you to thank for maintaining my Duchy."

"Hardly, Lord," she said, stepping forward and fussing around the bedclothes.

"I would like to see my children," he said, when she had made him recline.

"Of course, Lord. But there is no hurry. You should recover first."

"There is little time. I need to see to the southern defenses, and construct two new forts along the Dive. Then there is Maine to think about."

Matilda frowned. "Lord, you have beaten back Henri. Is it not time to step back from battle? Let peace prevail?"

Peace? Peace?! Something in his look must have registered with Matilda and her brows knitted.

"...For a time, Lord. Until you are ready to consider... new conquests."

A fit of spinning pulsed through his head, ran down to his stomach and bloomed into sickness. He gulped down bile, fixed his feet. *Might not be able to get on a horse. Can try a bout with the sword though.*

"Peace?" He struggled to calm his breathing. "No peace. Not now. Not yet."

The fever might have claimed him. He would have been dead, gone, leaving his sons younger than he was when his own father had died. And with Henri beaten but not so beaten that he could not take advantage. Anjou too... with the pair of them slicing away at Normandy like it was a shoulder of venison... There would be nothing left. For all that he'd done, Normandy was on a knife edge. Could not rest now.

And then there were those who had claimed loyalty to him while lying in wait for an opportunity... Betrayers. Backstabbers. Would his boys Robert, Richard and young William have to wake to see their guardian murdered? Or would it be their own throats the knives slashed across? He had a sudden memory, faint but powerful, of seeing a child's face buried in bloody earth. No. It could not happen. He would not let it. And he knew that Matilda would throw herself onto a knife rather than see one of her children harmed. Good heaven, the power of her love for them was terrifying... But she was vulnerable as anyone, and had thrown herself in danger's way as it was. She had governed while he had been feverish. Had deflected the difficult questions until he had recovered enough to show he was in control again. But how would the nest of vipers that were Normandy's barons react to Matilda's diplomacy and wit should his strong arm no longer lay behind it?

No. The job was not done yet. Not until Normandy, and the Duke of Normandy, commanded too much power, might, influence to attack. He needed a buffer against Anjou— territory that would act as a moat or rampart. He needed the support of the Church. And perhaps even a promised crown.

***

In another day, William could walk across the chamber without collapsing. In a week, he was able to walk around the curtain wall. In two weeks, he was itching to hit something, so grabbed a blunt-edged sparring sword and made his way to the courtyard to see who might be available to spar with. Two squires were fighting with swords, laughing and joking as they danced around each other looking for an opening, striking a blow, neutralizing their opponent's moves. William felt a sudden surge in his chest. *Oh to be a young nobleman with nothing to worry about but bruises if you didn't move fast enough.* He approached, watching for a few moments, enjoying the fight. It might have been him and Fitz, not so very long ago.

One of the squires caught William's gaze, and obviously realized who he was, as he stopped and let his sword arm drop, leaving him open to a downward swing by the other, which thumped into his shoulder. The squire winced but did not utter a sound. The other, a tall, rangy youth laughed, "Why did you stop, you nonentity?" then spun on his heel as he noticed, belatedly, that he was being watched.

"You focus too much on your opponent in battle and you'll get a sword up your arse," William said, trying to sound harsh but unable to disguise his smile.

"Lord," the two squires said, bowing their heads.

"Would one of you mind sparring with me?"

"No, Lord," both of them said, again in perfect synchrony.

William looked at them. The squire who had taken the hit to the shoulder was evidently in some pain, though he was trying not to show it. "You, then," he pointed at the other. The first squire looked momentarily disappointed, then relieved. He bowed his head again, and sidled away, trying not to hold his damaged arm until he was far enough away.

"I would be fighting him if you hadn't bruised his shoulder," William said as he tied his helm under his chin. They began maneuvering. "He noticed what was around him better than you did," William added.

"Yes, Lord," the squire said. "I will remember in future."

"Good." Well, that was a good start. The squire had not been discomfited. Some young lads would have sunk into despondency at a harsh word from their Lord. Not this boy. William aimed a testing blow at the squire, who deflected it easily with the flat of his sword, and turned the movement into a blow of his own while skirting back so William's own momentum was against him. In a few moments the old fluidity had come back, and William was swinging and parrying, thrusting and grappling joyfully as though he had not spent weeks abed. The blood was coursing, now.

The squire was good, William acknowledged. He was using his height and long limbs to give better leverage to his strikes, his lean frame to keep his movement fast and graceful. William was just as tall but bulkier, more powerful but slower. For the first ten minutes he barely got a blow anywhere near his target. The squire was vulnerable to a two-handed thrust that he lacked the power to deflect, though, but soon adapted to that and avoided the move with his greater speed, pivoting onto his back foot and twisting his torso out the way, then countering.

William's ears were thundering with blood, and his chest was heaving to suck enough air in. He laughed, despite his frustration, and the young man laughed back, grinning as he changed direction to counter William's next strike. But William had one last play. He feinted the two-handed thrust at the squire's torso, then as the youth rocked back and swung his sword up for a high strike, switched the grip of his right hand and drove the sword downward at his adversary's front leg. Blunt though it was, the sword pierced the squire's stocking. William whipped the blade out and stepped back.

The squire shrugged and chuckled, stooping to rub his leg. "Well done, Lord. In battle I'd be well and truly skewered. I didn't see that coming."

"No, you didn't," William smiled. "If you had, you'd have had every opportunity to skewer *me* while I went for the leg."

"Oh yes, I see. Again, Lord?"

William rubbed his face. His head was starting to feel light, and he had to fight the sensation that he was tipping to one side. "No, not today. Soon though."

"Yes, Lord." The squire seemed disappointed, though he had gone rather pale and seemed to be struggling a little to breathe.

William unlaced his helm and took it off, welcoming the rush of fresh air. His hair was sodden with sweat. "What's your name, squire?"

The youth finished removing his own helm, revealing a mop of reddish hair. "Wulfnoth, Lord."

"The Saxon?" William blurted. He had not recognized the boy. And he spoke Frankish with a Norman accent!

Wulfnoth shrugged, an expression of discomfort on his face. "I suppose."

Well. So Saxons could fight, if they were trained properly. That was worth knowing. "Thank you for the bout, Wulfnoth. Very satisfactory. You fight like a Norman."

The boy's grin returned immediately. "Thank you, Lord."

CHAPTER 13

It could be avoided no longer. For almost three years, most of which he had spent in the field, William had managed to dodge the need to hold a Conseil de Duc. Now, with the fighting against Henri and Martel done for the time being—and an heir and two more sons now secure in their succession—there was no excuse any more. There was plenty to deal with. Treacherous nobles who had crawled back begging for mercy had to have their punishment decided. Those killed in battle, to have the fate of their assets and dependents decided. The faithful had to be rewarded.

There was one benefit. It meant he could call on his former guardian. He'd not seen the Baron of Wacey in years, and had not realized how much he had missed his mentor and friend.

"Ralph! It's good to see you," he yelled as soon as the baron was brought to his cabinet. "We've missed you at Falaise." He stepped towards the baron, ignoring the vicious stab of pain in his leg that returned every so often.

Ralph came forward, stiffly, clasped his hands. "I'm sorry William," Ralph said. His voice sounded weaker, thinner than William remembered. "The truth is I have been unwell. I still am. I gained a wound at Val es Dunes, you may recall.

It was just the kind of knock you can get in a battle. But it has never really recovered. I feel so much less than I was. I would not have been able to help you much more, I fear."

William looked at Ralph, seeing him for the first time. His former guardian's hair was now almost entirely white. The baron was much thinner than William remembered. It was as though decades had passed instead of just eight or nine years since he had left William's service. When had this change come upon him? Had he always just seen Ralph as he had been when he first took on the guardianship? He had been suffering, and as usual, William had been oblivious. And ever since Val es Dunes? His stomach turned.

"Ralph. I'm so sorry. I didn't know." William looked at his feet. Focused on his own problems as always, and never seeing what was going on outside them. Was Ralph telling him he was... declining?

"Don't worry. I am quite well. Just not as fit as I used to be. Not nearly. But I am enjoying my estates, or as much of them as I can get to these days. I may have ridden to hounds for the last time, but nobody lives forever." He smiled. "Consider the benefits. When I do die, it will be without issue, and my lands will revert to you."

"Ralph... I..." Everything seemed to be falling.

"Don't look so miserable. A year or two ago it looked as though Geoffrey Martel or Henri Capet might have been the beneficiary. I am glad it will be you. You have faced more than I thought you would have to, and withstood every blow. Well, almost." He nodded at the William's leg. "You're limping a little. Nothing serious, I hope?"

"No, no. I took a cut in the leg with an axe at Varaville. It became inflamed, I was feverish for a while..."

Ralph nodded slowly. It seemed they had neither of them escaped unscathed. "How does it go with the Duchy?"

Changing the subject, Guardian? William was grateful, anyway. "It seems the Duchy is secure. Reasonably so. As much as at any time since Grimoult and Hammond tried to murder me."

"I remember." Ralph smiled again but there was no humor in his eyes. After a moment he relaxed. "You've done well. Your father would be proud of you, I've little doubt."

William had more doubt. "In truth, I've been lucky. More lucky than I deserve. You heard about the battle at Mortemer?"

"I did. A great victory for your Grace."

"Indeed, but it was not mine. It was blind luck. The local barons came out and managed to repel Rainauld's army. I can claim no credit at all. It was the barons' victory—Eu, Mortemer, Giffard, young Warrenne."

Ralph threw his head back and laughed. He grasped the front of William's tunic and shook it. William stood, wondering what to say. Was Ralph losing his reason as well as his health?

"You do not see, do you?" said Ralph when he'd recovered his breath.

"See what?"

"Those barons fought for you."

"They fought for their lands, surely? Their people?"

"My boy. You never listen to a word I tell you! They might have locked themselves up in their castles and let Henri take your territory, then changed their allegiance when the dust had settled. They might even have changed sides and joined your enemies. They fought because they'd rather have you as their overlord than Henri or Geoffrey."

William frowned. "You think so?"

"I do. And they might have learned a few things from your military campaigns too. You are the commander who hasn't lost a battle. You won your own fight at Varaville, yes?"

A slaughter more than a fight. William was glad Ralph hadn't been there to see that. Henri couldn't get away fast enough to see what befell the few men who had been unlucky enough to be trapped between the rising tide and Norman vengeance. "It wasn't much of a battle, truth be told."

"Sometimes that's the best way," Ralph said, seeming not to understand William's meaning. "Alençon, Domfront, recovered with minimal bloodshed, I hear."

"At Domfront, not so much blood. It was possible to secure peace through offer of leniency. At Alençon... It was necessary to make a strong point."

"Quite, quite. Military prowess shows you are a man not to be trifled with. But more important than that, you are now the Duke who people look up to. They trust you. It was that fact which secured your victory at Mortemer."

William felt his face flushing. He looked at his shoes again. "I won't leave it to chance next time."

"I know you won't. The key is that you can count the support of your barons when you make those plans which leave nothing to chance. I have to admit too," Ralph went on, "I was wrong about looking to your cousin Edward for an example. England is a mess these days. Although perhaps things would have been different if Edward had had sons. You've done well there too, I hear."

"Yes. Robert. And Richard. And young William." William smiled, as he could not stop himself doing whenever he thought of his youngest in particular. "They are healthy and strong, the physicians tell me. Though Robert is very noisy."

"His father's son, then. I would give you one last piece of advice though."

"I would gladly accept it. What is it?"

"Don't make any of them bishops at least until they can walk unaided."

***

William had been expecting, and dreading, as fractious, bad-tempered a Conseil as he had held after Grimoult's trial. To his surprise the barons and bishops who filled the great hall were quiet, respectful, deferential even. Perhaps it was the presence of Matilda to his right making them better behaved. Perhaps it was the increasing prosperity that relative peace and security was bringing to their estates. Perhaps it was just that they'd heard the stories about Alençon.

Today, all the trouble came from his own magnates. Friends.

For a start, before the Barons arrived, Montgomerie had repeatedly prodded him about Maine. It was as though he was aware of something William was not, but would not admit to it. William had no particular intention of making any pronouncements about Maine today—there would be enough business to attend to. Obviously the county represented unfinished business for Normandy, and in the long term William had no intention of letting Anjou control it unchallenged. And equally obviously, Montgomerie had hopes of recovering his wife's territories. But beyond that, the reason for Montgomerie's probing was unclear, and William felt a tightening in his stomach at the thought that his friend was maneuvering on his own account. He would have to watch Montgomerie—and that wife of his, the odious Mabel de Bellême—and the realization gave him no pleasure.

The first business was to deal with those French nobles captured in the recent fighting at Arques and Mortemer, deciding ransoms, giving them their parole if it was felt they could be trusted, allocating a host in Normandy if they could not. Despite the many bureaucratic annoyances he had to contend with since his return, William could barely disguise his satisfaction. The ransoms would swell his coffers by no small sum, and the idea of taking gold from Henri added considerably to William's pleasure in the matter. Plentiful but practical sums were extracted from those nobles taken at Mortemer, to be divided among the barons who had saved the Duchy. God willing, the gold would bind them to William even more closely, and there were further rewards to come. William was particularly impressed with Guillaume de Warenne, now eighteen, who had commanded his family's army in the field and, by all accounts, fought with intelligence and courage. He thought of himself at that age, and colored at the recollection of life as a string of hunts, feasts and girls. Still, he had taken to the field at Val es Dunes at the age of 20, and not done too badly at that.

De Warenne was just a skinny boy, but he held himself well and spoke plainly. William found himself liking the lad, and wishing he had a daughter he could give him in marriage.

Now it was the turn of Norman nobles who had risen up with his uncle, William of Arques, and been defeated. A queue of them, brought in, one by one, to confront their liege lord. Some had resentment in their eyes. Some shame. Most, resignation. All gave the oath of fealty once more. The knights and lowlier barons were allowed to go more or less as free men. The greater, and those whose treason had been more pronounced, had to give further assurances. They would be required to swear on Holy Relics—Bishop Lanfranc had suggested some time ago that it was always worth having such relics nearby when a vassal was required to make a particularly important vow, and a chest containing various saints' bones and possessions now occupied a prominent spot in front of William. One or two had to give a surety or give up hostages to ensure their future good behavior. All gave up some land or paid a penalty.

Everything went without interruption until Hugh de Grandmesnil was brought up before William. He did not know de Grandmesnil particularly well—the baron was around William's own age, and like William had become head of the household while still in his minority, but beyond that, he could not recall.

He had tried to look into the histories of all those to be brought before him today, but there was never enough time. So when the charges against de Grandmesnil were read out, and Roger de Beaumont, a few places down the bench issued an angry bark, William racked his mind to recall what in the family's background might have led to Beaumont's reaction.

"Er, Hugh de Grandmesnil," Fitz said, rifling through some parchments. "Sworn knight of William of Arques. He abandoned the siege at Domfront and returned North with your uncle, but laid down his arms and gave himself up with twelve mounted men before the action at Arques.

"Do you renounce your treachery and promise in all things to be faithful to your liege lord?" William asked, trying to keep his voice level despite the rush of emotions that crowded in at the recollection. Anger, still fresh, at his uncle's betrayal at the sieges of Alençon and Domfront. Guilt, at what he had done afterwards. Shame, at the stories that circulated still.

De Grandmesnil knelt, about to give the oath, when Beaumont stood, and faced William.

"I urge you, Lord," he said, face white, hands trembling, "do not listen to the treachery of this man. He has already moved against you, and merely gave himself up to save his own skin."

William blinked. What was Beaumont doing? "Cousin, what—"

"Lord, I refute these charges!" de Grandmesnil cried. "I am faithful to your Grace, and prepared to swear it." Anger flashed briefly in eyes, quickly replaced with disquiet. He looked pleadingly at William.

"His father stole the Risle Valley when I was fighting in your service, Lord," Beaumont hissed before William could interject, "and it took years for my family to recover the land from the Grandmesnils' control."

William stared. He had never seen Beaumont so angry. He gestured at the baron to sit. Beaumont's beard seemed to bristle, but he obeyed.

"Is it true?" William asked of de Grandmesnil.

The knight bowed his head. "It is, Lord, and I am sorry for it." He looked up. "Although historically, the land belonged to my family, and was—"

"Enough," William snapped. "That's not my concern. I demand loyalty from every noble within my Duchy, and your support for my uncle, who plotted against me and openly turned against me, does not speak loudly of your loyalty."

"Lord," de Grandmesnil replied, "I knew nothing of the secret plottings against you, had I done so, I would have spoken against it. This I swear."

"He can't be trusted," Beaumont snarled. "None of them can. You don't remember what it was like, your Grace. You were just a child, and many barons and knights, even if they didn't rise up against you, ignored their responsibilities and took what they could get their hands on!"

"My Lord, historically—"

Will none of them obey? "Enough!" William bellowed, and his voice echoed around the high ceiling of the hall. He turned to Beaumont. "I will have no more of this. We shall come to a just solution. Now please, Cousin, peace."

Beaumont's face was a shade of purple, but he sat back and folded his arms. William turned to Fitz and Montgomerie, who leant around Matilda.

"Any suggestions?" William asked. "The fellow seems genuinely contrite, and Heaven knows we need as many knights as will fight for us."

"It's true about the Risle Valley," Fitz said. "The Beaumonts and the Grandmesnils have been arguing over it for generations, but it's rightfully Roger's now. The de Grandmesnil estates are not large, nor particularly rich."

"I can't demand even more land if they don't have much."

"Why not seize it all and just give it to Roger?" Montgomerie suggested. "If the family isn't powerful, where's the loss?"

"If he'd stayed to the bitter end with Arques, then perhaps, but he didn't even fight us."

Montgomerie shook his head. "What can you do to resolve it then? It seems you must either offend Beaumont or de Grandmesnil, and I know which I'd prefer."

They were interrupted by Matilda gently clearing her throat. "Horses," she said, when she had their attention.

William gaped at her. "Horses, my Lady?"

She nodded. "I am led to understand that the de Grandmesnil family made its name in horse breeding. I believe they still have several fine stud farms. Their coursers are prized in Flanders. They might provide some means of compensating Beaumont while leaving de Grandmesnil's lands intact."

"Horses, you say?" They could never have enough decent warhorses. It seemed like a solution.

William turned to de Grandmesnil once more. "Sir Hugh," he said, "Will you undertake to provide a supply of your best horses to Beaumont and his mounted knights for as long as he is in my service?"

"Yes, Lord!" de Grandmesnil nodded enthusiastically. "Within our ability to breed them, of course. But our chargers will not be found wanting."

"And will you undertake to recognize Beaumont's claim on the Risle Valley and swear never to take so much as a perche of it?"

"I will, Lord."

He turned to Beaumont, who looked a little calmer. "Cousin, you have been a faithful and strong companion. If I could give you more lands and wealth here and now, I would. Be patient, I beg you. There will be opportunities soon enough." He hoped that last statement was true as he addressed the hall: "I demand loyalty, but in turn I promise that loyalty will be rewarded. Serve me and fight for me, and your estates will grow. Now, Sir Hugh, your oath of fealty."

"I promise on my faith that I will in the future be faithful to the lord," de Grandmesnil said, clearly and quickly, "never cause him harm and will observe my homage to him completely against all persons in good faith and without deceit."

"Good. Go, a free man, and let's have horses enough for all the wars in Christendom."

Before turning to the next piece of business, William happened to catch the eye of Ralph, who was smiling gently, though he was not sure whether his former guardian was looking at him or his Duchess.

Either way, it gave William a brief glow in his chest, which was not unwelcome. It seemed another obstacle had been cleared. He realized he was tired. Not the bone weariness of being on campaign for weeks, but a sort of smoke filling his mind, a strong compulsion to close his eyes. How much more of this was there? If the lines on the list in front of Fitz was anything to go by, there were still many hours' worth of matters to deal with.

And the next matter was Gui of Ponthieu, who had been Count for mere weeks when he was captured at Mortemer. His predecessor, Enguerrand, had fared less well, dying in front of the castle at Arques when Henri's cavalry had been ambushed. It seemed he had been kicked in the head by a horse. Rumor had it that his sister, watching from the walls, saw him die and had gone mad, though William thought that very unlikely unless her eyesight was as strong as her constitution was weak. And William's own sister had hardly been happy about it. Adelaide had been married briefly to Enguerrand until the Pope had made his displeasure plain. He shifted uncomfortably in his seat. Poor Adelaide. It couldn't be helped. Gui had also lost his younger brother at Mortemer, which can't have done anything for Ponthieu's sister's sanity.

But in any event, there was Gui to deal with. Gui, who had been fool enough to fall into William's hands, but evidently not fool enough to get himself killed.

He was young, perhaps twenty, thin, pale and stooped. He did not look to be of the cloth that a Count should be cut from, but then he had spent most of his lordship in captivity. It took a push from Gallet to make him kneel.

"Do you renounce your treachery and promise in all things to be faithful to your lord?" William had lost count of the times he had asked that today.

"No," Gui said. "I don't."

What? Had William heard him right? "Did you say 'no'?"

"Yes. That is... I swore fealty to Arques. He is my brother-in-law. I followed him as my oath required."

"I was your brother-in-law too." William kept his voice soft, feeling the rage building that would make him shout, or worse.

Ponthieu shrugged. "That marriage was annulled."

William winced. That sacrifice had been another part of the price to his own marriage's recognition by Rome, a bargaining chip thrown on the table by Lanfranc. He had not spoken to Adelaide since. He doubted she would want to speak to him, anyway.

Fitz stood, clearly having less success at controlling his temper than William. "But Duke William is your overlord!" he said. "To whom your ultimate loyalty is due!"

Ponthieu met their gaze. "Isn't that to the King? Who you fought against, Lord?"

A couple of years or months or weeks ago, William would have been tempted to kill the man where he knelt. Instead, he just gaped. What in the name of all the Saints' holy whores was he doing?

Fitz was gaping too. "The King. Attacked. Us." he stammered. "William of Arques repudiated his liege lord and engaged an alliance against him!"

Gui shuffled his feet. "Well. None of that was my concern. My own liege lord commanded me, and I answered. To go against him would have been to break my oath. I should not have to do penance where I have not sinned."

"Cut his hands off!" Someone shouted from the back of the hall. Half the assembled nobles gasped in shock, the other half rocked with laughter. Once again, part of William, buried deep inside him, thought he should be leaping up and killing someone. Matilda had turned pale beside him. Fitz was goggling and issuing sounds from the back of his throat.

"Enough," William sighed. "The Count has made his views plain. Put him in a cell."

"Very well," Fitz said. "For how long, Lord William?"

"Until he's ready to pay me homage."

"Can we seize his lands?" Montgomerie asked.

Fitz shook his head. "Oh, his uncle, the bishop of somewhere or other is managing them in the Count's absence."

"Hmm. That's a shame. Who's next?"

Ponthieu was dragged away in silence. In comparison, the part William had dreaded in the preceding weeks, dealing with Mauger, was surprisingly easy. In this he was helped immeasurably by the oleaginous clergyman's absence. His uncle had slipped away from Arques and fled to the island of Guernsey, where, it was said, he had named the place of his landing 'Saint's Bay'. That morning, a council of Norman bishops had ordered that he be stripped of his offices, those to be redistributed. A fellow called Maurilius, who Lanfranc had written to him to recommend, and Matilda seemed very impressed with, was appointed Archbishop. In truth, William did not mind having too many holy men around him, as long as they were genuinely holy. The new fellows were as unlike Mauger as it was possible to imagine. Odo's religious duties had no doubt become a lot less interesting with all these men of God surrounding him. Ah well, that might not do the lad any harm.

The last piece of treachery to deal with was the greatest. His uncle, William of Arques. Without satisfaction, William declared that he would be stripped of all his titles and lands —which were held of the Duchy anyway. He was about to order the former Count exiled when William looked at him and realized how utterly defeated he was. Only then did he realize how much Arques' insurrection had been motivated by desperation. Arques looked tired. Beaten down.

As indeed he was. William remembered the prideful, arrogant nobleman he had been not so long ago, and realized that his uncle had always expected William to fail. He had agreed to back down and accept the lordship of Arques and Talou only to bide his time. When William was attacked by Geoffrey Martel and held his own... Then Arques had panicked. Realized the Duke was becoming stronger, not weaker. He had treated with the King and withdrawn himself to his castle as a last gamble, hoping that it would be the last drop that made the river burst its banks. He had failed. He must have known he'd failed, probably even before William's cavalry had broken the King's relief effort outside his walls.

"You may remain within Normandy, if you wish it," he said. Arques looked up at him. No malice, or anger, just surprise. "If there is any nobleman here who will house the Count of... My Uncle, that is to say, please declare yourself."

"I shall be pleased to do the bidding of my Duke and give succor to the, er, gentleman," said a voice from the mass. The speaker stood. For a moment, William wondered what the fellow had stuck to his face, before he realized it was Eustace of Boulogne, still wearing those bizarre mustaches.

William stifled a laugh. "Very well, thank you Cousin, your generosity is most appreciated. It is settled. My uncle shall retire to Boulogne."

"Thank you, Lord," the former Count said, slowly, softly, and William was not sure how to read what was behind the words.

***

While the reunion with Ralph had been somewhat bittersweet, another that day was entirely happy. Bishop

Lanfranc had returned from Rome and entered during the latter stages of the conseil as if he had never been away. It was all William could do to prevent himself from leaping up and embracing the cleric. Lanfranc just gazed upon the scene of William's triumph over traitors and enemies, his features still, as if it was the most commonplace occurrence imaginable.

After the conseil had finally concluded, Lanfranc approached William and bowed. "Lord, I have good news."

"Your presence is good news, Bishop," William smiled. "Truly, it is wonderful to have you back."

Lanfranc responded the compliment with the slightest of nods. "Your marriage is officially recognized, Lord. I have the dispensation from Rome. Sadly, each time it appeared his Holiness was close to agreeing with our viewpoint, he died, and the work started again. But several recent cardinals are former students of mine, and see things very much as we do, and eventually his Holiness was persuaded."

"That's magnificent." William let out a long sigh. Finally! He did not realize how much the matter had still been weighing on him, but in truth if the Pope had decided not to approve the marriage, it would have thrown the Duchy into yet more turmoil. "I don't know how I can repay you."

"Lord, your support for the Church, and your kind consideration of my pupils for offices of the Duchy, is reward enough."

Typical. William grinned "Nevertheless, this is momentous." He would find something to bestow upon Bec. He would ask Matilda for suggestions.

"Thank you, your Grace. In any event, I understand there may be developments afoot that could, if handled with the requisite skill, enrich both your Duchy and the Church, and I find myself well placed to assist."

William had missed Lanfranc's keen mind and eye for an opportunity. He smiled. "Really? Do go on, Bishop Lanfranc."

CHAPTER 14

It was a typical wooden fortress, of the kind any Norman knight worth his salt could throw up in a few weeks. In time, there would be a stone keep here, maybe one day a stone outer wall, but for now, the wooden rampart and bailey atop its cone of earth made the statement it needed to. The castle of Saint James de Beuvron said to Conan of Brittany and Geoffrey of Anjou that anything East and North of this was Norman, and Normans would fight for it.

"All this could have been yours, you know," William said to Gallet as they rode through the gates. "Sure you haven't changed your mind?"

Gallet took an unappreciative glance around. "I'm holding out for Archbishop of Rouen." He threw a scrap of dried meat to his dog, Odo, a lean, scruffy-haired hound, probably a cross between a hunting hound and a stray, that had attached itself to him during a previous campaign. The dog caught the treat and gobbled it right down, but continued to stare at Gallet and William with beseeching eyes.

"You'll want an estate one of these days." William answered, ignoring the dog. "You can't soldier forever."

The knight snorted. "When I'm more dangerous to our boys than the enemy, then you can make me the Baron of Saint Armpit de Shithole if you like. So who will you give this to? Odo?"

"Which one?" William smiled despite himself, giving a sidelong glance in Lanfranc's direction in case the cleric had taken offense at Gallet having named his dog after the Bishop of Bayeux. Predictably, Lanfranc seemed to be in his own world. Well, William would ennoble Gallet one of these days if it killed him. He would have tried to make Gallet Count of Ponthieu if Gui had not come to his senses and grudgingly sworn allegiance after a lengthy stay in a Falaise cell. "I haven't decided. Come on, it's starting to rain. Let's go in."

Today he had more important business to attend to than who would hold the title of this outpost. Gallet deserved better anyway. They dismounted, handed their horses over to grooms, and made their way to the hall built within the outer palisade, largest of a handful of buildings. Lanfranc excused himself to see to the chapel, which was as new as everything else round here, and just as barely finished. William cast a glance after him, wondering if it would help to pray for the hoped-for outcome of this little expedition. Whatever his views before, having been stuck between Matilda and his chaplain Walkelin during the construction of the abbeys had showed him that prayer actually seemed to work some of the time. At the very least, it helped to calm the mind after a long journey.

But today there was no time. The hall was as new as everything else around here, the posts not yet dulled by weather, the straw of the thatch bright gold. Inside, a few bolts of wool in Normandy colors had been hung to make the place seem a little grander. The floor was littered with wood shavings, from the hurried construction of tables and benches, and peasants were still bringing in rushes to provide a carpet.

"All right," William said when they'd had a look around. "I suppose this will have to do. At least Count Herbert didn't get here ahead of us."

"He may not get here at all," Gallet reminded him. "For all we know, Geoffrey has already realized the Count has fled, and overtaken him. Or others closer to home have."

William nodded. That last barb was a reference to Montgomerie. William hated keeping his friend in the dark but he knew that if Montgomerie or Mabel heard that Herbert of Maine had fled from Geoffrey Martel's overlordship, and intended to cast himself on William's mercy, they would not have been silent on the matter. Especially as Lanfranc had negotiated the sanctuary, circumventing Gervais, the former Bishop of Le Mans, Mabel's relative and currently kicking his heels at Caen since his own flight from Geoffrey.

But all of that depended on Herbert turning up. It took until sunset before the picket reported a small mounted party making its way along the road from Poilley. William, Gallet and Lanfranc took their place at the head of the hall with a pale, freckled scribe from Bec, and the detachment of soldiers who had accompanied them formed a guard. William hoped it was all impressive enough.

He needn't have worried. Herbert, little more than a boy, entered with his tiny entourage, looking haunted. His cloak was threadbare, his breeches spattered with mud from the ride, and his general appearance gave William a brief moment of guilty satisfaction. Herbert had lost his father and his county all at once. William had, after all, managed to hang onto his Duchy when his own father had died.

They exchanged the usual formal greetings between nobles, faintly ludicrous in this rude outpost. *What choice do you have?* William thought, *bearing in mind that you fled here from house arrest after your relationship with Geoffrey turned out not to be so cozy as you thought.* But as Ralph had often reminded him, the office was always worthy of respect even if the man did not seem to be.

"Truly," William said, when the formalities were dispensed with, "I am sorry to see you brought low in this way, Count Herbert. As you know, I am no friend of Geoffrey Martel—he has tried to take from me, as he has taken from you. You have my protection while you stay in the borders of the Duchy. How might Normandy further assist?"

William was expecting a request for armies to fight Geoffrey, and prepared himself to negotiate. He would not commit forces unless it was in his own interest, and Herbert was in no position to bargain.

"My Lord, will you also give protection to my sister, Marguerite?"

William's eyes widened. "You brought your sister with you?" *On a dangerous flight from captivity across hostile territory?* At least Geoffrey couldn't use her as a hostage.

"Yes, Lord. She is my only surviving kin. I would not trust to leave her with anyone else. She is only eight."

Lanfranc cleared his throat. "Is she betrothed to anyone yet, Lord?"

Herbert frowned. "That dog Anjou wanted to marry her to one of his sons. A contract was drawn up but it was not with my agreement."

"Then it is not legitimate," Lanfranc smiled. "She is free to marry... Say, his Grace of Normandy's son?"

"She is free," Herbert confirmed, guardedly. He looked at William. "You have a son, Lord?"

"Three, actually. Robert, Richard and Young William." And Matilda was already carrying another child. Please God, perhaps a daughter this time. He dragged his mind back to the matter at hand. "What did you have in mind, Bishop Lanfranc?"

"A marriage between Robert and Marguerite would tie your two great houses together, in equal love, great lords of Maine and Normandy," he said, spreading his hands expansively, then knitting his fingers together. "To that end I have labored with all my wits, my pains and strong endeavors, to bring your most noble selves to this bar and interview, face to face and noble eye to eye." The bishop continued in that vein for several more minutes. William reflected that the bishop's language had grown richer while he was in Rome, much as his coffers had. At the end of it, it seemed that Robert was betrothed to the girl Marguerite, and their children would be Lords of Maine. William, as Herbert's relation by marriage, would of course help the Count regain his lands and titles—when it suited him to—which would be held of William. There would be grants of land too, which William sorely needed to reward those who had already helped him in his earlier campaigns.

Herbert just looked relieved. William found himself wondering if the man even wanted to be Count. But he was born to it. What else was there?

"Thank you, Lord William," Herbert said. "I consent to all terms of reason."

As well he might. It was the best he could hope for. He would get to take up his titles and Maine would remain within his family.

Lanfranc smiled again, in that placid way of his. "Most gracious, Lord. And it only remains for you to pay homage to his Grace and become his man." The smile faded slightly.

"And to confirm—though I wish you many prosperous years in your Lordship, should, God forbid, it end before Robert and Marguerite be blessed with issue—his Grace the Duke will become your heir."

Herbert looked up sharply, panic in his eyes. Did he think they were going to cut his throat as soon as he'd signed his county away? William could not blame him for that. Geoffrey hadn't worried about the accepted proprieties when he'd walked into Maine with his army, on no better pretext than the old Count dying before the new was quite of age. And no doubt Geoffrey was less concerned with the proprieties of arranging an alliance through marriage before absorbing Maine into Anjou, however he had allowed Herbert to retain his title thus far.

"Count Herbert, there is no need for disquiet," Lanfranc said, that bizarre calm across him. "It is necessary that we make arrangements for all eventualities, after all. You would not wish for the county to fall into legal uncertainty before the agreed succession can be established."

Herbert relaxed slightly, but remained on his guard. He glanced at William. Was he thinking of Alençon? Or Varaville? Perhaps it had seemed a good idea to bind himself to the victor of battle after battle, but now, when he had to sit before the ruthless Duke...? Unbidden, he knelt, bowed his head, and said: "I promise on my faith that I will in the future be faithful to the lord, never cause him harm and will observe my homage to him completely against all persons in good faith and without deceit."

The words were easily said, but William was glad to hear them. It was settled then. The two parties, Normandy and Maine, elected to spend the night at Saint James before setting out for Falaise the following morning. William found himself standing alongside Gallet and his dog at the ramparts, looking out into the night.

"That was a lot of talk for nothing," the knight said, ruffling his hound's ears. "You haven't got one more perche of Maine than you did before. We're going to have to fight anyway."

"Let's hope not," said William. "This talk is important, believe it or not, especially if it saves bloodshed."

Gallet looked at him skeptically. On this matter though, William knew he was probably right. With the existing order acknowledged, the Church was more likely to support a military expedition with gold and even more valuable blessings that would attract support from other nobles. With the rightful heir Herbert in charge—for now—it would be harder for others to invade. As William had learned, painfully, winning on the battlefield was only part of what made a victory.

***

William's mind revolved ever more rapidly. He'd retired to his pallet in the hall at Saint James though he felt not the slightest touch of tiredness. He lay in the dark, seeking for sleep—God knew he needed the rest, there would be another long ride on the morrow—but continually returning to plans of attack into Maine. And what would come next if, God willing, he was successful. It would be no easy matter to defeat Martel, but that was not what exercised him most. If he was to rule in Maine, it would have to be through right, not at the point of a sword, through fortresses and garrisons. The nobles there, even the small folk, would have to accept him as overlord, and eventually, his children as lord. He would have to engage Matilda to help win them over.

At some point William must have drifted into a doze as he snapped awake in the sudden awareness that something had changed. A little like the moment at Valognes all those years ago, and the thought sent a shudder through him. What was it that had disturbed him? He examined the sounds and sensations that had reached him here in the dark. And then it hit him. The wicket gate had opened.

It was, in all probability, nothing whatsoever to be concerned about. A servant from the nearby village coming or going. A guard stepping out to take a shit. But sleep had been completely banished, and they were on the frontier of two hostile territories here. William pulled his clothes on and stepped out into the night.

He hailed the guard at the gate. "Why was the gate opened?"

The guard looked surprised, then embarrassed. "Sorry to have wakened you, Lord. A knight from Count Herbert's household arrived with an urgent message for his lordship."

Not so very unusual. "Hm. All right. He had the right credentials, I take it?"

"Oh yes, Sire. He carried Count Herbert's seal. And he spoke like he was from Maine all right. Funny sounding bugger."

"Very well. If there are any more visitors, come and tell me would you? No-one's supposed to know we're here."

"Yes, Lord. And I'll make sure Hugo is quiet when he leaves."

A memory stirred, something William could not quite place. He turned back to the guard. "This knight, what was his name?"

"Hugo of Reviers, Lord."

Christ's wounds! Surely it couldn't be? "Wake Gallet, tell him to come straight to Count Herbert's chambers. You!" he shouted at another guard who had just appeared, probably from making a circuit of the ramparts, "with me. Bring that torch."

They ran to the small building where Herbert and his retinue were sleeping and burst through the door. The flickering light of the torch revealed a knight with Hugonide livery on his surcoat standing in the midst of the sleeping Maine party. There was a shape on the floor by the door. An insensible Norman guard.

The knight registered a look of alarm which he quickly mastered. He was in his middle years with graying hair, and thin, but looked wiry and tough. He was dressed and equipped as any envoy might be, except for the wine skin he was carrying. Snuck in and realized the Count was not alone? Disabled the guard while he pondered what to do? "My Lord. Sirs. What can I do for you?" he said confidently, as though this was any normal meeting in a great house somewhere. The men of Maine were beginning to stir and wake, confusion in their eyes, and William thought he saw a look of calculation cross Hugo's face.

"What are you doing here?" William said. "What happened to him?" He motioned to the unconscious guard.

The knight smiled. "I am here to deliver a message to my Lord Count Herbert. That is all."

"And you can deliver your message while creeping around in the dark? What happened to the guard? The one who was supposed to escort you here but is now lying on the ground? Drop that wineskin if you please, I do not like the idea of what might be in it." *The same poison as fed to Grimoult du Plessis perhaps? Which left him seemingly well, but coughing up his own lifeblood in a few hours?*

The knight's expression turned from polite curiosity to something implacable. He snapped into motion, hurling the wineskin at William's head, spinning and diving to the side. God! A flash of pale leather, the swish of air as it passed, a struggle for balance as William had lurched instinctively away. In the instant William had been off his footing, a dagger had appeared in Hugo's hand, and he was lunging for Herbert. The Count rolled off his pallet just as the assassin reached it, another second and William, leaping, barreled into him. Shouts of alarm and shock battered his ears. Scrabbling for the knight, feeling his hot breath. Devil's horns, where was the dagger? There were powerful hands tearing at him now, and in a moment they had closed around his throat. Another second and the false knight had rolled him onto his back. Red burst behind his eyes, pain bloomed in his head. Then there was a great roaring snarl and something impossibly fast cannoned into the assassin, knocking him off William. He caught sight of a lean form biting and tearing at the false knight before the red blotches swelled to block out everything, turned black, and all was quiet.

CHAPTER 15

When Ælfgifa had first arrived back at the great house at Wintancaestre, she had been surprised and delighted to find her old nurse, Beddwen still installed in the nursery. Beddwen was as thin now as she had once been plump. Her rosy complexion had over-ripened into the brown, wrinkled aspect of a winter apple. Her once abundant dark hair was now fine and almost totally white. Still, Ælfgifa would have known that lilting voice anywhere—even if Beddwen's first word on beholding her had not been "Mwyalchen!"

Ælfgifa had forgotten that she was a grown woman of almost thirty and flown into Beddwen's arms as if she were still a child of ten, raw from the ceaseless scolding of her mother. Beddwen still had charge of the noble children and stood for as little nonsense as she ever had, but she was stooped now, and moved slowly. Instead, she marshalled a bevy of under-nursery maids in tending the younger children of the estate. It had been soothing to Ælfgifa to stop with her old nurse a little each day, to renew their relationship as one of friends rather than child and guardian. It was with a heavy heart that Ælfgifa went to Beddwen that day. She knew that the Cymri woman was sick—so sick she was unlikely to see another winter—despite Beddwen's pains to keep her condition to herself.

She stood in the nursery doorway, vacillating as she had when she was a child—wanting affection but not the chiding that went with it. Beddwen made her way slowly to a stool near the window and lowered herself onto it with obvious pain, oblivious of Ælfgifa in the doorway. Though her eyes remained tearless as always, Ælfgifa felt them sting and her throat close. She wondered what sensible choice she had ever made that had turned her onto the path she now had to tread. Had she been seeking nothing more than approval—her mother's, Harold's, Ealdgyth's, God above, even the Duke of Normandy's?—all this time? All her knowledge and study and cleverness. All the political game playing. The lives she had manipulated or even ended… what was any of that worth? Was that what Beddwen had seen for her young charge twenty years ago?

"Gifa child, I may not be seeing so well as I once did, but I know you are standing there. Will you be coming in or no? You're all too scrawny a thing to make much of a door." Beddwen smiled towards her, eyes rheumy, cauled with the milky growth some older people got if they lived long enough.

Ælfgifa found herself next to Beddwen and then seated before her without recalling how she moved. She had no idea how to say what she had come to say. Instead she reached out and took one of Beddwen's withered hands in her own.

"You'll be going then? Doing what your brother asked of you?" Beddwen said it mildly but Ælfgifa felt defensive.

"I do not know what else to do, Beddwen," she pleaded.

"You could be telling your brother 'no'. Be saying to him that he can send another emissary if he's a fancy to sue for the hostages the King sent to Normandy after all this time."

Beddwen smiled and patted Ælfgifa's hand. "I am knowing you will not."

"It is more complicated than 'aye' or 'nay'." Ælfgifa shook her head. "I have been torpid, useless these last years." She sighed. "Harold never meant for me to come home, I think. Not so soon. In any case, if my stock is still good with his lordship in Normandy, then it makes sense to send me. Beddwen, you wouldn't have Wulfnoth or even Håkon reared forever amongst strangers, would you?"

"Oh, Mwyalchen. As God is knowing I love you and Wulfnoth, and better than all my charges, though it is a sin to be having favorites, I only ever wanted you both to be happy. Do you not think that Wulfnoth and Håkon have finished their rearing by now? Young men of twenty-two or so they'll be. Honor is a wonderful thing in its right place, *Carriad*. Do not be thinking that you are responsible for the honor of others."

"Are you saying that Harold...?" Ælfgifa found she could not finish.

"Is as fine a man as it is possible to be. Given the full complement of God's gifts, wasn't he? Tall, handsome, clever, brave, ready with a jest. All men fall in line and love him. All women desire him, or so I am hearing. But I am wondering about his honor, see? What brother is sending his young sister to smooth a path for him with a potential enemy? He loves you, no doubting that. But he'll use what tools are best for his purpose whether that be a stranger or a beloved sister. But there. I've told you nothing you don't know, my clever one. Perhaps you are right to act when Harold asks. I am an old woman. I feel how far I am drifting from the world." Beddwen embraced Ælfgifa then, arms like the starved branches of winter trees. "Kiss me farewell, as you came here to do."

"Beddwen, I…"

"Hush, *Carriad*. We'll meet again at God's pleasure. I full know I will not live to see you again. To have the time we have had was more than I looked for."

Ælfgifa kissed her old nurse and just hung on to her for a moment. She did not correct Beddwen or make promises. She had heard the cough and seen the hastily concealed blood Beddwen spat up after. She wondered wildly if she could go back to her handsome, charismatic and ruthlessly ambitious brother and tell him 'no' after all. In her heart she knew she would not. She herself craved knowledge if not power. It was not for her to sit and wait.

"I don't want to say goodbye," she said in a choked voice.

"Then don't, *Carriad*. Hope that the next world will be kinder and always remember I love you," Beddwen said, her voice betraying how tired she was.

"I love you, Beddwen. Always," Ælfgifa said with rare emotion coloring her voice.

Beddwen looked surprised and amused but patted the younger woman's arm. "Well, I am knowing that, Gifa. Always, I know that."

CHAPTER 16

William opened his eyes. Blood-red blotches swam in his vision. Where was he? There was a fog shrouding everything that had happened. Lying on the floor. Why?

The moments before he had lost consciousness flooded back in. The assassin. About to attack Count Herbert. Just then a face lurched over his, and he recoiled.

"My Lord? Are you all right?"

Gallet. Thank God!

William tried to speak, but the words came out as a rasp. His throat burned. He became aware of a chattering cacophony. Everyone in the room was speaking at once, and the dog started barking too. William tried to quiet them, but his voice just whistled out of his mouth.

"Silence!" Gallet shouted, and the room stilled. William propped himself up on his elbow. Next to him, the assassin lay on his side, the tip of a short spear penetrating his chest, his throat a bloody mess, and blood pulsing sickeningly from both wounds into the floor rushes.

Curse it, William thought. Now they might never know who sent the killer. He sat up and rubbed his throat. It felt as though it had swelled up so much he could barely get any air through to his lungs.

Herbert was looking at him, eyes wide, wearing an expression that swung between gratitude and severe disquiet.

The Count's seneschal found his voice just then. "How could you allow this to happen, Normandy?" he yelled, voice filling the packed room. "An assassin allowed through to my Lord's bed! Is this how you treat nobles who are supposed to be in your protection?"

"My apologies, Count Herbert," William rasped, ignoring the seneschal and addressing the Count directly. "The assassin bore your official seal, and so he was let through. You can check his clothing, he will have it. As soon as we realized something was amiss, I came personally to check."

"It was fortunate you did," Herbert said, reluctantly. He nodded at Gallet and the dog, Odo. "Were it not for your bear here, and his hound, you would have died at his hands too." One of Herbert's party pulled the spear from the assassin's back and pushed the corpse over with his foot, then began rummaging in the pouch hung from the man's waist. Herbert examined his face. "I've never seen this man before."

William also looked. He did not recognize the man either. But his name... He was certain it was the same name given by the man who was suspected of murdering Grimoult. And the method appeared to be exactly the same.

"You should have been more careful anyway," the seneschal grumbled, examining the wax seal passed to him by his companion, then handing it to William. It did indeed bear the mark of Herbert's signet. "Martel was bound to make an attempt on my Lord's life."

Martel? William raised his eyebrows, but quickly wiped the surprise from his face. Of course they would think Martel was behind it! If only he could be so sure.

Mumbling further apologies and promising to double the guard, William and Gallet left Count Herbert, called servants to have the body removed and retired to the hall. The dog trotted after them as if nothing had happened. There was still blood on its nose.

"It's lucky they think it was Martel," Gallet said, keeping his voice low.

"You think it wasn't?" William asked, knowing as he said it that he thought the same.

Gallet fixed him with a cynical look. "Why would Martel wait until the entire party had left Maine only to attack them inside a Norman castle? No, this comes from closer to home."

"Did you recognize the assassin's name?"

"I didn't hear it."

"I did. 'Hugo of Reviers'. There's no such knight, but I've heard the name before, some years ago. Someone going by that name had seen Grimoult du Plessis shortly before he was taken ill and died on the morning of his trial by combat."

Gallet whistled and nodded. "Hmm. So it could have been Mauger. I'm certain that foul creature was behind Grimoult's death."

But you don't think that, either. "I doubt it was Mauger. Even if he did have the reach, what did he have to gain? He's far more likely to try to have me killed than Herbert. No, I don't suppose the assassin was anyone's man. A killer for hire, I dare say."

"Hmm." Gallet nodded, but offered nothing more.

They were both thinking it, so William elected to come out and say it. "Montgomerie?"

Gallet nodded again. "Or his wife. Probably his wife. The Bellêmes haven't lost their ambition, even now they're down on their luck. Especially now, in fact."

"Montgomerie wouldn't..." William said, sounding less sure than he would have liked.

"He and Mabel have their own people in Maine." Gallet patted the dog's head, then scratched his own. "I can't be sure they hadn't heard about the meeting, though I did my best to keep it quiet. I have a feeling Montgomerie knew something was afoot at the Conseil. I know you two grew up together, but he's beginning to meddle in things that oughtn't concern him. What does he want, anyway?"

William shrugged. "More than he already has." Didn't all men want that? But it seemed that Montgomerie was no longer satisfied with the prestige that came from the legal ownership of lands currently held by another Lord. Nor was he satisfied with the prospect of William's help to recover those lands. Perhaps Montgomerie dreamt of carving out a new barony from the Bellême estates. Could it be that he even entertained hopes of becoming Count in his own right?

William's throat seemed to be doing its best to choke him. He had been betrayed by his men before. By his uncles and cousin. But never by a friend. And the betrayal could not just have caused his death, it could have ruined a delicate negotiation and sparked yet more war.

***

It was an unusually quiet ride back to Falaise. Everyone seemed locked in their own thoughts. For different reasons, both the men of Maine and those of Normandy feared an attack from Angevin raiders. It was with no small relief that William saw the familiar towers nudge above the horizon of the gently rolling landscape.

It would have drawn too much attention to have Montgomerie summoned to him, so he quietly sought the Vicomte out, suggesting they take a turn outside the walls.

"Where have you been, Lord?" Montgomerie asked, apparently trying to sound breezy. "Your plans seemed very secretive. You haven't been hunting without me, have you?"

William tried to keep his tone even. "No, sadly. Matters of state. We had to be careful. Correctly, as it turned out." He avoided the temptation to look at his friend to see the effect his words were having. "Everything went as well as could be expected. Except that an assassin tried to kill the nobleman I was treating with, and nearly killed me too."

Montgomerie stopped, and William looked at him. His face was horror stricken. "Duke William... I... Did you escape harm?"

"Yes, fortunately. Thanks to Gallet, and his dog. He saved my life, not for the first time."

"Oh. I. Good. That is..."

"I was negotiating with Herbert, Count of Maine. As I suspect you know. It was Mabel, wasn't it? Who sent the assassin to kill him?"

"Lord?" Montgomerie's face went white.

William felt his face become a mask of stone. The anger was at bay, for now. "Don't try to deny it. I know the assassin was from Normandy. I know he was the same man who murdered Grimoult. Or I'm fairly sure of it." *Just tell me it wasn't you. Tell me it was that demon of a wife of yours, who you married for her land.*

"Yes. It was Mabel." Montgomerie looked down. "But I won't claim I didn't know she was going after Herbert. Or that I tried to stop it."

"Why not?"

Montgomerie looked at him with such fury in his eyes that William took half a step back. He understood. It was a look that said *you dare quest for power in your own right and prevent your people from doing the same?*

Yes! He wanted to shout, *because I am not questing for power for me, but for my whole Duchy and everyone in it!* He could not have his own grands squabbling over each other's holdings. It was that which had nearly brought down the Duchy in his childhood.

"You will not be Count in Maine," William said softly, slowly. "You know I will help you recover your wife's lands. There may have been some sort of independent barony in it, but not now. Can you not see I cannot reward disloyalty? I cannot have my grands pursuing their own agendas!"

"No, Lord." Montgomerie looked away, and William was sure there would be defiance in his eyes.

"I do not do this for my own sake," William added. *No, if I had acted only on my own account I would have done little but hunt and would have probably died in some wench's bed when a friend or ally cut my throat.*

"No, Lord."

William sighed. "All will be well. Keep your faith in me and there will be lands and titles aplenty."

"Yes, Lord William. At your gift."

Christ's nails, was that it? Montgomerie wanted something that was his, and not handed down by his Lord's munificence? William laid his hand on Montgomerie's arm. "Look, Roger. Cousin. Everything I have I owe to you, and Fitz, and Beaumont, and Gallet. You've earned all the rewards you have of me. Every one. They are yours by right, not gift." *And there's nothing a man may take that he does not earn.*

Montgomerie managed a weak smile. "Yes, Lord."

William bit his tongue so as not to remind Montgomerie what happened to his enemies. They parted with William only a little less uncertain of things than he had been on the way back from Saint James. *Is that true?* he wondered to himself. *Is everything you're doing about being a good Lord? About governing well? Maintaining the balance of order? Or are you just finding excuses for being as grasping as Montgomerie and Mabel?*

And would the people of Alençon believe him if he insisted he wasn't? Would the people of Maine?

***

It fell out as William had predicted when Count Herbert died of a fever the following year. Despite an elaborate show of legal right, prepared with care as usual by Lanfranc, the nobles of Maine had chosen to bypass the agreements made by their erstwhile lord, and install some distant relative through marriage. *'Count' Walter is half-Saxon, by the Saints' pustules, and still he is preferred to the Bastard of Normandy,* William thought, and had gathered his armies and thundered into Maine, to take what was already his.

This time it would be different. There would be no sieges, with all their slow horrors. He would not force a battle. He simply moved his army into the land around Le Mans, and began to feed off it. Livestock was taken, of course, crops were burned, but no man who did not resist was harmed. Le Mans opened its gates. A few nobles, those who still put their trust in Martel, held out, of course, and found their castles invested. Geoffrey of Mayenne proved a skilled opponent. William was almost sorry when the inferno consumed his castle as he waited in vain for Anjou to come to his rescue, and he surrendered without condition. For all the arguing of priests and scholars and men of law, it had taken nearly two years in the field.

And so, once again, it came to this—great piles of parchment and *quartauts* of ink, and many hours of talking, Fitz and Lanfranc bustling round him with orders and charters and endless Latin. Land to take away, land to give. Loans to repay, penalties to demand. Lanfranc suggested a change from the usual wording of the charter—rather than the recipient being noted as *fidelis*, or faithful, they would be described as the man of the *dominus*, or lord. William couldn't see what difference this would make, but to Fitz it seemed a revelation. "They will not be able to sell or pass on the land without your permission, Lord!" he explained. "All tenure depends on you."

"If we had to do all this anyway, I don't know why we went to the bother of raising the army," William complained.

"You have more power now because of it," Fitz said. "Between war and law, we can dictate the best terms."

"Patience, Lord," Lanfranc counselled. "Now you have Maine, *and* the legal right, it will be that much harder for your enemies to try to take it back. They can make no complaint to the King or the Pope." He half-smiled. "And moreover, you have shown Martel to have weaknesses. Fewer will be inclined to trust to him to protect them should they raise their hands against you."

Fitz nodded in enthusiastic agreement, then William noticed a pained expression cross his cousin's face.

"What is it Fitz?" he asked.

"What is what, Lord?"

William noticed Lanfranc giving Fitz the slightest nod. "You clearly have something on your mind, besides all this," he gestured at the thousands of meaningless marks on hundreds of pieces of vellum.

"It's just that... well, you aren't the only one doing so well at accruing power, Lord," Fitz continued, looking more uncomfortable by the moment.

"Of course. You speak of Martel?"

"No, Lord. Of England, in fact. We have intelligence from churchmen there, and spies at Wintancaestre and Lundenwic. Harold of Wessex is sending embassies to kings and magnates far and wide, even as he acquires yet more lands and titles of his own."

What's that to me? William shrugged. The family of Wessex was powerful and their star continued to rise, even after the death of Godwin. This was no surprise.

"Lord, we know you have ambitions in England," Lanfranc chimed in.

"Perhaps." William rubbed his brow. "It's hardly the time to think about what might happen in years to come."

"That is exactly what we must do," Lanfranc said. He nodded at Fitz again.

"It is said that Harold is gathering allies and is considering sending an embassy to you, my Lord."

"An embassy?" William snorted. "A fine thing for Wessex to send greetings when he has yet to return the hostage I graciously allowed home. And who has been kept away these ten years!"

Fitz pursed his lips, once again looking as though he would rather be anywhere than here. "Lord... we are given to understand that is exactly what Harold means to do."

"He will return Ælfgifa?" *Finally!* Fitz and Lanfranc were all very well for counsel, but he had missed that sparring, being forced to confront truths that had been hidden from him with a judicious word, even an expression on that unearthly face. He noticed the bleak expressions on Fitz and Lanfranc's faces. "And why would that be such a bad thing?"

Fitz wrung his hands. "It did not go unnoticed when the daughter of Wessex was last here that your lordship was often seen in conversation with her. It is not... proper, Lord."

"Nonsense!" *Where could such idiocy come from? Ah, Mabel de Bellême spreading her poison, no doubt.* "Your... concerns are noted, gentlemen. But I hardly think you need worry."

"Of course, Lord, of course," Fitz said. "But perhaps, if indeed the Jarl of Wessex merely wishes his sister to deliver an embassy, she should be allowed to do so and leave?"

"I allowed her to leave once, and that decision cost me valuable advice." William felt his chest tighten. Was this jealousy? Small-mindedness from those he relied on to be honest and wise? He spat "perhaps if she had been here these last years, I might have seen a way to have won Maine without a fight."

Lanfranc steepled his fingers, glanced at Fitz, yet remained as unreadable as ever. "We fear that the presence of the Saxon woman so close to your Grace could prove... deleterious."

William frowned. "You don't mean to tell me you believe all that nonsense about her being a changeling, or touched by the devil?"

"I cannot say what the Lord has in mind in this case, your Grace, though I doubt He has any great favor for the Saxon. But consider her... priorities. She is a daughter of Wessex, after all. Why should your Grace consider that she would value your interests above those of her family?"

The family who packed her off to live as a prisoner in a foreign country, then walked back into England at the head of an army without a thought for the consequences to her? The family who had surely not recognized her worth the way he had?

"I wish I could be certain my own counsellors valued my interests so highly," William said, standing and walking from the chamber.

CHAPTER 17

Ælfgifa reined in her mare and looked towards Falaise, rearing out of the mist ahead of her. The town was a scant mile away. It seemed she and her escort would reach the castle by nightfall after all. Her heart stuttered in her chest but whether from anxiety or excitement she could not tell. Already she missed Wintancaestre but she couldn't deny that there was a steady beat of anticipation at the thought of seeing Falaise again. She wondered if after so many years William would even remember her or their strange friendship. He must be well settled with his lady and doubtless some children by now. And Wulfnoth, her little one who had not been little when she left him last even. Would he be pleased to see her?

Just once I would like to come to a place again where once I resided and be glad without reservation, Ælfgifa thought crossly as they rode up the main thoroughfare to the castle. *Just once I would like to experience pleasure in renewing an association without all the tangled negatives that continually catch in my net.*

There was a short wait as they were challenged before riding into the castle grounds proper. Ælfgifa had argued that, while sending word ahead might be the courteous thing to do, William would know soon enough why she was there, so it would be better to let her make her case in person. She had no great hopes for success but at least she might see Wulfnoth and Håkon. Harold had charged her with another task. It was that which had excited her interest, in spite of her reservations. At some point in the future, Harold wished to make personal contact with William. He had listened with great concentration to everything Ælfgifa could tell him of the Duke's character and inclinations, sifting through the information and probing for possible weaknesses. Added to the store of information Ælfgifa had faithfully communicated in the years she was a hostage, Harold had a shrewd idea of how to play the Duke should it become necessary. The riddle for Ælfgifa was just why Harold should be so interested in William. As rivals for the throne went, William's claim—even if it were endorsed again by Edward—was weak. The Witenagemot would never countenance a full-blooded Norman ruler. She felt sure that Harold had more to fear from Harald Hardrada of Norway or even their own brother Tostig. There were other claimants circling now that Edward's health was failing and he was almost certain to die without an heir.

Then again, was Harold wrong to have marked out William for future friendship? In his rage years ago, Edward had rashly promised William a crown. Dubhne had told her that William knew of this offer, if it could be called an offer. What man is offered a kingdom and forgets it? *Certainly not William*, Ælfgifa decided. Not someone who had spent his life fighting to secure a Dukedom and who had been canny enough and lucky enough to survive the steps necessary to do so.

"Lady Ælfgifa?" a voice interrupted her musings, causing her to turn. The page went pale as he glimpsed her face and cast his eyes resolutely at his feet. "The Duchess bids you welcome and asks you to dine with her and her husband tonight, if you are not too weary. Lady Matilda has ordered a room and water for washing be prepared for you, if you would follow me, Lady?"

Ælfgifa raised her brows at this. William had had no time for the niceties of a well-run household but it was clear his lady had now well and truly set her stamp upon Falaise and its people. She nodded to the trembling page, biting back a sigh of exasperation. She supposed the lad could not help his reaction to her face but really it became wearing after so many years. Her irritation vanished when she beheld the room Matilda had ordered prepared for her. This was no lowly cell as she had been herded into last time, but a spacious, commodiously furnished room. It was well lit and had a decent fire crackling in the fireplace. Surely this room was meant for visitors of state? While Ælfgifa wasn't sure of the intention behind the gesture, she decided to make the most of the room and the chance to bathe and change.

She had scarce finished tying off the ends of her plaits when a gentle knock at the door sounded. A servant had been sent to say that if she was refreshed, then the Duke would see her in the lesser audience chamber. Ælfgifa took a few deep breaths as she made her way down the corridor. That William was willing to see her so soon was both a compliment and something potentially more forbidding. She remembered well his temperament and thought this haste was as likely to be curiosity and annoyance as eagerness. No doubt only Matilda's instructions to the servant had allowed her the brief respite she had enjoyed.

A least he has learned not to overturn his lady's instruction on household matters, Ælfgifa thought, smiling to herself, and entered the chamber.

There was evidence of Matilda's influence here too. The chamber might be lesser in terms of size but it was richly appointed with carved wooden seats of some reddish-hued wood and fine Frankish tapestries on the walls. There was a sideboard furnished with goblets and a carafe of wine. William and Matilda sat in matched, carved high-backed chairs. The candle light picked glints from amongst the tapestries here and there: semi-precious stones and gold thread. Ælfgifa was impressed. Not with the display of wealth and power but with the cleverness that had gone into it. This room might accommodate a mere dozen people but she doubted many of them would realize that it was much easier to create an illusion of power and riches in a small room than a large one. William's restless vassals must be half won over the moment they set foot in here. She wondered if William appreciated how truly crafty his wife was. Ælfgifa swept a deep, graceful curtsey and then glanced up at the Duchess. There was a gleam in those level eyes, a subtle hint of humor in the curve of her lips. For all her piquancy and slender figure, no one would mistake the Duchess for anything but a woman of influence any more. Ælfgifa found herself giving Matilda the barest hint of a wry nod, like one swordsman acknowledging another. The hinted smile on Duchess' lips deepened.

She reads me in return, Ælfgifa thought. *There might be some pleasant sparring here.*

"Please, Lady Ælfgifa. There is no need for such formality," Matilda said warmly, making it quite clear that formality was indeed required. Ælfgifa smiled to herself and glanced at William. There was no mistaking that black scowl. "We are very glad to see you here at Falaise once more."

"Just what does bring you back, Ælfgifa?" William demanded, undermining his wife's attempt at a courtly reception. "Ten years is a devilish long time to be away when I grant you leave to pay respects to your father on the condition you return!"

Ælfgifa caught the irritated look Matilda shot at her husband, which William missed entirely. Not that she blamed Matilda. It seemed that when surprised or inconvenienced William would fall back on habit over whatever manners Matilda had coached him into. Well and good, as far as Harold was concerned at least.

"Your Lordship will doubtless recall, being blessed with an excellent memory as well as a fine strategic mind, that I was forced to make my promise to return conditionally on the command of my king and my family. My brother, the Jarl of Wessex, Hereford, East Anglia and regent of Gwynedd, has only now seen fit to send me to Normandy. I am come with a message on my brother's behalf, Lord. Will you hear it?" Ælfgifa suppressed her glee. It was insanity to enjoy provoking this man so and in front of his wife too, but there it was, and she had missed it.

Matilda rested a hand on her husband's arm but William leaned forward in his chair and fixed Ælfgifa with a glare. "It seems to me, *Lady,* that your kinsmen have never been greatly skilled at making you do anything you do not wish to."

If only you knew, Ælfgifa thought. "I assure you I am an obedient daughter of Wessex," she said marring the truth with a tone that suggested she was anything but. Even Matilda was looking at her in consternation now.

"Ha!" William sat back. "What message have you brought then?"

"My brother, Harold, wishes to sue for the release of our youngest brother and our nephew. The king commended them to your care some ten years since—a duty admirably carried out—but they are not now political hostages nor is such needed to keep Wessex and England's monarch on the best of terms. Harold respectfully requests that they be allowed to return home."

If Ælfgifa expected an outburst of anger for this piece of borderline insolence she was disappointed. William regarded her with a cunning expression. "Did my cousin the king also make this request?"

Ælfgifa kept her expression calm. "No, Lord. It pains me to bear bad news but my brother-in-law is not in the best of health. More and more, Harold has been entrusted with certain aspects of the kingdom's welfare."

"Would adding two green boys greatly increase your kingdom's welfare? No, don't trouble yourself for an answer. I can release no hostages based only on the words of one acting as my cousin's seneschal." William smiled then and Ælfgifa knew what he would say before he spoke. "We shall wait for those instructions. Send a bird to my cousin if you will. Meanwhile, I insist you remain as a guest in Falaise."

He locked gazes with Ælfgifa and she was surprised to see something like acquisitive satisfaction reflected in his eyes. Whatever his reasons, William wanted her here.

"Very well, Lord," Ælfgifa said, curtsying again. "I accept your kindly offered hospitality."

"It was not an offer, Lady."

"Oh, I am well aware of that, Lord," Ælfgifa said with a sly, needling smile. "But I shall accept it in such wise, nevertheless."

William drew a deep breath and then half-chuckled. "You always were the most provoking imp."

"My Lord—" Matilda hissed under her breath.

Ælfgifa laughed frankly. "Then I hope your lordship is not greatly disappointed at my failure to mend my ways. My Lady," she added, curtseying more respectfully to Matilda.

As she took her leave of the pair, Ælfgifa couldn't help a pinch of conscience. Yes, William believed he had won. Had in fact taken something valuable of Harold's, perhaps, and he must see the sense in that, for if he had not realized the extent of Harold's wealth and influence before, she had certainly laid it out for him. What William did not see was that Harold had meant for her to be detained. Ælfgifa had realized that the moment her brother had bade her act as his emissary. Once again she was a game piece deployed to best advantage and she could hardly blame love for her brother for preventing her from seeing it this time. No, Ælfgifa would play the part intended but Beddwen's last words about honor weighed heavy on her and she found herself wishing it had not been so easy to plant herself as a spy in William's household once more.

***

At times over the next six months, Ælfgifa would find herself pausing over a task she had been focusing on, whether cutting lady's bedstraw or grinding herbs, writing with a crow's feather quill or setting a stitch of embroidery, and she would be caught with a feeling of unreality. Like vertigo. As if she had come full circle while in fact never having left Falaise at all. That sense of spinning, of being moved and trapped at the same time inevitably drove her out of doors where she would clutch at the nearest wall and fight for breath. She wondered if she was ill, if some canker had set in deep within her to make her see her life in this way. No matter what she did, no matter how hard she worked nor how minutely she occupied herself, Ælfgifa could not shake off the feeling that all her choices were coming back to haunt her. A murder of crows coming in to roost. She did not believe in the Sight, but she did know that there were patterns that connected events and that if one followed the threads one could predict with accuracy what their outcome would be.

Matilda was courteous and made Ælfgifa welcome amongst the ladies. She even seemed to enjoy the more robustly intelligent conversation Ælfgifa contributed, but there was no deep friendship there. Matilda was as guarded with Ælfgifa as Ælfgifa was wary of the duchess. To Ælfgifa's genuine disappointment, Helisande was not at court nor was she likely to be in the near future, having apparently gone to Valognes to look after her sick father.

Then there was the Duke himself, who took to appearing in the herb garden when Ælfgifa was working as if their routine had not been interrupted by a decade of estrangement. This time Ælfgifa did not find herself pining desperately for England. Having seen Wulfnoth and Håkon, she thought that neither of them would especially wish to return, making her errand a double folly. Or it would have been folly if she had not had another goal. Edith wrote to her and replied to Ælfgifa's own missives. Most were innocent enough exchanges of news, but some bore the careful pricked messages of concealed intelligence—which code Ælfgifa had taught her sister-in-law long since. William had either grown more secure or was complacent of her intentions. *Or*, Ælfgifa thought with a pang, *he does in fact trust you.* She felt slightly ill when she let herself think of sending information on troops and supplies, on William's enemies both open and covert. It was all very well to tell herself that she only gathered information, but she was not a child watching others out of survival anymore, and she could not absolve herself of how such information she relayed was used.

The perversely enjoyable task of smoothing Harold's way with William was less of an issue for her conscience. William had clearly registered just how powerful Harold had become and made Ælfgifa's task easier by quizzing her about her brother—and the rest of her family—whenever the opportunity presented itself.

Today was one such opportunity. William was at home for a change and had taken up his usual place on the stone bench while Ælfgifa tied back woody stems in preparation for winter. It had been close to a year since she had arrived back at Falaise. William never asked if a message had come from king Edward requesting the release of the hostages. Ælfgifa thought he had probably never been expecting one.

"Harold is the second of your brothers then? What happened to the first?" William said.

"Sweyn? He, er, committed an offense that caused Harold to declare him *nīthing*. My father supported the decision. He was bringing the family into disrepute with the people and with the King." Ælfgifa paused and swiped the back of one hand across her forehead. "I heard that he undertook a pilgrimage to atone for his crimes and was killed on the road."

"*Nīthing?*" William asked in puzzlement. "And how coolly you speak of a brother's death!"

Ælfgifa shrugged. "Sweyn was near twenty years my senior, I knew him but little and wished to know him even less. A bully, a braggart and an unpredictable, uncertain ally. I was glad he was removed from power in his Jarldom." She paused, trying to think of how to explain such a Saxon concept to William. "*Nīthing* means 'no thing', an outcast. But not merely one to be shunned. To declare someone

Nīthing is to make them an *un-person*. Anyone might murder them without fear of the least repercussions."

"That's..." William looked aghast.

"Barbaric?" Ælfgifa suggested sweetly.

William shook his head, but not in disagreement, she thought. "Just what did your eldest brother do to deserve such a fate?"

"He was a kinslayer. Before that, he abducted an Abbess from her convent and raped her. His intent was a forced marriage and gain of her lands. She was very rich, you see." Ælfgifa eyed the Duke. "I know not how it stands here in Normandy but those crimes carry great weight in England. It is against the Danelaw to force a woman—any woman, no matter her circumstances of birth—into marriage. Rape carries a heavy fine and a punishment determined by the liege lord of the area. Killing kin unlawfully is thought to attract the kinslayer's curse. Most families would cast out the murderer."

"Then your brother, Harold, and your father, weren't being especially ruthless?" William asked.

"More ruthless than many would have been. *Nīthing* is not a punishment used often. To be outcast from your lands and people, to have your life worth less than an eye blink? Most who are declared thus have committed multiple offenses of the same weight." Ælfgifa met William's gaze steadily. "Once was enough for Harold. For some crimes, once should be all that is necessary." She watched as William nodded, unconsciously in agreement, and thought about the stories she'd heard. Of the severed hands and feet.... Of the circumstances of his betrothal to Matilda....

"Besides," Ælfgifa said, shaking herself. "Sweyn was a blithering idiot."

"Lady Ælfgifa, surely you don't mean to say that you think the punishment for stupidity should be death?" William said slyly. "Must we all be as clever and learned as you? If so I would fear for most of my retainers!"

Ælfgifa chuckled darkly, flattered despite herself. "I think stupidity is its own punishment and often ends in death, Lord. I meant Sweyn—who was no great wit, it is true—was especially stupid to believe he could gain lands and wealth through a forced marriage. The lands and money a woman comes dowered with are hers until the day she dies. She then passes them on to descendants or other beneficiaries of her choosing. They might enhance a husband's standing, but they never become his property."

"Why in God's name have a dowry then?" William demanded.

"To show the wealth, value and independence of the lady, of course. Women choose husbands based on their suitability as managers and caretakers of their own lands as well as their likelihood in fathering healthy children. Good connections are also a consideration. Are these not considerations for a man seeking a wife? Why would a woman settle for any less?" Ælfgifa could see this version of marital transactions did not sit well with the Duke and was rather enjoying his reaction. "Women are not chattel in England, Lord. We may choose our husbands, own land and property, divorce ourselves of poor marriages in order to seek better ones."

"Gifa, I have no idea whether you are mocking me or not, but I'll thank you to stop these wild tales." That was the other change. The Duke's adoption of her pet name without even noticing.

"They are not tales, Lord, I assure you."

"England must be full of men run mad! Or were they mad already and so they allowed such folly?"

"Should you ever meet my sister-in-law, I beg you will not voice such an opinion to her. For all her beauty, Edith has a hastier temper than mine and a creativity for revenge that makes even me tremble." Ælfgifa swallowed any irritation at William's reaction. How would he know any better, with the laws being different in Normandy and the Latin church holding greater sway here?

She was about to say something needling to provoke him further but a voice crying out "Lord Duke!" forestalled her.

Ælfgifa turned to see one of the novices from La Trineté, red-faced, breathless and sweating in his habit, standing outside the walled garden. "Lord, a message..." the novice gasped, holding out a small sealed scroll that was surely fresh from pigeon flight.

"Take it, Lady," William ordered. "Tell me what it says."

Already alight with curiosity, Ælfgifa did not bristle at his peremptory tone but passed a water skin to the novice and broke the seal on the message. She and William moved deeper into the herb beds, away from the ears of the recovering novice.

The message was in Frankish. The hand poor but legible, clearly written in some haste. Ælfgifa's heart lurched in her chest as she took in the words. Surely this was no part of Harold's plan? He should have been gaining support around England for a further six months yet. She swallowed hard and read the missive aloud.

"Duke William of Normandy,
Gui of Ponthieu has caught some noble fish in his net. The Saxons were shipwrecked and taken captive by Ponthieu's men. One of them is Harold of Wessex. This news was thought to be of great interest to you."

There was no signature. There did not need to be. Ælfgifa would have eaten her kirtle if William didn't have at least some semblance of a spy network in place. Now was the moment where she would learn whether these last months of gradually working on the Duke, making him receptive to Harold as a potential ally, would pay off. She held her breath as she watched the words sink in. William's expression fixed grimly. Later Ælfgifa would wonder if it was the detested name of Gui of Ponthieu that tipped the scale. For now she was merely relieved.

"A horse!" William shouted as they emerged from the herb garden. "A horse and an escort. Quickly now!" Servants and grooms fell over themselves in their haste. Ælfgifa grabbed a passing stable hand. "Saddle my mare. I will be going with his lordship."

She glanced sideways to find William watching her but instead of growling at her for such high-handedness, he gave a short, swift nod. Either she would be useful or William felt she had a right to come. Just then Ælfgifa did not care which.

CHAPTER 18

William refused all offers of refreshment and clean clothing following a long ride through heavy rain, but demanded to see Count Gui of Ponthieu as soon as the party was admitted through the gate of Beaurain castle.

"My Lord William, welcome," said Gui when he had appeared, none too quickly, and knelt in a surly fashion. "I only lately received news that you were coming. To what do I owe the... honor?"

Gui had not improved, either in appearance or temperament, since he had emerged, pale and squinting, from a cell at Falaise so many years ago. It was the last time William had seen his vassal, and he would have happily made it longer. The Count seemed to have shrunk, being even more skinny than before, bowed with it, and his hair both lank and thin. To see such a pathetic figure glowering was almost comical, but William was in no mood for humor.

"Ponthieu," William nodded as cursorily as he could manage, after being led to Gui's cabinet. Ponthieu knew damned well why he was here. "I wish it had not been necessary to come myself. You have, I understand, seized—kidnapped—a number of men, at least one of them noble, who were shipwrecked at the mouth of the Somme."

Gui affected to look stung, as he had at the Conseil all those years ago. *Fortunate that you're in your own castle,* William thought. *In mine, that performance earned you two years as a prisoner.*

"I have apprehended some trespassers on my territory, if that's what you mean," Gui replied. "Saxon dogs. Brigands, raiding the coastline, no doubt, harrying my people."

If anyone had been raiding and harrying it was Gui. William was rarely free from complaints that Gui had been encroaching on the land of his neighbors, robbing, pillaging, interfering with passing shipping, and occasionally outright piracy. He always denied it and there was little enough proof. Until now.

"One of those *brigands* is one of the most powerful men in England," William spat, "a man you would do well not to make an enemy of." He leaned forward until his face was uncomfortably close to that of Gui. "And a man you would do well not to make into an enemy of mine, either."

Gui moved his head back a touch, swiveling his eyes uncomfortably. It would be well for him if he was beginning to realize how much he had bitten off. "Perhaps. But the fact remains they were trespassing…"

"They were shipwrecked in a storm, you had no business detaining them." William slapped the table. "Your duty as a nobleman was to give them succor and help them on their way."

"We couldn't understand them," Gui said, looking anywhere but at William. "How was I supposed to know who they were? And anyway, if one of them is noble I'm entitled to a ransom… a reward for ensuring their safe return."

William just narrowed his eyes, and Gui did not push the point. He was clearly lying about knowing who the men in his dungeons were. "Safe? I want to see the Jarl of Wessex. To ensure his good treatment."

Now a flash of panic crossed Gui's eyes. "But of course, Lord. I will send for him to be brought to us. In the meantime, are you sure you wouldn't like some food or wine after your journey?"

Stalling for time so Harold can be cleaned up and made presentable, no doubt. "That won't be necessary. I'll see him where he is. Don't trouble yourself. Have a guard lead me there."

Gui paused for a moment, probably considering whether to try to deflect William, but one look should have told him the Duke was not in any mood for games. Even more downcast than before, he called for a guard and instructed him to lead William. Not surprising, William thought, that Gui suddenly knew exactly which cell Harold was in, despite moments ago claiming not to know who any of the men were.

Blinking to accustom his eyes to the almost total lack of light, William waited while the guard opened the door and stepped through. It was a small cell, the kind a petty knight might be held in while awaiting ransom, not a great magnate and brother-in-law of a king. Saint Spirus' innards! Gui was a barbarian, and William began to wish he'd never pushed him into paying homage.

The only furniture was a wooden bench, and as William's eyes adjusted, he saw there was a man lying on it, dozing, perhaps. At any rate, he had not been disturbed by the clattering of the key and screeching of the door hinges. William cleared his throat, at which the other looked up, startled, and jumped to his feet. His bare feet. William realized with horror that Harold must still be wearing the clothes in which he had been shipwrecked. His hair hung loose about his face, flashing reddish wherever it caught the light of the torch outside.

William realized he barely spoke a word of Anglish. "You are Harold of Wessex, yes?" he said in Latin. "I am William. Duke of Normandy. I am here to release you." He prepared himself for a tirade on the shortcomings of Norman hospitality.

Instead, the other smiled broadly. "My Lord of Normandy!" He bowed, stiffly. "Well met, if rather unexpected. I have long desired to make your acquaintance. My sister Ælfgifa spoke well of your lordship. May I ask what brings you to Ponthieu? Your man Gui will have a face like a smacked guppy if you mean to make off with his prize catch."

William stared for a moment. Here was a man who had been shipwrecked then thrown into a cell, and they were exchanging greetings as if they were preparing for a May morning hunt. There may have even been a mocking note in Harold's voice, but whether it was directed at himself or William, or just the Saxon accent to his Latin, the Duke could not be sure. "Jarl Harold... forgive me, I'm not sure of the form of address." There was no point in talking around the issue, even if Harold had so far proved a model of courtesy. Gui had put him at a disadvantage, and that had to be rectified. "Allow me to apologize for the behavior of my vassal. This is not how I would have wished us to meet. I'm relieved to find you whole and in good spirits. I trust you have not been excessively mistreated? And," he growled, "I assure you, Gui will be lucky to have a face with all its features intact if he complains."

Harold laughed, an open, hearty chuckle. "A man after my own heart too, it seems. Nay, Ponthieu did not treat me ill although the man might look into hiring a better cook. The food was atrocious." They both laughed at that.

William could not help but be impressed at Harold's sangfroid. "No, it's a little more than the food he serves that offends me about Gui, if the truth be known. I hope we can provide better for you at Falaise."

There did not even seem to be anything false or showy about Harold's manner. Here was a man who could make the best of any situation he found himself in. "I imagine more does offend you about Gui—I believe I was meant to be a dainty tidbit and you have ruined his sport. The man will look like he's been chewing dandelion root for a month when you tell him you intend to offer me better lodgings."

William smiled grimly. "Don't worry about Gui. It's not so long since he was enjoying my hospitality at Falaise himself, though his room was rather small and the door rarely open. He may find himself spending a summer in his old accommodation if he continues to act more like a pirate than a Count."

Harold grinned, then his comradely smile faded, just a touch. "So Lord, I am here—where I should not be—and while that is more at God's convenience than mine, I will beg your pardon for my intrusion. Is there anything I might do for you, Duke William? You will excuse me if I ask after my sister—she was uncommonly long about delivering my missive. A full year now I think on it. Is she well? How does my young brother and nephew?"

William could not blame Harold for asking so many questions. While William was at a disadvantage in terms of social niceties, Harold was at a disadvantage in every other respect. Nevertheless, William could not help but be impressed that the Saxon was thinking of his family when his own circumstances were so poor. And mentioning Ælfgifa first? Any thought that Harold had sent Ælfgifa away because she lacked value evaporated. Harold clearly loved his sister. And perhaps knew her capabilities just as well as William did. If not better. "Your sister? She does the things she wants, when she wants, I find, though she has been of great service to me, for which I would thank you if I didn't think she would take offense." They laughed again, politely. "She's well enough," William continued. "You can ask her yourself, she came with me here."

Harold looked genuinely pleased at that, William noticed, which seemed to confirm his earlier musings. "Yes, Gifa does like to be useful," Harold smiled. "Still," he added, "she is much regarded by her family. And by you also, Lord."

William nodded his assent. The Saxon was about to speak again when William interrupted him. "Your offer of help is actually somewhat timely," he said, quickly. There was an advantage to be had, and he was not about to lose it. "I'm currently engaged in a bit of fighting with my Western neighbors. Since I've heard only good things about your military skills, it would be helpful to me if you would come along with your men, perhaps. I hear the Bretons have a bit in common with the Wealas you've been in action with."

"The Bretons?" Harold went on, looking thoughtful. "Yes their tongue is similar to that of the Wealas though I imagine they don't cling to the old ways so much. I don't speak it so well as my sister, of course, but I have the measure of them. Let me see... their current commander would be Duke Conan of Brittany, second of his name, would it not?" He looked William square in the eye. "You may count on me, Duke William. I have never shied away from honest battle at the side of one I would wish to name as a friend."

A friend, eh? Those were always valuable, and rarely offered so readily. "Interesting," William muttered, adding, "That is about the Bretons. I can't understand a word they say. It's hard enough to talk to those who do want me there, and most of what I get from the others is saliva. Yes, Conan is Duke there, at the moment anyway, though who knows who will be next week or the week after? Your assistance will be most welcome. As will your friendship. Especially if it comes to open battle. I've had quite enough of breaking down walls."

"You must indeed, though I confess I would very much like to see your men in action. A different kind of warfare altogether, compared to what I am used to."

William smiled to himself at the memory of Grimoult shouting *you fight like a Saxon!* at him on the field of Val es Dunes all those years ago.

"I have found that the trick with the Wealas is to allow them to keep their internal struggles and petty kingdoms," Harold went on, evidently warming to his subject. "Once you have proved that you are the leader of the wolf pack, they'll bare their throats but there's little need in getting caught up in their internal struggles unless it affects you. To that end I would say a public and humiliating defeat of this Conan must be the order of the day. You shall defeat him, Lord, and his people's loyalties shall transfer to you as the strongest leader. They are barely better than the savage Pretani folk who live in the north of Britain in that way."

"Hm. It will be too much to hope for a clean fight." William thought back to the raid to Dol Combourg the previous year. If only he'd stayed to finish the job. But Geoffrey Martel, ever the opportunist, had started to threaten in the South again, and William withdrew, considering he'd disrupted Conan enough and made a point. He was wrong. "It's true what you say. The worst thing for peace is weakness. If Conan is a wolf, he is a sick wolf, and allows others to snap at him. He's shown himself unable to put his own Duchy in order, so mine suffers. It cannot be allowed to continue. I'd like to defeat him any way I can, if it comes to it."

"I suppose we must hunt him down as with all wolves." Harold made to speak again, then paused, looked down at his torn, salt-stained clothes, his bare feet, and issued a short laugh. "Perhaps I should see about basic equipment such as boots before I am carried away in my own schemes!"

"Ha! Boots you shall have," William replied. He'd demand Gui's if he thought they would fit. "And a hauberk, and horse. A man of mine, Hugh de Grandmesnil breeds the most impressive coursers and destriers..." He stopped himself. It had been a clever stroke of Matilda's to bind de Grandmesnil to the Duchy through his horses. Now every Norman noble wanted one, and through the gold he had secured thus, had expanded his stud farms. The Baron had proved a skilled cavalry commander, too. William had to take care not to become boring on the subject. "You'd think being a good lord and looking to your own territory would be enough. If only our neighbors would let us, eh?"

"My Lord William, there are so few men with the mettle and the wit to see things as they ought to be. Still, there is reason for good cheer—two men of our caliber shall soon settle this limping wolf. And, if I may say so, it sounds as if you have the finest horses for many leagues. I would most certainly welcome something fine-blooded enough to have more than two gaits that wasn't the planking of a longboat!"

That was gracious coming from a man wearing rags and standing in a dank cell. "I hope you will consider me at your service," Harold added, bowing stiffly.

One of the greatest men in England at William's service? This was a prize catch indeed, to use the Saxon's phrase. "It would be my pleasure to do so, Jarl Harold."

"Then if you would be good enough to remove me from the stench of that half-bred cur Ponthieu, I would be glad to join your lordship in Falaise."

"That would be my pleasure too. Guard! Open the door."

Gui did not complain at William's insistence that he would take the Saxon prisoners with him, but looked so surly that the Duke paid him a ransom anyway. The last thing he needed was another embittered noble looking for any opportunity to hurt his liege lord.

They stepped into the courtyard, Harold blinking at the brightness, though in truth it was a grey day. William wondered that Gifa was not there immediately to greet her brother... ah, there she was, hanging back a little. Why would she be so reticent? Because she doesn't want to make a show of her importance, perhaps? Playing the insignificant minor sibling, who means nothing to the Jarl.

Harold, however, raced towards his sister with a yell of joy the moment he laid eyes on her, and her brief expression of consternation was swamped with pleasure as they embraced.

William insisted Harold ride with him at the head of the column as they left, and the Saxon's relief was obvious as they passed beneath the gates of Beaurain. Until William turned to him and asked, "So, how does my cousin the King?"

CHAPTER 19

The Couesnon flowed slowly by William and his captains, barely rippling at the fetlocks of their horses.

"Ha!" Gallet snorted. "They think to repeat your victory at Varaville!" The men around him laughed, good naturedly. They were a tight command group now, blooded at Mortemer, in Maine and now in Brittany. Young de Tosny, William's erstwhile squire, had passed over his right to bear William's standard when Old de Tosny died because he wanted to fight closer to William! Walter Giffard had gladly accepted that honor instead. De Grandmesnil had proved as skilled at fighting on a horse as his family was at breeding them, and despite Beaumont's griping, all had accepted the Baron into the small knot of William's closest military supporters.

They gazed across the shining sheet of water in the estuary, to their right the hulking mass of Mont Saint Michel rising out of the sea. Ahead of them, on a gentle rise behind the far bank, a column of mounted men in loose order, lances couched. They were as yet distant, but a flash of color dancing here and there showed their gonfanons attached. They were ready and waiting.

William raised his hand towards the newest member of the assembly. "Jarl Harold," he said, "you see we have a welcoming party."

"Yes," the Saxon grinned. "Now I'll see one of your cavalry battles, I hope." The Saxon's enthusiasm was infectious. Genuine curiosity, none of the sometimes false bravado of the Normans.

"You may, if they decide to give battle."

Harold knitted his brows, surveying the scene. "Hmmm. They will give battle, I think. There is plenty of room to maneuver the horses. No particular advantage to either side in the terrain, but you will have the river at your back. And perhaps they are thinking of Varaville as Sir Gallet suggests, and that you will be trapped by the rising tide. But the situation is different here, I think."

William smiled. "Go on."

"The Dive was deep, fast flowing and strongly affected by the tide. This river... The Couesnon..." His mouth twisted around the still-unfamiliar Frankish words. "It is broad, very shallow at the mouth here, slow. The road goes right through, so it must be fordable most of the time."

"Indeed. We could fight in the river if we have to."

"That is well. Let's try not to, eh? I'd hate to let my borrowed armor go rusty."

The men laughed again, and William ordered the charge. They began at a trot, urging the heavy destriers up to a gentle pace. The feeling of a great weapon gaining force as the speed gradually built sent a thrill through William, as it always did. The water splashed from the horses' hooves sending flashing jewels of water flying. They raised the pace to a canter. William gripped his lance, shifted the position until it was just so.

The Bretons were moving now too. Not coming straight in, but working inland. That could be dangerous, if they could push the Normans into the sea.

"They're trying to flank us!" William shouted, "wheel left!"

The line slowed a little, almost to a stop at the far left, while the right increased to a gallop to keep the rank together as they turned. It was a hard maneuver to pull off at the best of times, harder still while riding through a river, and the line flexed, but it stayed whole, and began to straighten. They were committed now. "Dex Aie!" William yelled, spurring his horse to a gallop, keeping up with the right flank that was now at full pelt.

The others were shouting battle cries of their houses, but what was that dreadful racket? The usual noise of the first charge was punctuated by someone banging their shield. William glanced to his right. The Saxon, of course. "Ut! Ut! Ut!" Harold yelled, and caught William's eye, grinning wildly, a lock of red-gold hair that had escaped from beneath his helm shining in the sun. William rolled his eyes but smiled back.

They were coming out of the river now, onto sand, wet and firm underhoof. The Bretons were coming down off the gentle rise of the bank. William could already see there were not as many of them, and they were not in good order. Overconfident. If they had any sense they'd be regretting their deployment.

Just then, William sensed rather than saw a few men go down to his right, a flash of something tumbling. No time to look back. Souls in Damnation, were there archers beyond the rise? He glanced around. No one else down, no arrows thudding into the ground ahead of them. No time to worry about it, not while there was a gap the enemy could exploit.

"Close up the line!" he bellowed, gesturing madly, and the men to the right began to drift toward him. There was a riderless horse now in the rank, he noticed, keeping to the line as though it had a ghost for a rider.

They thundered into the Breton line. William felt his lance strike home perfectly—his adversary was not wearing mail, and the point ripped into his chest like an arrow into a hart. As the Breton tumbled, already dead, from the horse, William hauled the spear back, and managed to hang onto it. He wheeled his horse left, and bore down on another Breton who was advancing on an unhorsed Norman. William broke his spear on the Breton knight who fell, landing with a horrible snap, and did not move again.

Part of the Breton line had remained intact and William saw them pull up. He yelled an order to reform to all those who could hear him, just as he caught sight of the enemy commander. They locked eyes. For a moment, William thought he was going to turn the remainder of his force and run. It would have been the sensible thing to do. Conan did not have cavalry to waste. But William knew what would happen. Honor was at stake. The Bretons charged again, brandishing spears or swords where they still had them. One or two rode in unarmed. They didn't take long to deal with.

The battle had disintegrated into small pockets of fighting. It took the best part of an hour before it was finished completely. As always, a brief euphoria of victory was swamped by a horrible sickening feeling—wondering who they had lost. He realized with a lurch of the stomach that he hadn't seen Gallet since the initial charge. Or de Tosny. Or Harold, for that matter. Saints and Martyrs! He looked for his standard, and rode for it.

"Giffard," he puffed when he had caught up with the standard bearer. "Have you seen Gallet anywhere? Or de Tosny?"

"De Tosny was thrown in the first charge," the knight said. "It looked as though his horse and a couple of others pulled up. Maybe they got into some soft ground. It got a bit boggy when we came out of the river. My horse didn't like it much, but we got through all right."

By the Holy Spirit's arsehole, this was the last thing he wanted! "What about the Saxon?"

"Haven't seen him."

William spurred his horse, aimlessly looking for his men, shouting their names.

"Down there, your Lordship!" someone called at him, pointing back at the river. He cantered in the direction indicated, where a number of figures on foot—he counted five, no, seven—were slouching towards him.

To start with, he didn't recognize them—they were all plastered, head to foot, in thick mud. Then one of them grinned at him—Gallet. He looked at the others. De Tosny was there, thank the Saints. And Harold. In that instant, William was overwhelmed with gladness. The thought of having to break the news of their deaths to Helisande and Ælfgifa was too much to bear.

"I must apologize, Lord William," Harold said. "I fear my borrowed mail may take a week to clean."

When they'd found a place to set up camp before marching on Dol, Gallet sidled up to William, his shaggy hound trotting at his heel. It was the first chance he'd had to talk to the knight properly since the battle. William asked him what had happened as the dog sniffed his boots and sprawled by his feet.

"It was bloody lucky your pet Saxon was there, though it gives me a pain in the bowel to say it," Gallet said. "We might have lost some good men."

"How?"

"Quicksand."

"What?!"

"Yes. The horses must have sensed it. Five or six of them just stopped and the riders came off. A couple of horses went down, mine being one. The last I saw of him he was joining the line as though he were pleased to be rid of me, the big hairy shit."

"So you weren't stuck?"

"I wasn't, and neither was your man Harold, but young de Tosny was, and four others. Couple of Fitz's men and one of Raoul de Ryes' I think. Well, there they were, up to their waists, thrashing round and getting deeper, and there I was, with the Saxon, lying on the mud trying to heave them out, and yelling at them to keep still, and of course they weren't listening..."

"By God and the Devil!" What a way to die. Being killed in battle was one thing. Even taking a wound that might rip you open and take hours or days to kill you... But to die by sand, slowly sucking you down, crushing the life from you...

"It got so they were up to their chests and weren't getting any deeper, thank Christ, but the tide was coming in, and nothing we were doing was working. The men started to panic again. Well, I can't blame them."

"What did you do?"

Gallet looked very serious for a moment. It wasn't a familiar look. "What did I do? Nothing. I'd about given up hope. Harold though... He steps forward, and do you know what he does?"

William rolled his eyes. "I don't know, he heaved them out two at a time? Christ's festering wounds Gallet, you're not telling a tale in the alehouse now!"

"No, but Harold might as well have been! He started telling jokes. Jokes, can you believe! Or what passes for jokes in England." Gallet smirked to himself, no doubt at the memory of one such. "Something with the way he was telling them, in his godawful Frankish, these shitty Saxon jokes, and within a couple of minutes de Tosny and the others had stopped panicking and started pissing themselves laughing. Of course, he had our full attention by then, so when they'd stopped laughing he tells them, very calm and careful, to keep their bodies still but kick their legs about and make a gap between them. Turns out that breaks the suction, or something, and bit by bit they could lift themselves back up. With a bit of hauling from me and Harold, we finally managed to get everyone out."

Gallet started repeating the Saxon jokes and chuckling to himself, and though William didn't find a single one funny, he found himself laughing in sympathy and relief, and that evening he and Gallet got roaring drunk on stolen Breton wine.

***

Ælfgifa rode towards the rear of the column. She could not lay a finger on why exactly, but since Harold's arrival and rescue by the Duke, she had felt grumpy and out of sorts. She knew she need not ride back here with the dust from those in front being kicked up into her teeth. Harold would have made a place for her at the front even if William had not. In fact Ælfgifa was certain that William would have raised no great objections. Her place in William's household and on the march to meet the Duke of Brittany in battle, was so

215

nebulous, and the respect accorded her so great—or should that be infamy?—that she might ride wherever she chose. No one would challenge her.

Ælfgifa had not intended to ride into battle but no mention was made of her staying in Falaise. Harold had seemed to take it as decided that she should accompany them, if not into the field, at least as part of the Duke's general staff. Pressed into service as a scribe, a translator, a healer and makeshift surgeon, there had been plenty for her to do. And if William had been too taken up with her brother and the campaign to ask for her advice, Harold had certainly sought her out. Even while she enjoyed the art of conveying much that must not be overheard or misinterpreted whilst saying those things that seemed entirely mundane to a casual listener, she had felt peevish and slighted. She supposed it was the covert way in which Harold now solicited her advice. In England it had been an open secret that the Jarl's sister had great influence with him, equal perhaps to that of his official advisors and his wife. While Ælfgifa understood the need to appear man enough to scorn the advice of a woman and a deformed, pitiable sister here amongst the Normans, Harold's readiness to deny her still rankled.

William's men had fallen under Harold's spell as quickly as the Duke had. *Why exactly did Harold need to banish me to Falaise if everyone loves him no matter what?* Ælfgifa thought irritably. She refused to admit to herself that she felt side-lined which was what vexed her. As if it were not bad enough that her own acceptance had been won by tooth and nail and straining her wits to breaking point, Harold had strolled in with a ready smile and a jest or two and they fell at his feet like eager puppies. Ælfgifa felt the beginnings of a headache gripping her temples. *You ought to be past such sibling resentment at your age,* she scolded herself. What did it matter? Harold was supposed to befriend William. That had been his plan. He would then gradually ease William into accepting that he, Harold, was the best choice for the English throne. There was sense in the maneuver. Such reasoning was unlikely to weigh with Hardrada after all, and Harold likely did not wish to fight a war on two fronts when the time came.

Privately, Ælfgifa thought that Harold had grossly underestimated William's tenacity, that deep insecurity that made the Duke restless and uneasy. That would do so until he had a near untouchable kingdom. But then that was Harold's problem—he certainly wasn't paying much attention to her at present.

They had chased Duke Conan from Rennes and had ridden hard upon Dinan. The final battle was upon them and Ælfgifa did not doubt they would be victorious. Then Harold's mission would be accomplished—albeit much earlier than he had intended. There would be no further occasion for charm from Harold then, save for leave taking. So why did she feel so uneasy? Ælfgifa couldn't imagine Harold would leave her behind having got what he wanted, or having laid the ground work for it at least. Yet disquiet whispered through her. William would not give up an ambition so easily as that. She felt sure the Duke would take some measure to keep a hold on Harold. Only a fool would not do so. Even if Harold were without wealth and power, he would be useful to a man eyeing the English throne.

Then there was Lanfranc. Ælfgifa did not like the man. She was certain that feeling was mutual. He was one of the few not caught by Harold's charisma. The feeling that he was working up some scheme to present to William was like an itch she could not reach. Worse, her fears were too unformed to bring to Harold's attention. She had hissed a general warning in her brother's ear but he had smiled soothingly and patted her head. Her brother was in danger of believing his own legend. William certainly had less time for spiky conversation with Ælfgifa now that her brother was here. Aware that she was being missish and juvenile, but unable to stop and thoroughly miserable, Ælfgifa scowled ahead between the flicking ears of her mare.

***

The Norman army swept through Brittany. After the fighting by Mont Saint Michel, it seemed Conan was determined to avoid battle. William initially headed South West, towards Dol, which the Duke had abandoned by the time they reached it. They had marched on Rennes, to discover that Conan had abandoned that too, and fled North West to Dinan.

Instead of a pitched battle, the Norman force expended its energy on anyone that got in its way, and no small number who tried to stay out of it. They burned every town and village they came across, putting men to the sword and women to worse. It had been a dry spring, and the houses and crops burned readily. Sometimes you could see the path the army had taken by following the columns of smoke back to the horizon and beyond. William knew Matilda would be displeased, and would no doubt talk him into praying for the souls of those innocents who had died by his hand, and giving yet more money and land to the church. It seemed small recompense, but the slaughter was, in any case, necessary. If Conan was any Duke at all, he would be provoked to come out and fight. If he didn't, the people would likely welcome the end of hostilities and bow to whoever had the power to end their torment. Meanwhile his

218

army had to eat, and the land could not sustain both the army and the folk who called it home.

Occasionally they came across small bands of skirmishers —either Conan's men deployed to slow William down, or local menfolk, petty knights and their armed men, fighting for their own homes and people. William could not help but notice that Harold and his squadron of Saxon infantry took much more of an active part when fighting against these Bretons than they did in terrorizing the smallfolk. It would be refreshing to have that luxury. William did not mind too much—it meant more plunder for his own men and those of his captains. By this time they had gathered to them a number of Breton nobles who had joined William when they saw which way the war was going. He even had three of Conan's nephews fighting under the Norman standard now. If only the Duke saw sense and surrendered, all this need not be necessary.

The weather was good, the ground dry, and the army made good progress. Before long, they were before the wooden bailey of Dinan castle. William offered battle on the fields in front of the castle, and when that was refused, offered to discuss terms of a mutually agreeable surrender. That was not accepted either.

"It looks as though we're back to siege warfare," Gallet grumbled when the second refusal came back.

"This I am most anxious to see, Duke William," Harold said. "Siege warfare is not such a craft in England as in Normandy, I think. Will we build siege engines? Throw up earthworks? Interdict their supplies?"

William nodded, noting the smiles of his captains. "Oh yes. All of that. We may be here a very long time, and you may learn a very great deal of Norman siege craft. Before that, however, I intend to try something a little faster to act."

That night, under cover of darkness, William directed great piles of oil-soaked brushwood to be stacked against the outer ramparts, which was achieved without too much loss. Fire arrows lit the bonfires, and before long, the bone-dry outer bailey was beginning to catch.

Harold frowned. "Won't the fires burn out before the rampart is weakened appreciably?"

William smiled grimly. "That's not why we set the fires. See how much smoke there is? It's choking. Their men will have to pull back from the wall."

"Ah. Giving your men more freedom to move."

"Yes. We'll attack the gate if we have to, but with luck we won't need to. They'll either give in or burn to death."

Harold cast him a look that William wasn't sure how to interpret, but at that moment, as if to demonstrate William's point, Gallet ordered a rank of archers forward. They shot more fire arrows, this time curving well beyond the outer wall. Flames could be seen leaping up inside the bailey, as wooden shingles and thatch caught. William nodded to de Grandmesnil, whose men started to bring up a battering ram, but before they had moved it half a dozen toises, the gates could be seen opening. A mass of people boiled out from the door. William tensed to give the signal to attack, but in a moment it was obvious that this was no armed sally, but a headlong escape. Within the hour, a sullen Conan came before William and handed him the keys to what was now a smoldering ruin.

William became aware that Harold was looking at him in a sidelong way. He met the Saxon's gaze.

"Would you really have let them all burn in there?" Harold asked.

William shrugged. "It was up to Conan. If he hadn't have come out, it would have been on his conscience."

***

After extracting terms from Conan, and oaths of several different kinds, the army began to withdraw from Brittany, past gutted villages and ruined crops. At Rouen, William stood his force down, and released his nobles to return home with their remaining men. In truth, remarkably few had been lost. The contest had been somewhat one-sided.

William had just finished offering a prayer of thanks at the cathedral when he looked up and saw Lanfranc waiting nearby. The cleric fell in with him as he walked from the cool shade of the church into the blinding Spring light, the racket of a victorious army thronging the square before breaking into its constituent parts. The bishop seemed content to walk with him, but the way he wrung his hands lightly suggested there was something on his mind. William turned to his adviser. "Is there something I can do for you, Bishop Lanfranc?"

The bishop acknowledged the question with a gentle nod. "Actually, Lord, my thoughts are of what you might do for yourself, for Normandy."

Always this diagonal approach. "Yes?"

"The Saxon. Jarl Harold. You knighted him, I believe. Presented him with a horse. A mail coif."

"That's right. He fought well, was among the best of my knights, it seemed fitting to accord him with the rank he befits."

That slight huff from Lanfranc might have been a laugh. "Jarl Harold is, of course, in his own land of a rank equivalent to that of your own."

William frowned with momentary irritation. "He's not in his own land, he's in mine."

Lanfranc pursed his lips. "Yes, Lord. But in his own land, Harold might aspire to higher office yet."

What in the Saints' bladders was he getting at? Could the man never say anything directly? "You mean he might become King after my cousin's death?"

"Yes, Lord. Precisely so."

"And?"

Lanfranc breathed out through his nostrils and steepled his fingers. "As things stand, Jarl Harold is obliged to you, and you to him. Were he a Norman knight, or even Angevin, Breton, Frankish, you might consider giving him higher office. Lands. Titles. Perhaps even a contract of marriage with a sister or daughter."

"Well, yes. And I'd be pleased to do so. But he isn't Norman."

"No. And therefore, when he leaves these shores, as soon he surely shall, your obligations will mean little. Yet there are measures you might take to secure further... advantages. Should Jarl Harold's star rise even further. To bind him to your Grace. To make his ascendancy your ascendancy, Lord."

What in Heaven's name was Lanfranc getting at? Edward had offered him the throne of England, but that was some twelve years ago, and William had given little serious thought to taking up the throne in recent times, if he ever really had. It had chiefly been of use to him as a means of enticing supporters with vague offers of land and wealth at some point in the future. But Maine and now Brittany had provided plenty in the way of spoils and rewards for loyal service.

That said, if a man who was one of the likely candidates to succeed Edward, if this ludicrous 'Witenagemot' had any sway, was bound to him—in fealty, perhaps even in marriage—William might not become King of England, but perhaps, in time, England could become part of a Norman Duke's territory.... And in the nearer future, having the King of England as his man might provide a powerful alliance against a resurgence from France or Anjou. Geoffrey and Henri were dead these three years past, and for now their successors lacked their forebears' energy—King Philip a minor and Count Geoffrey the younger seemingly an idiot—but who could say what the future might make of them?

"Harold has not yet paid you homage," Lanfranc said

"I've no doubt he will." Why wouldn't he? They had fought together, and Harold had said numerous times that he was at William's service, and had been as good as his word. The band of Saxons had been a helpful addition to his force.

Lanfranc made that familiar knowing half-smile. "Even so, there may be ways of making the matter more binding."

"More binding than an oath?"

Lanfranc seemed to ignore the question. There were schemes and plans going on in that head of his. "You will rest in Bonneville-sur-Toques on the way back to Falaise, Lord?"

"Yes."

"The church at Bonneville is home to various Holy relics. If it were to be put to Jarl Harold that he swear on them, he could hardly refuse. And in swearing on Holy relics, could hardly go back on it. Without direst consequences."

William sighed. He supposed it wouldn't make any difference to Harold. "All right. Make the arrangements."

CHAPTER 20

Ælfgifa heard varying tales of the great victory as they broke camp at Rouen. That Conan had been forced to hand over the keys to his castle at lance point, for example. Sifting through the overexcited account from the runner who had been sent to request Lady Ælfgifa dispatch news as soon as possible, she had decided that this rather exaggerated account meant that the Bretons had been forced to surrender. She rather thought the vast amounts of oily black smoke she'd seen roiling in the distance back at Dinan castle had more to do with the victory than any heroic charge. Of course the runner had no useful intelligence for her, such as to whom she was to address this news. In a fit of pique she penned a note to Edith, pricking a sardonic message regarding her husband's prowess at the edges of the parchment. That done, she supposed she ought to seek out the Duke or Harold and acquire all the information the runner had not recalled.

"And now his lordship has knighted him!" The excitedly raised voice came from a small knot of younger soldiers. Ælfgifa paused, all too sure they meant Harold. *Knighted? Whatever for?* It was in poor taste if Harold had accepted— he was the equal of the Duke in status and had certainly cleared the debt inherent in William freeing him from

Ponthieu. "'Course his Lordship showered him with gifts and horses." Ælfgifa bit back a smile at the mental image *that* conjured up and listened harder. "...could work all my life and not afford armor such as that! Mind, this Saxon lord deserved it. No barbarian, whatever the rest are like. Saved his lordship's men from quicksand."

"Gor, that's a horrible death!" Another soldier shuddered.

"How did he do it? This Jarl? Once the quicksand has you that's it. All you can do is watch the poor buggers be sucked under..."

Ælfgifa turned away. The increased pain in her head made her unclench her jaw. Just when she'd thought Harold's star couldn't rise any higher. She recognized that part of her irritation was resentment but under that the whisper of disquiet undulated like a sleeping serpent. She had survived by being invisible most of the time. Harold being so completely noticeable made her uneasy.

Although, she considered, *how exactly Harold could hide his excellences I don't know. It will blow over and we will go back to England, leaving a few strange tales behind us.* But Ælfgifa could not shake that sense of foreboding.

***

The morning after William's war party arrived at Bonneville, Lanfranc announced to the nobles that there was to be a ceremony at the church. No-one questioned what it was for. There had been so many services of blessing and thanksgiving and celebration of this or that local saint on their travels that most submitted with a roll of the eyes and more or less polite silence, although there were a few raised eyebrows at the display of holy relics, usually stored in a stout chest beneath the altar and brought out only on the most important holidays. There was a sound behind him, an

225

urgent shuffle of feet and a hissing voice, and William looked over his shoulder with some alarm, but the disturbance had already passed. Latecomers, evidently.

Harold had initially responded in the same manner as the others, coming along unquestioningly, though his brows clouded slightly when William called him to the front, and glanced around at the assembled nobles looking on in expectant silence. De Tosny stepped forward and handed William a gleaming hauberk and a war-helm set with a jewel above the nasal. William had made a gift of some fine pieces of armor and other attire to Harold already—a coif, mail leg-guards, and of course, boots—but these items were the culmination. The completion of the set.

"Jarl Harold," William said, clearly and loud enough that his voice echoed around the stone pillars a little. "You have provided a great service to me. Brittany and Conan are no longer a threat to the peace and prosperity of Normandy. I thank you for your brave and resourceful actions. When we met you regretted your lack of war gear, thanks to your rude treatment at the hands of my vassal. I hope this hauberk and helm will compensate your loss."

Harold took the hauberk, weighing it appreciatively in his hands, and the helm, turning it over. There was still a twinge of uncertainty on his features, but it was lifting, as he began to sense that the ceremony was to honor him. As indeed it was, in the Norman fashion. Indeed, as he spoke, he almost seemed amused. "My Lord, I must thank you again for such uncommonly fine armor. And for the great honor you did me in numbering me amongst your knights. But tell me, noble cousin, why have we come here and what manner of objects are these?" Harold gestured at the relics laid out before them —dusty bones and withered organs.

"It is only right for one who has offered his service to be richly rewarded," William acknowledged. "These objects? Why, they are the holy relics of Bonneville. Here is the fingerbone of Saint Eustache, with which he blessed the people of Carcassonne after the Lord liberated them from the Basque paynims. And these are the vocal chords of Saint Bernadine of Tours." Or was it the other way round? Lanfranc had described them to him earlier, but after a while, one bit of a saint starts to look much like another. There was a fragment of the true cross, a piece of Saint James' shroud.... "Most Holy objects. What better can there be on which to swear an oath?"

Harold smiled indulgently. Did they have the same saints in England? No matter, it meant the same, surely. "Holy objects indeed." His brows creased slightly again. "I must ask you to repeat yourself, Duke William. My Frankish is not near so good as my sister's. I thought you said 'oath'?"

"I apologize, Sir," William bowed his head a little. "In any case, it would be proper to conduct the ceremony in Latin." He changed to the church language, trying not to trip over it too much. "An oath. Yes. Of course. You offered me your service, did you not? And have carried it out admirably. I simply require an oath of homage. A simple thing, but one that fixes my obligation to you, and your bonds to me. As we were here in Bonneville, it seems right to cement the pledge upon these relics, do you not think?"

"I see," Harold said, showing no reaction. Yet was there a hesitancy there? "I am unfamiliar with your customs yet, Lord. And while I am glad to have been of service to you, I would be uneasy swearing anything without knowing the proper form." His demeanor returned to something close to its usual affability, but there was still a slight stiffness to his shoulders. Was he trying to get out of it? Such a straightforward thing as an oath of homage, after everything they had been through? "Let not my ignorance of your customs mar a great success with clumsy words. What if I should give offense? Will you accept my heartfelt pledge of friendship and my fealty to you as Duke of Normandy in place of an oath? Truly I should hate to blunder before you or your fine companions."

It was hard to imagine Harold shaken by anything, let alone something so commonplace as an oath of homage. Yet perhaps William had not appreciated how differently this might be done in Saxon lands. Hard to imagine, but perhaps Harold—the man who had joked in the face of quicksand and a rising tide—needed reassurance. And yet he must understand the necessity of this? "You need not fear giving offense, Jarl Harold," William said, as comfortingly as he could. "Only a refusal to acknowledge the bond between lord and vassal could do that," he smiled, "and I am sure we need not have any concerns on that score. We have fought side by side on the field of battle. You have aided my enterprise, I have freed you from captivity—there can be no greater proof of our mutual regard. It only requires this formal step. I understand your uncertainty. A simple statement will suffice, to pledge on your faith that you will be faithful to your lord, never cause him harm and will observe your homage in good faith and without deceit. Do you promise so to do?"

The explanation seemed to have helped, as Harold's discomfort melted away. "Then Lord William, excuse my clumsiness. I will take it from the Saxon form if you do not object?"

Before William could reply, Harold had knelt before the altar, and placed his hands upon it by the relics. "I offer my oath upon my honor as a Jarl and custodian of England," he said, "upon the names of Cnut the great and Edmund

Ironside my forefathers, from whose teachings and principles I sprang as surely as from their blood, that I, Harold Godwinson offer fealty to the Duke of Normandy on this day, in the presence of these... holy relics. I shall suffer no insult against Normandy. His enemies shall be my enemies. His good shall be my good and I shall uphold it on this sacred soil until my last breath."

Harold turned back to William. "Do you keep faith with me, my lord, and I shall keep faith with you."

William gestured Harold to stand. It was not the precise form of words he would have chosen, but it seemed to fit just as well as the conventional form. He relaxed a little. "Perhaps our lands are not so different, when all is said and done. Gladly I accept your oath, Jarl Harold, and swear that for all the years you are my vassal I shall do no injury to your body nor your possessions, justice or honor. That which you should do easily, I vow not to make difficult, and that which you should do, I shall not prevent, while you are faithful to me."

"I am glad we should be bound in such a manner, Lord. Perhaps now we have satisfied custom and the priesthood we might drink to the fortitude of our vows like men?" Harold looked to William, perhaps for a signal that the ceremony was at an end, but then seemed to look past him and muttered something in Anglish. "Forgive me," the Saxon said, switching back to Frankish, "but I cannot help noticing how that sour-faced fellow scowls so. Does he not share our joy?"

William looked over his shoulder. The figure Harold had indicated was the Bishop of Bec, standing with his arms folded. William usually had trouble telling what the cleric was thinking, and now was no exception, though his face did not bear the beatific smile he usually wore when William had followed his advice. "Bishop Lanfranc? I don't believe he has ever displayed any joy, and don't expect him to start now. Truly, he could argue night was day and have you rising with the moon and retiring with the sun before you knew what you were about, but joy is beyond his wit." Saints, but it was dry in this church. The idea of a drink was suddenly appealing. He exhaled slowly, letting out a tension in his chest that he did not realize had built. "I will submit to Saxon custom in this matter of a drink to our vow. Come, I find churches less oppressive places than I used to, but will gladly exchange this one for a tavern and put up with a flea in my ear from Matilda for it."

"A bishop, eh?" Harold was by now back to his warm and friendly self. "Well I won't waste good ale on him by inviting him along then. The clergy are all very well in their place but that place is rarely beside a barrel of good ale or a fine vintage. No doubt your excellent Lady will understand on this occasion." He leaned forward, adding "should she ever come to hear of it," with a wicked grin.

"Hm." Some chance of that. "My Lady would get to hear of it if a bee landed on the wrong flower half a league outside Caen, but some things are worth the trouble."

They approached the stony faced figure of Lanfranc, who raised a finger and murmured, "Lord, might I—"

"Later, Bishop Bec," William said as he brushed past, and he and Harold strode out into the light to find a place to drink, discussing the favored formation of cavalry on difficult terrain.

***

Ælfgifa had wearied of riding. Wearied, even, of writing missives and sitting quietly behind curtains, in meetings of strategy. She'd looked forward to a proper rest at the small town they had reached—Bonneville-sur-Toques. From here

230

she supposed, she and Harold, and her brother's men would head for the coast and return to England. Ælfgifa felt flat, somehow, and still that sense of unease lingered.

"Lady Ælfgifa," cried a loud, friendly voice. She whirled and found herself facing Helisande's husband, Gallet.

"Sir Gallet," she said, dropping him a small curtsy. "I am surprised to see you linger here when you are no doubt eager to return to your wife. I was sorry not to have seen her. Will you pass on my best wishes for her health and happiness, and tell her Falaise was not the same without her?"

Gallet's grin broadened. It was impossible not to like this loud, blunt, no-nonsense man. "That I will, Lady, with pleasure. I shall be going there soon. Just want to see the oath taking."

"Oath taking?" Ælfgifa replied in confusion.

"Yes, Lady. Only a select group, the church being small. I'm sure you'd like to see your brother swear on the relics though. Come, I'll take you."

"My thanks," Ælfgifa said distantly, wondering what in the world Gallet could be talking about. He escorted her into the back of the tiny church and then muttered an apology about needing to stand with his lord. Ælfgifa gave him a vague smile of thanks, already focused on the strange tableau before her. Several indeterminate objects had been laid on the stone altar. Before them stood William and her brother. In that moment Harold reminded her sharply of Wulfnoth when her younger brother had tried to wriggle out of punishment as a small boy. To anyone else, doubtless Harold was presenting the same pleasant and affable facade as ever. Ælfgifa knew him better. Harold was in a tight spot and scrabbling to get out of it.

Well, this ought to be interesting, she thought. Then she registered William's words and went cold. William was asking her brother to swear the oath of a vassal. If she had not known Norman custom so well she would have thought it a shocking insult. As it was, she could see all perspectives at once. William had rescued Harold from Ponthieu. Had knighted him. In William's eyes—probably in the eyes of all the Normans—that made him Harold's liege lord. But Harold was a Saxon. The oath taking of their people was different and a Saxon Lord never knelt to give an oath to another. In a flash of insight she knew that the objects on the altar must be holy relics. William... no someone else. Lanfranc perhaps? Anyway the intention was to make Harold swear fealty and perhaps homage to a Norman lord on Norman holy relics.

All of this was wrong!

Harold was not at liberty to swear any such thing. Any oath he made must be upheld by his people. And Harold was in the service of King Edward. Then there was the small matter of swearing on the bones of a person who was not acknowledged a saint in England. The Duke would take this very seriously but... To Ælfgifa's horror, she saw that little quirk of the mouth that meant Harold regarded the happenings as a fine jape. She must have made a little sound, desperately wanting to help Harold out of his predicament whilst biting down on the words that wanted to escape. A hand seized her upper arm and a voice hissed slowly in her ear, "If you interfere in this now, God shall curse you worse."

Ælfgifa glared up into Bishop Lanfranc's face, so icily calm on the surface but the anger in his eyes was unmistakable. "Tell me that in your scarce passable Latin and I may half-believe you! Otherwise trouble me not, you ignorant fool." She tried to wrench her arm free from his grasp but he was surprisingly strong. No one saw them scuffle in the dark at the rear of the church. Lanfranc, almost nonchalantly, raised his other hand and struck her across the mouth. Ælfgifa tasted blood and the room erupted in white hot flames of rage. She stamped on his foot hard. With a muffled yelp he let her go. Ælfgifa stumbled back a step and then whirled on him again. "By the hand with which you struck my thrice cursed face, be bound by the affliction visited on me!" She snarled, too angry to think clearly about what she was saying. Lanfranc paled, the tightly controlled anger melting into genuine fear, but Ælfgifa went on. "There will not be a god in heaven but you will die roaring. I swear it!"

She lurched away from him, determined to stop this charade even if she had to pretend a fit of the vapors but it was too late. William had maneuvered Harold into a corner and from his tone was becoming impatient with Harold's hesitation. Later she would wonder why she could not think of anything that would stop this. Later she would look back on her desperate scuffle with Lanfranc and wonder at her fury and her ill-considered words—cursing a bishop? But *then*, there was nothing but the silent, roaring disquiet and Harold's words of fealty hanging on the still air.

"I offer my oath upon my honor as a Jarl and custodian of England, upon the names of Cnut the great and Edmund Ironside, my forefathers, from whose teachings and principles I sprang, as surely as from their blood, that I, Harold Godwinson offer fealty to the Duke of Normandy on this day, in the presence of these... holy relics. I shall suffer no insult against Normandy. His enemies shall be my enemies. His good shall be my good and I shall uphold it on this sacred soil until my last breath. Do you keep faith with me, my lord, and I shall keep faith with you."

Ælfgifa raised her head and stared at Harold in disbelief. Where had that... that *horse shit* come from? And all that talk of swearing after the Saxon fashion? That was no oath-taking she recognized. She looked from William to Harold and back again. She saw the camaraderie betwixt them. Saw William's relief and triumph and Harold's partially concealed smugness and her stomach twisted sideways. She wondered if Harold even knew what he had done.

***

Gallet led the two nobles, with various other Norman seigneurs and knights, great and petty, and the shaggy lurcher that barely left his side, quickly through the streets. He made directly to a nearby house that looked little different to the others on the outside, apart from the game of skittles taking place in the alley beside it, but within was full of drinking men, casks of wine and the stench of God only knew what. To Harold's mild disappointment, they didn't have any ale, and laughed when mead was suggested, but he happily accepted a flask of cider. William chose wine, which he noted with a scowl was probably from Burgundy, but drank it happily enough. Toasts were made extravagantly in various languages and styles, Norman and Saxon, and before long William felt a pleasant glow spreading through him.

"We should bind our great houses more closely together," he said to Harold. "In equal love," he added, remembering a phrase Lanfranc had used during the meeting with Herbert of Maine. Poor, dead Herbert. Ah, well. "Marriage!" he declared.

"I regret to inform your Grace that I am already spoken for twice over," Harold replied with a smirk, upon which Gallet started to laugh so hard he began to choke on his wine.

William ignored the knight. "That Danish paynim wedding of yours? That doesn't count. No, you shall have my daughter, Adeliza. She's a charming girl, quite lovely, kind, accomplished. And she'll be of age in just six or seven years."

"Your Grace honors me too greatly," Harold said levelly. "And should you not ask your daughter first?"

That had William laughing himself, too hard to speak for a good long time. "Ask her!" he wheezed. "I've seen what happens when you give a girl the choice. No, my Adeliza will do as she's told. What say you?"

"Even so, in great, and increasing respect to your Grace, is it not right that a prospective husband at least meet the girl before agreeing? It is custom in England..."

"England! We're not in England," William replied, recovering himself a little. "All right. Plenty of time to sort that out anyway. But what about on your side? Have you any sons or daughters that..." A thought struck him like a beam of sunshine. "Gifa! We'll find someone for Gifa! All those years with her own people and still not married. It won't do."

"Ah... I had not thought..." Harold looked by turns bewildered, horrified and amused.

"We can find a Norman noble for her," said William, warming to the subject. There would be a decent dowry from Harold, no doubt, and William could throw in that villa by the Orne. Her husband would get used to looking at her, and conversation would prove diverting in any case. Anyway, she would spend plenty of time at Falaise advising, reflecting the truth back to William in ways he could not see at first glance. "What about de Tosny, he's not betrothed yet is he? Or the youngest de Ryes? Gallet?"

William spent the next while arguing with Gallet about which of the magnates or their sons were eligible. He swore he knew all this, but it seemed hard to recall and tell them all apart for some reason. And then he had to lie on the floor where he had a lengthy discussion with Gallet's lurcher, whose name he had forgotten and therefore addressed as 'Monsieur Chien'. When he turned back to Harold, the Saxon was slumped on the table, snoring, and could not be woken. Ah well, whatever it was they were talking about, he could deal with it in the morning.

CHAPTER 21

Ælfgifa looked up from the makeshift desk, carefully corked the ink she had prepared and set down the goose feather quill. Then she pushed herself abruptly to her feet, skirts swishing angrily about her ankles as she paced the narrow confines of the tent.

"Gifa..." Harold's voice trailed off. He looked as though he was only just resisting holding his head. Good. She hoped it was pounding. What had he been thinking? First the fiasco of the oath taking and then drinking the ale house dry... well, she might have understood that. But to make promises whilst in his cups?

"Do not say a word, brother," Ælfgifa said in a voice that promised retribution. How could he have acted so? Under the fury was a thick layer of humiliation. Just which lordling would William offer her to? After having cowed him into obedience under threat of violence, before silencing him with a fat purse and lands... Who had he selected to bribe into marrying the deformed, unfeminine and outspoken Saxon princess?

"We must talk about it, Gifa. We cannot anticipate a proposal of this nature unprepared," Harold said sounding infuriatingly reasonable. Ælfgifa did not want to talk about it. She wanted to scream about it. She wanted to punctuate those screams by throwing large, heavy objects at Harold *and* William. Then she wanted to explain to them that she was not, in fact, for sale at any price. It would be a long lecture.

"Who?" she finally managed to choke out past her rage.

"Er, Ralph somebody? De Vasey? No that cannot be right." Harold fumbled, well aware that he had crossed the line.

"It will not be Ralph de Wacey. He is past sixty and deathly ill. There are half a dozen other Ralphs. Three of them are my junior by more than ten years. One of the others is of very uncertain loyalties, one prefers the companionship of his fellow men in bed which is well and good but not for me, nor I for him, I imagine. The remaining Ralph would as soon marry a viper as take me to wife. He very nearly told me so when I stitched up his leg."

"The mangy cur!" Harold exclaimed.

"For God's sake, Harold, you became so drunk that you made a rash promise that I would marry one of William's men! A Norman! Do not trouble your indignation on my behalf, I pray you." She stopped pacing and rubbed her temples. "Did you sign anything? Make any definite bargain?"

"No!" Harold exclaimed. "I obey the law, Gifa. You know this. Give me credit for some sense."

"The way you have acted the past few days, you deserve none. Besides the Dane-law does not hold here," Ælfgifa said. "Very well. I have no wish to marry. I will not marry, no matter what advantage it gains you. Do not look like that, Brother, even inebriated it will have passed through your mind, I have no doubt. We will wait and see if William renews that offer. If he does, I will answer and you will not interfere, understood?"

"Yes, sister," Harold said, eyes tightening with pain at his pounding head.

"And Harold? I will make this very clear now. I am going home to England."

"Very well, Gifa, as you say," Harold grumbled, waving her words off. "Have you anything for this vile headache, now?"

Ælfgifa raised an eyebrow. "I'm sorry, brother. I never learned how to treat the effects of too much wine. Do not worry. It will work itself out in a day or so." Her tone was sweet and deadly. With a low groan of pain, Harold flung aside the tent flap so he could lurch out and empty the contents of his stomach on the ground.

Ælfgifa's rage collapsed into irritation. No doubt even the mortification would fade soon enough. William could not be insensible to her preferences. He had never treated her as if she were any other woman. She doubted he recalled that she was a woman at all much of the time. He would forget and in a day or so, she and Harold would be on a ship bound for England. With these thoughts she comforted herself and tried to appease the unyielding knot of foreboding in her gut.

***

In the morning, of course, there was more to attend to, and by the time William had shaken off the worst of the thick feeling in his head, the sour taste in his mouth and remembered the business of a husband for Gifa, neither she nor Harold were close by. William resolved to ask Matilda for suggestions when they returned to Falaise.

For now, the important business had already been sealed, thanks to Lanfranc's timely suggestion. William had secured an oath of homage from Harold, on holy relics, no less, and promises of marriages to tie their houses together. This, with his promise from Edward all those years before, gave him cause for gladness. Perhaps he would be King, or have the new King accept him as overlord. More likely he would receive generous grants of land, and in time his sons or grandsons would be kings of England as well as dukes of Normandy. It was a legacy he could finally be proud of. Securing the borders of Normandy was vital, and finally fixing the Norman lordship of Maine was an important step, but it was no more than the completion of his father's and grandfather's work. It was wonderful to be able to say that— not so long ago, even holding onto his father's possessions seemed to be more than he could hope for. But now fortune had dropped a greater opportunity in his way.

After the return to Falaise there was more urgent work to do, keeping him from discussing the matter any further with Harold. The abbeys at Caen were nearing completion and it seemed scores of decisions had to be made there and then, lest some catastrophe befall the whole Duchy. William left Lanfranc to consider the matter of England and what might happen when Edward died.

Then there was some trouble with the boy Robert, who, it was claimed, had his tutors in torment and was terrorizing the other nobles' sons. Even, it seemed, his brothers, Richard and Young William, and that would not do. William had tried to grab a moment to speak with his eldest boy, but it was not easy to find much time. His mother did not help, truth be told—Matilda seemed blind to Robert's moods and sometimes violent temper, and resisted all efforts to discipline him. He hoped there would be time enough to see to his family when things calmed down after the war in Brittany.

Finally, there was a moment when he and Matilda found themselves alone in their private chambers. He considered raising Robert's troubles, but the Saxons would be leaving shortly, and he wanted her advice on the marriages. "So, Lady," he said, loosening his boots in the hope of gaining some relief from the blisters he had gained in the field and which had not yet subsided. "I wished to ask you about this business of a husband for Ælfgifa."

"A husband for Gifa?" Matilda smiled, then laughed. "Whyever would you suggest such a thing?"

He frowned. "Well. To keep her here. And for her own good."

Matilda laughed again. "Oh, my Lord," she said, "Gifa doesn't want a husband, and I doubt we'd find one who would be good for her! Just finding a man with a mind halfway the equal of hers might take us until Domesday."

William's chest tightened. He had meant to do a good thing for a friend, and here was his own wife, laughing at him! "He doesn't have to be a match for her mind," he muttered. "And what does it matter whether she wants a husband or not? You didn't want one, as I recall."

A look of something like anguish crossed Matilda's face for the briefest moment. Oh Lord, the way he'd behaved.... He stammered a reluctant apology.

She sat next to him and laid a hand on his arm. "Marriage suits many people, perhaps most. Even you, my Lord. But not everyone. Do not force this on Gifa, I pray you. If she wants to go home to be with her family, why not let her?"

Because she is valuable! Because she is as valuable to Harold as she is to me. William had a sinking sensation— that with Ælfgifa at his side, Harold would be powerful indeed, especially when it came to the negotiations that would inevitably follow Edward's death.

Then there was the unshakeable feeling that once Ælfgifa had left, he would not see her again in Normandy. There would be no more meetings in the herb garden. No more conversations that were like an unsolvable puzzle at the start and by the end felt like surveying the whole world as a bird could. No more of her sharp tongue, dancing wit, a challenge to his authority that always remained just on the right side of a slap to the face.

He tried again. "Do you not think she would value the companionship of a husband? And the occupation of the mind that would come from an estate? It strikes me that she is hard to befriend but as firm as Caen stone when friendship has been struck. The right man.... Devil take it, woman, she ought to be happy, shouldn't she? Once in a while?"

"Gifa's happiness is not in your gift, husband," Matilda said, softly. "You will make up your own mind on this, as in all things, but this is my advice. Do not try."

She was right. Of course she was right. The trouble was, William thought, so was he. He tightened his boots again and went to find Harold.

***

Ælfgifa spied her brother and the Duke oblivious in earnest conversation as she headed towards the herb garden for what would be the last time. Despite her fiery assertions to Harold, she felt a plummeting in her gut. Here, isolated in Normandy, there was no Danelaw to save her if Harold chose to make an exception and sell her... She sank on to the stone bench feeling sick. The small knife she used to gather herbs, rattled in the trug as she dropped it at her feet. In annoyance she tried to shake herself out of her fears. Yes, Harold was ambitious. Yes, no doubt she would be an advantage to him here—if she were housed at Falaise at least—especially if the

Duke and her brother kept up close relations. But Harold would never force her into marriage. He was not like Sweyn. No, but he had not hesitated to use her in other ways... so was 'never' over-reaching her understanding of Harold's regard? *I will walk to the coast and swim to England before I allow such a thing,* Ælfgifa thought defiantly. And yet how powerless was she here? How toothless was her recourse for justice if she were entrapped so?

She pressed the palms of her hands against the cold stone of the bench and by degrees grew calmer. There was no trap if she did not allow it. She might overturn all Harold's plans in a moment by confessing to William of all the intelligence she had gathered here on her brother's behalf. Her fate then would surely be torture and death. Could she prefer that to being forever a prisoner? Could she act so selfishly just to assert her own will, her own right to direct her own path?

Do you keep faith with me, and I shall keep faith with you...

And then Harold passed the entrance to the garden without seeing her and later she saw William heading towards the great hall. Neither sought to speak with her privately. There was no surprise announcement at board and on the following day they rode to the coast and set sail for England. As Normandy fell into sightless distance behind her, Ælfgifa slowly began to relax, although she would not feel truly easy until she was once more at Wintancaestre.

It occurred to her clearly for the first time, just how great her fear was. Not of pain or death. Not ridicule or cruel words nor even of being an outcast of sorts. No, her fear was that she would be removed from events, powerless, voiceless, helpless and shut away, to live out a dreary existence of low interest, day on endless day until she wore out and died. So great was this fear that she had never allowed herself to confront it before. Now it returned to her often and never failed to start a cold shuddering within her. *Never*, she told herself. *Such a thing will never come to pass. I vow it. Nothing shall ever induce me to such silence of voice and self.*

CHAPTER 22

Ælfgifa looked up from her careful stitches at the sound of raised voices. It sounded like her brother and Edith but that couldn't be right. She had never heard them argue. Disagree perhaps, and regularly, but never to the point of presenting anything but a united front. She sat up straighter in the recessed window seat and let her embroidery fall to her lap. Since she had returned with Harold from Normandy a year ago, she had become adept at carving out small chunks of her day where she could not be found by clamoring nieces wanting their hair braided or grubby nephews with pockets full of frog spawn or even the quieter older children who had an interest in learning, demanding she correct their work. As much as Ælfgifa loved the house at Wintancaestre and even secretly enjoyed being *wyrm-fanthu* to so many children, there were times when all she wanted were her own thoughts. Sometimes—today for instance—she wanted no more than quiet and work she could do with her eyes shut if need be. She found embroidery soothing now compared to the harder labors of growing, gathering and preparing, and the myriad of other tasks. It was pleasant to let her mind drift when it was so often occupied with tactics, strategy, judgments and reparations—all those things needed to help run such a huge estate. She had thought perhaps that she was the only one feeling the strain, the impending sense of purpose as Harold careered like autumn wind around England, gathering more and more support.

Yet she could very nearly make out what Edith was shouting. Edith never shouted. She never had to. Harold sounded peeved and impatient when he replied. Not like her brother at all. Feeling hot and uncomfortable at eavesdropping on what was possibly a marital dispute, Ælfgifa rose and started towards the open gallery door, intending to shut it. She did not get the chance. Edith swept into the room and demanded, "For God's sake, Gifa, tell your brother what a fool he is being!"—for all the world as if Ælfgifa had been involved in the quarrel from the start.

Harold had followed his wife in and now leant his tall frame against the closed door. His mouth was set in a grim line, all usual traces of mirth absent.

"I find myself for once having to own that I do not understand," Ælfgifa said dryly.

"Tostig has finally gone too far with his tax reforms. His people are in revolt and if he does not quell the rebellion soon, he will lose his Jarldom," Edith said, still battling her anger.

"I'll admit that news is not a great surprise to me but I hope that Tostig is not the brother you wish me to speak sense to. I have no influence there!" Ælfgifa cast a glance at Harold. *What am I missing here?*

"My lord and husband has received a plea for aid from your greedy, useless brother." Edith said, mouth compressing into a white line.

"And you said no, did you not, Harold?" Ælfgifa glanced at her brother again.

"Of course I did. I am not such a fool as that!" Harold snapped.

"So what then?" Ælfgifa asked in puzzlement.

Edith gave a harsh little laugh. "It were not enough that Tostig should fail in his charge so utterly as to have his brother refuse him aid. No, my husband, the most influential man in England, has allied himself with the rebels and intends to fight with them. Against their liege lord. His own brother."

And like that the pieces snapped together for Ælfgifa. She fixed Harold with a scowl. "And what exactly do you intend to do with Tostig once you win, brother?" she asked, although she thought she already knew.

Harold gave her a faint smile. "You are both of you too wise not to have guessed it. I will have Tostig exiled. It will not be hard. He is a brute who has spent his time terrorizing his folk rather than courting their good opinion."

"Harold, pay me the great compliment of not attempting to pass off your motivations as altruistic," Ælfgifa said caustically. "I doubt not that you do feel the plight of the downtrodden. I am equally certain you feel it a good deal more readily since Tostig will not throw his support behind you and has his eye on a prize you crave for yourself. He even has a supporter or two amongst the Witenagemot, does he not?"

Harold scowled, mouth twisting in dissatisfaction. Ælfgifa nodded. "I suppose it does remove an obstacle. But Harold, *exiling* Tostig? I doubt not that the rebels will win with you supporting them and most likely with little cost. Why not reason with Tostig? Outright threaten him, if necessary. He will be so relieved to keep his lands... would it not be better to have him owe you a favor, however grudging? When the time comes, demand that he throw his support behind you then. It would only strengthen your claim to the throne. You can negotiate such terms as would mean he had to treat with his people fairly and they will remember you for coming to their aid."

"Listen to her, Husband," Edith chimed in.

"No. Not this time. He is too much of a threat. You have both always spoken sense but this time you cannot see it is best the threat is removed. Perhaps as women you have some tenderness of heart for family." Harold was looking away so he did not see the incredulous look that passed between Edith and his sister.

"My tenderness of heart tells me that you had best hope Tostig dies in this fight then, brother, or be willing to kill him yourself," Ælfgifa said bluntly. "Do you let him live and he will run straight to Hardrada, who also looks to England's throne with a covetous eye. That is an alliance you can ill afford."

"Gifa, I am not going to kill our brother," said Harold sounding exasperated. "You have the blood of a serpent to suggest it."

"A tender heart but cold blood to fill it? You cannot have it both ways, brother. You know we speak sense or you would not be so annoyed!"

"She speaks truly–" Edith began.

"Enough!" Harold raised a hand as if to push through a contentious mob, not fend off the words of his sister and his wife. "Enough, you have both said your piece."

"And what then, Harold?" Ælfgifa said.

"Why then, Gifa, I will do as I think best!" Harold wrenched the door open and slammed it behind him.

Ælfgifa looked at Edith uncertainly. "I could follow him? He may see reason yet?"

"Nay, sister," Edith said wearily. "We have excited his stubbornness. He will do nothing we ask now. Let us hope he thinks better of this foolish scheme."

Ælfgifa nodded but privately she thought it unlikely. Ever since Brittany, perhaps even before that, Harold had started to believe he was invulnerable. That he could not fail. He made no distinction between what did happen and what could, not any more. She had tried to reason with him on the voyage back from Normandy a year ago. Had tried to make him see how the Normans would have taken his actions—allowing William to knight him, acting the part of a vassal, worse—swearing a vassal's oath on their holy relics.

Harold's response had been deeply sarcastic. She could recall it word for word. "Sister, did you not listen to the words I spoke? I swore on holy relics that are not holy—those saints are not saints in our church! I made a vow based on the blood and principles of two men who are not my forebears. And I swore to uphold my oath on the sacred soil of Normandy only. That only leaves me with the rest of the world to do as I please in. In short I gave a pretty speech, that sounded well and promised nothing other than that I should consider the Duke my friend as long as he considered me his, and that I should do as I saw fit otherwise." He'd snorted in derision.

Frustrated and beyond exhausted, strained almost to snapping point by the weeks of riding and the constant mental drain of battle plans and logistics and tactics and recording the whole festering mess in Latin and Frankish, not to mention sending missives hither, thither and yon at the snap of Harold's or William's fingers.... After all that, Ælfgifa had flared up. "The duke will not see it so, brother. The duke is no petty lordling. He has scraped his land and his wealth back from scavengers and wolves with tooth and nail. When he accepts an oath from a vassal—anyone he considers a vassal—he expects it will be kept." She'd drawn a shuddering breath. "William has spent his entire life fighting for what he considers his. Do not think he will gladly surrender a dearly desired prize or release you from what he believes to be a binding oath simply because you point out that your clever wording promised nothing. In William's mind you have promised everything. He saw you as you wished him to. As I prepared him to. But he is no fool, for all that he takes a linear path and has not your quicksilver tongue and charm."

"What would you have me do, Gifa? I was tricked!" Finally Harold had shown a flash of temper.

"I would have you remember what you have done. Of course it was a trick. His pet bishop saw to that. But before you don a crown, if the Witenagemot favor you, recall that William—your *friend*—will act against treachery, real or perceived. You cannot do anything in haste. You—"

"God save me, Gifa, I never thought to hear you carp on like a fish wife. I have half a mind that you like this Norman Duke. Perhaps more than like. Considering what you turned down—"

"Have a care, brother." Ælfgifa had felt that every word was a blade. That she might slice Harold to ribbons. "You tread on worse than quicksand when you open that topic to me."

Harold had had the good grace to look a little ashamed. "Still, Gifa, it raises questions."

"I do like him. God help me for I have been his friend but half the time and spied on him the rest, I could not help liking him. But I never, not for one moment, underestimated him." She had rubbed a hand over her face. "It is done now, I suppose. You will have time to think of the best light to present things in, should they come to fruition."

Harold had smiled at her broadly then and wrapped an arm about her shoulders. "If? Some faith, little sister! *If* indeed!" She had not had the heart to berate him again. "You know," Harold had gone on, "I liked the man too. He was grim. He was abrupt and he had a god-awful temper at times. But there is something admirable in that tenacity. That will for success."

Looking back now, Ælfgifa sincerely hoped Harold would not have cause to regret those words.

CHAPTER 23

It fell out as Ælfgifa had predicted. Harold and the rebels won, and Tostig was ousted from his Jarldom and sent into exile. There were already whispers that he had presented himself to Harald Hardrada of Norway. It sat ill with her. She still felt Harold had made the wrong choice, although she was willing to admit giving Northumbria to Morcar to rule was a bold and inspired move on her brother's part. Morcar was the brother of both Harold's second wife, Aldythe, and of Edwin, the Jarl of Mercia. In one stroke Harold had garnered the full support of the North, whilst at the same time stamping out the possibility of a civil war that would weaken England. Ælfgifa supposed that even King Edward, sick and distant as he was, must surely approve of Harold's ploy.

Of course that did not mean she had to put up with his insufferable smugness over the matter. Harold was underestimating Tostig and failing to keep nearly close enough a watch on Hardrada. She had no desire to travel to Norway, but she wondered now why Harold had been so set on placing her in Normandy. Did he have other spies already in Norway? Idle speculation. The fact remained that Tostig combined with Hardrada was a dangerous alliance. Harold should have arranged an accident to befall Tostig before he ever left England's shores. Ælfgifa paused in her thoughts, drawn up in horror at her coldness, her callous willingness to kill a man if he was a political danger. It did not matter that Tostig was very nearly as vile as Sweyn had been. He was still her brother. Was she so willing to turn kinslayer herself? *Perhaps I should be nīthing,* she thought, troubled that she was unable to summon up any guilt for her musings.

There had been little snow over midwinter. Instead the days had dawned iron-skied, the ground sheened with hard and bitter frost. It almost looked pretty—until you set your boot upon the path and the cold ate into your bones. Shivering in the morning light, Ælfgifa was unwilling to go back inside. That restlessness, the sense of foreboding, hung over her again without any cause and she could not settle to needlework or making tinctures today. So she was not surprised when a voice called from behind her. She felt as though she had been expecting it. Was almost relieved it had finally happened.

"Lady Ælfgifa?" It was a novice from Wilton Abbey. For a moment Ælfgifa was catapulted back in time to the herb garden at Falaise, William standing behind her, a grim and solid presence, while she read the tiny scroll of parchment that had arrived from La Trineté. Then she was back to here, now, Wintanceastre. Foreboding gripped her again, chilling her more greatly than the frozen ground. Her fingers closed numbly around the tiny scroll the novice offered her, and she knew it contained bad news. *Death?*

***

Ealdgyth didn't say a word when she saw Ælfgifa. Merely took her sister by the hands and drew her into an embrace, more frank and more unguarded than any Ealdgyth had offered since Ælfgifa was a child. Ælfgifa twined her arms around the Queen, feeling her sister shaking against her. Harold might as well have been a block of wood for all the attention Ealdgyth paid him. Not, Ælfgifa suspected, that Harold minded at all. The king was dying. A slight from the soon to be widowed Queen would not trouble him at all.

"How is His Majesty?" Ælfgifa said softly.

Ealdgyth pulled away, pale and dry eyed. She took Ælfgifa's hand. "Come."

Ælfgifa had naturally never been in the King's chamber before. It was comfortable and well-appointed but could hardly be described as decadent. A good fire burned in the hearth and there were beeswax candles to light the room. A priest had been sitting with the King, and two holy sisters from the convent at Westminster quietly moved about the room, taking away uneaten food, changing linens, strewing herbs meant to ease breathing on heated braziers. Edward was unrecognizable. A long, skeletal figure who barely made a hump under the finely woven blankets and furs. His skin was yellowed on his shrunken flesh. The nail beds of his fingers were faintly blue. Most of his flowing white hair had fallen out leaving a few limp hanks. Ælfgifa listened to Edward's stertorous breathing and shook her head slightly. The king looked dead already. She met Ealdgyth's gaze. *I cannot heal this. This is age. This is God's will. I have no cure for this.*

Ealdgyth nodded, once. A small, grateful smile on her lips. Ælfgifa thought that her sister had not really hoped for any improvement or help.

"Has His Majesty been like this long?" Ælfgifa said, determined that if she could not help she would at least try to ease Edward's passing. She had never liked the man but he was not a monster. She would rest easier if she did what she could.

"Since before midwinter." Ealdgyth swallowed.

"I can give him a draught to put heart in him and ease his last hours. Shall I prepare one?"

Ealdgyth nodded. "Do it."

"Very well. You must sit and talk to him, sister. He can hear you yet, I believe." The last kindness—letting someone know they were not alone as death drew them inexorably from this world into whatever waited beyond.

Ælfgifa had been so focused on the scene in front of her that she had not registered Harold's presence until she almost walked into him. She shot him a cross look and moved past him to the door, intent on getting what she needed from the still room. To her annoyance Harold walked with her.

"Is this the end, Gifa?" Harold said in a low voice. "Edward will not recover?" There was a vein of suppressed excitement in his tone.

Ælfgifa raised an eyebrow at her brother. "Have you nowhere else you need to be just now? As I recall you make a poor still room assistant."

"Gifa..."

"He will not live. But if I can get enough of this draught into him he may rouse a little. Temporarily. Enough to bid his wife farewell. He–" Ælfgifa stopped abruptly at Harold's sudden grip on her arm. There was something unpleasant and unnamable in his eyes.

"Do it. Make him drink it. Rouse him!" Harold said. Before Ælfgifa could voice her disgust at Harold's tasteless comments, he was gone, leaving her to fetch and prepare alone.

***

They fed Edward with a rag soaked in the tonic Ælfgifa had made, just as she remembered doing for Wulfnoth so many years ago. True to her prediction, Edward's color improved and he stirred feebly. Ælfgifa heard one of the nuns exclaim that it was a miracle and couldn't bring herself to explain that this was the beginning of the end. The king's breaths were numbered. She watched as Ealdgyth sat by his side, speaking softly to him. He seemed to answer after a fashion, enough that Ælfgifa saw a strange tenderness pass over her sister's face. Then the king grew agitated, one hand clutching at his chest the other reaching into the room. His speech was indistinct and slurred. Ælfgifa knew his heart was working harder than ever, and she shooed the nuns and priest out of the room.

"I think he wants... Harold?" Ealdgyth murmured in bewilderment.

I expect he does, Ælfgifa thought, already stepping aside so her brother could rush forward. Harold did not see the venomous glare Ealdgyth shot him for pushing her aside. Ælfgifa shut out Harold's words. They would be the usual mixture of truth and lies and charm they always were. But the memory she could not shake ever after was how Edward struggled to speak whilst Harold knelt at his head. How Edward's gaze roved the chamber until it landed not on Harold. Not on his wife. Not on some unseen figure his dying mind conjured. But on *her.* She knew he had seen her. If felt as if he had seen her clearly for the first time in his life, despite all her years at court. Edward's eyes sharpened in clarity, his mouth twisted in something between disgust and revulsion, and for a moment his voice came more strongly.

"Command... obey me. You. I place them with... you. Commend my dear wife and my kingdom, to your protection. The protection *only you...*" Edward made a last effort, his gaze demanding that Ælfgifa understand his meaning, "can give."

Me? He's asking me to care for the country and the Queen? Surely he is raving? But he was not. She knew that. Utterly bewildered, she watched as Edward turned his head to Harold and said clearly. "God's will be done." And then he died.

***

If the death of an ordinary person brings silence, a creeping hush as if they were only sleeping and might be disturbed, the death of a king brings an uproar. There was rushing and noise and exclamations. Somewhere there was weeping. Ælfgifa stood apart from this storm, still caught and held by Edward's last words. *The protection only you can give.* What had he meant? Her influence with Harold and other powerful notables? Her ability to play the games of court so effortlessly? The seed of ruthlessness that burst into bloom when she was pushed to make a choice? Had Edward actually seen her, seen what she was capable of all these years? Or had his mind conjured some other likeness or visage, which had overlaid her own, in his last moments? Whoever he had seen, his dying words, his last order as her king, was to do all in her power to protect England.

There were many hands to do what was necessary for the body of the king. Ælfgifa was not needed. She drifted out of the king's chamber, down the corridor. She found herself outside in the early dawn light, gray and sulky in a granite sky. It was cold on the bench and she had forgotten her cloak, but she felt her wits returning. Ælfgifa didn't look up as a long shadow fell across her. "Brother," she said in greeting as he sat next to her. She knew what was likely coming.

257

"Gifa, your tonic did well. Just such an end and such last words as I hoped. I can rest more easily now, I think. It would have troubled me not to have Edward's blessing." Harold leaned back comfortably.

"Yes, Harold, and if Edward had given you his blessing you would have it. As it was, he blessed no one and he placed some strange and surely impossible charge on me!"

"What on earth do speak of? You were there, Gifa. You heard Edward name me his successor," Harold said sitting rigidly upright again.

"Harold, he did not name you. Nor was he speaking to you at the end—save perhaps for when he said it was God's will. He was speaking to me. Or to whoever he thought I was. Though I am at a loss to puzzle out his meaning," Ælfgifa said.

Harold laughed, uncaring of if he should draw attention or disapproval from the early rising servants. "Did you think he was making you king of England, little sister? That is the first truly addled thing I've heard you say. And while I'd have you as king over many a real man, it was to me he gave the crown."

"Brother, can you hear yourself? The crown was never in Edward's gift. I doubt not the Witenagemot will find for you. You will be king. Is that not enough? Must you take a dying man's last words as well? He commended the care of the kingdom and his wife to... to *someone* in that room and it wasn't you." Ælfgifa shuddered as she remembered that fixed and furious stare. "It were best if those words were never mentioned, Brother." She glanced up but Harold was not listening. Not really. He had heard what he wanted to hear and who else would ever question that interpretation? If she could just shake the restless feeling that she had been given a task, a burden....

She peered heavenward. A broad slash had appeared in the winter clouds and through them shone a star so huge, so bright and fierce that her breath caught in her throat.

Harold looked up at her gasp and saw immediately what had transfixed her gaze. "The Star, Gifa. *The Star*. Here we are in the week of Epiphany and the very star that led the Magi to a stable shines above us! I must call the Witenagemot. Now. Immediately. That star will lead them to great wisdom and me to glory!"

Ælfgifa had been caught by a growing sense of dread at the sight of the star. She was not superstitious but here was a sign of ill-omen if ever there was one. "That star is not for you, brother. That is a warning!" But Harold had already moved away, too full of restless energy to wait for true dawn before he began his plans.

***

It happened so fast Ælfgifa felt as if she stood in a storm tide. The Witenagemot was called. In truth it was the final of many Witenagemots—there had been nine lesser gatherings over the last two years, representing the church and the old kingdoms. All had found Harold to be the favorite. The Witans who gathered here were representatives—ealdormen, thagns, Lords, Abbesses and bishops. The wisest and most influential men and women of Saxon England. It was luck that they were all gathered at Westminster, in Lundenwic for the feast of Epiphany or Harold might have had to wait a month or more. It may have been the shortest Witenagemot in history. The answer was unanimously in favor of Harold.

Ælfgifa tried to rein Harold in. Tried to make him see that holding the coronation the day after Edward's death was unseemly in its haste. That some, who knew Harold less well might think him a usurper. She might as well have

259

counselled the fire not to burn for all the good it did. Never had Harold been in such high spirits: never more sought-after or popular. And never had Ælfgifa been so full of irrational creeping fear and dread.

All the while, that brilliant, evil star made a slow passage across the January sky.

CHAPTER 24

The celebrations for the feast of Epiphany at Rouen were only just over when Gallet brought news from a spy who had hotfooted it from Lundenwic. King Edward had fallen sick and was not expected to last out the week. No sooner had that news been received that a brief message arrived by pigeon stating simply that a royal messenger was on the way from the English court, and could be expected at Falaise within days. That evening, a strange sign appeared in the sky. A star seemingly, huge and bright, with feathers like an arrow's fletching behind it, pointing North and West. After vespers, a crowd gathered in the square gazing at the star and wondering what it portended. William had never seen anything quite like it, and a tension in his breast told him that whether the star was a sign for good or ill, it would bring change.

Fortunately, the feast meant all his magnates were on hand. William resisted the temptation to call a council there and then. There was little as yet known with certainty, and he would only need to gather them again when the full facts were clear. Even so, he discussed the likely outcomes with Lanfranc and Fitz informally, and informed Montgomerie, Beaumont and Gallet that he wished them to remain close by after the court had returned to Falaise—and the latter, to muttered curses, that his dog was not invited. When the English emissary was reported to be approaching, William gathered the men, and Matilda, together in the small audience chamber in the Ducal manor.

There would no doubt be time enough to consider a response. There were numerous claimants to the throne, of course. Harold and William, obviously, but also a boy related to Edward by the name of Edgar Ætheling, Harald Hardrada the Norwegian king, Harold's brother Tostig. There may have been a few others that would come out of the woodwork that William didn't even know about. While it was common for there to be some dispute over a crown on the death of the old monarch, none could remember a kingdom with so many candidates for its ruler, so much uncertainty surrounding its future. William was only certain that both he and Harold would have their parts to play, and together, both could emerge the stronger.

The Witenagemot would have to discuss, and one thing that William had learned in his years as Duke was that when many powerful men gathered to talk, and so much was at stake, conclusions were not to be quickly reached. It was a pity that Edward's Norman magnates had been elbowed out of the Witans during the spell when the old Jarl Godwin's power was at its height. It would have been useful to have allies in that cockpit, but no matter. The new Jarl of Wessex was bound to him, and as such he would have influence.

The messenger, who described himself as a Serjeant of Wintancaestre, was brought before them, prostrated himself before the nobles, and rose to deliver his message. He cleared his throat theatrically, and began "honored Duke William, I bring news from King Harold Godwinson of England."

"Wait," William said, his voice sounding wheedling in his ears, "You say *King* Harold?"

The Serjeant nodded, keeping his expression neutral. "Yes, Lord."

"Surely you mistake," William frowned. "The old king, my cousin... the Lord rest his soul," he added, mainly for Matilda's benefit. "He is but lately dead. Pray tell me when his Grace the King... the former King, Edward... ah, left this world?"

"On the fifth day of January, Lord. At Westminster."

Christ's Nails! Less than a week ago. And the succession had been discussed, settled and bestowed already? It could not be right. Harold had formal obligations to William, of course, but were there not also the bonds of friendship? Of men? And what of Ælfgifa? Had they intended to communicate with him but been overtaken by events?

"There is no other message? None preceding the greetings from... His Grace?"

The herald briefly displayed confusion in his eyes, but quickly recovered himself. It must not be the first time he had delivered news that was not expected, wanted, understood... So no message from Harold to declare his intentions. Not a single word. Nor from Ælfgifa, giving William any indication of what was planned—he, who had given her a home for years and a station befitting her abilities! Who had shown her friendship and told her things he had told no-one else?

"But Lord Harold is King *elect*, yes?" he said, a horrible plunging sensation beginning to run through him as he considered what the messenger might actually be telling him. "Surely the matter cannot be concluded yet?"

"Lord. Harold is crowned King of England. He bids me–"

William raised his hand again, fought against his arms, his teeth, his legs, which had tensed as if his entire body was forming a fist with which to crush this insolent Saxon. "And has my cousin even been laid to rest? When was *King* Harold confirmed? When was he *crowned*?"

The emissary raised his chin and looked straight ahead. "On the sixth day of January, Lord. King Edward, God bless and keep him, was buried in the church of Westminster. On that day also, the Witenagemot met, and nominated Harold king, whereupon he was crowned in the same church, Lord."

A pulse of nausea bloomed in his midriff. It was happening again. Was there nothing that was owed to him that he need not take at the edge of a blade? Was he always to be the bastard of Normandy, valueless, to be cast aside?

The room seemed to tumble away around William, even as everything remained in place, and a sudden peal of thunder echoed in his ears. The Serjeant continued with his message, but his words turned to meaningless noise, like the echo in the ears after a battle. He gestured again for the man to stop.

It could not be! And yet, William knew, it could. A man of Harold's energy would not wait for the world to catch up with him. May Christ make his overactive cock drop off! He should have known all along. Great men do not wait for fate. They seize it. What marks the greatest men is that their grip holds. A sound like the snarl of a cornered wolf emitted from his chest. "Go on," William said to the messenger. "Deliver the rest of your... embassy."

The messenger spouted the usual platitudes. Greetings from King to Duke, meaningless nonsense about Royal friendship and courtesy.

Of Harold's obligations to William, of the oath that was made and accepted, nothing was said. It was as though

Harold had never come to Normandy. Never been shipwrecked and released by William. Never been accepted into his service, fought by his side, drunk himself into a stupor toasting his fealty, offered to marry William's daughter...!

Betrayal. The memory of it flowed through him like the Orme in flood. His cousin, Burgundy, rising up against him, condoning murder and treachery. His uncle, Arques, abandoning the field of battle and making common cause with his enemies. His cousin Montgomerie meddling in Maine. Little men. Petty men. He would grip them by the throat and choke the life from them and trample their corpses one by one until all men left showed him some respect!

"This is not... this is not...." William pushed himself unsteadily to his feet and took a step forward while the world spun and candle flames guttered.

"Good Herald," Fitz said to the messenger, who was maintaining his composure evidently with effort. "We thank you for carrying out your office in such wise, now I pray you, leave us while we consider our own greeting for K... the Lord of Wessex for you to return. You will be given refreshment should you wish it, and we thank you for your patience." He gestured to a page to lead the messenger from the room.

The door had no sooner closed than William felt the rage reach boiling point. "That wretch!" he yelled. "Filthy worm! Parasite! Saint Gertrude's flaccid tits, does he think to cheat me and laugh in my face? I should have left him to rot in Gui's dungeon! No, I should have had him flayed and thrown back in the Manche!"

Everyone else remained silent while William hurled every insult he could think of at the distant figure of Harold. He had thought the man was his vassal. He had thought the man was his *friend*. Eventually, he ran out of curses and slumped back into his seat. The silence that followed was like the dark of night in midwinter—thick, impenetrable. Everyone looked at their shoes. Even Matilda did not dare to cross the gulf of his anger while it was so wide, so lightless. He knew he should never have let Ælfgifa leave, but that faithless Saxon lord had beguiled him. He had trusted Harold. He had liked him. And now they both smiled even as they slipped the blade into his gut.

This is what you get for thinking powerful men are your friends. The ties of blood mean little, and the ties of friendship, less.

"I am sorry, Lord," Fitz said, finally, lifting his white face. "He has treated you most impolitely."

"Impolite?" William exploded again. "Is treason impolite? Is betrayal? Would it be impolite to receive a lance in your back from a sworn man?"

Fitz's mouth flapped a few times. Choosing the correct answer was clearly troubling him. Eventually, he said "it is infamous, Lord. It is... ill treatment beyond imagining. But Harold is now in England. He wears the crown."

"*My* crown," William barked, feeling the heat of his voice, in his face. "He wears *my* crown. The crown promised to me by my cousin, in good faith, and which that foul traitor promised to help me attain."

Fitz's eyebrows rose. "My Lord, I don't think–"

"You never do think!" He staggered to his feet again. "None of you saw this. None of you warned against it. What action did you take to prevent Harold usurping my rightful throne! None!"

A room full of mouths gaped back at him as though he was a mother blackbird with a nest of feeble, pleading chicks. All except Lanfranc, whose lip curled slightly, the only amendment to his usually stony expression. The edges of William's vision started to blacken.

Matilda stood. "My Lord," she said, voice thick with uncertainty—even she'd never seen him this deep into his fury. William's nails dug into his palms lest he grab her by the braids and finish what he started that evening at Senlis. "Your honor is intact," Matilda continued. "All can see how impiously Harold has acted. He will be punished for his transgressions, in this world or the next."

William stared at her, blinking. Yes, punished. But.... Fitz pursed his lips, stood, quickly stepped over and placed his hands on William's shoulders. "Duke William," he said, looking directly into William's eyes. "We are with you. Your council stands with you. We will decide now on what action to take, and we will support you. First, we need to establish what to say to the herald. What message he will bear back to Harold. It is important that whatever we do now is considered carefully. Everyone here is loyal to you, Duke William. We will help. Together." He dropped his hands and stood there looking sheepish.

The roaring in William's ears began to fade. The world began to stabilize. Fitz was right. Of course he was right. Harold was counting on being far away with a sea between them. In the spirit of friendship they had parted in, no-one had any reason to suspect that Harold would act like such a churl, and as for breaking an oath of homage before it was ever even called upon....

"We may still prevail upon Harold's good sense," Fitz said. "Send to him reminding him of the promises that he swore to. Show patience, but let him be in no doubt you do not intend to let him escape from his obligations."

"He won't just give up the throne," William said, taking his seat again. "Not after going to the trouble of getting crowned the day he was confirmed."

"No, but he could still compensate your Grace for the loss, and the insult."

"Harold has broken an oath sworn on Holy Relics," Lanfranc broke in. "He faces excommunication if the Pope hears of it. Which he will. All the other claimants to the throne are barbarians." He turned to William. "The new Pope, Alexander, my former student..." he smirked very slightly, "will likely endorse your right, Lord. Most likely. It has concerned his Holiness for some years that the Saxon church holds to heretical ways. One example is the Archbishop of Canterbury, the leading churchman in the land. Stigand, a Saxon. He is not recognized by the Pope. Your Grace recalls Robert Champart, who was ejected from the office of Archbishop against the wishes of the mother Church?"

"Of course." It was, after all, Champart who had brought the offer of the throne from Edward. "What of him?"

"If the heretic Stigand performed the ceremony to crown Harold, then it is not valid. Harold is not yet King."

"Send an embassy to His Holiness right away!" William demanded. "We may yet secure something worthwhile from this slippery Saxon."

Lanfranc bowed. "Yes, your Grace." He took his leave. The others looked to William.

"And if he still refuses to acknowledge you, Lord?" Montgomerie asked, daring to put the question that was probably on everyone's minds.

"Then we'll fight," William answered.

"Good," Gallet said. "I was getting sick of all this talk."

CHAPTER 25

Every time William prepared for battle he remembered how tough the fighting was. Organizing the forces. Keeping them in order. Fixing tactics. Motivating the men. Then facing the fear down. Not disgracing himself in front of his men. Adapting to a changing situation.

And every time he prepared for battle, he forgot how difficult it was dealing with his nobles beforehand.

The invasion of England would be the biggest military mobilization Normandy had seen since William had been Duke. Perhaps since Rollo arrived here a century ago and founded the Duchy. It needed men, weapons, ships. All that could only come from willing vassals, and it meant money, which itself could only come from willing vassals. All his previous campaigns had involved raising forces from only part of the Duchy. Building an army fit to subdue England would inevitably draw on the whole of Normandy, and even from his supporters elsewhere, in France, Brittany, Poitou and Maine.

"Lords of Normandy," he announced. "You all know why you're here."

He looked around the assembled faces. Once, he would have seen insolence, suspicion, disgust, even outright hatred in many of their faces. More recently respect, loyalty, and possibly fear. Today, the barons just looked weary. They tended to be better behaved since Matilda had taken her place at his right hand. These days, he would not hold such a council without her, and not just for that reason. For all the rarity of her interventions, they were always valuable.

There were those he could always rely on, of course. Apart from Fitz, Beaumont, there with his eldest son Robert. His half-brothers, Odo ridiculous in his most ornate bishop's garb and Robert of Mortaigne, who looked hauntingly like their mother. Then there was old Hubert de Ryes and his sons, the three legitimate and Eudo FitzHubert. Walter Giffard, Hugh de Grandmesnil, Ralph de Tosny. The young Guillaume Warenne who had already won him a famous victory. The newly knighted Roger de Mesnières, uncomfortable in these surroundings. Eustace, with his ridiculous mustaches.... Montgomerie, he was still suspicious of, but who had done nothing to worry him overtly since the business in Maine. Precious few others whose loyalty could be taken as read.

"We are here because of the foul treachery of the Jarl of Wessex, Harold, who broke the sacred ties of homage and an oath sworn on Holy relics, seizing a crown that had been promised to me by my cousin Edward, through ties of blood and fealty..."

There was one fewer face among those who he could rely on for support. Ralph de Wacey, his former guardian, and supporter of all his enterprises, even if from afar, was not there. Would never be. William's summons had been answered with a message that Ralph was too ill to leave his bed. William had worked through the night to tie up loose ends with orders to have a palfrey saddled and waiting for him in the morning.

As he had stepped blearily into the courtyard, another messenger arrived. Ralph had died the previous evening, having slipped into a sleep from which he never woke. William searched his feelings and yet was finding it hard to accept that his former guardian was gone. The man who had schooled him with endless patience to be the Duke he now was. When it struck William that never again would Ralph lovingly chide his wilder behaviour, or find some memorable lesson in the world around them to impart, he wanted to scream. And yet more than half of his mind was filled with tallies of archers and infantry, with provisions, with supplies of seasoned wood to be transported to boatyards with the facilities to construct a fleet of ships, and it crowded his grief to the margins. Normandy had only a handful of vessels capable of carrying soldiers and stores to England and, if necessary, fighting their way across the sea to deliver it. They would need hundreds.

William continued his address to the council, setting out the army's requirements. The number of men they would need—five thousand knights, ten thousand other men at arms; the number of ships—eight hundred and fifty; of horses—two thousand....

He could see he was losing more of his nobles with each new requirement. And they went on. Quintals of grain and meat. Talents of wine. Seasoned timber for the construction of fortifications. The expressions on the faces of his nobles turned from weariness to alarm. At the conclusion of his petition for assistance, the chamber fell into quiet.

After a silence that had long since become oppressive, Geoffrey of Mortagne spoke up.

"Your Grace. You have been most ill-treated, it is true," he said. "But I have lost many men fighting for Normandy. It has cost me dearly. My lands have been fought over, crops destroyed, livestock killed and stolen, my people carried away or driven off. We've been fighting for years. Against Henri, against Martel, Arques, Conan. Your borders are secure, your Grace, while my knights are worn out. I pray you, let Normandy prevail in security and peace."

More spoke up. Each repeated a similar tale to that which Mortagne had told. William had to admit that there was truth in their words, even as he felt the sting of them. Was he not the lord who had led them to victory after victory? They had suffered in the fighting, yes, but they would benefit from safety, from the removal of threats like Anjou and Brittany, would they not? But though each campaign had raised its armies from only part of Normandy, over the last fifteen years, there was not a perche of it that had not been fought over at least once, and sometimes several times. As William looked around the chamber, he realized that not one of those barons had not suffered through the loss of money and damage to their estates. Most had lost friends, and not a few, sons. Even those who were more enthusiastic about the idea of invading England regretted that they lacked the funds and the men to help.

"It need not be necessary to fight." William wished he sounded more certain of himself. "But it will be necessary for Harold to know that we are prepared to fight. The Bishop of Bec is currently negotiating with the Pope's representative, and should Harold be excommunicated for his breach of faith, as he surely will, he may be persuaded to give up the crown he falsely wears and retire to his several Jarldoms." William did not believe for a moment that Harold would do any such thing other than at the point of a lance, but here he only had to make the first step, to gain the funds to start building a fleet. The rest could follow later. "And should we secure a Kingdom, or grants of land and titles, those who aid me will be rewarded."

William knew it was the wrong thing as soon as he'd said it. Everyone here knew he had been dangling English estates before potential supporters for years. It had ceased to have any value, and reminded everyone that although he had been promised a throne these twelve years, he was no closer to sitting on it now than he had been then.

The conseil broke up with no agreement. Most of the nobles protested that they could not help, entreated William to consolidate his existing successes, focus on Normandy. Several times he found himself on the point of resolving to do this, before the thought of Harold's betrayal swum back into his mind, with the impossibility of letting it stand.

"What will you do?" Fitz asked when the inner conseil gathered later that day.

"Talk to them again," William said. "Individually. We'll go to them, and persuade them one by one. Start with the lowliest, the newest knighted—Roger de Mesnières, him first, and see how the grands like it when they think they're going to miss out. Draw up a list of English estates and their wealth, as much as is known about them. We can't wave vague offers around any more, I think we will need to make specific promises of Jarldoms and estates to buy my barons' support. But let's make a virtue of their reluctance—this way I can really reward those who have shown the most loyalty."

CHAPTER 26

Ælfgifa glanced up as Edith sighed once again. They were attempting to embroider borders on a ceremonial robe for Harold but neither of them had made much progress. Ælfgifa was finding the exercise to be especially pointless since she felt certain that Harold would not be wearing the trappings of state any time soon. Eight months had passed since Harold's coronation and it had been no smooth transition. Neither she nor Edith had seen him for some months themselves. After the coronation, Ælfgifa had persuaded Harold, with some difficulty, that he should send an envoy to the Duke of Normandy. Grumbling, Harold had finally agreed but he had rejected all of his sister's suggestions as to how to word the message. In vain Ælfgifa had tried to make Harold see that he must refer to the oath he had sworn two years ago. That it would be a powerful insult to a man who did not suffer such slights lightly and who was deeply marked by past betrayals, to be overlooked in this way. Surely Harold could see that a little careful diplomacy now would save him a great deal of trouble in the future? Did he not already have to look to his flanks with Hardrada and Tostig and various other lords, both petty and mighty, showing a disturbing interest in the throne? Had Harold not heard the murmurings that he, Harold, had slid onto the throne before Edward had even left the seat cold? Had Harold not heard that the haste with which the Witenagemot was called, with which a decision had been made and worst of all, with which Harold had held a coronation, was being regarded as deeply suspicious? Surely a little judicious flattery to soothe William now—along with a generous present of gold, grain and rare items such as spices and amber—would go a long way to ensure the Duke was not nipping at Harold's heels anytime soon.

In the end, Harold had grown tired of Ælfgifa's lectures. He pointed out that the oath was no oath at all and that since she credited William with more intelligence than most men he surely knew it by now. If he did not then he lacked the necessary guile to be king of England or to meet Harold in battle. As for sending a gift—why that implied homage and future gifts to come. It would be a bad practice to start such a thing now and excite expectations he had no intention of fulfilling.

"But it buys you time," Ælfgifa had argued. "You know Hardrada will not rest. You will likely have to settle that issue with him sooner rather than later. I do not claim to know the first thing about leading an army in battle but I know to a man how many you can call up in the *fyrd*. No general chooses to fight two wars simultaneously!"

"Would you like me to make you a general, Gifa?" Harold had said sarcastically. "God's teeth but you go on. The *fyrd* is some fourteen thousand strong if called in full."

"Yes, Brother, but how many can you call up so quickly? They do not all serve at once and even then you cannot hold them for longer than two months. You would strain your supporters' confidence greatly if that were the first thing you did as king. If you allow a generous estimate you might manage a force of seven thousand which you will have to divide or did you think that William and Hardrada might each wait their turn?" Ælfgifa had flashed furiously.

"Sister, there *is* no war as yet. I doubt not there will be battles ahead but even you cannot be so farsighted as all that. God's blood but you are a doom-crow these days. Full of womanish fears. Is this what happens to intelligent women when they are not able to marry and bear children? Perhaps you should have accepted that offer–" Harold had pulled himself up short.

Ælfgifa had drawn a deep breath, holding onto her temper through sheer will power. "I need no farsight to see that two powerful men who believe you have taken what is theirs will come to try and take it back. Flatter the Duke, Harold. Send him gifts and good wishes. Do it or we will all regret it."

But Harold had not. Now he and his fleet were garrisoned at Wihtwarasburgh, watching the sea and waiting for the ships they had heard William was building. Harold was a master of sea-faring combat and they would have the advantage of knowing the tides and coasts. Her brother was certain that he could beat William in a battle by sea. Ælfgifa thought he was right, but William and his fleet did not come. Seven months since they had received word that William was building ships, and the foulest weather imaginable. Enough that the Duke had evidently not been able to set sail. Autumn was drawing in and the Channel would be even more impassable. At least until Spring. Ælfgifa imagined that supplies must be running low on the island of Wihtwaras. Harold would have to disband the *fyrd*. They might see him back here in Wintancaestre any day now. She would try to persuade him to diplomacy again, though what good it could do now she did not know.

A message had come a few weeks since from Morcar, Jarl of Northumbria. Ælfgifa's exiled brother Tostig had been raiding the coast ceaselessly. Ælfgifa knew Tostig was testing Morcar and his brother Edwin's ability to defend their Jarldoms. She felt certain it would not be long before Tostig tried a more direct approach.

***

Harold and his personal housecarls arrived the following day. It gave Ælfgifa no pleasure that she had been right in both her predictions. Her brother had been forced to dissolve the *fyrd* stationed at Wihtwarasburgh due to low supplies. He had left a token force to guard the coast under their brother Gyrth's command. Harold said that he thought it unlikely that William would set sail now. The weather was too poor to allow a crossing without risking all of his ships. Now the focus must be on Northumbria. Tostig and Hardrada had taken Eoferwic. Edwin and Morcar had been defeated.

Ælfgifa did not stay to hear battle plans nor to witness leave takings. Harold had come to gather as many thagns and their men as possible. And this time she was not going to be left behind. Someone needed to accompany Harold and speak sense to him. With a packed saddle bag slung over her shoulder, she saddled her own mare and waited until she could join the throng marching north to Eoferwic.

***

"Well, Gifa, since you came to advise unasked, do not spare me your words now," Harold said drily. Beneath the hood of her cloak, Ælfgifa grinned. She had thought Harold had made her out at the cooking fire the night before but as he had said nothing she had not been sure.

She rode up beside Harold. "It is our present predicament that you wish for my opinion on, is it not?" Harold gave a terse nod.

It had gone their way to start with. The Norse army had raided Eoferwic and taken hostages, then, in the way of their people, had retreated to a camp closer to their ships where they felt safer. Hardrada was clearly not going to gamble everything on one successful battle. She thought he had intended to escape by sea and return to harrying them once more in the face of serious opposition. Ælfgifa could only assume that Morcar and Edwin had acted like a prize pair of fools to have lost Eoferwic so quickly in the first place. Hardrada had also expected Harold to attack from the sea and clearly Tostig, who should have known better, had not thought at all. The Norse army had been taken completely by surprise. Harold's troops had slaughtered them, all of those on the West side of the bridge over the river Derwent. It appeared that the Norse army had been crossing to reach the old Roman road from Eoferwic to Lundenwic, never expecting attack to come from the land.

Ælfgifa glanced around. The air was thick with the tang of blood. Her mare shifted under her restlessly. There was nothing like a hacked up pile of fresh corpses to let your enemy know you meant to defend your kingdom. After what she'd seen in Brittany it would take a very bloody battle to make Ælfgifa flinch. The problem now was that the remainder of the routed Norse army was on the other side of the bridge, a choke point being effectively held by one man. Or giant. It was unsurprising that a superstitious whisper rippled through the troops at the sight of him. He was huge, built like a bear and standing near seven and a half feet tall.

He also seemed to be out of his mind with rage, foaming at the mouth and roaring as the legendary *berserkir* had once done. Ælfgifa wondered which plant root he had chewed to ascend into a state where he did not notice the cuts and arrows, nor feel any weariness. The giant wielded the biggest Dane axe Ælfgifa had ever seen. The haft was as tall as she was, she'd wager, and the giant had cut down twenty men with it already. Their advantage was lost now. Blocking the bridge had allowed the remainder of the Norse army to form a shield wall. They would not be cut down like winter wheat as the other half of the Norse army had.

First they needed to cross the bridge and no one could get close enough to the giant to kill him.

"Well?" Harold snapped.

Ælfgifa regarded the scene dispassionately for a moment more and then chuckled. "He is mortal enough. One good blade in the right place will do it. You must kill him, brother."

"This is your vaunted wisdom? Kill the foaming giant?" Harold swore. "If it were that simple, sister, we would have done it already. God's blood but you pick a fine time to lose your head!"

Ælfgifa met Harold's gaze coolly. "Bring me a barrel, the pig boy and a long spear—a good one mind," she called the instructions over her shoulder and one of Harold's housecarls obeyed in puzzled silence. "Brother, I think you had better send five... no, seven men against the giant on my command."

"It's too narrow to get at him with a dozen men whilst he carries that festering axe!"

"That is because you are attacking at the wrong angle," she smiled a closed cat's smile at him. "And brother? Make sure those men are not ones you desperately wish to retain. They *will* die, most like."

Ælfgifa felt Harold watching in astonishment as she led the pig-herd—a boy of fifteen—upstream from the bridge and concealed him in a barrel. The pig-herd gave her a nervous smile as he accepted the spear she handed him, paling as the barrel rode low in the river. It was easy to convince him. In another life, Ælfgifa might have felt ashamed at using the boy's hero worship of the *Great Harold Godwinson* to convince the lad into a foolish attempt at heroics. But time was of the essence. With the help of two of the *fyrd*, Ælfgifa pushed the barrel into the current. She signaled to Harold—his expression lost with distance, though she could imagine it all too well—and felt a surge of satisfaction as her brother waved his chosen group of seven into a useless charge against the giant. At least Harold was still willing to listen to her on some matters. One man was cut down immediately. The soldier behind him survived the giant's next swing because he slipped in his comrade's entrails, falling so that the blade swept harmlessly over his head. The barrel drifted unremarked by Saxon and Norse alike, bobbing in the current until it passed beneath the bridge. There was a flicker of movement that Ælfgifa would have missed if she hadn't been looking for it. She gave a grim nod of satisfaction. The pig-herd had obeyed her instructions to the letter. The giant on the bridge roared, bringing the axe high for a mighty downward swing and then stopped, mouth stretched wide, eyes staring in shock as they filmed over with death. Ælfgifa imagined the surprise that Harold's expression would now hold, not understanding yet what was happening as he watched the great axe fall from the giant's nerveless fingers to tumble into the frothing current. The spear she had given the pig-herd was wedged up between the lathes of the bridge, impaling the giant through his gut and nailing him in place as his great weight carried his body down the length of the spear, to slump dead on the bridge. The spear point emerged from the giant's back, glinting darkly with blood.

Ælfgifa heard Harold order his army across the bridge, and smiled grimly to herself. Two of the *fyrd*, a stocky dark haired man and a woman with arms a blacksmith might envy, fished the barrel from the river. Ælfgifa helped the grinning, pale and shaking pig-herd from the barrel. She said something kind without paying much attention to her own words. Praise for a job well done. As she returned to Harold, her brother shook his head at her. "If you had truly wanted the throne, Gifa, I would have been seriously worried." They kicked their horses into a trot and crossed the bridge.

***

"You ought to talk to them first, brother," Ælfgifa said, as she surveyed the shield wall ahead. "Perhaps if you offer Tostig his Jarldom in return for turning on Hardrada we might break the wall without a drop more of the *fyrd's* blood spilled."

"I had thought that. Tostig must be shitting himself having seen what the Nords will do on his lands. He must realize that Hardrada is in charge now." Harold's expression hardened. "All the same, Gifa, Tostig has to die now. If he does not then I will have allowed a traitor to attack the King of England."

"Oh, he will not *take* your offer, Harold. He's far too craven and indecisive to attack Hardrada. We need only make Tostig hesitate for an instant. Hardrada is paranoid and unpredictable. He may kill Tostig for us. Either way, setting them at odds before we fight can only be to our good."

Ælfgifa had donned breeches and a long tunic several days ago for easier riding. She now lifted a crude leather helm and nasal into place over her tightly plaited hair and pulled her cloak around her.

"Gifa! What are you doing?" Harold hissed.

"Going to talk to the enemy on your order, Your Majesty," she grinned at him. "You cannot say that I am not qualified to give offense in every respect. Besides, dressed like this they will take me for a boy. Tostig has not seen me in near twenty years."

"But you have no armor."

"Nor am I like to. The women in the *fyrd* are all much taller and larger than me. There is none that will fit."

"Gifa, what if you are killed?" Harold said, looking distinctly uneasy.

Ælfgifa shrugged. "Use it as an excuse to rally your men and crush the Nords. I've healed half the *fyrd* at one time or another it seems. Of course, I *will* expect a magnificent funeral." She clucked to her mare and sent the horse trotting towards the enemy lines. She felt rather than saw Harold hastily signal two of his housecarls to flank her. She heard the hoofbeats coming up from behind and smiled to herself.

Hardrada and Tostig were mounted on horses stolen from Eoferwic, and had positioned themselves slightly to the side of the main shield wall with a group of their most trusted supporters. They looked like little boys caught with their breeches down. Ælfgifa eyed them scornfully. In a way she supposed they had been.

"I am come to offer terms from King Harold the Second of England," she said in a low-pitched, carrying voice. "Tostig, exiled traitor Jarl of Northumbria, lay down your arms and bid your followers do likewise. You shall be forgiven. If you turn on the Norse pretender, Harald Hardrada, your Jarldom shall be returned to your care."

Ælfgifa paused. As she hoped, Tostig hesitated. She watched the expression of rage petrify on Hardrada's face. Tostig swallowed and said hastily, "and what will you offer my noble ally, King Hardrada, if he turns on *me*? If he lays down *his* arms?"

Ælfgifa tightened the reins and wheeled her mare in a wide arc trotting back and forth in front of them for a few moments, allowing the tension to build. She pulled the horse to a halt right in front of Hardrada and said in a low pleasant voice, "he shall have six feet of ground...." She eyed the Norwegian king up and down disdainfully. "Or perhaps a little more, as he is taller than other men."

She swung her mare out of the way, laughing as Hardrada roared his fury, startling his own horse and almost losing his seat. "You should bring your own horses to battle," Ælfgifa continued conversationally. "You can never tell how flighty the stolen horse of your enemy will be. Or how loyal." She set two fingers to her lips and gave the piercing whistle that stable lads across England used to train horses. The one that summoned them in from pasture, promising grain and warmth and shelter. The bay gelding surged forward under Hardrada and he almost fell a second time, thrashing to get the horse under control. "Even our horses are loyal. Pity about our cur dogs." She let her gaze rest on Tostig for a moment and watched as her brother grew red with rage.

"You've delivered your message, boy," Hardrada snarled. "Now go and ask Harold if he came to fight or exchange insults."

Ælfgifa smiled. "You have no loyalty between you, only necessity. Your force is split, with a third of the remainder guarding your ships. You are outmatched, outnumbered, and out of your depth. You will neither of you live to see the next sunrise. Die well. Or not."

She turned the mare into a full canter back across the field, the housecarls following close behind.

"That wasn't a messenger. That *was* Harold." Tostig's cry was almost inaudible over the drumming of her mare's hooves but she caught it. Sheer instinct made her fling herself low over her horse's neck as an arrow seared the air above her head. A moment more and they were out of range. The *fyrd's* shield wall parted, let her canter through, closing behind her.

"Well?" Harold said.

"They took the bait but sadly not the offer, brother," Ælfgifa laughed.

A wry smile came to Harold's mouth. "Go to the back, across the bridge if need be. You are starting to make the men nervous and main battle is no place for you."

"Since my knowledge of sword play consists of 'insert the pointed end into your enemy' I have to agree with you, brother. I will keep out of the way." It made a difference to be doing, Ælfgifa decided. Perhaps she was more like Harold than she had thought. She could understand his reckless courage better now, his urge to laugh mid-battle. Smiling a little more cynically, she moved back to an area where she could treat the wounded, and the dying could be laid out.

***

Ælfgifa sat by the hearth fire in the great hall at Eoferwic. Harold was hearing pledges of allegiance from Olaf Haraldson of Norway and Paul Thorfinnson, Jarl of Orkney. After today she doubted it would take much to hold them to those pledges, for a time at least. The battle had raged for several hours but the Norse Army had broken before the *fyrd.* Eystein Orre, who had been left in charge of the Norsemen guarding the ships, had force marched the men to assist the main Norse army at Stamford. Many had dropped with exhaustion when they arrived. The rest had fallen with their comrades, including Orre. Hardrada had been felled by an arrow through the throat. Tostig, when he was found, had been trampled but Ælfgifa thought he had died long before Norse and English boots made a bloody mess of him. There was a small but deep wound under his left arm, through the pit into the heart. It was the only wound that had bled greatly. Ælfgifa thought Hardrada had cut his losses and stabbed Tostig as battle began. She supposed she took a share in the responsibility for Tostig's death. Her words had killed him. There was no guilt though. Only the pleasant, warm aching tiredness that came after hours of toil, healing and stitching, dragging men and women away from battle. The enjoyment of being clean and dry after being so covered in filth and blood you hardly knew yourself anymore.

Three hundred ships had carried the invaders to England. Only twenty-four were required to carry the survivors home to Norway. The ground had soaked up blood like a greedy primordial deity until it could not ingest any more and the field was a wet, crimson-brown sludge, littered with broken corpses. It was a victory but not without cost.

Ælfgifa supposed Harold had even been eager for an actual fight after all those months of waiting fruitlessly for William. She took a sip of ale and stared unseeing into the flames. There was much merry-making underway in the hall behind her. Edwin and Morcar had been freed and Harold was embracing them magnanimously. Ælfgifa rolled her eyes. If the idiots had not charged out to meet the Nords in a head on battle in the first place this might not have been necessary. Still, at least one threat to Harold's rule was vanquished so perhaps it was just as well. Her actions today seemed madness in retrospect. But then had not the ends justified the means? *You did tell me to do whatever I could do, Edward,* she thought, *whether you meant me or not.*

Perhaps because she was one of the few people in the hall not drinking or wenching, or in the case of the shield-women —and some of the men—petting pretty young ceorls of both sexes, Ælfgifa was the first to see the messenger, standing dripping and breathless in the doorway. His eyes searched the seething room. Looking for Harold. Looking for the King. Ælfgifa's heart sank. She remembered that last night, she had caught a glimpse of that same evil star, more distant, less brilliant but still filling her with deep foreboding.

CHAPTER 27

Matilda turned a pleasant smile on the stinking, filthy throng as she rode by, offering a word of encouragement to the occasional, favored individual. The men so blessed would invariably bow deeply, offering a cascade of thanks and praise to their mistress. A few fell to their knees in the mud. William had given up wondering how she did it, and was just pleased she could.

They passed by knots of cavalry and infantry training and drilling, provisioners assembling stores, fletchers making arrows, an army of carpenters sawing and adzing, creating the timber sections that could be quickly assembled into forts. As far as the eye could see, the army was preparing for war. And everything was falling apart.

They moved away towards William's encampment. "All seems to be going well for you, my Lord," Matilda said brightly. "The Holy Enterprise is impressive to behold."

"It's a disaster, my Lady" he snarled. "We've been here too long. The fleet took too long to assemble. Even with your thoughtful contribution." Matilda had bought and fitted out a ship to lead William's fleet, quite without his knowledge—the *Mora* was beautifully built and decorated, the stem adorned with the figure of a golden child, who looked remarkably like Robert had in his fifth or sixth year, holding a bow and forever aiming it at England. The unexpected arrival of the ship into port, with Matilda standing at the prow, had near caused a riot with men rushing to the wharf to prostrate themselves before their munificent Duchess. William could have probably staged the invasion then by ordering the army to swim to England. "The winds were against us so we moved here to Saint Valleri. Now the winds have turned against us again, blowing a gale in our faces or flat calm." He shook his head and looked down. "It's been like that for weeks. We're barely holding it together."

"But everything is ready. It merely needs for the conditions to fall into place. You will prevail, my Lord. God wills it. See the army you have assembled."

He snorted contemptuously, then regretted it. Matilda was on his side, even if no-one and nothing else was. He softened his tone. "An army without a battle to fight can be just as dangerous to us as to our enemy. We're keeping them under control at the moment, but we won't be able to do so forever. Much longer, and they'll start to drift away. Desert. Start robbing and killing the locals.... Then I'll lose the backing of those Barons whose people and land suffer. Then the rest will follow. And the problem will be solved as I will have no army."

As so often, Matilda surprised him. "Have you asked God for help, my Lord?"

"God?" So simple a thing?

"Yes. Who could help more?"

"That's the problem. People are starting to say God is not on our side." He clenched his fists around the reins. "By the Saints, I have the Papal banner! What more do they want?"

Matilda smiled. "The smallfolk and fighting men have a great faith, touching in its simplicity and strength. They will know in their hearts if God supports this enterprise. Perhaps if you considered a gesture to demonstrate His grace? Or that your own faith matches their own?"

"I am the Duke, is that not enough?"

Matilda tilted her head a little. "Who is the Duke before the splendor of God?"

At William's request, the nuns of Saint Valleri brought out the saint's holy relics in their wooden chest, to the middle of the field where the preparations were being made, and a fine altar cloth was laid over it.

Matilda laid a hand on his arm "Let us pray, my Lord."

"Here? Now?"

"Yes, my Lord. In the sight of all your people."

William nodded his head and smiled indulgently. "A... one who was once a good friend to us told me that in England, a Lady may rule an estate while her husband is away. That small folk and women may talk to a Lady of matters that may need to be addressed, where they may refrain from talking to a man. If I am to be King there, we should consider their customs our own, where they are civilized. My Lady, I wish you to rule Normandy in my stead. That is, if you are content to. Beaumont may help, if you wish it."

Matilda smiled gently and nodded her assent. The two of them and their chaplain, Walkelin, knelt in the mud and prayed for what felt like hours. After a while, William realized the sounds of hammering and chiseling, swordplay and horsecraft, had died away. The wind whispered gently over them. When William raised his head, opened his eyes, all there was to see, for as far as could be seen, was a sea of bowed, bare heads of kneeling men, gathered around the shrine. His face felt oddly cold. The breeze playing on the tears pouring down his cheeks. A fair wind for England.

***

William watched the archers wading ashore. It seemed to be taking them an inordinate amount of time. The leading ships had hit ground a long way out from the shore, and even at high tide, the coast did not shelve nearly steeply enough to get close in.

He turned to the *Mora*'s captain. "What's the bottom like here? Sand?"

"Mud, Lord. Very soft mud," the sailor answered.

Saints' Pustules! He looked back across the bay, in the forlorn hope that by the time he looked back, the archers were ashore. "Are all the ships accounted for?"

"All but two, your Grace," the captain said.

"Do you know which vessels?"

The man started wringing his cap in his hands. "No, Lord."

It was not a fair question to ask. Most of the ships were built on exactly the same lines, and in the shadows of the dawn, any devices and pennants they displayed could not be distinguished, even at relatively close quarters—and the anchored longboats were spread out all across the bay. "Hm. Try to find out, would you?"

"Yes, Lord."

The first rank of archers had still not reached the shore, the awkwardness of their movements apparent even from here, and the second line were not yet half way to the beach from the leading ships. There was no sign of any opposing force on the shore, but they were horribly vulnerable to an ambush. If there happened to be a force, even a small one, hiding in the grass that fringed the beach, they could fall on the archers as they came ashore, bows and quivers raised awkwardly above their heads. "Does this place have a name?"

"The Saxons call it Pefenesea, Lord."

Pefenesea. They had landed at the wrong place. A bad place.

But how long would it take to re-embark the archers, stand out into the Channel and look for another place to land? He looked round for fitzOsbern. "Fitz? A word, if you please."

Christ's wounds. There was every chance Harold's fleet was putting to sea even now.

Fitz staggered forward. His face was white, possibly tinged with green. "My Lord," he said, swallowing.

Poor Fitz. "What's the matter with you?" The faint scent of vomit reached William's nostrils, answering the question before Fitz could.

"Sea travel does not agree with me. When can we go ashore?"

"Not yet." He gestured towards the archers. The first line, under Roger de Mesnières, was just reaching the shore. William's stomach tightened. This was the moment when a defending force would fall on those attacking. He thought back to Varaville, the slaughter on the banks of the river Dive. Another great victory. *Ha*. How easy it was when everything was in your favor. "This isn't a good landing site."

"No, Lord." Fitz struggled against his obvious discomfort. "The water is too shallow, the bottom too soft. It will take many hours to bring all the men and supplies ashore. We can be sure of losing a good number of horses if we try to land them here. Men too."

"Hm." The sun was just starting to poke above the horizon. There would be no more hiding in darkness. This might be their only opportunity. Everything since Valognes twenty years ago had led to this. If they turned back now William could not help feeling it would be to an inevitable decline. "If we put back to sea, even assuming that the wind stays in our favor, the Saxons could be sailing by now. Harold will have had news of our arrival for a couple of hours. There's no guarantee we could find somewhere better before they found us." It was a miracle that they had met no Saxon ships already. And miracles were not to be refused so lightly. Another would not be forthcoming.

The horror of returning to sea was written on Fitz's face, but he didn't give voice to it. There was another possibility, neither of them were referring to. The possibility that they might cut their losses and return to Normandy. Their army was still intact. They had lost only two ships. It meant they could try again.

In reality, though... After months of waiting, all the efforts it had taken to secure the nobles' agreement, the struggles with the weather. And Harold would doubtless be better prepared the longer he had to secure his position. There would not be a second invasion.

"I need to see for myself," he said. Fitz nodded, and called the captain to take them closer inshore. The oarsmen carefully stroked the *Mora* forward, picking their way through the other anchored ships. William saw men in them slumped over their oars, faces glum. After finally leaving the French coast, they had got within a few toises of the English shore only to find themselves sitting in boats kicking their heels while the vanguard plodded ashore. He could almost hear the mutterings about evil luck, bad omens, God setting his face against them again.

The *Mora* gave a barely perceptible lurch, sagged forward again, then dragged softly to a halt.

"That's as far as we can get, your Lordship," the captain called from the prow. "I don't want to push her any further in case we can't get off the mud again. Would you like me to call a skiff over to take you farther in?"

William waved away the offer and clambered over the rail. The bottom only seemed to be a pied or two under the surface of the water, but he sank up to his chest. "Come for a swim Fitz," he called, "the water's lovely."

Fitz groaned, and lowered himself over the side. They sloshed and heaved their way towards the shore, and within a minute or two, William was exhausted. It felt like hours until the water started to become a little shallower and the edge finally looked as though it was getting closer. The two rows of archers had made it ashore now, the first fanning out to search the shore for any spies or armed men, the second forming a defensive line, arrows nocked. God willing, they'd kept their bowstrings dry.

"At least if we're rushed now, we would have half a chance to get away," Fitz panted, dragging his feet through the sludge ever more slowly.

"Only if we're rushed from the shore," William replied. He glanced behind, out to sea. "We might still be attacked from the sea."

"Normandy!" Fitz shouted as they reached the shore, letting the vanguard know that the Duke was one of the two bedraggled figures lurching towards them. The archers lining the shore made a gap that William and Fitz staggered into. They were covered in mud but in good trim, with their hair shorn, wearing short jerkins, bows partly bent. The nearest archers turned, bowed their heads, muttered *Lords*, just as William's boot caught in the mud and he sprawled on the beach, throwing his hands out to stop himself. He heard the intake of breath from all nearby as he pushed himself back to his feet. Cocks of the Holy Martyrs! Now there would be more chattering of bad omens and ill signs. No sooner had he touched England than he was covered in it. He looked at his hands, covered in Saxon mud.

He turned to his men. Raised his barked, filthy hands. And shouted "By the splendor of God, I have grabbed England with both hands!"

Fitz laughed. The archers nearby cheered, and the cheer rippled along the line skirting the shore, most of them no doubt unaware why they were cheering, caught up in the hysteria. The sound echoed across the waters of the bay.

CHAPTER 28

A trumpet sounded just as William and Odo had finished their *matins* prayers, followed by shouts that a small party was approaching. William and his half-brother walked to the top of the earth bank skirting the harbor to see what was going on. Fitz and Robert de Beaumont, Roger's eldest, were already there, questioning the sentries. In the dawn light, a small group of horsemen could be seen approaching along the track worn by the constant coming and going of Norman raiding parties in the last few days. Flags fluttered from lances held in the air. Flags of truce?

"Do you recognize the banners," William asked, squinting into the dim light. "Is it him?"

His stomach twitched slightly at the thought. It would be an embassy of course, Harold would not come himself. Would he? He surely did not lack the nerve.

"House... Wessex," Beaumont said.

So it was him! A meeting William had ardently wished for these ten months.... And no doubt where Harold went, Gifa would be trailing in his wake, speaking counsel to all whose ear she had secured, advice that may be madness and sound like sanity, or the opposite.

"...But not Royal standards. I see others," Beaumont went on, almost to himself. "East Anglia, I think. And Kent."

"Ah. Harold's brothers," Fitz added. "Leofwine and Gyrth, I believe. It's undoubtedly an embassy from the K... from Harold, Lord."

God curse it! He was too cowardly to come after all. The disappointment was like a stone in his chest. "So, the traitor dare not show his face, eh? He sends his brothers crawling to me to plead for him."

"Do you want to hold them outside, Lord?" Fitz asked. "We can ride out and treat with them before the walls so they don't see too much of our forces. It would doubtless help them if they knew our strength in archers and cavalry, as they have none."

William smiled grimly. "No. Bring them in. I want them to see."

The two brothers were brought to him. One had Harold's eyes, the other his red-gold hair. It was all William could do not to have their heads returned to Harold separate from their bodies, but he mastered himself. They introduced themselves to him with a long list of honorifics—each held at least half a dozen Jarldoms, it seemed. William paused before confirming his own identity, watching them glancing at the earth walls protecting the longships, and with more disquiet, the sturdy timber castle already complete, and the thousands of men and horses, the many quintals of supplies.

"Duke William," the fair-haired one who had introduced himself as Gyrth—evidently the senior—said when invited to state his business there. "I am commanded by King Harold the Second of England to order you to return all captives you have taken, restore any possessions seized to their owners and leave these shores."

So even now Harold refused to acknowledge him. William leant forward. "It will be hard to restore burned Autumn crops to the ground, though perhaps not so hard to restore livestock which are already working their way through the guts of my men. In a manner of speaking. Were I minded to fulfil your request regarding captives, that would be easier. There are none." No, just corpses littering the countryside. No-one who had not fled or hidden had been left alive, as well Harold should well know. "And if I do not comply?"

"Then face war."

William laughed bitterly, and the others joined in. He swept his arm around at the fortifications, weapons, soldiers. "I came prepared for war. In fact, it will surely not surprise you to hear, I was expecting it. If it comes to war, I am ready, and it will take more than the threat of it for me to turn tail now." His lip curled. "Perhaps your brother needs a lesson in diplomacy. He might ask your sister Ælfgifa, as she seems to know more of statecraft and warfare than the rest of your family combined."

Gallet snorted with laughter behind him, and he noticed with satisfaction both brothers flushing, rage in their eyes. William pressed his advantage. "I will tell you how it will be. Harold must maintain his faith and abide by the oaths he swore before God and man, or face more damage to his lands and more death among his people. Unless of course he chooses to fight to prove his right."

"Duke William," Gyrth snapped, "Harold holds the crown through right of blood, the nomination of the old King and the support of the Witenagemot. He was crowned with the blessing of the church. He vows to terminate all pacts and friendships with you unless–"

"Pacts? Pacts?" William jumped to his feet. "What pacts has he not already terminated? The crown is mine by right of blood and my cousin, the old King's grant." He forced himself to lower his voice, as soldiers were beginning to stare. "Moreover, as for the church, his Holiness, Pope Alexander has decreed that for the breach of his oath of homage, legitimately sworn on Holy Relics, Harold will be excommunicated unless he agrees to honor the *pacts* he should never have broken."

At the mention of excommunication, the two brothers looked at each other, and both appeared momentarily unsettled. Not that the Saxon church here adhered as closely to the dictates of Rome as it might, but the outright opposition of Pope to King was not a matter to be taken lightly. William wondered if they knew that Pope Alexander had been a pupil of one of his closest advisers.

"The involvement of the heretic Stigand in the coronation renders it null and void in the eyes of His Holiness," Odo chipped in. "The blessing of your church is worthless."

Leofwine frowned, glanced at his brother. "But Stigand didn't perform the ceremony—"

"Enough." William sat again, and leaned back on his stool. "I am content to have the matter judged according to the law, be it English or Norman. I am also willing to submit to the judgement of the Pope as to who should be King. Or to meet Harold in single combat. Kindly take my offer back to *Jarl* Harold."

Gyrth wrung his hands. "Impossible, he cannot agree."

"Cannot agree to single combat? Does he fear to meet me in the field?"

The Jarl smiled awkwardly. "Duke William, King Harold cannot pass over the Crown, by single combat or by any other means. The crown was bestowed upon him by the people of England. He could no more give it to you than he could take hold of the flaming star that appeared in the sky on his coronation and fling it at invaders."

"Very well. In that case, I have one final offer. Gyrth—you shall have all those lands currently held by Harold, and Leofwine, all the lands held by Godwin, your father. If Harold will not honor the compacts he made with me, then he will have nothing, for as a traitor and perjurer he deserves nothing but death."

The emissaries turned to leave, their faces red, and William called after them. "I almost forgot. Your brother Wulfnoth sends his regards and regrets that he could not be here. To tell the truth, I think he rather enjoys living as a Norman."

Leofwine and Gyrth stopped, but did not turn. William noticed that the elder had laid a restraining arm on the younger. As the brothers rode away, William could be certain of one thing. That within a day or two, he would be King of England or have lost everything.

CHAPTER 29

Ælfgifa could see that Harold had chosen the site to make his stand well. The hill was steep and combined with the boggy ground, would make a formidable obstacle in its own right. The *fyrd* had been increased in number on the desperate, hasty march south and now their number was close to nine thousand. Ælfgifa was not sure it would be enough. Something felt... off. She could not lay a finger on what though and talk of foreboding or gut feeling would achieve nothing save accusations of hysteria. She watched from a distance as earthworks were thrown up with haste. Harold had chosen a pitched battle. The hill was close to the old Roman road that ran through Southern England to Lundenwic. Whoever controlled the road, conceivably controlled the country. William would find it hard to advance in numbers without access to the road. All the same, Ælfgifa wished it was not all to be decided on one pitch and toss, as though they played knuckle bones with the kingdom.

If this battle was lost, then there would be no opposition. A message had been sent to the fleet but there was precious little chance it could arrive in time for the battle, unless William should hesitate to attack. Ælfgifa did not think he would. Physical courage had never been lacking in the Duke of Normandy. Besides he was no fool, he would know that further reserves of the *fyrd* had been summoned. William would not wait until Harold's army was fourteen thousand strong.

She turned back to her brothers. Leofwine and Gyrth were almost strangers to her now. She felt little confidence in influencing either of them. No, her work must be done on Harold, if she could convince him to listen to her. Gyrth, normally as devil-may-care as Harold himself, wore a grim expression and Leofwine looked troubled. Both men were seething over some insult the Duke had dealt them. Could they not see that insults mattered not at all, here and now? They'd delivered the Duke's response to Harold's overtures of diplomacy with barely controlled fury in their voices. Her brothers were primed for a fight, taut as bow strings. Potentially reckless and therefore dangerous to the men they would command.

"Harold, you must speak to William yourself," Ælfgifa interrupted them. All three men stared at her as if she had lost her wits but she ploughed on. "I mean it, brother. William was of a humor to be insulted. He did not want to treat with your Jarls, brothers or no. Only one man could settle this with diplomacy and that is you."

She could see the refusal gathering in Harold's eyes and spoke over him. "This is hurt pride. You made him look a fool to his people. William has been betrayed by many of his vassals over and over again. Whether you believe yourself to be among their number or not doesn't matter. William does believe it and so do his lords. That you were trapped into an oath that you took care to ensure meant nothing, does not matter. William believed it to mean everything. But this can still be rectified. Talk to him on neutral ground, flatter him into a better opinion of you. You may be able to make him see your point of view. Offer him something to save face. Pay the small price of swallowing your own ego, brother. As evenly matched as the *fyrd* is with William's army, the price paid in blood will still be far higher than an apology."

For a moment Harold seemed to waver. He had to know that his soldiers were not fresh after the battle at Stamford and then a forced march of over two hundred and fifty miles. Ælfgifa could see her brother, her king, weighing up their lives against his own unshattering belief in his right to rule. And she saw the moment when he decided would throw himself onto a Norman spear, rather than grovel to the Duke of Normandy.

"Gifa, little blackbird, your concern does you credit but we *will* win. I'd rather have this done here and now, one battle to decide all... my position will never be stronger. My reign untroubled because my greatest opponents will be defeated. William is no master of pitched battle. The land is against him and his army is uncertain. A defeat will send his Breton conscripts fleeing for their lives. The men of Flanders also. The *fyrd* will vanquish them. Do not trouble yourself."

"I hope you are right, brother, I truly do." Ælfgifa swallowed then fixed Gyrth and Leofwine with a glare. "Remember that all you need do is hold. You do not need to win. You do not need to chase down your enemy. You do not need revenge for an insult."

She could not stay. She turned on her heel and headed to where the healers were gathering—monks and nuns from the nearest abbey. She would be useful, not hole up in Hæstingaceaster as Edith and Gytha had. As she passed she heard Gyrth's comment, "Don't recall her being such a domineering little bitch..." cut short by the thud of someone cuffing her brother's head and a yelp of surprised pain.

Ælfgifa looked at the shield wall before she left. It was much larger than the thin line the *fyrd* had formed at

Stamford. There was something solid and terrifying about it. She could almost feel the Norman army breaking upon it. Instead of reassuring her, it made her more anxious. A single pitch and toss.

CHAPTER 30

Just as the first glimmers of the new day appeared in the East, the scouts that had crept out under cover of darkness returned. Harold was close, they reported. Surprisingly close. Less than four leagues, on a South-facing ridge at the top of a hill near the straight North road. Two hours march at most. William wondered at Harold's boldness. He had never been afraid to throw himself into a fight, but neither had he been reckless—and camping so close to the Normans bordered on recklessness. It would not take the Norman army much time or effort to get there, and while it was clear that Harold was not quite bold enough to attack William at his fortified encampment, he was still willing to give his enemy an easy stroll to give battle instead of half a day's forced march.

He considered and dismissed the idea of simply staying in camp and giving Harold the choice of attacking them here or leaving them within his Kingdom. Harold's position was undeniably good, according to the scouts' report—he had formed his shield wall between two stands of woodland, with a steepening slope leading up to it, and marshy ground to either side of the approaches. But the advantages of fighting today were overwhelming. The Normans would barely be able to forage for supplies with an army so close. They would be stuck here, and if Harold re-commissioned his fleet, as he was surely even now making arrangements to do, they could be attacked from land and sea simultaneously. That would all take time to arrange, but Harold's sudden appearance, mere days after his victory against the Norse—not to mention the speed with which he had managed to get himself crowned—suggested that the Saxon might just be capable of launching a seaborne assault sooner than William might think possible. Days, instead of weeks.

No, the weather was good. The ground wasn't as wet as it usually was at this time of year, and there was more in his favor today than there might have been. For the first time since he had heard the news of Harold's betrayal, William felt his mood begin to lift. Today, they would fight, and one way or another, it would be decided. Seemingly for no reason, Matilda, and his children, Robert, William, Richard, Adeliza sprung into his mind. Was he about to leave them fatherless, as his father had left him? He offered a quick, personal prayer not so much for success on the battlefield as for his family. It was too late to change course now. William realized that even if an angel had visited him at the birth of this enterprise and told him he would die in this venture, he would not have done it one whit differently.

Odo led prayers for Prime before the Papal banner, and the army knelt as one man within the earthwork, among their de-rigged boats, priests scattered through the mass repeating the prayers and blessings. A few swords and axes received a final sharpen, and men began to buckle on their weapons. William secured a small casket round his neck and had it blessed, quietly, by Odo. It contained the fingerbone of Saint Eustache, on which Harold had sworn his oath.

William patted his black destrier as it ate oats from a nosebag. He never named his warhorses—it was best not to become too attached to them, but this beast was the finest he had yet owned. Perhaps the best yet to come out of Hugh de Grandmesnil's stables, and he could not help feeling admiration, even affection for it. "I'm sorry my friend," he whispered, stroking its neck as it continued to munch, paying him no heed. "I fear you will not see the sunset. But you will help me win a kingdom, and I promise that if I can make your end fast when it comes, I will."

The horse snorted, shook its head a little, and went on eating.

The army did not hurry. It did not need to. A league from the site Harold had chosen to station his army they crossed two streams which, had they been under pressure from a nearby enemy, might have provided some difficulty. The ground was a little marshy, but William had encountered worse. His mouth twisted into a smile. At least if they encountered quicksand they'd know what to do.... Fitz looked at him quizzically. "Nothing important," William said. "Just thinking of which Jarldom I'll give you when I'm King." Fitz made the sign of the cross and started praying for his foolish Lord who would tempt fate even when everything was at stake. Hereford. Fitz would be Jarl of Hereford. That was Harold's latest acquisition, wasn't it? He would strip his enemy's holdings one by one and hand them to those who had proved most loyal until Harold had nothing.

It was the easiest march to a battle William could remember. Less than two hours since leaving Pefenesea, the army was drawing up in an open space among forested hills. And up there on the brow was Harold and his army.

"It's a bit tight," Gallet said with a grimace. "Not a lot of room for maneuver."

"It could be worse," Beaumont said. "And they have no cavalry. I wouldn't want to face a charge coming down that hill, but as they are without horse, it's not such a disadvantage."

"No archers either, from what I hear," Fitz added. "That's good too. They could outrange us by a good margin from that height."

"These heathens have no horse and no archers?" Eustace asked. "Why not?"

"It's not how they fight," Gallet said. "They do it shield-wall to shield-wall. Close enough to spit in your enemy's eye."

"We will crush them as surely as your Grace has triumphed in every battle," Eustace proclaimed. "This field will be the site of your greatest victory!"

"You realize they say Harold has never lost a battle, too, don't you?" Fitz muttered. "He's no fool, and he's just won against the Norse."

"The barbarian Norse are no comparison. We are civilized Christians!" Eustace puffed up and his mustaches bristled. The warlike swarm of armed and armored men didn't look particularly civilized to William, but he was more concerned with their ability to fight. He recalled Gallet's comment at one such moment as this that the first battle you lose is likely the last one you fight. When had that been? Varaville? Arques? Val es Dunes?

"We'd better get these civilized Christians into order," William interjected before his captains descended into bickering. "As we agreed. Eustace and Fitz, with your Flemish and Frankish on the right flank. Odo, with Count Eudo and his Bretons on the left." William would lead the central 'battle' with Gallet, and the rest of his grands forming the command. There was a clear chain. If one fell, the others would know who to report up or down to. And if necessary, who was giving the orders. William glanced up at the ridge.

Banners were flying, and the line of painted, circular shields were visible. Harold had brought his line forward.

No going back now.

They'd been here long enough to get into order, and no sign of Harold wanting to parley was apparent, so William gave the signal to begin. The commanders of the three battles brought their archers to the front, and formed a line, which began to move up the hill. William could hear the men laughing and joking as they went, no doubt enjoying the novelty of not facing a barrage of arrows in return. Few of the archers had any armor more effective than a leather jerkin, which might just stop an arrow at extreme range from penetrating—mail was too heavy and constricting for most archers, not to mention too expensive—so it was no doubt refreshing to go out into the field in relative safety. They sauntered forward until their commanders judged they were in range, then, casually, each pulled a bundle of shafts from their quivers, stuck them into the ground within easy reach, nocked one and drew.

William gave the order for the infantry to follow at a distance as the archers began to shoot. The battle had begun.

***

As the first hour or two of the battle passed, William felt a sense of frustration and impatience creeping up on him, and fought it down. That could be a dangerous thing. But it was a strange kind of battle so far, with little sense that anything was happening. It might have been an archery competition, with the Saxon shields as the targets. If it weren't for the bellows and jeers of derision from the Saxon shield wall, that is. The Norman arrows were curving up the hill and disappearing at the Saxon rank with no discernible effect. It was possible to make out that some of the shields appeared to have more than a few shafts sticking out of them, and now and then there was a ripple in the wall, possibly representing a man falling and the line closing up with reserves moving forward when needed. But other than that, the Saxon army seemed to be no more affected by the hail of arrows than if the shafts had been made of straw.

William saw a man in the short tunic of an archer picking his way through the line of infantry and running towards the commanders. "My Lord," he puffed when he had approached. "I'm sorry to report, but we're using up our arrows at a fearful pace. We're nearly halfway through all those we have with us."

Good God, halfway through their arrows? And without so much as a dent in the Saxon line? "And there are no further supplies here?" he asked. "How can we be running so low?"

"The rest are back at Pefenesea, Lord. We didn't think we'd need any more, and Lord fitzOsbern said we should hold some back in case Harold came at us from the sea." He wiped his brow and huffed. "It's them Saxons not having any archers, you see, Lord. Usually we'd have the other lot's arrows coming to us, and we'd have plenty to shoot back at them, but we've only got our own today."

"Eternal Damnation!" William shouted, momentarily letting annoyance overcome him. "All right," he went on when he had recovered his composure. "Stand the archers down for the time being. We'll fight it their way. Send the infantry forward." He turned to de Grandmesnil. "And ready the cavalry."

The three wedges of infantry started to move forward, and a great roar went up from the Saxon ranks. A rhythmic banging started to drift down the hill, soon joined by the chant of *"Ut! Ut! Ut!"*

"I wonder what they mean?" Gallet said, and William chuckled.

"They seem to be very impressed with someone called 'Oot'. Any idea who that might be?"

"Perhaps they're trying to say 'Eustace'. I hear they were very taken with his mustaches."

William ordered the reserves and the command to creep forward again, to keep them in contact with the battle. As he did so, the infantry launched forward, and the crash of shield on shield, the increase in roaring from Normans and Saxons alike was momentarily deafening, even at a hundred pieds' distance.

Now the battle had started properly, but William took no satisfaction from that. In most of the fights he had been in, he had been closer to the action, if not right in it. Now, he had precious little idea what was happening. Most battles in Normandy were somewhat more mobile than this—even the sieges!—and it was possible to see which side was dominating, when a change in fortunes occurred, when a new tactic was employed. This Saxon warfare, though.... Being stationary was its purpose.

And being stationary was Harold's purpose. He only had to hold. If that shield wall held, William's army would break on it like the waves on a rock, and long before the rock had worn even a single ligne, the tide would be ebbing, never to return. If the grumbling from Gallet and Beaumont was any indication, others were finding it just as frustrating as he was.

Was he fighting Harold's battle, the way Harold wanted? "Are you up there?" William muttered to himself. "What are you doing? What do you see?" As he said the words, he couldn't be sure who he was addressing them to—Harold, or the Jarl's sister. He had a sudden sense that Ælfgifa was near. Surely not—she would not be so close to the fighting. And yet... her skills as a healer would be in demand behind the Saxon line. Not to mention her other skills. Perhaps it was not so preposterous.

"De Grandmesnil," William called, and the baron edged his horse over to where William stood. "Prepare for a cavalry charge."

"Lord?" De Grandmesnil frowned. His confusion was understandable.

"To the left, I think. The ground looks best there. Between the center and left battles."

De Grandmesnil's brows knitted. "I expected to deploy the cavalry only if a breach appeared in the wall."

"I know."

"And, pardon me, Lord, but I see no sign of any such breach developing."

"No. I know. But the day is passing, and we're playing into Harold's hands with this wrestling of footsoldiers." William outlined his plan.

De Grandmesnil tried hard to hide the horror in his eyes. "You want us to charge uphill, at a disciplined shield-wall, wheel—tightly, mind—throw spears while turning, and withdraw down that slope?"

"Yes, that's exactly it." He paused, allowing that to sink in. "We need to reverse things. Make a gap with the cavalry that the infantry can exploit."

"I haven't heard of it done this way before."

"We're doing it first, then."

De Grandmesnil raised his eyebrows, puffed his cheeks. "It won't be easy. We'll take losses."

Gallet laughed "What's the use of training so hard if we're not going to make use of it? Come on Hugh, at the sight of this lot coming up the hill at them, they'll clench so hard they won't be able to piss for a month."

"I'm more worried about ours," de Grandmesnil replied. "It'll be like they're being thrown against the wall for no purpose."

"Perhaps I wasn't clear. I'm coming with the charge. I'll lead it if you like."

Young Beaumont moved closer. "My Lord, I must humbly advise against doing so. The risk to your person is too great. Far too great"

"The risk to my person is great whatever happens today. I'm no use back here. You know what to do if I fall."

"Yes, Lord, but–"

"Save it for later, we need to hit them harder than we are now."

The cavalry walked their horses around to the rear of the reserves and archers before moving into formation. There would be no time or space for the traditional gentle start, building up to speed as across the vast fields of France. Messengers darted forward to the commanders of each battle, informing them of the change of plan. William prayed they would get the idea and pull the infantry back before the cavalry got there. One message not fully understood and they'd be tripping over their own men. A memory forced its way into his mind—Harold on horseback, charging at the Bretons, laughing. Well, he'd be laughing now if William managed to charge his own footsoldiers down.

The messengers were returning. It was time to go. He caught Gallet's eye, and the knight nodded companionably. It always came down to this.

William shouted, and the battle cry of Normandy echoed over English fields. They gave their warhorses all the spur they would take. The destriers reared and planted their hooves in the receiving earth, and the cavalry poured out from behind the reserves. This time, they were in a column rather than a line, a snake rippling up the hill, only four horses in front of William.

For what seemed like an age, all William could see ahead was the backs of their own infantry and for a moment was convinced that he was going to pile into his own men. Then, almost as the first horse was on them, the left and center battles parted, and beyond the gap, Saxon shields. William hefted his spear. The leading horses turned, seeming to teeter on the edge of the ridge, and wheeled away, and there was nothing between William and the Saxon line. He caught a glimpse of bearded and mustachioed faces, flashes of scale and mail, a line that had not been intimidated into breaking by a hundred heavy warhorses charging at it, and hurled his spear into the center of the mass. William heaved on the reins, pulling his warhorse to the right, desperately steering clear of the shield wall, and back down the hill through the gap in the Norman line.

The cavalry eased up slightly as they withdrew downhill. William chanced a glance back over his shoulder to see that the infantry battles had rushed back in the gap with a cheer, but the melée seemed static again. The Saxon line had held the first charge.

"They're still there," Gallet puffed at him as they reached the bottom of the hill, and beckoned for new spears to be brought to them.

"It's early yet," William replied, breathing hard, struggling to get his breath back. "No-one ever won a battle on the first charge."

"I wish someone would tell the minstrels that."

"All we need to do is cause one part of the line to break. A gap a few men wide and we can get in."

Quickly they spurred the horses again, and leapt back up the hill. The Norman infantry opened up once again, and for the second time, William hurled his spear into the Saxons' wall with all the force he could muster, screwing up all the fury and betrayal he could direct at Harold into the throw. He turned the horse away again, just as a huge Saxon stepped out of the line right ahead of him. William hauled at the reins and put his full weight onto the right stirrup, hearing nothing but the thudding of blood in his ears. The Saxon was swinging something above his head—a great, two-bladed battle axe. Swinging down, meeting his onrushing horse, and struck at the charger's shoulder.

Holy God! The horse lurched, stumbled, head plunging. For an instant, William thought it was going to tumble, but the beast staggered upright, and lumbered down the hill, dropping heavily on its front left leg. The horse was tiring, wounded, and the cavalry sweeping round from behind were starting to overtake him. Just as William thought he would make it to the Norman lines, the horse's left leg collapsed and his mount dropped from under him.

Floating free, sky dark, light, dark, and then a thumping blow to his right side. And once again William grasped England with both hands.

His head rang like a bronze bell. Through the ringing the sound of horses thundering either side of him, then men shouting, weapons clashing. He grappled with his scabbard buckling, pulled his sword free, half expecting a mass of Saxons to fall on him at any moment. His vision cleared and revealed everything around in chaos. Half a dozen horses lay on the ground before the shield wall. His own was dead, its neck broken. The infantry this time had not fully rushed back into the gap. The Bretons on the left bowed away from the Saxons, formed a loop.

Just as William knew it would, the loop shattered and began to flow back down the hill towards him like water sloshing out of a pail. The second line of infantry, advancing behind, fleetingly resembled men fording a river in flood before they were carried back by it. It was a river of Bretons. Oh, Saints and Martyrs. This was the end.

Curse them all. This time there was no anger. Just disappointment, thick in his gut.

No. No pity. William clenched his teeth. Fix the wall. Win the battle.

It was then that William first heard of his death. The Bretons massing towards him were yelling all manner of things—among them he heard *The Bastard's fallen! Duke William is Dead!*

Not dead! Fallen, but not dead! He fumbled with the lacing under his helm and wrenched it off his head. "Look at me!" He screamed. "I'm alive! I am the Duke! Look at me!"

A number of the soldiers running towards him, around him, saw the mad figure standing in their midst, bare-headed, and slowed, stopped, turned back to face the Saxons, though many did not.

Just then, William saw he had the break in the English line that he had wanted so badly, with no forces to exploit it. The English right had begun to push forward, and then pursue the fleeing Bretons. "Hold!" William shouted. "Form a line!" The soldiers who had gathered around him started to shuffle into a line, to brandish their weapons — short spears, mainly, the odd sword. A sound of hoofbeats, and Odo and Gallet pulled up beside him, shouting his name.

He turned to them "Odo, bring the reserves up now! Look, the Saxons are leaving their line. Gallet, get the cavalry, quickly, and ride them down!"

Gallet nodded and turned, shouting for de Grandmesnil and the battered remains of the cavalry. Expertly they formed up on the move, wheeled round and charged, full pelt at the advancing Saxons. The Saxons had been intent on the fleeing Bretons, cutting down stragglers mercilessly and pushing forward at a rapid march towards the knot formed around William. "Hold!" William yelled, feeling the nervous energy, the fear, vibrating in the men either side of him. They readied their weapons and locked eyes with bearded, red-faced men brandishing axes, just as the Norman cavalry ploughed into the Saxons' flank, shattering them from a unit into a cloud of confused individuals. A few moments later, Odo at the head of the infantry reserves arrived and tore into the reeling English. A few of the Saxons who had broken their own line made it back to their shield wall. Most did not.

The field was now littered with corpses and the grassy slope was hacked to shreds. The reserves had plugged the gap in the Norman line, William saw with a torrent of relief. He shouted a word or two of thanks to the men who had stood with him, and bade them join the left battle once more.

"Why didn't he attack?" William panted at Fitz when he reached the rear of the Norman position. "He could have rolled up our line like a parchment scroll."

"Harold doesn't need to win," Fitz replied, shrugging. "He just needs not to lose. Why risk throwing everything at a single charge when he can just stand there. If we haven't broken him by nightfall, he might as well have rolled us up."

"I'd have attacked. Opportunities like that don't come along very often."

"You have nothing to lose, Lord William. Harold has everything to lose."

"Hm." He shouted at an auxiliary to bring him a fresh horse, and in a short while was mounted again, and back with the cavalry. Just then, he noticed Young Beaumont trotting towards him, holding two standards under his arm. He threw them to the ground by William's horse.

"Recognise those, Lord?" the knight laughed.

William peered at the mud and blood-stained flags. Could it be? The standards of East Anglia and Kent, each stitched with the wyvern of Wessex. "Gyrth and Leofwine?"

"Yes, Lord. Both dead. I saw the bodies."

Could it be? Among those Saxons stupid enough to break their own line the two brothers who had brought the last peace offering. Fools! A sneer twisted on his lips. Perhaps they had not forgotten the slight he had dealt them the day before, and let their anger lead them to their deaths. That was a tactical advantage too. Harold had lost two of his commanders. The battle would be harder to manage, and the chain of command confused. The Saxon was bleeding. Good!

"Another charge, Lord?" de Grandmesnil asked.

William cast his eye over the army, mixed in his brief experiences at the front line and considered. "No," he said. "Everyone is tiring. I'm going to order a brief withdrawal. Give the men a chance to rest, eat, drink. But not long enough that many more men can turn up for Harold." That was important. Scouts had reported that members of the *fyrd* were still drifting in. Not enough to replace the men lost in the last charge, but this was the kind of battle where every man would count. "And besides, I want to give Harold time to receive the news that his brothers are dead."

He called Gallet over. The knight was streaked with blood and muck. They all were, but it suited Gallet somehow. "I have a task for you," William said. "I want you to go with the footsoldiers in the left battle. Take command—I give authority. You saw what happened when they collapsed."

"You want me to make sure it doesn't happen again?"

"No. I want you to make sure that it does."

***

The Norman line pushed forward again, and in a moment the sound of clashing weapons, shouts of triumph, fear, pain, anger rang out over the battlefield. William nudged his horse —his fourth of the day—to the bottom of the slope and waited for the moment to charge. He felt a twist in his stomach. It was nearly time for Gallet to launch the feint. Like so much today, this year, it was a gamble. This was perhaps the biggest gamble of them all. It would be too easy for the feigned retreat to turn into a real rout. They had never trained in this maneuver. It relied on everything being right.

There it was! The left of the line started to warp again, and the battle turned and streamed down the slope. William looked for Gallet but could not see him. He caught a glimpse of Eustace sprinting away from the battle, eyes as wide as his screaming mouth, until a stone hurled by a Saxon caught him on the back of the head and he sprawled headlong in the mud. And yes, the Saxons were hard on their heels. "Dex Aie!" William called and spurred his horse. Hooves thundered in churned-up ground. Horses and men panted, sending jets of steam into cooling air. Behind them, the archers, out of action for so much of the day were running forward, preparing to loose their final arrows over the Norman forces, plunging down into the Saxon lines.

As before, the Norman cavalry and infantry tore into the Saxons who had been foolish enough to leave the line. William swung his sword carefully, with devastating accuracy, slicing down into leather and flesh, thunking even off steel helms hard enough to kill or topple. Those who did not go down under his sword went down beneath his horse's hooves. Many men had allowed themselves to run out of the protection of their shield wall, perhaps hundreds. As the momentum of the cavalry slowed, William saw just how many had fallen. The field was thick with English dead.

And just like before, the impregnable shield wall was beginning to close up behind the men who had rushed out. William's heart dipped. But as well as the corpses, a great many battered, arrow-riddled shields now lay on the ground where they had been dropped by the charging men, out of reach of the Saxon lines. There were great gaps in the line where no men held a shield at all. And William thought he saw fear in staring eyes and ashen faces. The English were down to their reserves. The weakest, the cowardly now found themselves near the front, and with precious little protection. Saint Abstemious' guts! God bless Gallet, he'd drawn them out beautifully. William wondered briefly where the knight was. "Where's Gallet?" He shouted at Giffard.

His standard bearer shrugged. "Haven't seen him since the feint."

William sighed. No time to seek him out and thank him, they had to press the advantage. He called the archers to move forward and to fire higher. With a shout the leatherclad line moved up, confident now in their safety, or reckless in bloodlust. Every arrow was telling. More and more men were falling in the Saxon lines now. "Normans, fighting a Saxon shield wall and winning!" he muttered. Giffard smiled wanly back.

But were they winning fast enough? The sun was already low in the sky. William's heart plunged again. It was working. They were chipping away, but they could not fight in darkness. The fight would become a game of chance. The cavalry and archers would be useless. They would be at the mercy of a force with far greater local knowledge, and the chances of finding their way back to the safety of their fortified camp were too small.

There was an answer to that. A simple one. William unclenched his fists, tried to calm himself. Remember the state that he felt before battle—that calm descending, seeing things from afar, knowing the best way to fight and win. To keep the anger at bay and not be slave to the blood.

They could withdraw. Make a cavalry charge to cover the retreat of the footsoldiers, then wheel and follow. The ground would be difficult to withdraw over, but they had already passed it that day and knew the best ways. Moreover, it would be harder ground to advance over, especially for a pursuing force without cavalry. Withdraw while they still had the light. Back to the camp at Pefenesea. Send to Harold for concessions. Go home, honor intact.

No. Concessions, Harold would not agree to, and would not honor if he did agree. In days, his army would be near twice the size it was now. And there was still a chance to settle it here. Now. Today. Even now they would lose men returning to the camp and may end up having to give battle in even worse circumstances. It was not the safe choice it seemed.

To the end, then.

"Another charge," he called to de Grandmesnil.

The cavalry massed for the attack. William inspected the spear he had been handed. An unfamiliar design, and the shaft dyed with gore up several pieds of its length. He was preparing to wield a Saxon spear, probably bathed in Norman blood. Such was the day. There was time for another charge, perhaps two. William kicked the horse into a gallop, and it lumbered up the hill, jibbing this way and that, aiming between the knots of archers pouring their deadly projectiles into the enemy wall. He did not shout this time—his voice was all but gone.

The horse was tired but gamely kept up its gallop as the slope steepened. The lines approached. The Norman footsoldiers held, then began to charge as the cavalry drummed past them. William readied his spear. Once more threw it into the mass of men, saw a soldier fall, the wall close up.

Again. Once more.

The shadows stretched almost the length of the hill now. This would be the last charge. William nodded to de Grandmesnil, and they turned their panting horses up the hill.

Ahead, a bristle of spears, half-wrecked shields, the tops of helms. A ripple ran through it from somewhere on the right. Oh Saints, was the Norman line failing again? They would not repair it now, not so late in the day. But the movement was in the Saxon wall. There it was, sagging near one end, then the center. A breach! There, another! Men were dropping shields, axes. They were running. The Saxons were running.

"Bring me Harold," William called, spurring his horse madly. His voice was a scrape, lost in the cacophony as the Normans swarmed across the line they had battered against all day without winning a single ligne. "Bring him to me alive!"

***

A battlefield after a battle was never a pleasant place to be. Blood-soaked ground, in the darkening light looking almost black. Legs and arms, even heads punctuating the churned earth. The wounded, dying men, some swearing, some crying for a surgeon, some wailing regret for their wives left poor behind them, some muttering upon the debts they owed, some upon the children they had left. It all swirled into one horrible sound, like a dream of purgatory, reeking up to heaven.

"I am afraid there are few die well that die in a battle," Fitz said to William as they moved through the scene, putting right what they could. They would have to return to the camp soon, but there were more pressing things that were worth risking the darkness for.

"You think he is dead then?" *Pray God is was not true.*

"De Mesnières saw him fall," Fitz answered. "He died bravely."

"They all did." *Curse this darkness.* It was hard to tell Saxon from Norman corpses in this gloom, never mind one from another. "This one. Here. Help me, will you?"

They turned the body over. William wiped the mud, grime, blood from the face. "It's him." His voice sounded flat in his ears, like someone else's.

Gallet. A spear driven into his back, the snapped-off tip pushing right through his chest. William stood looking at the knight until he lost all sense of how long he had been there. "He saved my life," he said.

"He saved the battle," Fitz said. "He will be honored."

"How?" William heard his voice catch. "He wasn't even a noble. Just a knight at arms."

Fitz didn't reply.

He should have had a title. Lands. Most of all he should be alive. He had a wife and children. They would always be looked after, just as they would never forgive the Duke who led him to his death. Still, Helisande had proved useful once before as companion to a noble Lady. Perhaps she could do so again. Perhaps the presence of a friend would make life easier for that Lady in the world that was to come.

"Have the body taken back to the camp. Look after him, Fitz."

His steward bowed and hurried away to make the arrangements. William gazed down from the ridge at the last glow in the West. All this was his now.

Somewhere around here was the last remnant of the man who had sought to keep it from him. His followers might yet regroup and fight a rearguard action, and the Normans were not yet out of danger. But it was beyond question that Harold was dead. Many Saxons had seen him take a mortal wound, some said an arrow to the face or eye. And many Normans who had fought through the last circle of English, to find the body of a red haired man lying on the ground, still with some life in him, and had hacked him to pieces. That mustachioed idiot Eustace had boasted of how they had slashed and stabbed at the body, ruined his face. William could not even look on the expression of his rival as he had died.

There was one more, scant consolation. The deaths of Gyrth and Leofwine. Harold would have died knowing his brothers preceded him. That Godwin's sons were almost extinct. That would have to be satisfaction enough, for the time being.

They would need to recover the body as final proof that the Saxons' king was dead, had been overthrown. For now?

Let him rot.

ᏇᎻᎪᏢᏆᎬᎡ 31

This will be the stuff of tales, Ælfgifa thought distantly as the three women stepped through the mess of battle, along the path that had been cleared for them. *This will become a song told by skalds and bards before the day is out.* Edith was just slightly in front of Ælfgifa and Gytha. Her black hair flowed down her back and swayed past her hips. She was well past forty and had borne six children, but she was ethereal. Untouched by the stench and carnage. Bloodless as the moon and as quietly radiant. It was as if an ancient goddess had set foot on the battlefield, sowing shame for the actions of men. As if her grief had illuminated her. She was dry-eyed and grave. And any man whose gaze she caught, immediately looked down—in respect or shame, Ælfgifa could not tell.

Gytha walked more slowly but she was as upright and strong as ever. More than a trace of her great beauty still remained, golden and rosy instead of white and shadowed, like Edith's. Her face held more judgement, more anger, but she too was composed.

Which leaves me, Ælfgifa thought. *I must be the crone in this triad. Perhaps I shall not appear in a song.*

They stopped before a party of men, still in armor, still streaked with blood and other fluids. Ælfgifa felt her mouth settle into a flat line. William had hastily washed his face and hands at least. She met his gaze and for a moment there was a flash of something like guilt or remorse in his eyes, then it was gone and his blocky features hardened. There would be no pity here.

"My Lord," Ælfgifa said in Frankish, trying to keep the edge from her voice. The breeze freshened for an instant, catching the cloth that covered a dead man's face. A Norman. For a moment she was distracted. Surely that was Gallet who lay there, battered and still but utterly recognizable. Gallet was dead. A hard, clawing sadness gripped her. She had losses in both camps and no one else would ever understand. No distancing now, no stepping away into cold detachment when she needed it. How strange that she should stand here in this blood drenched hell, thinking of how she had dandled that man's children on her knee. Had in fact eased one of them into the world. The sadness clenched harder as Helisande came unbidden to her thoughts.

Ælfgifa recognized the effects of shock in herself and forced her attention back to the Duke of Normandy. "Lord, this is my mother, Gytha Thorkilsdöttir, and my sister-in-law, Edith Swannesha. We have come for the body of our fallen King, Harold."

William's eyes flashed dangerously. "Have you, Gifa? And what pray do you expect of me?"

Ælfgifa opened her mouth to say that it was reasonable for the fallen of either side to be returned for burial but Edith was already speaking in accented Frankish. "Who is this man who addresses you so familiarly, Sister?" she said in a cold voice. Edith knew exactly who William was, Ælfgifa was sure. The lack of recognition was designed to infuriate William. She saw the barb strike its mark.

"I am William, Duke of Normandy, and King of England. Victor at this scene of fate and your husband's body is in my gift!" William snapped.

Edith regarded him with cool disdain. "William the Bastard. That *is* what they call you, is it not?" She glanced around almost indifferently. "This is a table set for mongrel dogs, not a scene of fate." In that moment she was every inch a queen and William might have been a serf at her feet. Ælfgifa had never considered how beauty could be so dreadful a weapon before. She had never admired nor feared for Edith more.

"The coronation has yet to take place, Duke William," Gytha spoke up, her old asperity not lost in her own fragmented Frankish.

"We want no quarrel, Lord," Ælfgifa said desperately. "With your good mercy we will take Harold's body and go. This is a time for mourning, whether Saxon or Norman, surely?" She stared at him, refusing to look away. *Please. Please do not make this a petty instrument of vengeance.* William looked away first. Then something that was dark kin to a smile curved his lips. He said to Edith, "If you want your husband, you must first find him, Lady. I have a pile of the most likely candidates. And their parts. Things do not stay attached in the heat of battle." He gestured to a row of sack covered corpses behind him. These had not been laid out respectfully as Gallet's body had. "Have you some way to tell which is your husband, that does not require his likeness intact? We none of us could be sure which was him, though a dozen of my men say they saw him fall."

Edith became paler and swayed a little as if struck. Ælfgifa moved to her side and took her hand. "Let me see them and you shall have an answer." Edith's voice was surprisingly strong. William moved back and gestured the women forward. Ælfgifa did not think anyone saw how much Edith leant on her, she was so graceful. But as one sack was whisked from a body with a severed arm and a collapsed skull, then another from a man whose face had been cut away entirely, then another and another, raw, shreds of men revealed in a ghastly parody of a May-fair conjurer's trick, Ælfgifa felt her muscles scream under Edith's increasing weight. Each freshly revealed horror was a further blow. Finally, Edith gave a soft cry and dropped to her knees by a corpse whose face was ruined beyond recognition. A hand and a foot were missing, forcing Ælfgifa to remember a story about William and a pollarding knife she had heard a long time ago. She wondered if he was enjoying this spectacle.

"This is my husband," Edith said clearly. Ælfgifa looked, trying to be objective. The height would be about right and the hair, when it was clean, might be a faded red-gold. Edith had parted the clothes on the corpse's chest and laid one hand over some mark or scar there. "This is Harold. I am certain."

"And who should know better but his concubine?" William said. "Take it away." Several men moved forward to wrap Harold's body once more and for a moment Ælfgifa did not understand. Then she saw that they were taking the body away not handing it over. Two men held back a struggling Edith who was swearing in Anglish. Gytha, grappled feebly with a third man, her insults only too clear despite the language barrier. Ælfgifa knelt in the mud, blood staining her skirts and realized a fourth man was on hand to subdue her. He held his hands out gingerly as if afraid to touch her. She gave him a look of deep scorn and impatience, turning to William once more. *Why? Why in God's name?*

Gytha stopped her struggles and spoke. Slowly, painfully in broken Frankish and Latin. "Lord, I am a wealthy woman and this will have been a costly campaign. I will give you my son's weight in gold if you return his body to me for burial. Please, I beg you. Let me have him."

Edith had gone still, eyes wide with hope and fury.

They do not see, Ælfgifa thought. *They do not understand. Harold insulted William in a way he cannot forgive. Harold's death means that some part of him will have always cheated William. He may not realize it, but the Duke will always wonder, in a dark corner of his mind, if he has truly won. It was not enough for Harold to lose, or for William to win. Harold had to be sorry and now he never will be.*

William stopped in front of Gytha. "Lady, I have just become King of England. Can you offer me a greater amount of gold than that?" He turned away. "Besides, did not your Harold have enough gold in life? I won't have it on my conscience that he will have yet more gold in death. It was his avaricious grasping for a crown that was promised to me that has caused all your sorrow. He will be given a Christian burial without honors and that is more than the traitor deserves. Be content with that and leave me!"

Ælfgifa braced herself for a tirade of curses from her mother but for once Gytha was silent. For the first time in her life, Ælfgifa realized that she was seeing her mother weep. She had not even cried openly when Wulfnoth lay so near death as a child. Now Gytha took no pains to hide her tears. Perhaps her weeping was more in fury than grief. There was vengeance in her eyes. Gytha and Edith held on to each other as they made their way out of the camp but Ælfgifa lingered a moment. Rising to her feet and fixing William with an inscrutable stare.

William's haughty posture wilted. "Well, Gifa? Say what you will. You do not usually spare anyone that forked tongue of yours." She could tell he meant to bark it at her, make her scurry away perhaps, but Ælfgifa was beyond fear or sorrow or fury. There was only that cold, crystalline place of reason from which to answer. Finally it had come, the clearness and distance, to save her.

"You could have been a better man. Better than Harold. Better than you ever expected of yourself. Instead, this." She gestured to the partially cleared battlefield. "A man who does not master himself loses, no matter what battles he has won. And to sit like a covetous old miser over my brother's remains..." She shook her head. "You cannot have what you wanted from Harold. He can never kneel at your feet and grovel and pledge obedience. He would die first—as we have the proof. So tell me, was your pride worth it? Worth the cruelty to his widow and his mother?"

She turned and started to walk away, half expecting to be struck down for her words.

"You make no mention of cruelty to yourself, Lady Ælfgifa?" William called. There was anger in his voice but also a genuine note of enquiry.

She glanced back. "I have lived my life inside the cruelties of others. They do not touch me nor will they silence me. I thought better of you. Harold had many failings but he was never spiteful. You are no king. You are a dog in a manger."

CHAPTER 32

There is nothing a man might have that he must not take. William surveyed the walls at Escanceaster appraisingly, with the eyes of one who has seen many defenses and broken down not a few. Roman, in origin, much rebuilt and repaired. Poorly maintained. There would be opportunities to smash a gap in the crumbling mortar and rain-eroded stone big enough to drive an army into, and put to the sword anyone who resisted.

But he had never believed in breaking down walls to defeat people who might, by the simple expedient of waiting, defeat themselves. Doubvres had surrendered in eight days. Escanceaster had been encircled almost twice as long. Too few of the Saxons' cities had walls that were in good enough repair to keep an army out, most had no walls at all. They had no network of fortresses dotting the countryside where armies could regroup and launch counter attacks. The smattering of hilltop earthworks they had found had been abandoned generations ago. They could not win that way. Would not. If they resisted, Norman horsemen would sweep across the land burning and killing. It was what they did best.

Even so, these Saxons were fighting him at every turn. Resisting him. It didn't have to be that way. He had treated with their nobles. Allowed them to keep much of their own land, and faced the ire of his own in doing it. Confirmed many Saxon lords and bishops in their titles and holdings. He had offered to abide by their customs. Been crowned in the church that Edward had built and in which he was buried. He had even had Matilda—gentle Matilda, who loved and understood the smallfolk—crowned Queen, at Harold's old seat of Wintancaestre in the hope that she would have the same ability to pacify Saxons as she had showed in Normandy. The nobles and bishops had shown sense initially, after that foolish attempt to place a child, Edgar Ætheling, on the throne. The heretic bishop Stigand, of all people, had surrendered to him at Wallingford, and in a moment of liberality, William had allowed him to keep some of his bishoprics. Not the Archbishopric of Canterbury—that was for Lanfranc. Others who had submitted, he had shown mercy to, even generosity.

And then they turned on him, whipped up by Harold's witch of a mother. They could have had peace under their new Lord. They had chosen conflict, division, punishment, death.

For the first time, William was glad Ralph was no longer alive to see how wrong he had been, about everything.

He remembered a day at Falaise, having fled for his life, and being chided for his failures by his guardian. Back then, the failure of Normandy contrasted with the success of Edward's England. Peaceful. Prosperous. England, it now appeared, was like Escanceaster. Impressive from the outside, but rotten to the core and crumbling from within. *Because you cannot trust an oath sworn by a Saxon.*

By now most of the food would be gone. Before too long, the warhorses would be slaughtered for meat. Then the inhabitants would be eating the cats and dogs, then killing and betraying one another for a scrap of food or a sip of filthy water. William could build his siege defenses. Place an army here, and wait. Wait until Domesday. Let them fester and die one by one until the whole city was nothing but a vast charnel house. Perhaps he would maintain it thus. A city of the desiccated corpses of his enemies. It would make Alençon look merciful. But it would not end war.

He had almost regretted his words to Harold's women after the battle. His refusal to release Harold's body. Even though he had been duped by Harold, and had no-one else to punish for Harold's transgressions, tricking the grieving womenfolk had given him no satisfaction. The truth was he had needed Harold's body, and he had needed them to identify it. But when all was said and done, he could have been honest with them, as no Saxon would be honest with him. Except one, perhaps, in her way.

The manner in which Gytha had poisoned the fragile peace and become a rallying point for Saxon resistance wiped all that away. And even Gifa had turned away from him. What truer test of friendship could there be than war? It was only to be expected that she had failed. He had too. They had sworn no oaths to each other. Before all this, they had not needed to.

Still, the one thing that kept a chink open in his heart towards those hiding behind Escanceaster's walls was the rumor that the old king's sister, a changeling and sorceress, was there too. It made sense. She had been with her mother that day, and it seemed the ties of family were stronger for some than others. *A mother can be like a weapon*, she had said once. This mother was like Greek Fire, destroying everything, friend and foe alike.

"Majesty!" A soldier had approached while he was in his reverie. "A message from the city. They request a parley."

"So Gytha wants to talk, does she? After setting the country ablaze."

"No, Lord. The message is from another."

CHAPTER 33

Ælfgifa was running out of patience. By all rights William could have the city razed to the ground—not that that would be necessary. After the battle at Senlac Hill, after that endless march through the battlefield with Edith and Gytha to find Harold's body and face William for what she had thought would be the last time, Ælfgifa had come to her senses and urged her mother and sister-in-law to flee. They had headed for the ancient walled city of Escanceaster and there they had remained holed up for nigh on two years, grieving for Harold and their wounded, ransacked country. England was changed, perhaps forever. Only time would show how much. They had managed to get word to most of Harold's kin and many were able to escape abroad. Ireland. Flanders. It did not matter so long as they were free.

Ælfgifa's original plan had been for the three of them to escape overseas as well but Gytha suffered a nervous collapse and Escanceaster was as far as they had managed to go. There was no love lost between Ælfgifa and her mother but she felt that she could not simply leave Gytha behind. She had encouraged Edith to take her remaining children—those too young to have left already—and go into exile. She did not think she would ever see Edith, the sister of her heart, again.

Gytha had recovered and, while frailer of body now, was as sharp of mind as ever. It was then that Ælfgifa had realized that her mother had spent those weeks of silence, lying in bed, not only growing stronger but becoming more bitter. Her hatred and acrimony hardened. She had lost three sons at the battle on Senlac Hill. Gyrth and Leofwine had died beside her favorite son, Harold. Her remaining son was still held captive in Normandy and Gytha was blind and deaf on the subject of it having been Godwin and Harold who sent him there. If Ælfgifa could have died five times over in place of her brothers, both dead and captive, that would have suited Gytha very well.

But there was a worse problem with Gytha remaining. The people of Escanceaster wanted Norman rule as much as the next Saxon outpost—not at all. When Gytha realized that she had become a rallying point, she encouraged the people of Escanceaster, emboldened them, set them afire with her words of valor and liberty. Where a prudent person would have cautioned them to treat with their new lords, Gytha whipped them into a frenzy until all Escanceaster was in open rebellion. William had acted swiftly. Escanceaster had been under siege for more than two weeks. It was painfully obvious that the city could not hold. Already food was scarce. Gytha had unleashed a storm in Saxon hearts and minds but failed to see that their bodies needed sustenance.

Ælfgifa reached the place where her mother stood on the curtain wall, hidden from view below. She hesitated, wondering what the best approach to take would be.

"Well?" Gytha snapped.

The direct approach then. "Mother you have to leave. Now, or at least tonight." Ælfgifa met Gytha's fierce, glittering eyes with an implacable expression of her own.

"We will last perhaps another week. Maybe two. By then we will be eating the dogs and horses."

"Nonsense," Gytha said turning away to look out over William's camped forces.

Ælfgifa refused to be dismissed. "If you go now, Mother, then you have a good chance of making your way overseas to Edith. If you wait a few days more, then there is every chance someone will sell you to William to curry favor and a decent meal."

"The Saxons will never betray me!"

"Betrayal is a relative term, is it not? Put loyalty up against hunger, desperation, torture and death, and betrayal looks like its natural bedfellow, inevitable as the tide returning." Ælfgifa took a deep breath. "It's over, Mother. All you can do now by staying is ask these people to die for you. Most of them are not even soldiers."

"William the pretender will grow tired—"

"No, Mother. He will sit there as we starve. He will wait as we kill each other and eat our own dead and die of disease or shit ourselves to death from tainted water. He will wait patiently as our bones turn white in the sun and snow. You do not understand siege warfare. I do. And the Duke is an expert—he has spent his entire life breaking sieges, taking walled cities that thought they could resist. We cannot win at this type of warfare." She looked Gytha in the eyes and said steadily, "and we cannot live on your hatred."

"You are unnatural. Always, you were strange and calculating. You have no proper feeling..." Gytha nevertheless sounded shaken.

"That's as may be, Mother, but we cannot eat your ill-opinion of me either." Ælfgifa grasped Gytha's shoulders and Gytha flinched at her touch. "Mother for once in your life listen to me. Hate me and revile me if you will, but be ready to leave by nightfall. Ulfstaen will get you away safely."

"And if I refuse?" Gytha said but all the fire had left her voice.

"Then Ulfstaen will have to insist. This is not a negotiation, Mother. This is a command"

Ælfgifa turned to go but Gytha's words caught her and held. "What will you do... Daughter?"

"Do you care?" Her mother just looked at her. Ælfgifa shook her head. "Someone must surrender to William. I have already sent terms. So who better than me? Let us hope he will be satisfied with one hostage and agrees to harm no one else."

"Ælfgifa..."

"Yes, Mother?"

Gytha seemed to be warring within herself. "You should never have been my child."

"I am well aware of that." Her mother's words no longer had the power to wound her. She felt unutterably weary.

"No. I mean... I want to be able to say I am sorry I could never love you as a mother ought, but..."

"But you cannot say it because it isn't true." Ælfgifa smiled mirthlessly. "Do not make yourself a liar on my account, Mother. God speed."

***

William agreed not harm any of the citizens of Escanceaster, nor to raise any of the standing levies in return for the city's honorable surrender and for the Lady Ælfgifa to commit herself to his keeping. Ælfgifa, sitting in the cell to which she had been brought, considered that the transaction had been fair. It was point for point what she had requested in her message to William. She had waited the allotted three

337

days, to allow Gytha plenty of time to be away, and then surrendered. So far as she could see, William had kept his word. It would have been a fine piece of irony if he had forsworn himself. On the other hand, she had not expected to be locked up like a criminal. The cell was clean enough. There was even a pallet and a blanket. Ælfgifa had been there three days now. Surely William knew this was the way to get under her skin. Deprive her of freedom and information. She wondered if she would go mad. Somewhere, in the great halls above, William thrashed out the details of the rule of the city with its Witan. It mattered not that she must now consider William an enemy, she felt... left out. And annoyed with herself for the sentiment.

The sound of footsteps outside her cell made her look up. Muffled voices and then the scrape of a bolt drawing back. Ælfgifa lurched to her feet and came to an abrupt halt as William himself entered the cell. The guard did not look happy about leaving the Duke—the King—alone with an enemy, even a surrendered one. Still he could hardly suggest that William was no match for an undersized Saxon woman without giving great offense. Ælfgifa felt a perverse sense of merriment coursing through her as William looked around the bare, damp chamber in dismay.

"My lord Duke of Normandy," Ælfgifa welcomed him with sly humor. "Will you not sit down?" She gestured to the rickety pallet. "Or perhaps take some refreshment?" She swept a hand out to indicate an earthenware jug of brackish water. "The guards have not brought food yet but I can assure you the scraps are always of the finest quality. The bread never more than two days old at most."

"Gifa, I did not come here to play games," William finally snapped.

"Is it so, Lord? But you see you have played a most amusing game with me, surely now it is my move—such rich accommodations you have provided me with, should I not play the hostess?" Ælfgifa smiled at him sardonically.

Color rose in William's cheeks and a flicker of embarrassment passed over his face. "I told my seneschal to see that you were put somewhere suitable. I can see now that his ideas on what constituted suitable differed from my own."

"It is of no consequence, Lord. Not when you have deigned to see me so quickly." Ælfgifa was pleased to see another wave of blood rise in the Duke's face at her needling.

"If you do not wish to be here, then your fate is in your own hands," William said, struggling for an even tone. He clearly had something he wanted to ask her. Perhaps he had hoped a little rough living would soften her up. Foolish of him to expect her not to notice what he was doing.

"This reminds me greatly of the room I had as a child," she mused aloud, as much to irritate him as to draw out the conversation. He was an impatient man and he always revealed more than he meant to when he felt he was being thwarted.

"Lady Ælfgifa! Did you attend what I said?" William snapped.

She turned a small, close-lipped smile on him. "I did. *Lord.*"

"You mean, I think, *Your Majesty.*"

"I always say exactly what I mean. *Lord.*" Ælfgifa watched him carefully. *What can you do to me now?*

"If you decided I was your king, then you might have much finer rooms." William sounded almost as if he was wheedling and this intrigued her far more than any attempt at bribery.

"I fail to see the connection, Lord."

"Gifa, we need have no quarrel. You are guilty of nothing more than being a loyal sister and daughter, whatever it cost you." William locked gazes with her. "I value loyalty. And I value good counsel. Unhurried, considered, intelligent counsel from someone who has the ability to see all sides at once—well, that is invaluable. Those qualities are rare. Found in so few people."

It hit Ælfgifa then, what William was asking, and she wanted to laugh bitterly. "You wish for me to serve you as I did my brother. You want my perspective and advice."

"And your loyalty. There would need to be an oath taking."

We're back to that then, Ælfgifa thought.

"I know you. You would not forswear for you would never swear to anything you did not intend to do." William went on.

"Just an oath?" Ælfgifa said drily.

"And in return you would have a title, lands, wealth... a husband if you wished for one. You could not be officially recognized as an advisor of course, not being a woman and a Saxon..."

"Of course." Ælfgifa raised an eyebrow.

"But you will have funds to create the most coveted herb garden in Europe. You already made a start at Falaise." William was entreating her now. She did not fully understand the avid gleam in his eye. It was not lust but kindred to the feeling perhaps. A wish to acquire. To own. Was she that valuable?

"And of parchment and inks and gold leaf? I would want to write a herbal at some point," she said evenly.

William waved her demands off. "Whatever materials you needed for your work. Any of your work."

Really? God's blood. Advisor, herbalist, scribe, sounding board and general dogsbody. If I had four legs and a swift gait I do not doubt he'd add 'courser' to the list. Ælfgifa read the Duke's expression. He meant it. He would even find some poor Norman lord to take her as a wife if she desired. It was not just her accomplishments he wanted, she realized. It was her lack of fear. Her willingness to speak her mind and not tiptoe around him, ill temper and all. The Duke had probably even come to enjoy the odd spikey rejoinder. To like having someone he could quarrel with without recourse. *Friendship. He wants my friendship as well as my usefulness. He does not understand that you earn friendship, you do not purchase it with the wealth and land and titles you stole in the first place.*

"And if I decline your generous offer?" Ælfgifa asked with heavy emphasis on the word generous.

"You are too wise to do that. Not when you can see the benefits. Not when you have nothing to lose and everything to gain." William paused. "To... displease me thus would be most unwise, Gifa."

"As you say, Lord. Perhaps I might have some time to consider all the angles of your most kind proposal."

William scowled. "You may have the night. There is a *conseil* on the morrow. I will have your answer then." He rapped on the door and the guard, looking relieved, opened the door and let him out.

Ælfgifa sank onto the pallet. Not thinking about the offer —she had made her decision. Thinking on how to phrase her answer.

***

The *conseil* seemed to take forever but Ælfgifa was too glad to be out of her cell to mind much. It was similar to a

341

Thing except that there was a very definite sense of who was allowed to speak and who was not. Most of it seemed to be taken up with awarding grants of land to Norman nobles. It should have infuriated her but she had learned to divorce herself from the proceedings. Part of why William's offer tempted her was the opportunity to influence such events. She knew she could do it. The right word here, a judicious bit of flattery there, the truth always poured in William's ears and her own network of whisperers...

"Lady Ælfgifa." William's voice jolted her back to the present.

She stood before him and curtsied.

"You stand accused of no crime save that of being loyal to your family, a vile nest of traitors. Your family is gone and We are minded to take you into Our household. What is your answer?" He watched her, as she drew a deep breath. For a moment it seemed possible. She could stand behind him, unseen but correcting the reins of power with deft touches. The uprisings would die down. She would teach him how to understand her people, how to appeal to them, command their loyalty if not their love. England might have a stable rule for another ten, twenty, thirty years. An untroubled reign and William would listen to her as Harold had not...

"I thank you for your generous consideration, Lord. I regret that my answer must be no." Ælfgifa gazed at him levelly. Watched the fury transform his expression.

"No?" William almost hissed. "Your answer is no? Well, Lady, shall we hear your reasoning?"

"Very well. You would require my loyalty bound by an oath. I cannot swear such an oath. I will not swear such an oath when I do not believe I will keep it. My loyalty belongs, and always shall belong, to my family, be they dead or departed from these shores. My loyalty is to my people and not mine to swear away for any comfort offered." Ælfgifa found her words had dried up. It did not matter. No need to add that William would usher in a way of life she could not countenance. An inequality she would never embrace. A religion that thrived on fire and blood that she could never serve.

William's voice was choked with rage. *Rejection?* "You make a poor choice, Lady."

"My Lord, there are no good choices, only those choices which must be made."

"Then you have presented us with a dilemma, Lady. What are we to do with you instead?" William's eyes glittered dangerously, his temper very close to the surface.

"You will do as you choose but if you were minded to hear my request, I should like to be sent to my sister, Ealdgyth. She will succor me." Ælfgifa knew the answer would be no as soon as she asked. She had taken something William wanted. He would now take from her.

"With the Dowager Queen? Our late cousin's wife?" William sat back. "No. No, I think not, Lady. As far as Saxon hearts and minds go that would be all too much of a good thing in one place." For a moment a hint of genuine anxiety appeared on the duke's face and Ælfgifa realized it was not mere pettiness that made him deny her. He believed that she, assisting Ealdgyth, would form another rallying point for the Saxons. That she would wield political power outside his control. "No, considering your skills, Lady, We have a more fit place for you. Were you not once told you would make a fine monk? Doubtless you would be almost as good as a nun, if you learned to curb your tongue, that is. In fact We can think of the ideal situation now. A rather remote convent. Still I am sure the good sisters will welcome you."

His eyes hardened on her. "No doubt they will find you...
useful." The pause was exquisitely timed.

Ælfgifa knew her expression hadn't flickered. She could
tell because William smothered a flash of vicious
disappointment. But her face, lips, hands, everything below
her neck in fact, had gone numb. This was to be her
punishment. To be locked away. Removed from all sources of
information. Ascribed a life of tedium where she must bury
her mind...

She made it through the doors of the great hall. And
down the corridor with her escort. And back to her cell.
William knew she chafed at lack of freedom and at boredom.
His counter offer contained plenty of both. Ælfgifa wondered
if in the years to come, having acted as her conscience bade
her would be comfort enough.

***

The sun had barely been up two hours and William was
hungry already. After all these years, he still had no appetite
on the morning of a hunt. Even this one, the first of the
Spring. William paced the hard earth of the forest clearing,
waiting for the huntsmen to return. He passed a group of
young nobles clustered around his son William, laughing and
joking, and put his head down, but one of them called to him.

"It is good to see you returned from England, Lord," the
knight said. "How does the Kingdom?"

William looked up to acknowledge the platitude and his
heart leapt, his hand almost flying to his dagger. He calmed
himself. "Wulfnoth," he said, nodding to his hostage. For a
moment he had thought it was Harold standing there,
greeting him in Frankish, an open, friendly smile on his face,
instead of his old enemy's younger brother. "Well, thank you.
It seems some your former countrymen are determined not

to be peaceable, but things seem a little quieter now." Should he tell the young man more? Give him some news of his sister? Later, perhaps.

The sound of hooves signaled the return of the huntsmen. William motioned to his groom and mounted his horse with care. The mare barely reacted to his presence. He always spared her the spur these days, even if it meant someone else got the kill. Mostly, that still fell to him. He was the Duke of Normandy, after all. Especially now there were not as many grands as there used to be. Poor Fitz, killed on campaign in Flanders a month ago... William still expected to look up and see his old companion. Faithful, uncomplaining servant. There would be no songs about his exploits, no chronicles of his life.

William shoved the thoughts back and bade the huntsmen approach to discuss the state of the game, picking through handfuls of fewmets. Studying the droppings was hardly a pleasant business, but there was still no better way of ensuring the hunt went as well as possible. He identified a likely creature. "How about this one, young master Ardfoot?"

"Ah, yes Lord," the huntsman smiled. "A fine hart we tracked to the South. Eight years old, or thereabouts. A hart of twelve tines, in full fat. A fair distance, and he will give good sport."

"I do not doubt it. Very well, shall we start?"

"By your leave, Lord."

The party trotted gently out of the clearing, making their way to the South. The huntsman blew the first call on his horn, and the acknowledgements came back from the parties around the forest.

It was a good hunt. It lasted many hours. The stag gave them the slip completely twice, but William had time, and faith in his huntsmen. His son and the youthful nobles seemed to be chafing at the slow pace of the hunt. William rolled his eyes. They didn't understand. But even he was tiring by the time they finally brought the stag to bay, and it took some effort to dismount from his mare, and his hands shook as he undid the longbow's fastenings, groped for an arrow, nocked it... The stag was still there, front hooves planted wide as if it were preparing for one last leap. It was a large, muscular creature, with huge, elaborately tined antlers. Fine indeed. Today, it had met its match, and had nowhere left to run.

As calmly as he could, William drew the bow back, aiming for the hart's chest. The string creaked almost as much as his muscles as it reached the greatest tension, and he released the arrow. One was all it took. He broke the hart carefully, giving the best of the meat to the huntsmen.

As the party rode back to the town, the master huntsman approached, a grin all over his ruddy face. "Well done, Lord, very well done! It was marvelous skilful how you did drive him towards the other party!"

William acknowledged the compliment, thanking the man for his service. He deserved it. Valognes was a well-run estate these days, not least due to Gallet's widow Helisande, now a wealthy matron, who ran his household here, surrounded by a pack of rough, rangy hounds. The bastard pups of Gallet's lurcher, Odo, no doubt. Not that William saw much of Helisande on his visits. She always seemed to have an excuse, to be busy with something, and he did not push the matter. Gallet's death weighed on him every day. That his children were strong, intelligent, wild, and might one day be happy, was only partial compensation. The eldest boy was already in the Varangian Guard in Constantinople. They would go far. Far from Normandy.

News of the hunt appeared to have preceded the party. As they rode back into the streets of Valognes in the late afternoon, it seemed as though the whole town had turned out to catch sight of the Duke who had become a King. *Dominus Rex.* The good lord, who provided for them, and sat at the top of an ordered, secure world.

They had not seen the harsh winter in England. The whole villages, even small towns—anywhere suspected of harboring rebels—that had been burned to the ground, the inhabitants either slaughtered where they stood or sent out into the snow. The people here—healthy, smiling people, cheering their Duke—had not seen the thick pillars of black smoke punctuating the sky from horizon to horizon. Had not smelled the burning thatch, timber and flesh. Had not heard the screams of pain, fear and insult. William did not know the Anglish for 'bastard'. It was probably just as well. Those Saxon lords who had refused to submit to his rule had risen up. And then those who had submitted to him rose up too. Nearly the whole of the North had been in revolt at one point, and then the cursed Wealas had joined with them...

William caught sight of Wulfnoth, and called him over. "I've been thinking," he said. "I don't see why you need to remain in Normandy any more. You've served your time and I have no need of hostages any more. I need people I can trust in England now. You could have land, a title. Perhaps you could be a Jarl in time..." He staggered to a halt at the stricken expression on Wulfnoth's face.

"Lord, I... thank you for... I am grateful... but I have lived in Normandy these twenty years. I do not think there is anything for me in England any more."

William resisted the temptation to raise his eyebrows. Perhaps the young man—not even all that young anymore— had heard more than William had realized. It was true, there was not much left of the England that Wulfnoth had grown up in. Everything from the language spoken in the great councils to the boundaries of the territories, and the titles of those who administered them and the great cathedral Lanfranc was building in Canterbury was different. Much was still the same of course, but with every challenge to his rule, William had found himself having to bypass or crush one more aspect of Saxon life. They had been so different, after everything.

And Wulfnoth had no family that he could reunite with. One condition that William would have imposed, had the boy been willing, was that he could not see Ælfgifa. She had made her choice, and her penance must be complete.

"Very well," William nodded. "I understand. If you change your mind, you have only to ask. If not, one of my sons will surely have a place for you in his retinue."

"Thank you, Lord," Wulfnoth said, relief in his voice as he bowed in the Norman style.

***

For a long time Ælfgifa played a game of 'if'. The convent William had selected for her was nearly sixty miles from any other settlement. It was a retiring order in Kernow, devoted to study and prayer, and as William had predicted, they found her useful. Ælfgifa, never immoderate in her desires, learned to want even less than she had before in her life and she played 'if' while she did it. 'If' as she tended the garden. 'If' at prayers. 'If' always 'if'.

What if she had succeeded in persuading Harold to approach William with more consideration? Or if she had made Harold speak to William before the battle? What if she had stayed in Normandy after the campaign in Brittany? Or if she had not rescued the situation with the despicable

Eustace? Surely Edward would have punished him. There would have been no skirmish in Doubvres. Her family would never have been exiled. Edward would never have threatened to offer the crown to William...

If. If. If.

After a few years she made a resolution to stop. To live the narrow remains of her life well. She would not fall into despair or rehash the past. It was done now and she had no power to affect anything. Eventually, Ælfgifa accepted this and managed to find some contentment. There was just one faint hint of wistfulness, one wish she still held but buried so deep, she did not recognize it herself.

Ælfgifa had not expected ever to hear from William again. Thoughts of rescue had had to be abandoned as soon as she was imprisoned, for sanity's sake. So to find Bishop Odo of Bayeux waiting for her in the hall was an intriguing surprise.

"Ah, Lady, er..." Odo looked profoundly uncomfortable to be speaking with her. Ælfgifa suppressed a smile and inclined her head. No need to curtsey. She was no lady now.

"Lord Bishop," she said. "To what do I owe the honor of your presence?"

"William... the Duke... My brother... hang it all! The King of England has a commission for you." Odo finally managed to spit the words out. She did not bother to hide her smile this time though there was nothing of humor or pleasantness in it.

"Does he? Well, I am always at the service of his lordship," she said, words thick with irony.

Odo frowned at her use of the incorrect title but did not challenge it. "He requires a record of his campaign in England. A full and faithful account, neither omitting nor blurring any detail, to be worked in the finest dyes and wools. Faithfully stitched to show his great victory."

"A tapestry," Ælfgifa said. She was about to say something scathing about William's great victory when a faint flutter under her breast bone pulled her up short. This was what she wanted. To tell the story... to tell *all* of the story. This was a great work. Something she could pour her life's energy into. Already scenes bloomed in her mind. Fifty panels at least. Rich colors. Judicious tituli in Latin to punctuate the tale. And within William's version of the truth, she would conceal her own. The sense of triumph was as savage as it was surprising.

Ælfgifa smiled at Odo, for once showing her teeth in predatory anticipation. He visibly recoiled and she laughed. "Lord Bishop, you may tell the Duke of Normandy that it will be my *pleasure* to do just as he wishes. I will have the finest of our needle-workers engaged for the task."

Odo had clearly had the wind taken from his sails by her ready agreement, though he was not fool enough to believe that this was a sign of repentance or obedience. He got hastily to his feet. "Well and good, Lady... er..." Odo flushed and swallowed. He did not look a bit like William. Ælfgifa decided he must take after their mother. "I will tell his Grace... er, His Majesty."

Later that day, Ælfgifa received the first message from her sister Ealdgyth since she had been sent to live in this convent.

"Dearest Gifa,

I write to entreat you to undertake a task for me..."

Ælfgifa read the rest of the note and could not stop smiling.

Finis

Ælfgifa's eyes flashed open in the dark, heart thundering, blood humming in her veins as it had not for years. Not since she was still a young woman. A blade of moonlight sliced through the unshuttered window of her cell, cutting a path through the shadows to lie at the foot of her hard cot. It was long before *matins* and she could not imagine why she had awoken. There had been no sound, no alien scent. Nothing to disturb the monotonous, grinding wheel of day and dark, prayer and fast and toil that had become the calendar of her days. At first Ælfgifa could not name the emotion that held her enthralled, it had been so long since she had truly felt afraid. Indeed, it had been many years since she had felt anything except a wry, mocking acceptance of her lot—save that visit from Odo years since. And yet she knew with certainty that she was required elsewhere.

Automatically, she rose and dressed, the draught that seemed to have no source caressing her bare neck with cool fingers below the ragged, cropped ends of her once thick hair. A wimple and veil covered the tattered remains of her last shred of vanity. She paused at the door of her cell, wondering which way she should go. In the years since she had come to the convent, she had developed a knack for knowing what was happening all around her without paying direct attention. The barest hint of disharmony pulled her attention to into sharp focus. A stranger in the grounds or a sickness in one of the sisters, would send her unerringly to investigate. The novices whispered that Lady Wessex had the *Sight*. The old lie neither wounded Ælfgifa nor amused her any longer but she took no trouble to correct them. How were they to understand that it was merely a matter of paying attention to what your five senses told you? That she was not gifted with supernatural power but instead, like an aging spider sitting in the center of her web, knew when a filament was disturbed by an outside agency. Something disturbed the peace and sanctity of the convent now.

The tapestry. Ælfgifa was sure and slipped silently down the hall without troubling to strike a rush-light. There was someone in the tapestry room. Someone who did not belong there nor in the convent for that matter. Her heart beat fast and she found her breath coming short and harsh. The door to the chamber set aside for the purpose of creating the largest piece of embroidery Ælfgifa had ever heard or dreamed of, stood ajar. The flickering light from within told her that more than one beeswax candle had been lit and that someone paced the length of the tapestry, examining it. She wondered if they noticed the subtle stories told within and beneath the main one. The ambiguity as Harold swore an oath that was no oath. The confusion at Edward's death—to whom did he commend his kingdom? Did the intruder see the mocking way certain nobles—both Saxon and Norman— were depicted? Did they see Ælfgifa herself, carefully disguised behind a blank, unmarked face as Bishop Lanfrac struck her and she cursed him? Did the intruder understand that within the faithful account, there were threads of honor and betrayal, misunderstanding and accord, humor and sorrow, and a world lost? A kingdom changed forever— diverted from its course in history like a river turned on meeting a boulder. She shook her head. How could anyone read the story she had written there? Was it enough that the story *was* there to be read?

Without disturbing the shadows, she slipped into the chamber and regarded the tall figure, now slightly stooped with age, as he stood with his back to the door and peered at one especially brilliantly colored scene.

Seeing the King's silvered hair, the tremor in his hands as he held the light close, the way he needed to bend towards the tapestry to see it more clearly—these markers of age made Ælfgifa feel her own years. She was younger than her mother had been when Gytha had borne Wulfnoth but as if each stitch, each image and scene had been a living creation, so much of herself had gone into the tapestry that she felt herself to be much older. *My great work, in the end, has been within that narrow catalogue of talents William once allowed women,* she mused. *And the King? Where is his great undertaking?*

"Does it meet your lordship's requirements?" Ælfgifa asked. No need for him to know that Ealdgyth had commissioned the tapestry also, setting Ælfgifa to supervise the task. Her mouth felt strange and she realized that she was almost smiling. How long had it last been since she had smiled? When Odo had visited to commission this great work some years ago?

The king turned sharply, still swift on his feet for all his age and increasing girth. His expression was dark with something like fury and then he saw who spoke. The scowl cleared. "Ælfgifa?"

"For my sins." She performed the graceful half-bow of a postulant rather than a curtsey.

"You look just the same!"

Ælfgifa raised an eyebrow at this assertion. It had been more than a decade since she'd last seen him. Since he had sent her here, to be shut away. She could not quite keep the bitterness or the sarcasm out of her voice as she replied. "It is the benefit of being born so hideously ugly. One has nothing to lose as age and infirmity approach."

To her surprise a rueful smile tugged at the corners of William's mouth. "You regret your choices, Lady?"

"I have no reason to regret anything anymore, Lord. As you see, I am hardly in a position to interfere further here."

She regarded him gravely and her conscience smote her. "You offered me a different path and I did not accept it. That it sat ill with me does not lessen the honor you did me. I would not have chosen this," she indicated the stone walls of the convent, "even if I could not accept the role you offered. But I cannot say your ruling on my refusal was unjust. I should perhaps be flattered, but I have learned not to require much excitement in life."

The William she had known would have been battling with his rage at such needling, keeping control with visible effort. The man in front of her merely smiled with unfathomable weariness. "Ælfgifa, I am well aware that I presented you with an impossible choice. I reckoned without your familial loyalty—they used you to a man after all. I have missed your insight but I can admit honestly, here in a house of prayer, in the smallest hours of darkness that I am relieved you did not take up my mad request and become an advisor—however unofficially." He turned back towards the tapestry and Ælfgifa moved to stand near him. "I can also admit that I have reached an age where being able to sleep at night is almost worth more than even your counsel. At least allow me the compliment of being the only man to truly recognize what a dangerous creature you are."

Ælfgifa inclined her head slightly, blood hot in a face that had been a frozen mask for too long. For the first time she could recall, she could think of nothing to say. Her eyes lit upon the scene William had been surveying.

"Do you find the likeness pleasing, Lord?" she repressed a sudden, wild burst of mirth.

"Eustace," William said. "You always did have a wicked streak. Although it is uncannily like, I must own."

She did laugh then. It felt as if something were breaking loose inside her. She was once again drawn up to a great height, looking down not just on the events of now but on the events of before and the shadowy passage of yet-to-be. How small it all was. But even a tiny pebble casts ripples that are felt across the lake. England was forever changed under Norman rule. "Was it worth it, Lord? Now you sit secure upon a throne—albeit from Normandy—can you rest now? Was it enough?"

"I do not think any of us will ever know, Lady," William replied. "I find those last words you spoke to me come back to me more and more as the years pass. 'There are no good choices, only choices that must be made.' You were right."

Ælfgifa met his eyes for a moment. *You have conquered a land and a people you do not understand any more than they understand you,* she thought. *Worse for you is that you know this.* "Would your own choices be different, Majesty?" she said, giving him the acknowledgment of royalty for the first and last time.

William paused so long that she thought he would not answer. When he did, his gaze was fixed on the motionless embroidered figure of Eustace forever galloping away from battle, mustaches and all. "I think perhaps it is better not to look at my choices. The past is... better left where it is."

Since little can be done about it in any case. Ælfgifa nodded. "Perhaps that is just as well." Gathering her serenity once more she said, "Will you return? When the work is finished? It wants but one more panel. Odo's instructions were *explicit* on your behalf." *And so were Ealdgyth's.*

"Perhaps, if I should pass this way," William said, turning towards the door. "I will take my leave of you, Lady."

"My sincerest wishes for a safe journey, Lord," Ælfgifa replied. He would not return. She felt sure of it. The past was a book he had no wish to read from. After William left, she turned back towards the tapestry. There were so many pages missing from the book, or rather only hinted at. Truths that were only given a half-life here. Soon who would remember those truths?   She took the rush light and doused the candles, shutting the door against damp and draughts. Those who came after William, and Ælfgifa herself, would not know what they had lost. Perhaps if they didn't know, it wasn't so great a loss. After all, Ælfgifa reflected, she could hardly be sure that Harold would have made either a better or a worse king.

THE END

Appendix 1: Historical Note

The challenges of writing any historical novel are many and varied, and they differ according to the period, people and places being written about. Much of the challenge involved in writing about the 11th century, even when it comes to figures as important as dukes and kings, is how little information exists, and how little of that can be considered in any way reliable. We know a fair amount, in broad strokes, of what William I, Duke of Normandy and King of England, did. The details are scant and hazy though, and in some cases an event such as a battle or the birth of a child are so uncertain that they may have taken place at any time within a five year window or not at all. And while we know of William's actions, we can generally only guess at what motivated them, what thoughts lay behind them. In many cases there were markedly different versions of the same event to consider—for example, the exact site of the Battle of Hastings, which is still argued over today.

With those challenges come opportunities. Much of what happens in Oath and Crown happened in history, or at least, there is some historical evidence for them. These include the assassination attempt on William at Valognes, and the subsequent battle of Val es Dunes, which drew heavily from *The conspiracy of the Norman barons against William the Bastard, Duke of Normandy*, MXLVII by the Abbé le Cointe (translated by Edmund Goldsmid). Most of William's sieges and battles as presented in the novels are based on real ones, although the lack of detailed accounts of them means that considerable artistic license was required to flesh them out. The only slight alteration made to recorded history was that the Battle of Mortemer and the Battle of Varaville take place closer together than three years, as in history, and that events around them have been conflated for narrative purposes.

The sieges of Domfront and Alençon took place, as did the betrayal by William's uncle, William of Arques, the later conquests of Maine and Brittany, and Harold's swearing of an oath of fealty. The accounts of these draw on the nearest thing we have to contemporary accounts, including the Saxon *Roman de Rou* by Wace (translated by Edgar Taylor) and the Norman *Ecclesiastical History of Orderic Vitalis* (translated by Marjorie Chibnall), with due allowance for the agendas that these later mediaeval writers were working under. Some incidents and characters were informed by the Bayeux Tapestry, one of the most impressive pieces of documentary history and art that has ever been created. It is now widely accepted that the tapestry was created by Saxon needleworkers and artists.

Equally, most of the characters have some root in history. The only major departure on the Norman side is the character of Gallet, who in the account by the Abbé le Cointe was a jester or fool who warned William of the approaching assassins, much as happens in *An Argument of Blood*, but then disappears from the record. There is nothing to suggest he was actually a knight, or that he continued to serve William faithfully for many years. (The lurcher called Odo was also a figment of the authors' imaginations, we are sorry to say).

The character of Ælfgifa is certainly based upon an historical figure—the tantalisingly shadowy youngest legitimate daughter of Gytha and Godwin. Throughout historical record, Ælfgifa often pops up though it is hard to say whether it was the same person each time—there were several nobles of that name. Reports are conflicting. Some say that she died in infancy. Some that she entered a nunnery as her sister Gunhild did, dying around 1086 which would have put her at around seventy years old. Ultimately, considering the detail we have on the rest of Godwin's legitimate children, it is strange how much Ælfgifa's story seems to have been removed from the record. Of course one explanation could be that she did in fact die in childhood. Then again, if any of the 'Ælfgifas' who later crop up in historical record are her, it seemed likely that she was considered in some way defective. It certainly gave the authors a way into the Saxon side of the story. Once again, there was much fleshing out in order to present the reader with a fully formed character.

Nevertheless, it would not come as much of a surprise to us if certain things we think we made up turned out to be true, as numerous times during the writing, we found historical evidence for some event or character that had seemed to spring from our imaginations only.

Appendix 2: Biographies of Historical Characters

NB—characters with their names in bold appear in the books, those not in bold are only referred to.

The Saxons:

Royalty:

Edward the Confessor—King of England 1043–1066

Emma of Normandy—Daughter of Richard I, Duke of Normandy by his second wife. Mother of Edward, Alfred and Goda (Godiva/ Godgifu) by her husband Æthelred. After his death, she married was Cnut the Great and gave birth to Harthacnut and Gunhilda of Denmark.

Harthacnut—King of England 1040–42, son of Cnut the Great (sometimes spelled Canute) and Emma of Normandy by her first marriage. Harthacnut was Edward's younger half-brother.

The House of Wessex:

Wessex was the last of the great Jarldoms—originally the last remaining kingdom of the Heptarchy after the Danes invaded, before Alfred the Great, Edward the Elder and Æthelstan eventually united all of England as one kingdom

Godwin of Wessex (originally of Sussex)—Jarl of Wessex 1018–1052 (Father, probably Wulfnoth Cild, Thagn of Sussex, mother—unknown)

Gytha Thorkilsdóttir (JHEE-taa)—A Danish noblewoman—daughter of Thorkil Sprakling, Countess of

Wessex, wife of Godwin and mother to nine of Godwin's children

Sweyn Godwinson—(sevEHN) the eldest of the Wessex children. His Jarldom included Gloucestershire, Herefordshire, Oxfordshire, Berkshire and Somerset. Exiled in 1046. Declared *nīthing* (niðing) 1049, for his crimes

Harold Godwinson (also known as Harold II or Harold of Wessex)—Jarl of East Anglia, Hereford and later Wessex, King of England 2nd January–14th October 1066

Ealdgyth (also known as Edith of Wessex)—(ALD-jheet) Eldest Daughter of Godwin and Gytha, wife of Edward and Queen of England in her own right, 1045–1066. She was named Gytha presumably after her mother but changed her name to Ealdgyth or Edith when she married Edward

Tostig—(THOR-stig) third son of Gytha and Godwin, Jarl of Northumbria, killed at the Battle of Stamford Bridge, September 1066

Gyrth—(GERTH) fourth son of Godwin and Gytha, made Jarl of East Anglia, Oxfordshire and Cambridgeshire sometime around 1055. Killed at the Battle of Hastings

Gunhild—(GAHNH-hihl) Second daughter of Wessex. Entered a convent and very likely became Abbess due to her family and wealth but exactly where is not known. Died 1087

Leofwine—(LEOV-wine) sixth child of Godwin and Gytha. Made Jarl of Kent, Middlesex, Surrey, Hertfordshire and Buckinghamshire sometime around 1055

Ælfgifa—(ALF-ghee-faa) Third daughter of Godwin and Gytha. Very little is known about her and most is contradictory. She allegedly had lands of her own in England but there is no mention of a husband or children. Another source places her in Brittany at the same time Harold was shipwrecked and there is a mention of a possible alliance there—which never seemed to have come off. Some sources place her as having died as a child, others as living well into the 1080s in a nunnery. Considering there is at least some information available on all of Godwin's other children, for her to be such a shadowy figure is intriguing to say the least

Wulfnoth—last child of Godwin and Gytha (although Godwin appears to have had several illegitimate children who, in typical Saxon noble fashion, were taken into his household and raised with his legitimate children—even so far as to be given dowries and land of their own). Wulfnoth spent his life as a political prisoner in Falaise, Normandy. William the Conqueror issued orders on his deathbed for Wulfnoth's release in 1087. He was re-imprisoned by William II Rufus in England and died in captivity 1094

Edith the Fair—(also known as Edith Swannesha or Edith Swan-neck) wealthy Saxon noble woman, heiress to lands in Cambridgeshire, Suffolk and Essex. First wife of Harold Godwinson in the *more Danico* fashion—which led some historians to demote her to merely a concubine as it was not a Christian marriage—and mother to five of Harold's children.

The French:

Henry I (Capet)—King of France 1027–1060

William I ('The Bastard'/'The Conqueror')—Duke of Normandy, born c.1028, died 1087, Duke of Normandy from 1035, King of England from 1066. William was the illegitimate son of Duke Robert I and Herleva, who later married Herluin of Conteville. Robert had his nobles swear fealty to William before going on crusade in 1035, and nominated his young son as his successor, despite his illegitimacy. When Robert died during the return journey, William became Duke, despite the objections of several powerful nobles. During his minority, Normandy was in a state of chaos, and no fewer than four of Williams guardians were assassinated. He died in Normandy in 1087

Herleva of Falaise—mother of William I, and his half-brothers Odo and Robert, Count of Mortaigne. According to various stories she was the daughter of a tanner or furrier, though other versions suggest her father was a steward to the Duke

Matilda of Flanders—Duke William's wife, whom he married c.1053, though the marriage was not formally approved by the Church until c.1057. She was crowned Queen of England at Winchester in 1068, and died in 1083. She founded the Abbaye aux Dames in Caen

Ralph de Wacey—William's fourth and last guardian, son of a former Archbishop of Rouen. Ralph had actually been instrumental in the murder of one of William's previous guardians, but when asked to take on the role himself, did so with vigour. He led William's armies while the Duke was a minor

Gallet—(Or 'Golet') Some sources (e.g. William of Jumieges) speak of a 'Gallet' or 'Golet' (Wace) who was a favourite jester of William's, and who saved his life by reporting the approach of the would-be assassins at the beginning of the uprising of 1047–8. The role of Gallet as a favoured knight of William throughout his career until Hastings is entirely fictional, but his death at Hastings in the narrative is a nod to Taillefer, another fool or minstrel, who was said in some sources to have taunted the Saxons and been among the first killed in the battle.

William fitzOsbern—One of William's closest advisors, childhood friend and son to his former guardian, Osbern. He was instrumental in the organization of the invasion of England, and fought in the battle. He was rewarded with the Jarldom of Hereford, but was killed fighting in Flanders a few years later, in the chaos surrounding the death of Count Baldwin

Lanfranc, Bishop of Bec—one of William's closest advisors, a clever strategist and educator. He secured agreement from the Pope for William's marriage to Matilda of Flanders, though he initially disagreed with the match. One of his pupils became Pope Alexander II, which likely helped William secure support from the Vatican for the invasion of England. He was rewarded with the archbishopric of Canterbury after the Norman conquest, and built the first stone cathedral on the site of the current cathedral. He died at Canterbury in 1089

Roger de Montgomerie—one of Duke William's chief counsellors, and related to him through the wife of William's grandfather. He probably remained in Normandy in 1066 to help govern the Duchy in William's absence, but crossed to England in 1067 to assist William establish himself as King. He was rewarded with the Earldoms of Shrewsbury and Arundel

Mabel de Bellême—wife of Roger de Montgomerie, through which Roger inherited large estates in Maine. Mabel was known as a schemer and plotter in pursuit of power and revenge against those she perceived had slighted her. She was murdered in 1079 by men whose lands she had appropriated

Roger de Beaumont—a distant cousin of Duke William's, and one of his closest supporters, noted for his beard, an unusual adornment among the usually clean-shaven Norman nobility. It is not clear whether or not he accompanied William to England in 1066, but was instrumental in organizing and funding the invasion, and either remained in Normandy to help govern the Duchy or took on an organizational rather than military role in England

Robert de Beaumont—eldest son of Roger de Beaumont, he fought with William at the Battle of Hastings and was rewarded with the title of Earl of Leicester

Baldwin V, Count of Flanders—Duke William's father-in-law, Count of Flanders from 1035–1067

Hugh de Grandmesnil—Hugh was born to a family famous for breeding warhorses. He fought with William at the Battle of Hastings, and was made Sheriff of the county of Leicester

Eustace ('aux Gernons'—'The Mustaches') **of Boulogne**—Eustace was a relative of Duke William, and Count of Boulogne from 1049–87. Ironically, in view of his earlier enmity with the people of Dover, after the Norman conquest, Eustace later joined the people of that town to rise up and overthrow the castle's Norman garrison, for which he had his English lands confiscated by King William

Herbert, Count of Maine—acceded when his father Hugh died, but never took up his titles because Geoffrey Martel annexed Maine on Hugh's death, on the pretext that Herbert was still a minor

Conan II, Duke of Brittany—Ascended to the Dukedom while a minor, and, like William in Normandy, was subject to numerous uprisings and periods of disorder. His rivalry with

William may have led to his death from poisoning in December 1066

Guy of Burgundy—a relative of Duke William, the grandson of William's grandfather Duke Richard I, who the rebels tried to install as Duke in William's place, 1047–49. William besieged Guy's castle, forcing his surrender around 1051, whereupon he left Normandy for Burgundy, there attempting to overthrow his brother, Duke William of Burgundy

Geoffrey of Anjou ('Martel'—'The Hammer')—Martel was Count of Anjou from 1040–1060 and in that time fought wars with three of his powerful rivals, as well as the King of France (who later became an ally against Duke William). Martel never gave up his expansionist ambitions and only his death rendered Normandy safe from Angevin aggression

William of Arques (or Talou)—(Generally known in the novels simply as 'Arques') William's uncle, who had argued against William's succession when his father, Robert, died. He was later given lands and titles but to ensure his loyalty these were held of the Duke, meaning they technically belonged to William and could be taken away. He was exiled after rebelling against William, and was the last Count of Talou

Mauger, Archbishop of Rouen—an uncle of Duke William who plotted against him, in collusion with William of Arques. Although Mauger was a cleric, he was not known as a holy man, alleged to have a weakness for prostitutes and occult practices. He was deprived of his offices when the rebellion of William of Arques failed and fled to the Channel Islands, naming the place of his landing 'Saint's Bay'.

Appendix 3:
Main Battles of William of Normandy

Battle of Val es Dunes—c. 1047

Duke William and King Henri I of France defeat the army of Guy of Burgundy and the Norman barons who rebelled against William's dukedom, in a clash of cavalry at Val es Dunes, SW of Caen in Normandy

Siege of Brionne—c.1047–1051

Duke William's forces besiege Guy of Burgundy in his castle at Brionne. Guy eventually submits in 1051

Sieges of Alençon and Domfront—c.1049–51

Norman border towns open their gates to William's rival Geoffrey 'Martel' of Anjou. William besieges the towns and overcomes them in around 1051

Siege of Arques—c.1051–1053

Duke William's uncle, William of Arques (also known as William of Talou) rebels against his Duke, abandoning the siege of Domfront and securing himself in his castle. Duke William besieges the castle, successfully repelling an attempt by King Henri I of France to relieve the siege, by feigning a retreat and then ambushing the pursuing forces of the King. Arques surrenders in 1053–54 and leaves Normandy, putting himself under the care of Eustace of Boulogne

Battle of Mortemer—c.1054

King Henri I of France invades Normandy several times in the 1050s, with Geoffrey Martel's support. In 1054, the King's army faces Duke William to the West of the Seine, while another army under Counts Rainauld and Odo crosses into Normandy at Mortemer, in the North East of the Duchy, where they are defeated by the local barons. Henri withdraws from Normandy on hearing of the defeat

Battle of Varaville—c.1057

During another invasion by the King, half of Henri's army is stranded on the bank of the River Dive during an attempt to cross when the tide rises. Duke William takes the opportunity to fall on the half of the army that has not yet crossed and routs it. After this, Normandy faces no more invasions from France or Anjou

Conquest of Maine—c.1062–64

William makes an agreement with Count Herbert II of Maine to marry his son Robert to Herbert's child sister Marguerite, and that William will be Herbert's heir if the latter dies before the marriage can take place. Herbert dies in 1062, but the local nobles install Walter of Mantes, husband of Herbert's aunt. William invades Maine in response, and by 1064 Walter surrenders, accepting William's claim to the County

Breton-Norman War—1064

The Duchy of Brittany has been a rival of Normandy's for generations, but is unstable during much of William's Dukedom thanks to a struggle between the rightful Breton ruler Conan and his uncle Odo. William supports Odo, and later other challengers to Conan's authority, before invading himself in 1064. Conan seeks to avoid battle, and Norman forces range through Brittany chasing the Duke and laying waste to the land. Eventually, William catches up with Conan at the Chateau de Dinan where the Count surrenders.

Battle of Hastings—October 1066

After pacifying Maine and Brittany, William is free to pursue his claim to the throne of England, which he was allegedly promised by Edward the Confessor. Harold

Godwinson has himself crowned in January 1066, but William is not able to transport his army to England until September that year. He establishes a camp at Pevensey in Sussex, while Harold, who has just defeated Harald Hardrada's invasion at Stamford Bridge in Yorkshire, marched 240 miles South to intercept William, gathering troops from the *fyrd* along the way, establishing a position at Caldbec Hill or Senlac Ridge near Hastings, very close to William's position. Both armies appear to have been evenly matched despite being used to different ways of engaging in battle. William decided to give battle quickly, and after a very long fight, by the standards of the time, the English army was defeated when its commander, Harold, was mortally wounded—according to later accounts, by an arrow to the eye—and the shield wall collapsed.

Appendix 4:
Main Battles and intrigues of Harold Godwinson—Harold II of England

1045—Harold commanded a fleet of ships against Magnus the Good, king of Norway and Denark 1035–1047) Confirmed Earl of East Anglia and married *more daneco* the wealthy Saxon noble woman, Edith Swannescha.

1047—Sweyn, eldest son of Godwin, Earl of Wessex, is exiled for abducting the Abbess of Leominster. His lands were split between his brother, Harold, and his cousin, Beorn. Sweyn returned, attempting to recover his position and murdered Beorn, for which he was declared *niðing* (1049). This made Harold Godwin's uncontested heir for the old kingdom of Wessex.

1049—commanded a fleet, at King Edward's request, in aid of the German Emperor   Henry III, against Baldwin V, count of Flanders.

1051—following an insult from Eustace Aux Gernons, the people of Dover skirmished with the Count of Boulogne's men, killing several Normans. Edward decreed a harsh punishment, which Harold's father, Godwin — Earl of Wessex, refused to carry out, instead supporting his people against the Normans. Godwin and his sons, including Harold, were sent into exile. It is then that Wulfnoth, together with Håkon, Godwin's grandson by Sweyn (and possibly his youngest daughter, Ælfgifa), were given into the custody of the Duke of Normandy as political hostages. Edith of Wessex, Edward's wife, was sent to a convent.

1052—Godwin and Harold raised an army and forced King Edward to restore the family's lands, titles and wealth, and to release Queen Edith from the convent she had been sent to.

1053—Godwin dies of what was probably a stroke whilst dining with King Edward. Harold succeeds him as Earl of Wessex, becoming one of the most powerful men in England.

1058—Harold is given the Earldom of Hereford. He has now become the focus for anti-Norman rule in England, as Godwin once was, under the restored monarchy of Edward.

1062–1063—Harold led a series of successful campaigns against Gruffydd ap Llewelyn, King of Gwynedd and Powys, and later temporarily all of Wales. Gruffydd was defeated by Harold, who held him at bay against the mountains, and was killed by his own men in exchange for their safe passage. Harold then married Edith of Mercia, Gruffydd's widow, in the *Christiano* fashion. She allegedly had twin sons by Harold, although the evidence to support this is slender.

1064—Whilst gathering support for his nomination as king, (although some sources say that Harold was heading to Normandy to sue for the release of political hostages) Harold was shipwrecked at Ponthieu. William of Normandy demanded his release. Harold then accompanied William into battle against Conan II of Brittany. Interestingly, this is where Ælfgifa appears in historical sources once more. There is a suggestion that she was being offered as a wife to cement alliances, that she was present at the oath-taking between Harold and William and there is even a tiny depiction of an Ælfgifa in this scene in the Bayeux tapestry, where a bishop is seen striking her—perhaps to ensure her silence?

1065—Harold sided with the Northumbrian rebels and defeated his brother, Tostig, who was sent into exile. Harold appointed Morcar, his second wife's brother, as Earl of Northumbria in Tostig's stead.

1066—Edward the Confessor dies on 5th January allegedly commending his country and his wife into Harold's care. The Witenagemot (the last of many over the previous two years) elects Harold as King. Harold is crowned, probably at Westminster, on 6th January 1066. It may have been out of sheer convenience because all the notable Witans and Nobles were present for the feast of Epiphany. Halley's comet was first seen in the sky around this time, at its closest point to Earth, though it would be spotted on and off on its return journey for the rest of that year.

Harold amasses troops from the *fyrd* on the Isle of Wight in preparation for William's invasion. The weather was so poor, that after seven months of waiting, Harold was forced to disband the troops on 8th September because William was trapped in Normandy due to unfavourable winds.

The Battle of Fulford took place near York on 20th September Edwin, Earl of Mercia and his brother Morcar, Earl of Northumbria, were defeated by Harold's exiled brother Tostig and Harald Hardara—both of whom were claimants of the crown.

The Battle of Stamford Bridge—25th September Harold led his army on a forced march from London in four days (250miles) and caught the Norwegian army by surprise. So many were killed from Hardrada's army that of the two hundred ships that had brought the invaders, only twenty-four were needed to take the survivors back to Norway.

The Battle of Hastings—see above.

ABOUT THE AUTHORS

J.A. IRONSIDE

J.A. (Jules) Ironside grew up in a house full of books in rural Dorset. She loves speculative fiction of all stripes, especially fantasy and science fiction, although when it comes to the written word, she's not choosy and will read almost anything. It would be fair to say that she starts to go a bit peculiar if she doesn't get through at least three books a week.

She mostly writes fantasy and sci-fi. Often this leans toward the dark fantastic or dystopian forms of fiction. Occasionally there's some outright horror. Her passion for all things dark and dystopian stems from the fact that these narrative vehicles bring out the very best and absolute worst in people. She finds it endlessly fascinating to explore what it means to be human by—figuratively—putting her characters' backs to the wall. Often they'll even surprise her with the lengths they'll go to to achieve their goals.

As a keen martial artist, Jules has studied several disciplines but is most accomplished in Goju-ryu karate, which she has studied and taught for over twenty years. Her favorite things include books (obviously), slippers, cheese, and surreal conversations.

She lives in Gloucestershire, on the edge of the Cotswold way, with her boyfriend-creature and a small black and white cat, both of whom share a God complex. Her first book, paranormal mystery novel *I Belong to the Earth*, was published by Illusio & Baqer in May 2015.

For more information on Jules Ironside, please visit her website, **A Perfect Dystopia** .

MATTHEW WILLIS

Matthew Willis is stuck in the past, and likes to drag people back there for company. Fortunately, the past is a foreign country where very cheap short breaks are available. He occasionally breaks into fantasy and science fiction, stopping only to argue with people on Twitter about what actually constitutes science fiction. He lives in Southampton, roughly equidistant from the *Titanic*'s former dock and the airfield where the Spitfire first flew, sharing a Blitz-damaged house with his university lecturer wife Rosalind and an imaginary zebra. For some reason, finding inspiration in history is rarely a problem.

Matt was born in the historic naval town of Harwich, Essex, in 1976 and grew up in a nearby village, never far from the sea. Matthew studied literature and history of science at the University of Kent, focusing on Joseph Conrad for his MA, and sailed for the university in national competitions where he didn't always finish last. He subsequently worked as a journalist for *Autosport* and *F1 Racing* magazines, and he has written for *Aeroplane, Flypast,* and *The Aviation Historian* in addition to maintaining the blog **Naval Air History**.

Matt's first novel, the historical nautical fantasy *Daedalus and the Deep*, was published in 2013. His first nonfiction book, on an obscure World War II aircraft, was published in 2007. In 2015, his short story *Energy* was shortlisted for the Bridport Prize.

IF YOU ENJOYED THIS BOOK
VISIT

PENMORE PRESS
www.penmorepress.com

All Penmore Press books are available directly through our website, amazon.com, Barnes and Noble and Nook, Sony Reader, Apple iTunes, Kobo books and Smashworks and via leading bookshops across the United States, Canada, the UK, Australia and Europe.

An ARGUMENT OF BLOOD

BY

MATTHEW WILLIS AND J. A. IRONSIDE

William, the nineteen-year-old duke of Normandy, is enjoying the full fruits of his station. Life is a succession of hunts, feasts, and revels, with little attention paid to the welfare of his vassals. Tired of the young duke's dissolute behavior and ashamed of his illegitimate birth, a group of traitorous barons force their way into his castle. While William survives their assassination attempt, his days of leisure are over. He'll need help from the king of France to secure his dukedom from the rebels.

On the other side of the English Channel lives ten-year-old Ælfgifa, the malformed and unwanted youngest sister to the Anglo-Saxon king Harold Godwinson. Ælfgifa discovers powerful rivalries in the heart of the state when her sister Ealdgyth is given in a political marriage to King Edward, and she finds herself caught up in intrigues and political maneuvering as powerful men vie for influence. Her path will collide with William's, and both must fight to shape the future.

An Argument of Blood is the first of two sweeping historical novels on the life and battles of William the Conqueror.

PENMORE PRESS
www.penmorepress.com

Knight Assassin
The second book of Talon
by
James Boschert

A joyous homecoming turns into a nightmare as Talon must do the one thing that he didn't want to - become an assassin again.

Talon, a young Frank, returns to France to be reunited with the family that lost him to the Assassins of Alamut when he was just a boy. But when he arrives, he finds a sinister threat hanging like a pall over the joyous reunion. A ruthless man is challenging his father's inheritance, aided by powerful churchmen who stand to profit by his father's fall. When Talon's young brother is taken hostage, Talon has no recourse but to take the fight to his enemies.

All is not warfare, however; Talon's uncle Philip, a Templar knight, brings him to the court of Carcassonne, where Queen Eleanor has introduced ideals of romance and chivalry. There Talon is pressed into the service of a lion-hearted prince of Britain named Richard.

Knight assassin is a story of treachery, greed, love and heroism set in the Middle Ages.

PENMORE PRESS
www.penmorepress.com